Afterlife Crisis

A Beforelife Story

After ~~Mid~~life Crisis

A Beforelife Story

Rhinnick Feynman
~~Randal Graham~~

Published by ECW Press
665 Gerrard Street East
Toronto, Ontario, Canada M4M 1Y2
416-694-3348 / info@ecwpress.com

Cover design: David A. Gee
Author photo: © Anna Toth

LIBRARY AND ARCHIVES CANADA CATALOGUING IN
PUBLICATION

Title: Afterlife crisis / Randal Graham.

Names: Graham, Randy N., author.

Description: Series statement: A Beforelife story.
On title page, title appears as "Midlife crisis";
"Mid" is crossed out, and "After" is written
above it.

Identifiers: Canadiana (print) 20200232851
Canadiana (ebook) 20200232924

ISBN 978-1-77041-470-9 (softcover)
ISBN 978-1-77305-562-6 (PDF)
ISBN 978-1-77305-561-9 (EPUB)

Classification: LCC PS8613.R3465 A78 2020
DDC C813/.6—dc23

The publication of *Afterlife Crisis* has been generously supported by the Canada Council for the Arts which last
year invested $153 million to bring the arts to Canadians throughout the country and is funded in part by the
Government of Canada. *Nous remercions le Conseil des arts du Canada de son soutien. L'an dernier, le Conseil
a investi 153 millions de dollars pour mettre de l'art dans la vie des Canadiennes et des Canadiens de tout le pays.
Ce livre est financé en partie par le gouvernement du Canada.* We acknowledge the support of the Ontario Arts
Council (OAC), an agency of the Government of Ontario, which last year funded 1,737 individual artists and 1,095
organizations in 223 communities across Ontario for a total of $52.1 million. We also acknowledge the contribution
of the Government of Ontario through the Ontario Book Publishing Tax Credit, and through Ontario Creates for
the marketing of this book.

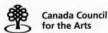

For S. & P.

Preface

It's okay if you don't believe in the afterlife.
The people who live there don't believe in you, either.

Afterlife Crisis is the second story in the *Beforelife* universe, a world that you might think of as the afterlife. The people who live there wouldn't think of it as the afterlife, though, because they don't think that anything comes before it. They call their world Detroit. Almost all the people who live in that world have forgotten their pre-mortem lives, and think that people simply pop into existence by emerging from the Styx and getting on with eternal life. Anyone who remembers having lived a mortal life is shoved into an asylum and treated for Beforelife Delusion.

This raises a question. Should you read the first story, *Beforelife*, before dipping into this one? A short answer is "no". A slightly longer answer is "yes". But another answer, and an altogether more correct one, is that it depends on what you want to get out of this book. Having read the previous paragraph you know all you need to know in order to string along with the story of *Afterlife Crisis*. You'll realize that many of the characters in the book are historical figures who now live in the world of Detroit without remembering who they were in the mortal world. You'll know why humans in Detroit are immortal — able to recover from any injury or illness — and why they cringe at the very thought of human mortality. You'll understand that the people of Detroit fail to realize the true nature of their world, and that the people being treated for Beforelife Delusion are the only ones who get what's going on.

There are other mysteries, though, that you'll have a better chance of piecing together after reading both books. Who is Abe, the all powerful leader of Detroit? Why are some people in Detroit, like Abe, able to reshape the world to suit their whims? Why does Rhinnick Feynman, the narrator of *Afterlife Crisis*, believe he's a character in a novel being penned by a cosmic Author? Why do some people reincarnate? Why does Rhinnick's pal, Zeus, seem to believe that he was a Yorkshire terrier when he lived in the mortal world? And why are there so many Napoleons cluttering up the scenery? Clues about these (and other) mysteries are liberally besprinkled throughout both books. And while you'll be able to piece many of them together by reading *Afterlife Crisis* on its own, those who really enjoy detective work might have a lot more fun by sifting through two volumes filled with intersecting clues.

For what it's worth, my mother can't imagine why anyone wouldn't want The Collected Works, so she suggests that you head to the bookshop and complete the set right now.

RANDAL GRAHAM

Chapter 1

"Zeus," I said, once the dust had settled, the chickens had hatched, and the chips had fallen where they may. "I don't mind telling you that, while we were still in the thick of it, and before the happy endings were strewn about with a lavish hand, there were moments when I felt things mightn't end so frightfully well. One might even say that Rhinnick Feynman, though no weakling, came within a whisker of despair."

"No kidding," said the honest fellow.

"I mean, one couldn't say that peril didn't loom. It loomed like the dickens. The tortured Napoleons, the corrupted ancients, the bone-chilling brushes with matrimony, not to mention the even graver threat of—"

But wait. I've gone off the rails. Eager to bring my public up to speed on current events, I've shot off the mark like a scalded cat and left the readership befogged. It's a snag I often come up against when starting a story, viz, the dashed difficult business of where to begin. No doubt you've found yourself in the same sand trap. I mean, if you bung in too much explanatory chit-chat at the starting gate, establishing what is known as "atmosphere," or sorting out who begat whom all the way back to the primordial soup, you fail to grip. You see your readers, if any, stifling yawns and reshelving the book before you can say "what ho?" Yet if you spring off the bat at a couple of hundred mph, without supplying the merest whiff of expositional what-nots, you leave your public at a loss and yelling for footnotes. And it now occurs to me that, in opening the tale of present interest with the above slice of dialogue, I have made the second of these two floaters, failing altogether to set the stage for the super-sticky affair involving Zeus, Isaac Newton, Nappy, Vera Lantz, Dr. Everard M. Peericks, and the Napoleon who had lately taken to calling himself "Jack" — a tale which my biographers will probably call "Rhinnick and the Newtonian Horror," or possibly "Feynman Conquers Science." But by whatever name the affair is called, after taking all in all and weighing this against that, I suppose that it's best to begin this story at the inception of my quest, if inceptions are the things I'm thinking of, and describe events in a roughly chronological order, allowing readers to string along and draw such character-strengthening lessons as they might from their perusal of my adventures. And so we begin, as it were, at the beginning. Let me marshal my facts, weigh anchor, and shove off.

The thing got started at the Detroit Riviera, one of the juiciest slabs of geography to feature in any travel brochure for the well-heeled jet-setter. I had repaired to this locale, staying at the appropriately opulent Hôtel de la Lune, in order to push along my top-secret quest — the one entrusted to me by Abe, Mayor of Detroit, first-born of the Styx, and ultra-powerful ruler of all he surveys. Stated briefly, the quest required yours truly to scour the landscape for a particular chump named Isaac, a government toady who was now, according to Abe, "the most dangerous man in the world." For some unspecified reason, this Abe, despite his highly touted omnipotence, needed the undersigned to act as his agent or right-hand man in tracking down this Isaac and laying his plans a-stymie. Why Abe couldn't do it himself, who can say? Perhaps mayoring kept him busy, perhaps he was occupied with matters of cosmic import, or perhaps he recalled that my last adventure had been settled by a dose of *Abe ex machina* and he feared displeasing the Author by dishing up something unduly similar in the sequel. But whatever the reason was, the quest had been thrust at Rhinnick Feynman, and Rhinnick Feynman had acquiesced. Once I'd assented to the gig, Abe had legged it into the sunset, disappearing to parts unknown with a view to hobnobbing with Ian, Penelope, and the City Solicitor — bit players in my prior ventures whom we can leave aside for now.

As for why the Riviera was my *point de départ*, as the Napoleons might describe it, well, it isn't any of the reasons you might expect. It wasn't the white sands, the smiling sun, the tropical breezes, or the frolicsome co-eds engaging in what is known as "beach volleyball." Far from it: we Rhinnicks do not idly wallow in creature comforts when entrusted with matters of globe-wobbling import. No, my choice of the Riviera as the Feynman HQ was one of those master strokes of generalship for which I am so widely known. Allow me to lay out the gist.

The nub of my quest, as already stated, was that I should sniff out this Isaac, discover how and why he was making himself a menace to pedestrians and traffic, and promptly ensure that he cease and desist. And if you've dipped into my memoirs to any extent, you'll know that I rarely saddle up for any enterprise of this nature without Zeus at my side — Zeus being my colossal gendarme and loyal retainer. But this Zeus, as you'll recollect, had recently had his memory wiped and marbles scrambled by a previous "world's-most-dangerous" chump and had himself toddled off to parts unknown. Well, it's widely known that every heroic quest requires a solid B story, and in this instance my B story was the reunion of self and Zeus with a view to rejoining forces and pushing along with story A, viz, quelling whatever storms were forming on the Isaac Newton front. So both the A and B stories hinged on hunts for missing persons — I had to find Isaac; I had to find Zeus. All pretty clear so far, what?

You may have already spotted the choice that faced me. When searching for multiple quarries, one can either charge about the landscape moving from Spot A to Spot B, and from Spot B to Spot C, and from Spot C to Spot D, if you follow me, shouting names, digging for clues, and crossing your fingers in the hope that your prey hasn't shimmied back to an earlier bit of the alphabet by the time you've hit Spot E; or one can find a likely roost, settle down for the long haul, and keep an eye skinned with a view to seeing one's quarry wander by. Perceiving that this second approach could save a good deal of trouble and expense, it was this course I adopted.

But where to roost? That is the question, and also the point where the patented Feynman genius came in. I joggled the memory and recalled hearing assorted specimens of the cognoscenti say that *anyone who is anyone* takes their winters at the Detroit Riviera. Reread that sentence if you must. Anyone (mark that word) who is anyone (mark it again) takes their winters at the Detroit Riviera. And while it is beyond doubt that Zeus and Isaac are as different from one another as apricots are from zebras, it remains true that they both fall within the textbook definition of *anyone*. So I installed myself where anyone who is anyone was apt to be, viz, the Detroit Riviera, and waited for nature to take its course.

QED, as the fellow wrote.

It was while I reflected on the inspiring ingenuity of this plan, seated on a hotel balcony and enjoying a meditative martini, that a rap on my chamber door signalled someone waiting without, seeking to revel in my society.

"Come in," I yodelled cordially.

He came in.

4

The "he," in this instance, was William, the hotel porter, bringer of room service, and handler of the Feynman bags; a well-groomed, balding, and officious-looking chap who brought to mind an emperor penguin that had been stuffed by an over-zealous taxidermist.

"Good afternoon, Mr. Feynman," he said, inclining the bean.

"Gunga Din!" I riposted, warmly.

"Gunga Din, sir?"

"Gunga ruddy Din," I said, rising imperiously, for the chap's carelessness had irked me. Circumstances involving credit checks, reservations, and other minutiae had dictated that I allow this hired retainer to penetrate my intimate circle, as the expression is, making him one to whom I had vouchsafed accurate data concerning the Feynman ID. But this information, I had explained, fell strictly within the established bounds of porter/portee privilege, and the name "Rhinnick Feynman" was not to be uttered in any venue where eavesdropping ears might overhear.

"I'm travelling incognito," I reminded the sieve-brained blister. "Or do I mean incommunicado? It could be one, or it could be the other. But setting that question aside for now, the name is Gunga Din. Not Feynman."

"Forgive me, sir," said William. "Just as you say. 'Tis in my memory lock'd, and you yourself shall keep the key of it."

"Right ho," I said.

"Good afternoon, Gunga Din," said William.

"Hello, William."

"I have a letter addressed to Mr. Feynman," he said.

I well-I'll-be-dashed. I mean to say, regardless of how assiduously a chap safeguards his identity, he can't be said to be travelling incommunicado if communicados keep arriving via the post.

"To whom should I have Mr. Feynman's letter delivered, sir?" asked William, raising the brow.

5

I snatched the missive and gave the servitor one of my austere looks, being too preoccupied with this mystery letter to deal with backchat from the help.

Upon inspection the letter proved, as foreshadowed, to be a letter. More importantly, my inspection revealed that the porter had not erred. Despite the pains I'd taken to keep a lid on the Feynman ID, the missive was addressed to none other than "Rhinnick P. Feynman esq., Hôtel de la Lune, Detroit Riviera." And while this was enough to shiver my timbers, as the expression is, you can imagine my chagrin when, flipping the envelope over, I saw that its sender was none other than Dr. E.M. Peericks, Chief of Psychiatry at Detroit Mercy Hospice.

I well-I'll-be-dashed once more.

"Is there a problem, sir?" asked William.

"I daresay there's a problem!" I riposted. "The sender of this communiqué is Dr. Everard M. Peericks, prominent loony doctor and principal wrangler of the inmates at Detroit Mercy Hospice; a fellow who, whatever his merits, is one who both Rhinnick Feynman and Gunga Din would like to steer sedulously clear of. His possession of up-to-date information re: my whereabouts threatens to subvert my whole foreign policy."

"Most disturbing, sir," said William.

It was at this moment, with a feeling that no further suspense was called for, that I opened the letter and ran an eyeball over its contents. What I read left me nonplussed. I reproduce the letter here, *in toto*, so as to assist your stringing along:

Rhinnick P. Feynman, esq.
Hôtel de la Lune
Detroit Riviera

Dear Mr. Feynman,
Re: <u>Professional Favour</u>

My name is Dr. Everard M. Peericks, chief of psychiatry at Detroit Mercy Hospice. I am writing to ask for your help with a current patient. This patient — one who has been with the hospice for some years now — has recently experienced a series of persistent and disturbing delusions in which you appear to play a prominent role. Despite our best efforts, we have been unable to persuade the patient that these delusions are the product of mental illness, rather than accurate memories of fantastical, impossible, and apocalyptic events. Until we succeed in convincing our patient that these memories are mere figments of a disturbed imagination, I feel that any attempt to treat the underlying condition is doomed to fail. This brings me to why I'm writing to you. It is my hope that, at your earliest convenience, you could visit Detroit Mercy, meet with my patient, and assist me in demonstrating that these memories cannot be real. You could help us prove that you were not involved in any events resembling those that form the basis of the delusions and ultimately convince our patient that these "memories" are nothing more than the products of a troubled mind. The patient has repeatedly attested that you are a person in whom the utmost faith can be placed, so I believe that your assurance that these events did not occur would be convincing and therefore invaluable in my patient's treatment and recovery.

I understand that you are a busy man, but I sincerely hope that you can soon spare the time to assist a person in need. The hospice address and my office number can be found on the card enclosed.

Yours faithfully,

Dr. E.M. Peericks
Chief of Psychiatry
Detroit Mercy Hospice

I handed the letter back to William, who'd been standing there in a respectful silence, displaying all of the quiet stolidity of a stuffed moose.

"What do you make of this?" I said, instituting a brief stage wait as he digested the contents.

"It seems, sir," said William, "that the doctor bids you to minister to a mind diseased, pluck from the memory a rooted sorrow, raze out the written troubles of the brain, and with some sweet oblivious antidote cleanse the stuffed bosom of that perilous stuff which weighs upon the heart."

"Obviously," I said. "That much is clear. But what's bothering me is all of this 'Dear Mr. Feynman' business, not to mention the phrase, 'My name is Dr. Everard blasted Peericks,' and this 'my job is loony-wrangler, here's where you'll find me' bilge. For this loathsome Peericks, I should explain, is no exotic stranger, but someone I've known for years and years. Our longish history of mutual association mightn't justify listing Peericks on the roster of my warmest friends and boosters, but we are far from being ships that passed in the night. We've rubbed elbows hundreds of times, and I've spent hours closeted with him in his office discussing matters of mutual interest. Yet here is this letter, written in formal, introductory tones as to one who is a man of mystery."

"Odd," said William, and I remember agreeing with him.

"I mean, why would Peericks address me as a perfect stranger?"

"I couldn't say, sir."

"Of course you couldn't. Don't be an ass."

"Forgive me, sir."

"And then there's all this guff about some deeply troubled patient. While it's no great shock to hear that there are members of the public who fantasize about yours truly, spending an idle hour imagining what it would be like to hobnob with me, or even to walk in the Feynman shoes, it's dashed unsettling to hear that some unfortunate goop has mistaken these widely shared fantasies for *bona fide* memories of—"

Here I broke off, not so much because I'd run out of things to say, but because the mystery, at least insofar as the deeply troubled p. was concerned, had clicked.

"Zeus!" I exclaimed.

"Zeus?" said William.

"Zeus indeed! The poor delusional inmate must be Zeus, a longtime pal of mine who went awol after having his brains scrambled — a long story, I won't go into it now. But suffice it to say that the aforementioned Zeus, a dear and esteemed crony, is one with whom it is my fondest wish to reconvene, if reconvening means what I think it does. Perhaps all of this 'troubled mind' and 'fantastical delusion' rot is the fallout of the mental whatsits which befell Zeus at the climax of our recent imbroglio with the forces of darkness — old memories climbing out of the wreckage, as it were. It all adds up. I mean, Zeus *has* accompanied me on some fairly apocalyptic undertakings, and Dr. Peericks, as narrow-minded an ass as has ever pushed a syringe, would be precisely the sort of fatheaded bimbo to chalk these memories up as delusions."

"I see, sir," said William.

"It still doesn't explain Peericks's odd behaviour," I added, stroking the chin. "I mean to say, it's not as though amnesia is contagious. As baffled as poor Zeus must be, Dr. Peericks's memory, at least so far as I could tell, seemed sound as a bell when last we held a tête-à-tête. Yet judging from this letter, every trace of yours truly has been washed from the doctor's mind."

"Highly mysterious, sir," said William.

"On the other hand," I added, for one likes to inspect all sides of a problem, "I did recently bean the blighter with a book called *Cranial Trauma*, bathing him in both irony and confusion. That might account for some general weakening of the grey cells. Or it may be the case that, if one spends one's professional life cheek-by-jowl with assorted loonies, sooner or later a modicum of their collective goofiness rubs off, if modicums are the things I'm thinking of."

"It is conceivable, sir," said William. "Perhaps, sir, if you assent to Dr. Peericks's wishes, and present yourself at Detroit Mercy, this mystery will be solved and all made clear."

I laughed. One of those hollow and mirthless ones.

"My dear, naive ass," I said, fishing an olive from my martini, "you can't go about Detroit deliberately seeking the society of psychiatrists, Hospice Goons, and other members of the mental health fraternity. Or rather you can, but what a hell of a life."

I couldn't explain to this officious prune that, even if Peericks truly had lost all memory of my sojourn at the hospice, Detroit Mercy still housed a squadron of nurses and Hospice Goons who, on catching the merest glimpse of Rhinnick Feynman, would waste no time in snatching up a man-sized net with a view to bunging me into a cell with padded walls. At the moment of going to press I retained the distinction of being counted among the residents of Detroit Mercy Hospice, and one who'd left that dungeon's grounds without the usual precondition of having the words "Certified Sane" stamped on my forehead.

"No," I said, suppressing a shudder. "I cannot go. I cannot assent, as you put it, to the doctor's wishes. I'll have to give it a miss. They won't get a smell of me at the hospice."

"But what about Mr. Zeus, sir?" said William. "He is, if one can trust this letter, suffering profoundly. And Doctor Peericks, a man who, by all accounts, is an eminent specialist, seems convinced that only you can ease his pain."

This held me. Indeed, it isn't going too far to say that this flowery-tongued boll weevil had touched a nerve. Those who have read my character sketch will attest that Rhinnick, whatever the cost to self, does not readily turn away from a pal in trouble. And here was Zeus deeply immersed in the mulligatawny, showing signs of recovered memory but unable to clear the mists. I was on the horns of one of those things you get on the horns of. A *dilemma*, I think you call them. I was faced with a clear choice between presenting myself at the hospice, facing the risk of a longish period of captivity which would shackle my efforts to find Isaac Newton, or giving the whole enterprise a miss and leaving Zeus languishing in this blasted doctor's care, thus cheesing any chance that Zeus's brain would reboot itself and render its host able to string along with my primary quest. A difficult choice calculated to baffle even the most astute philosopher.

But after a moment's quiet reflection, there was no choice. I could never abandon Zeus. Whatever slings and arrows I might face, whatever hidden dangers might lurk 'round yon corner, I had to pitch in and help my pal.

"William," I said, "your simple, manly words have penetrated. You have jiggled the Feynman conscience. I will go to the hospice, as you suggest, though the prospect freezes the gizzard. The doctor will be there. Matron Bikerack will be there. Mistress Oan, director of Sharing Room activities, will be there. Plus any number of Hospice Goons. The very idea makes me feel as though I had a whole platoon of spiders marching up and down my spine. Tell me, William — what was it you said the other day about the way a fellow feels when he knows he's jolly well got to do a thing but the more he thinks about it the less he wants to do it?"

"Sir?"

"It was when I mooted the notion of signing up for karaoke. Currents came into it, if I recall."

"Ah yes, sir," he said. "And thus the native hue of resolution is sicklied o'er with the pale cast of thought, and enterprises of great pith and moment with this regard their currents turn awry, and lose the name of action."

"That's the bunny," I said. "One of your own?"

"Yes, sir," said William. "You are, if you do not mind the observation, letting 'I dare not' wait upon 'I would', like the poor cat i' the adage."

"Very possibly," I said, although I hadn't a clue of how the cat element entered the conv. But the die was cast. I would go to the hospice, face the dangling sword of Damocles, and help Zeus. It was, I could see, the humane thing to do. And we Rhinnicks are sticklers for doing the humane thing.

I hitched up my resolve, reminding myself that in life it is not loony doctors that matter, but the courage you bring to them.

I laid my plan before William.

"I leave this afternoon," I said. "I shall bid farewell to the Hôtel de la Lune, ho for the open spaces, and make my way to the hospice, leaving not a rack behind, as I've heard you put it."

"I should remind you, sir," said William, "that you are scheduled to participate in this evening's luau feast. You had expressed considerable interest and seemed to be looking forward to it when last we spoke. Perhaps you might delay your departure for a day and enjoy one final evening at the waterfront."

"Once more unto the beach, as it were?"

"Precisely, sir."

"No, William. I leave at once. For if it were done when t'were done, then t'were well it were done quickly."

"Well put, sir," said William. "Indeed, I wonder if you would mind if I wrote that down, for future use."

"Not at all, William," I said, tolerantly. "Now remind me — which shuttlebus do I take to get to the IPT station? It's the second route on the B-line, isn't it?"

"I beg your pardon, sir?"

"2B, or not 2B? That is the question."

"I shall look into the matter, sir."

It was less than an hour later that I had packed the bags, donned the travel garb, uttered a few last-minute farewells, and left the Hôtel de la Lune, kicking the sand from the Feynman shoes and steeling myself for the coming storm, scarcely prepared for what I'd find at journey's end.

Chapter 2

It was an easy passage from the Hôtel de la Lune to Detroit Mercy — not a journey to be compared with some of my fruitier expeditions. I mean to say, one need scarcely jog the memory to find the episode in which I, along with assorted hangers-on, escaped from this very hospice and made the trek to Vera's emporium — Vera being a psychic pipsqueak who helped me out of a spot of bother. That trip, as has been recorded elsewhere, featured hot pursuits by Hospice Goons, a bloodthirsty Napoleon, police chases, armed drones, and other vicissitudes designed to blot the sunshine from my life. But the journey of present interest, as I was saying before I interrupted myself, featured nothing so goshawful. On the contrary, this trip involved no more than a proletarian ride on public transit, an uneventful whoosh through the Instantaneous Personal Transport — a teleportation thingummy widely known as IPT — and an easy jaunt along various roads and footpaths until I hitched up at the gates of Detroit Mercy.

Even these gates — which I'd been dreading ever since I'd first digested Peericks's note — proved no obstacle for Feynman. While they were, as expected, manned by a pair of Hospice Goons, these Goons failed altogether to raise the hue and cry on catching scent of yours truly. All they did was peep at my letter of invitation, grunt a pair of dismissive grunts, and bung me through the gates, all with the air of two Goons who saw

Rhinnick Feynman as a stranger in a strange land and one who could easily be dismissed as small potatoes.

And while you might expect me to chafe at going unrecognized while treading on my home turf, as the expression is, on this occasion I didn't, what with one thing and another. I had heard the one about gift horses and mouths, and so I left the guards behind me without trying to prod their memories and kickstart the merry reunions.

On entering the hospice I passed through the usual gauntlet of receptionists and administrative beazels, many of whom were known to me, but none of whom registered any trace of familiarity with the Feynman face. There wasn't a hint of "ahoy there, Rhinnick," nor anything along the lines of "rejoice with me, for I have found the lamb which was lost" — just a larger-than-average dose of "right this way sir, thank you for coming sir, the doctor will be right with you." It wasn't long before I found myself decanted into a chair in Peericks's office, where I was left alone to wait for the doctor and pass the time in reflective mood.

And I'll tell you why my m. was r. Having made my way past the phalanx of forgetful hospice workers, if phalanx is the word I want, I suddenly found myself with time to chew on the rumminess of my newfound anonymity. I mean to say, Peericks's letter had hinted that the doctor himself had come down with a spot of Rhinnick-centred amnesia, but recent evidence forced one to the conclusion that the affliction had now spread. As for the cause of this development — who could say? Was this some elaborate ruse designed to lure me back to the hospice with a false sense of security? Or might it be a recent revision by the Author, blotting out those earlier chapters of my life in which Detroit Mercy had been the Feynman abode? I think you'll agree that this called for a deeper and more thorough investigation.

It was while I sat musing on these matters that Dr. Peericks sauntered in and took his customary perch behind the desk.

"Mr. Feynman," he said, smiling.

"Dr. Peericks," I said cautiously, cocking an eyebrow and searching the chump for any sign that the well-dressed, debonair, and distinguished-looking visitor sitting before him had rung a bell or two, or tugged at the mental folders bearing the legend "Feynman, R."

"I can't thank you enough for coming," he said.

"Think nothing of it."

"We're so grateful that you've come," he said, beaming in my direction and seeming a good deal more bonhomous than I remembered. "We were becoming desperate. I hoped you'd be willing to help us, but hadn't imagined that you'd be able to make the trip so quickly. You must have left the moment my letter reached you. I—"

"The pleasure is mine," I said, falsifying the facts in order to push the thing along.

"I trust your trip was comfortable," he said, sticking to the cordialities with the stubbornness of a dog who has set his teeth on a favourite slipper. "Words can't express our genuine gratitude." And he carried on in this thanksgiving vein, polluting the atmosphere with copious "thank yous," "pleased to meet yous," and "we're ever so gratefuls," for the space of several ticks, allowing me ample scope to deploy the well-honed Feynman senses in search of any trace of reminiscence on the part of the louse before me. And the longer I subjected this psychiatric ass to my penetrating scrutiny, the more it became clear that, as his letter had foreshadowed, here sat a man to whom the undersigned was less familiar than summer snow.

It was at this point, having had enough of the preliminary *pourparlers*, that I decided to broach the issue in that direct way of mine.

"You don't recognize me, do you?" I said.

"Recognize you?" he said, taken aback. "Well, no. Should I? I — I don't think we've ever met—"

"Roommate of Brown?" I said. "Poster child for *ego fabularis*?"

"I'm sorry?" said the fathead.

"Devotee of the Author? Deliverer of ironical bumps on the head? Does none of this spark your memory?"

The man looked at me befogged. And I don't mind telling you that, now that the issue was laid bare, and the question of this sudden fad of blotting out all knowledge of Rhinnick Feynman was being mooted out in the open, I found myself nonplussed. I mean to say, one doesn't insist on universal acclaim, but one does hope to evoke at least a pinch of the Auld Lang Syne spirit when meeting up with one's former brain attendant. I mean, dash it. Here sat a medical man who had tootled around in the Feynman corpus collosum, seeking here a memory, there a delusion, all with a view to rendering some quackish diagnosis: a man, in short, who ought to have known my face as well as any. But here we were, vis-à-vis, as the Napoleons say, and this highly paid MD registered no more glimmers of recognition than a particularly forgetful goldfish who's been neglecting his brain exercises.

"I'm sorry, Mr. Feynman," said the bewildered pest, "I don't understand what you—"

"Perhaps this will prime the grey cells," I said, reaching into an inner pocket with all the skill of a conjuror and fishing out what I hoped might serve as an *aide-memoire*.

"Grrnmph," said the *aide-memoire*, perhaps better known as Fenny — a loyal hamster in whose presence Peericks had wallowed on many occasions.

Fenny's advent didn't go so frightfully well. Peericks made the face you might expect of a man confronted with unexpected hamsters, and a noise one generally makes upon accidentally swallowing a rather-too-elderly oyster. I took the hint and returned Fenny to store.

"Mr. Feynman," said Peericks, once composure regained its throne, "I don't know what you're trying to prove, but—"

"Never mind," I said, waving him off. "I must have been thinking of something else."

Here I let the matter drop. I mean, eager as I was to solve the riddle of my sudden loss of celebrity status, I reminded myself that I wasn't so dashed eager for the fallout that might ensue should I be recognized as one who was awol from the grounds. Besides, I felt it was time to switch gears and get to the purpose of my visit, viz, the business of helping Zeus.

"Now about this patient you mentioned," I said.

"Yes," said Peericks, who, if I read him correctly, now eyed me with a spot of wariness. I had the impression he was mentally thumbing through his loony doctor's handbook in search of a fitting diagnosis. "Perhaps I should tell you a bit about her case," he added.

"*Her* case?" I said, surprised.

"Yes, my patient. She—"

"You don't mean 'she,'" I said.

"Excuse me?" queried the fathead.

"You said 'she.'"

"I did say 'she.'"

"I should explain," I said tolerantly, remembering I was dealing with a goof who seemed to have lost a few of his marbles. "You employed the feminine pronoun in reference to this patient. An understandable gaffe, conventional grammar not being everyone's cup of tea. Probably not even taught in loony doctor school. But rest assured that 'he' is the mot juste when chirping about a chump who identifies as male."

"The patient is female," said the ass. "Her name is Oan."

I stared at the man wide-eyed, as the expression is. I don't mind telling you this revelation had landed on me like a crisp left hook to the mazard.

"What's the matter?" said the doctor.

"Did you say Oan?" I asked, bewildered.

"Yes," said the physician, "the patient's name is 'Oan.' It's spelled 'Joan,' but the J is silent and invisible."

"But you can't mean Oan."

"I do mean Oan."

"A droopy bird with a spiritual air and a marked disposition to fiddle with crystals, Vision Boards, healing oils, and similar garbage?"

"So you *do* know her!" said Peericks, leaning forward and making a face that had INTRIGUED written across it in large, capital letters.

It now occurred to me that the cagey thing to do would be to hold my cards close to the Feynman chest. I mean to say, we had already weathered a few exchanges which surely had this medical fathead wondering whether my brain was up to factory specs, and I didn't wish to add fuel to the fire. So rather than dishing up the full, sordid history of my entanglements with the crystal-toting weirdo under discussion, I simply said, "Oh, we've met," and hoped this would fit the bill.

Aiming to stave off any further cross-examination by the physician, I turned the tables by seeking particulars from him.

"I understood her to be your employee," I said.

"She was. Oan served as our Sharing Room director for more than thirty years. She's a great help to me and an asset to the hospice. Beloved, really. And she's wonderful with the patients. She's a great comfort to them."

I could have corrected the blighter there, pointing out that Oan was about as comforting as a kidney stone or a porcupine-quill blanket. And far from being beloved, she was pretty generally thought of as a blot on the hospice landscape and a fly in her patients' ointment. But I kept these observations to myself. Better to let the babbling gasbag buzz along with his story.

"She took a leave of absence some time ago," he said. "She said she was on a spiritual journey — something about 'reconnecting with the universe.' She didn't say where she was going, but when she returned she wasn't herself. There was an earnestness about her, a sense of urgency. And she had an incredible story. She told me she'd been involved with a group that she called the Church of O, and that she'd been witness to a supernatural duel. She claimed that the things she witnessed proved everything she'd been teaching in the Sharing Room all these years — that the universe can be changed through acts of will. You can see why I was concerned. She also said that she had seen proof of the beforelife, as well as someone or something called 'the Great Omega.' All delusions, of course. But she repeatedly insisted that a man named Rhinnick Feynman had been with her when she witnessed these events and that he could support her story. That's why we sent word to you."

Well, I suppose at this point I could have assured the old ass that he'd been supplied with accurate data, but I didn't. I was still a trifle shell-shocked to find that it was Oan who had been babbling about me in the hospice, rather than the Zeus for whom I'd budgeted, and I wasn't entirely clear on how to proceed. At the moment of going to press, I had half a mind to make an immediate exit in the direction of the Hôtel de la Lune, hoping to reach the Detroit Riviera in time for the luau. On the other hand, I wondered whether remaining *in statu quo* mightn't be the shrewder move, increasing the odds that I would divine the Author's will. I mean to say, the Author might have penned this whole 'return to the hospice' sequence with some quest-furthering plot twists in mind, and I might louse the whole thing up by leaving early. Trapped in this equivocal state of whatdoyoucallit, I just sat there twiddling my thumbs and staring vacantly into space. A moment or two later, perceiving that Peericks was still hanging on my lips and awaiting speech, I finally filled the dead air with a mild "oh, ah."

"That's why I asked you to come," said Peericks, earnestly. "Oan insists you were involved in the events she describes. She says you'll verify her story. That's why we'd like you to speak to her. She holds you in very high regard. If you could convince her that the experiences she describes weren't real, and that she imagined the whole thing, then she might accept that she's experiencing delusions. I should explain that my own expertise lies in treating conditions that give rise to delusions, particularly BD, a disorder in which the patient believes in the beforelife and—"

"I'm familiar with the condition," I assured him. And as I did, I realized this sudden swerve in the conversation presented an unexpected chance to peg two birds with one stone, taking a stab at plumbing the depths of this fathead's memory loss while also sniffing out some intel about my old pal Zeus.

"Speaking of BD," I said, striking a nonchalant tone, "I once knew a chap who had it. Went by the name 'Zeus.' He also thought he'd been a dog in the beforelife — some sort of terrier, I believe. I recall him mentioning something about once having cooled his heels here at the hospice — wearing the terry-cloth robe, eating the soft foods, and generally joining in the communal race toward mental health. I think he was here fairly recently. Tell me, Peericks, how does this square up with your data?"

"A Mr. Zeus?" he said, surprised.

"Just Zeus," I said. "Big chap. You couldn't have missed him. A grinning mass of beef and brawn who stands about eight-foot-six. Take a line through any shaved gorillas you've met, and adjust the scale upward. You'll generally find him messing about by lifting heavy objects, burying bones, or chasing postmen. Ring any bells?"

"I'm afraid it wouldn't be proper for me to discuss a hospice patient," said the ass.

"So he *is* a patient?" I riposted.

"I can't confirm that, Mr. Feynman. I'm sorry. Our rules concerning patient information are strict—"

"So if I were to inquire about this Zeus's whereabouts?" I asked. "Say, with a view to passing along his correspondence?"

"I'm sorry. Patient information is confidential."

"You told me about Oan," I countered, shrewdly. And although I fully expected this rejoinder to catch him in the midriff and leave him gasping, it didn't. Instead the dithering bungler tried to distinguish Oan's case and suggest that it was different. Specious, of course, but that's what the bungler did.

"You might be in a position to help us with Oan's treatment," he said.

"I could help you with Zeus, too!"

"I'm sorry, Mr. Feynman," began this serial apologizer, but I checked him with a gesture.

"Fine, fine," I said. "I understand you have your rules, arbitrary though they might be. So you can tell me all about Oan but not about Zeus. Let's take that as read. So answer me this, Dr. Peericks," I continued, lining up a long shot. "Has Oan reported any recent run-ins with heavily muscled chaps who think they're dogs and answer to names which rhyme with goose?"

This seemed to give the doctor a headache. He pinched the bridge of his nose before marshalling his strength and soldiering on.

"I'm sorry, Mr. Feynman, we do need to discuss Oan's treatment and drop this other matter."

"Say on, physician," I said, indulgently.

"All I ask is that you convince her that she's imagining the events I told you about — these meetings with the Church of O; the cataclysmic battle."

"Convince her that she's come a bit unglued, what?"

"Well, broadly speaking, but—"

"Gone off the deep end, I mean to say. Any number of screws loose—"

"We prefer to say our patients are—"

"A bit cuckoo? Potty as a whatsit?"

"Excuse me?"

"Of unsound mind, man. Try to keep up. You want me to confer with this Oan, lend an ear to her story, inform her that the whole cataclysmic battle sequence which she's been harping about can be written off as the babblings of a loony, and leave her persuaded that she is *non compos mentis*. This will allow you to flush the bats from her belfry and refill her bean with thoughts you find more pleasing."

I seemed to have said the wrong thing.

"That's not how we would describe the treatment process!" said the pedantic pill-pusher, huffing in an affronted sort of way. I silenced him with another one of my gestures. I further assured him that, whatever psychobabblish words he and his fellow mental health boosters might ascribe to the task before me, I had collared the gist and was happy to take the gig.

"So you'll help her?" he said.

I said I would.

"I'm so pleased," said Dr. Peericks, and so profound was his relief at my willingness to pitch in that his whole aspect seemed to transmutate before me, if transmutate is the word to describe a quick switch from officious bleater to one of those soulful, dewy-eyed types you sometimes see in the second act of musical comedies. I mean to say, a word or two of assent from yours truly and this Peericks's entire demeanour shifted.

One moment he was a bureaucratic doctor, oozing profes-sional detachment and medical whatdoyoucallit, and the next he had the aspect of a child of tender years who has recovered his long-lost dog. I had the distinct impression that if I didn't tread carefully I would soon be dodging a hug.

Peericks observed my gaze, and he must have noticed that I had raised a censorious brow at this unseemly show of emotion, for he now blushed prettily and twiddled with his tie, as though reluctant to unleash some slab of compromising data.

"It's just . . . you see . . . well, Oan's happiness is very import-ant to me," he said, his voice growing husky as he gazed over my right ear. "She's a wonderful colleague. She . . ."

"Of course," I interjected, having no time to sit through an employee evaluation. "I'm sure she's a first-rate caring nurturer and top-notch purveyor of spiritual doodads. Now point me in her direction and let's have a peek under the hood."

"I do hope you succeed," he said. "If she could be returned to me — or to us, I mean — if she could continue her work with the patients—"

"Right ho," I said, eager to get this show on the road.

"The patients are lost without her. She has such a way with them. So kind. So nurturing. A thoroughly selfless woman. The sort that no hospice should be without. I hadn't realized what she meant to me — or . . . to us — until she was gone. It has been so difficult without her, Mr. Feynman. For all of us, I mean. It has been like a cloud has settled over the hospice. Please," he implored, still with the soppy, melting tone, "do your best to help her. It would mean so much to me. So much to the hospice."

Well, I don't know about you, but I'm pretty astute, and I now began to knit together a few threads from our recent exchange. Follow these clues: Not only had this pestilential blister called Oan "wonderful" and "selfless" without choking on his words, not only had he claimed, in a husky voice, that her happiness was very dear to him, but he'd also managed to describe Oan's harebrained efforts in the Sharing Room as comforting and helpful. Helpful, forsooth! Add to this the fact he positively beamed at the thought of having Oan hauled out of storage, and then practically melted while musing about Oan's real or imagined merits, and a picture begins to emerge. If this wasn't a man whose senses had been dulled by smouldering passions, a fellow who, in other words, had been pierced by Cupid's arrow, then I don't know the symptoms. The man was besotted! And if the available evidence could be accepted as both admissible and credible, it seemed the object of this medical poop's affections was *Oan* — the dottiest self-deluded guru to ever light a patchouli candle and project her astral self. They say there's a broom for every corner, but I wouldn't have thought a freak like Oan could ignite the divine fire in any self-respecting bosom.

"Well, well, well!" I said, grinning.

"Well, well, what?" said Peericks.

My grin intensified.

"You're in love! You're in love with the old disaster!"

"What? Me? No. Don't be absurd. That wouldn't be . . . I mean, setting aside the fact that Oan is now my patient, and—"

"Ah!" I said, seeing all, and sagely tapping the side of my nose. "Another one of those specious rules. You're about to tell me that there is some official edict about the zookeeper fraternizing with the exhibits. Understood. But mark this. If Oan could be cured, if she could be certified as fit to mingle with the undeluded masses, then—"

"Then she could return to her duties," said the doctor, who seemed eager to move our discussion away from the theme of love's young dream. This was fine by me, as I had now thoroughly reconnoitred the scene and scooped up all the useful intelligence. This doctor's ghastly display of heart-on-sleeving had convinced me beyond all doubt that he had fallen base over apex for this Oan — something I wouldn't have thought possible. And as unbelievable as this hot news was, it had the promise of coming in dashed handy. I mean, here was a psychiatrist who was, I deduced, in a position to spill the beans about Zeus's coordinates, and here was I in a position to help that same psychiatrist pitch a bit of woo. If I could speed the blighter's wooing — possibly put him in a position to saunter down the aisle with his inexplicable choice of bridal fauna — then I might be able to leverage this good deed into a bargaining chip for Rhinnick, by which I mean a method of convincing this prescription scribbler to unseal his lips with respect to Zeus's whereabouts.

It was, I could see, the Author's plan.

"I'll be only too pleased to help," I said, now chomping at the bit.

And the doctor, little knowing that he had supplied me with state secrets which would allow me to dictate policies and tactics, led me out of the office and down the hall.

Life in the hospice is, as you might imagine, plagued by interruptions and notoriously difficult to plan. We had taken only a few steps Oanwards when the hospice intercom issued an urgent summons to Dr. Peericks, bidding the old pot of poison to report to some sort of mental health kerfuffle. The physician, unleashing a muffled *dammit*, asked if I'd mind flying solo for a space and conferring with Oan in his abs. I assured him, not untruthfully, that nothing would please me more.

And so within a couple of ticks he handed me off to a Hospice Goon, who led me up a staircase, through a doorway, and down a hallway or two before depositing me in Oan's quarters, a cozy little apartment halfway along the second floor. Within this room I was surprised to find not one, but two loonies blinking back at me. One of these, as you might have guessed, was the aforementioned Oan. The second was a distinctly charbroiled woman covered head to toe in ointment and wrapped in gauze.

Chapter 3

Well, I don't know if you've hobnobbed with a bird who has recently strolled through a fiery furnace or backstroked in a live volcano, but if you have you'll understand how these encounters grip the senses. I mean to say, the eyes are arrested by the subject's seared exterior, the ears by the intermittent crackling of charred skin, and the nose by a bouquet of cooked flesh and medical ointments — a mixture far too rich for the human nostril. And while the barbecued exhibit now confronting me was draped in a shroud of gauze, this shroud, though straining at every thread, failed altogether to shield yours truly from the affront.

I betrayed no sign of aversion. Whatever the provocation, Rhinnick Feynman does not recoil in horror when presented with members of the gentler sex. He stifles his revulsion, bears up, and chips in with all the suavity of the parfit gentil knight. Or rather he tries to. In fact, I was on the point of charming my two hostesses with a few well-chosen civilities when Oan, selecting this moment to press the larynx into service, beat me to the punch.

"Mr. Feynman!" she chirruped, beaming freely and looking as though she'd won a sweepstake or two. And while it is always gratifying to reap the public's adulation, in this instance I was less gratified than surprised. I mean to say, it wasn't Oan's welcoming spirit which sparked my interest, but the fact that someone in this Abe-forsaken place had ID'd me at first sight, instead of treating me like a mystery man known only in song and legend.

"Mistress Oan," I said, inclining the bean. And turning my gaze toward her flame-broiled compatriot, I topped this off with, "And your friend, err, Miss . . .?"

"We do not know her name, Mr. Feynman," said Oan, in that dreamy, droopy voice she always deployed in sharing sessions. "She rarely speaks. It's so very tragic. Dr. Peericks says she has lost all of her memories."

"Two chairs," said the exhibit under discussion.

"Two chairs?" I asked.

"It's very curious," said Oan. "She keeps repeating that same phrase. She started this morning. And when she utters those words she stares off into space, as though she hopes to focus her energies upon the Laws of Attraction — you know all about the Laws of Attraction, don't you, Mr. Feynman?"

"Yes, yes, of course, of course," I said, staving off a refresher course on Sharing Room philosophy. "And if she's appealing to those laws, she seems to be doing a dashed fine job. She wants two chairs, you have two chairs. Also a pair of beds and tables. Everything seems in order, what?"

"Two chairs," repeated the charbroiled roommate, bringing her knees up to her chest and rocking gently where she sat. It was at this point in the proceedings that my hamster, Fenny, apparently sought a change of scenery, for he climbed out of my jacket pocket and ran down my leg, staking his claim next to the overcooked popsy and grrnmphing amiably.

As Fenny inspected his surroundings — no doubt finding them familiar, as he'd lived with me in the hospice for many a long day — I found myself wondering why the Author had thought it wise to include so many variations on the theme of memory loss in the course of these first few chapters. He must have had some reason, but what it might have been eluded me.

Personal obsession, perhaps, or maybe an upcoming theme for a book-of-the-month club. But for now I filed this puzzle away for future consideration. Returning to matters of present interest, I spoke as follows: "Has Dr. Peericks any notion of why this crispy exhibit's memory has gone phut?"

"Two chairs," ventured the crispy e., while Fenny sniffed around her ankles.

"We haven't a clue," said Oan. "Doctor Peericks is doing his best. He's quite marvellous, you know. He has made a study of memory disorders. He's told me all about it. He has been reading about an ancient practice once performed on BD patients, a practice called—"

"Mindwiping!" I interjected, dredging up a term I'd learned during my last sojourn at the hospice.

"That's right!" said Oan. "It's terribly cruel. Dr. Peericks says it's inhumane, destroying a person's memory — all of their thoughts, all of their dreams . . . Oh, I do hope the doctor is able to help her."

"Talking of memories," I said, redirecting the conv., "tell me, Oan: what do you remember of me?"

"You ask the strangest questions, Mr. Feynman."

"Pray, indulge me."

"Of course, Mr. Feynman. I'd do anything to help you. I remember you very well. We met in the grotto, when you brought the Intercessor into the sacred caverns, among the adherents of the Church of O. You assisted the Intercessor in his work. You were a great help to him. A central figure in his ministry."

This was not the response for which I'd budgeted. Indeed, it isn't going too far to say that her answer left me fogged. Let me explain.

If you haven't recently thumbed your way through the Feynman archives, you may have forgotten that this Oan is a bird I've known for years and years — meeting her not in the so-called "sacred caverns," but smack in the middle of this very hospice, where Oan had served, as previously indicated, as Sharing Room Director. And in that capacity she had been face-to-face with Feynman dozens of times — many of these quite memorable, at least so far as I'm concerned. Suffice it to say this cavern sequence to which she alluded was only the most recent instance of Oan slipping into my orbit.

"You do recall meeting me in the sacred caverns, don't you, Mr. Feynman?"

"Oh, rather," I said, but as soon as the words had crossed my lips I knew I'd been too outspoken. The strict letter of my retainer with Dr. Peericks specified that I was to closet myself with Oan, listen to her remembrances with interest, and then denounce them in no uncertain terms. Deny every charge. Tell her to go and boil her head. Convince her, in short, that what she remembered about any past entanglements with yours truly amounted to no more than a mere whatdoyoucallit. But this hadn't occurred to me until I had "oh rathered" her recollections, giving her reminiscences the gold stamp of approval. I suppose I could have taken a stab at taking these words back, negating them with a quick, "whoops, I meant to say 'no, I've no idea what you're talking about,'" but I rejected this strategy out of hand. I mean to say, I'd just acknowledged a prior meeting in sacred caverns. Once you let a cat like that one out of the bag, you can't just stuff the thing back in.

"I just knew you'd remember me!" she said, clapping her hands and bouncing where she sat.

"Quite," I added, eager to move past this spot of unpleasantness, but my interruption failed altogether to stop her from polluting the scenery with hosannas.

"I remember meeting you and the Intercessor in the grotto," she continued, "as you conveyed him into the cavern

31

and made your way to the river's edge. I spoke to both of you by the river. You accompanied the Intercessor as he conferred with the prophet Norm Stradamus and stood by his side through the terrible battle between the Intercessor's forces and their enemies.

"I missed much of the battle encased in an amber shell," she continued. "But those adherents who saw the battle said you played a vital role, helping the Intercessor overcome those who would stop us from communing with the universe and unleashing the true power of the Laws of Attraction. You were said to be very brave. You are held in great reverence."

Here she paused for a space, inhaling a lungful of O2 and looking as though she was approaching the point of bursting.

"The Hand of the Intercessor!" she said — although "effused" might be mot juster, as she sat there beaming at me rather freely, like a dog eyeing its master with the expectation of imminent bacon. "Rapturous" sums it up nicely.

"It's an honour to be with you again," she added, eager as ever to cross the t's and dot the i's.

Since faulty memory circuits are becoming a theme in the present narrative, I should remind my public of the episode to which Oan had referred. This "Intercessor" chap Oan mentioned is a cove named Ian Brown, a garden-variety chump who had the pleasure of being my roommate at the hospice. This Brown, the mildest piece of cheese you could produce in a year of Sundays, was mistaken by Oan and the Church of O for some sort of harbinger or prophet of an otherworldly what-doyoucallit named "the Great Omega" — a bird who resided in the beforelife and bestowed gifts on her people. Dashed silly of them, I know. But when it came to pass that Ian and self stumbled upon the Church of O in its sacred grotto — a slice of underground geography occupied by these robe-wearing yahoos — a spot of drama ensued ending with Ian and his wife biffing off to parts unknown and yours truly cajoled by Abe into signing up for my current mission, viz, the quest to find Isaac and thwart his plans. For present purposes, though, the critical thing is that this Oan, a bird who had known me for years and years, had just reported an accurate memory of Feynman. I was eager to hear more.

"And apart from that?" I asked. "Do you remember anything else?"

"Of course I do," said Oan. "After the grotto, you were the talk of the entire assembly of acolytes — the finest example of what we aspire to be. You were the Hand of the Intercessor. The one who travelled at his side. An ordinary man who, through no special merit or talent of his own, managed to stand side-by-side with the Intercessor as he laid bare the truth of Detroit, showing us that the world truly can be remade through acts of will. *'If you believe it, you shall receive it.'* You brought the Intercessor to us. You were his aide. You are a blessing to all who know you. As we shared stories of your works, and wrote songs of your struggle with the forces that opposed the Laws of Attraction, I came to understand that I was meant to be by your side. Standing with you, I mean. Twin souls, united in pursuit of a single, all-important goal — serving the Great Omega and laying bare her hidden truths!"

That sounded like two all-important goals to me, but I was in no mood to quibble. Nor did I pause to take umbrage at the "ordinary man" rot she had spouted. Choosing to pick my battles, I pressed on.

"But do you remember anything about me before we met in the grotto?"

"Before the Intercessor?" said Oan. "Why, no, Mr. Feynman. We hadn't met. Why do you ask?"

"Dash it!" I said, having had it up to the eye teeth with this trend of deleting largish chunks of the Feynman history.

"I'd have remembered meeting someone like you, whatever the circumstances," she added, picking at her coverlet. "Someone so powerful, I mean. So influential. So in tune with the currents that shape our world. So thoroughly tied to matters of cosmic import; aligned with the Laws of Attraction and central to my own aspirations."

I'll admit I liked the note of fanatical adoration she was striking, but I remembered that my priorities lay elsewhere.

"And what of Zeus," I said. "Do you remember a chap named Zeus?"

"Zeus?" she said, eyes widening in a vacant sort of way.

"Big chap?" I prompted. "Stands about eight-foot-six?"

"Why, yes," she said, looking pleased to be of assistance. "He was a patient at the hospice."

Once again her choice of words raised my brow.

"Was?" I asked, seizing upon the critical bit of dialogue.

"Why, yes. He escaped from Detroit Mercy at the same time as the Intercessor. I'm sure you're aware the Intercessor was briefly housed in the hospice as a result of a most unfortunate misdiagnosis."

"Two chairs," intoned the roommate, apparently feeling that she wasn't holding up her part of the conversation.

"And Zeus's current location?" I pressed, ignoring the charred beazel. "Do you know where Zeus is now?"

"I'm sorry, I don't. I expect the police are searching for him. Dr. Peericks must be so concerned. Perhaps Dr. Peericks could tell you if he has been found."

Fenny seemed to see this instant as the prime time to scale the charred roommate's leg and settle into her lap. Dashed familiar of him, I know, but the ways of hamsters are subtle and mysterious. The roommate responded to the affront by gently scratching Fenny behind the ear, as though the two were long-time chums.

I turned my attention away from this cozy scene and continued with my remorseless interrogation.

"So, you remember Zeus. You remember Ian Brown. You remember them escaping the hospice together. But so far as I'm concerned — *nothing* before the cavern sequence. You haven't the faintest whiff of a memory of yours truly before we met in the sacred grotto."

"Of course I haven't," said Oan, a look of puzzlement spreading over her map. "That was the only time we met. The only time before *today* I mean. But despite that, Mr. Feynman, despite the fleeting entanglement of our auras, I was certain you would come to my aid. I had faith that the Laws of Attraction would guide you to me, that the reverberating fluctuations of the universe would once again draw your aura toward mine, and that if I opened myself to the infinite possibili—"

"Quite, quite," I said. "But if you want to be scrupulously accurate, what brought me to you wasn't the pull of any law of attraction or the entanglements of our whatdoyoucallits, but a note from Dr. Peericks. A note which says 'pop down to the hospice, take a peep at Oan, and tell her she's gone cuckoo.' I give you the gist," I added, waving off her look of dismay. "But what Peericks wants, in a nutshell, is for me to confer with you and convince you that those cavern memories you've been babbling about aren't real. Imagination, I mean to say. The mere somethingorothers of a troubled mind."

"But Mr. Feynman!" she began.

"I know, I know," I said, raising a placating hand. "You mean to insist that your memories are the straight goods, that the cavern sequence proceeded exactly as you've outlined, and that any suggestion that you're suffering from delusions is the overzealous babbling of a loony doctor eager to push his pet diagnoses and erase all the interesting bits of his patients' personalities."

"It's true!" said Oan.

"But where does that get you?" I asked, in that incisive way of mine. "Consider the outcome. You stick to your current story, spilling the goods about apocalyptic battles in hidden grottos, and Doctor Peericks clings to the view that you're several cards shy of a full deck."

"But surely, Mr. Feynman, if you were to—"

"If I were to string along, supporting the company line, as it were, lending your account of the cavern sequence a spot of corrugation—"

"Corroboration."

"—or a spot of corroboration, if you prefer, then what will the harvest be? Do you think Peericks will be moved? Do you think a man like him, so hide-bound and steeped in scientific drivel, will take my assurance as absolute sooth? Will he pivot on the spot, change his mind, and publicly declare that his original diagnosis was all wrong? Do you think he is likely to chuck his prior findings and fling wide the hospice gates on nothing more than the combined say-so of a resident of the loony bin and one supporting chump who Peericks views as a total stranger?"

"I hadn't thought of that," said Oan.

"Think of it now!"

"I see what you mean."

"He will not," I continued, for I didn't wish to leave the thing ambiguous, "see my words as concrete proof that your prior babbling should be taken as gospel truth, but will instead conclude that your certified goofiness has rubbed off on yours truly and infected the Feynman brain, leaving the undersigned in danger of a longish stretch in the hospice right beside you."

This held her. She chewed her lower lip for a space before responding. And when she did respond, all she managed to say was, "What shall we do?" in a tremulous sort of way, if tremulous means what I think it does.

I leaned in.

"It is vital that we secure your release," I said, giving the words as much weight as I could manage. For, while I'd typically be sanguine or insouciant about this loony bird's address, in the current circs my foreign policy rested on getting Oan declared sane and fit to consort with civilians. I was desperate to have Peericks point me in Zeus's general direction, and to secure that simple favour, I needed to push along the medical louse's loopy efforts to press his suit with Oan — a suit which couldn't be pressed so long as Oan remained *in statu quo*. Everything hinged on her release.

I couldn't explain all this to Oan. If I came out with the straight goods and told her of Peericks's tortured heart, she might respond with a cool, "What, that old toad? Thanks for giving me one good laugh for today," and dash my plans to the ground. Even when dealing with a droopy soul like Oan, one has to tread carefully in such matters, sidling up to the tender words by throwing in the fancy touches preparatory to paving the way for true romance. So I rolled up my metaphorical sleeves and started in with the preliminary spadework, doing my best to appeal to her soppy and sentimental sensibilities.

"We must secure your release," I said, emphatically. "You see . . ." I paused, seeking to strike the right note, "my entire future happiness depends on it."

"Oh, Mr. Feynman!" she exclaimed.

"I shouldn't tell you this," I said, sneaking up on the thing, "but . . . there is . . . an aching heart in Detroit Mercy."

"An aching heart?"

"An aching heart," I repeated.

"But why does it ache, Mr. Feynman?" she asked, dewy-eyed and hanging on my every word.

"Dash it," I said, for this was threatening to take longer than I had hoped, "you know why hearts ache, Mistress Oan."

She seemed to shimmy a bit. Her voice, when she spoke, was whispery.

"You mean . . . for love?"

"Absolutely! Right on the bull's eye. For love of you, I mean to say."

"Oh, Mr. Feynman!" she repeated.

"But the dashed difficult thing," I said, waving off the interruption, "is that this aching heart can't bring itself to make its feelings known. It yearns to speak, but must stay silent. It wants to speak the tender words, to make plain its true feelings, but so long as you are closeted here, diagnosed as a loony and cooped up in the hospice, this aching h. can't take the risk. Please don't ask me to say more."

"But Mr. Feynman!"

"No, no! I have said too much already. But know this: love waits for you, Oan, but cannot flourish so long as you stay bunged up in here."

As soon as I'd uttered them I knew the words "bunged up" shouldn't have come within several miles of any attempt at pitching woo, but I could see by her rapt expression that Oan had let the error pass. She was hooked, as I knew she would be. Tell a droopy bird like Oan that she has a tortured, secret admirer and she can't help but melt on the spot.

"So you see," I added, "we must secure your release."

"But whatever shall we do?" she asked, chewing the lower lip.

"I have a plan," I said. And the reason I said this was that I did, in fact, have a plan.

"And the best thing about this plan," I said, "is that it's not only 100% foolproof, but also simplicity itself in execution."

"How wonderful!" she said, and probably would have danced a step or two but for the fact that she was seated.

"The plan is this: You should lie to Dr. Peericks."

"Lie to the doctor?"

"Like a public servant applying for reimbursement! What use is sticking to the truth when the simple act of falsifying the facts can get you out of chokey?"

She didn't seem to see the wisdom of my scheme.

"But I can't lie to Dr. Peericks!"

"Of course you can. Simplest thing in the world. You just wait for his next visit and say, 'Oh, Doctor,' for I'm presuming you call him doctor, 'Oh, Doctor, Mr. Feynman has cleared the scales from mine eyes, and I now remember all. That cavern story I told you never happened.'"

"But, Mr. Feynman!"

"I foresee your objection. You think Peericks will take convincing. That's where I can assist you."

"No, it's—"

"I don't mind at all!" I added, seeing that the bird was becoming a bit stirred-up. "I'm happy to help convince the old placebo-pushing pillmonger that you've resiled — do I mean resiled? — from your conviction that the cavern sequence happened as previously described, that you witnessed the City Solicitor and Penelope doing their best to shatter the cosmos at each other, and that you and the Church of O had unearthed proof that the beforelife was real. Why, I shouldn't doubt that you'll be out within the hour."

"But I can't say those things, Mr. Feynman!" said Oan, although if you'd care to replace the word "said" with "shrieked," you wouldn't be far wrong.

"But why not? It's the surest path to freedom."

"But it runs counter to everything I've ever taught in the Sharing Room, Mr. Feynman. I'm not sure if you're aware of this, but I've spent years working with patients in the hospice, helping them find their truths, helping them focus the Laws of Attraction and align their auras with—"

"Quite, quite," I said, trying my best to avoid the headache which always manifested whenever Oan vented spiritual truths. "But what does that have to do with anything?"

"Authenticity, Mr. Feynman! It's the core of all I believe. We must speak our own truth, and be our authentic selves. Only by being true to our own narrative, and walking our true path, can we attune ourselves with the Laws of Attraction. Only by heartfelt authenticity can we perfect our way of being, clarifying our auras and communing with the world. *The truth of ourselves,*" she continued, her words now brimming with soulful whatdoyoucallit, "*is the only way to perceive the truth beyond.*"

"But dash it!" I said, feeling a good deal like a leaking balloon.

"I'm sorry, Mr. Feynman. I cannot abandon my truth."

I'd always known Oan was goofy, but I hadn't budgeted for loopiness on so majestic a scale. Had my own schemes not rested on securing this freak's release, I might have legged it at this juncture and written her off as a lost cause. Any lesser man would have done so. But we Feynmen are resilient. Where others clutch the hair and smite the brow, we soldier on.

I gave the thing the cream of the Feynman brain, and was rewarded.

"If you won't change your story," I said, "how about this: we stuff the ballot box. If Peericks won't believe the cavern story coming from you and me, let's give democracy a chance. Show Peericks that it is no mere duo which shares this memory of the cataclysmic goings-on within the cavern, but a whole platoon of more or less reputable citizens who can bear witness to the events. We flood the man with supporting evidence. Call the acolytes and the chorus. Call Norm. Call Llewellyn Llewellyn if you can. Dash it, wrangle the whole herd of those who were present—"

"We can't!" she exclaimed, derailing my train of thought. "Norm Stradamus and his flock have disappeared! I don't know where they've gone. Perhaps they've gone into hiding, or found a way to breach the veil between this world and the hidden realm of the Great Omega—"

"What about the City Solicitor?" I suggested. "He was there."

"He's gone, too," said Oan. And her lower lip got a bit more chewing done to it. "What about the Intercessor himself?"

"No, not Ian. And not Penelope or Abe. They've all biffed off to parts unknown. Dash it," I added, for I'd had it up to the eye teeth with modified memories and disappearing persons, "surely there must be someone else who could lend support to your story. Some other witness, apart from yours truly, who can bootstrap our story and lend it a dose of credibility."

"We could ask Sir Isaac Newton!" chirped Oan.

I gaped at the old bird. Slack-jawed, if you catch my meaning. And if you'd cared to describe me as thunderstruck, you wouldn't be far wrong.

Chapter 4

And I'll tell you why I gaped. Oan's remark had smote me like
a blow. Or do I mean "smitten"? In any case, the Isaac to whom
she referred was, if you'll recall, the White Whale to my Captain
Ahab, if that allusion means what I think it does, and it struck
me as sinister that he, the chief whatdoyoucallit of a quest I had
shelved for the nonce while on the hunt for Zeus, might weasel
his way into this slab of dialogue with Oan. Story A horning
in on Story B, if you follow me. And hitherto I'd always heard
him called "Isaac," or sometimes "Isaac Newton," never having
encountered a "sir" attached to his name. I instituted inquiries.

"*Sir* Isaac Newton?" I said, agog.

"Two chairs," said Oan's roommate.

"Yes. Sir Isaac Newton, the scientist," said Oan.

"You mean secretary."

"No, scientist."

"He's the City Solicitor's personal secretary."

"He isn't!" said Oan. "He's Detroit's most eminent scientist
and a professor at Detroit University."

"Surely not."

"But he is!" said Oan.

"He's a secretary!"

"No he isn't!"

"Grrnmph," said Fenny.

It occurred to me that life in the hospice had finally
unhinged Oan's little grey cells; not that they had been too well

hinged in the first place. Nevertheless, perceiving we could be at this all day, I gave diplomacy a go.

"Allowing, mistress Oan, for the fact that Isaac may no longer serve as personal secretary to the City Solicitor, for I haven't checked his cv in the last few days, I can assure you that in the fairly recent past he did fill that post, relying on it as the source of his weekly envelope."

"No, he didn't," insisted the misinformed halfwit. And she followed this with a claim that she could prove it. She instituted a bit of stage business in which she opened a drawer in her bedside table and fished out a rather futuristic-looking datapad, this gadget being festooned with more blinking lights and other indicia of high-techishness than the ones you usually see.

Never having set my eyes on this particular brand of doodad, I allowed an impressed "oh, ah" to escape my lips.

"Impressive little thingummy," I added, thinking no harm could be done by dishing out compliments.

"It's the latest in I-Ware," she said.

This confused me, largely owing to the fact that I didn't see her words in print. I mean to say, to the untrained ear it seemed she'd said "eyewear," and I looked in vain for a spot to hook the thing across one's ears. Oan must have noticed my puzzled expression, for she served up a couple of footnotes.

"Capital I, dash W-A-R-E," she said. "*I-Ware.* A line of devices produced by Professor Newton. They're ever so popular. But that's not what I wanted to show you. Please, look here."

She fiddled with the device for a space and summoned up an article from today's edition of the *Detroit Times*. She turned the device toward me for inspection.

And you'll understand my surprise when I tell you that there, on the palm-sized screen before me, was the unmistakable face of the Isaac of recent discussion, accompanied by a caption, which I now read aloud:

"Sir Isaac Newton, Lucasian Chair of Mathematics."

"That's right," said Oan. "He's been the Lucasian Chair for ages."

"Is that good?" I asked.

"Of course!" said Oan. "It's one of the most prestigious positions at the university."

"Two chairs," said Oan's flambéed companion.

"One chair," I corrected, tolerantly. "Lucasian, whatever that means."

Having quieted the peanut gallery, I ran an eyeball or two over the first few lines of the article. What they said left me goggling. I mean to say, when you know for certain that a fellow is a personal secretary, and you catch two lines of text identifying this self-same egghead as the "longtime holder of DU's Lucasian Chair," you goggle. It seemed, in short, that Isaac Newton was not the furtive skulker I'd been led to expect when Abe pressganged me for this mission, but rather a chump of wide renown who could be found by anyone willing to breathe the fug of a university.

This turn of events annoyed me. I mean to say, no one is more amenable to the Author's retroactive, editorial revisions in the manuscript than I, but you'd like to think that when He changes things which touch on what we might call "the central plot," He might keep His protagonist abreast. Common courtesy, I mean to say.

"So you see, Mr. Feynman," said Oan, "Sir Isaac Newton, who was in the cavern throughout the crucial moments, would be the perfect witness to verify our claims to Dr. Peericks."

"So why didn't you give that chump a yodel and ask him to corroborate your story, instead of me?" I asked, still peeved.

Here Oan blushed, and plucked her coverlet once more.

"I hadn't thought of it," said Oan. "And I wanted you, Mr. Feynman. I thought you'd be the most helpful. I thought that, meeting someone as brave, clever, and worldly as you — one who stands alone as the Hand of the Intercessor, I mean — that Dr. Peericks would be so impressed he'd accept our story without question. And I thought you and I might work together, that we might walk the same path and, well—"

I silenced her with a look.

"An understandable gaffe," I said, pausing to appreciate the "brave, clever, and worldly" sequence. It's not often that I'm given the old oil in this fashion, most of my circle being more inclined to the slam than to the rave.

"But why do you now proffer Isaac as a witness for the defence?" I asked, getting back to the nub; or the *res*, if you prefer. "Why should Peericks trust his word any more than ours?"

"He's a scientist!" Oan persisted, "a scientist known for careful and meticulous observation. And he's a hero to Dr. Peericks. Why, if he were to back us up, Dr. Peericks would be forced to accept the truth of all I've said!"

No doubt you've seen my objection coming from several miles away. This Isaac, whatever chairs he might now hold, is no straight-shooting corroborator of others' apocalyptic memories, but a snake of the lowest order and the principal villain in my quest. And Abe the First — a usually reliable source — had referred to this blighter as The Most Dangerous Man in the World. Isaac was not, in short, the sort of person to whom yours truly could turn for a spot of testimonial support. I put this objection to Oan.

"I'm sure he'd help you," said Oan. "First and foremost, Sir Isaac Newton is a scientist. A popular one. He isn't dangerous in the least — I can't imagine why Abe the First might have suggested otherwise. And the professor values truth above all else. He's famous for it and says so all the time. He'd be sure to think the truths revealed in the cavern are among the most important. They touch on the very heart of things — the nature of the universe, the fabric of reality, even the very Laws of Attraction — Professor Newton would surely want to make this known. I don't know why he hasn't talked about this already. I — why, that's it!" she carried on, in a great-scotting sort of way, "I'll bet he's also waiting for someone else, another reliable observer, to verify what he witnessed in the cavern. He may doubt his own perceptions, and seek further support for what he believes he saw. He lives for evidence, Mr. Feynman. Why, I'll bet he'd be excited to hear that you are able to verify his claims! Oh, Mr. Feynman! This is perfect!"

I stroked the chin. It was true that, if I could give this Isaac an authoritative footnote or two, lending credence to any observations he had made in the grotto, then he might be inclined to help. By adding my own voice to his, I might help the poor fish survive the rigours of peer review. This was, I could see, an idea.

"So you really think he'll help us?" I asked.

"I'm sure of it!" she said.

"But what of Abe's warning? Abe called this chump The World's Most Dangerous Man, and Abe isn't known for making mistakes."

This held her. But then she snapped the fingers again, experiencing a second eureka moment in the space of just two pages.

"An experiment!" she exclaimed. "Isaac has never hurt anyone. I can't imagine him meaning to cause anyone harm. He really is highly respected and very popular. If he's a danger to anyone at all, it must be the result of some experiment he's running. Perhaps some new chemical compound, or a new source of energy. Something explosive. Or maybe some kind of environmental danger. An unintentionally hazardous piece of I-Ware that he hasn't yet released."

"Some sort of science thingummy, eh?" I said, stroking the chin a second time. This squared with what I knew about Isaac. Even when he'd been the Solicitor's personal secretary, he was always inventing things. The IPT. Flexion Filing. Boson whips and whatnot.

"That must be it," said Oan. "It has to be some sort of dangerous invention, or an experiment with consequences that Isaac fails to foresee. Perhaps Abe sent you to warn him!"

Once again this loony bird, as dotty as she might be, had swung the jury in her favour. For whatever reason, the Author had taken this Isaac chump and retroactively rewritten his character sketch, replacing his prior role as a dreary personal secretary with that of a highly vaunted academician. How dangerous could a scientist be? I mean, they spend their days in lab coats tinkering with vials, computational devices, and electronic doodads. If he was undertaking some sort of lab experiment which posed a risk to all and sundry, why, I'd simply point out the danger, convince him to abandon this folly and pursue some less dangerous pastime, and Bob, as they say, is your uncle. Story A would be neatly tied with a bow in service of Story B: I would convince Isaac to cheese the tinkering and then use him to corroborate Oan's story, which would in turn have the effect of unsealing Peericks's lips, convincing him to spill the goods about Zeus's current whereabouts. Why, the plan couldn't be surer of success.

"You've convinced me," I announced.

"Two chairs!" said Oan's companion.

"Grrmph," said Fenny.

"How wonderful!" said Oan.

"The path is set," I said, in that inspiring way of mine. "I shall set sail for Detroit University, tell Isaac to put a sock in whatever experimental tinkering imperils the known universe, and convince him to wire Peericks confirming your views about the cavern and associated events. I should be back by nightfall."

"By nightfall?" asked Oan, registering incredulity.

"By nightfall," I confirmed. "I'll pop into the IPT and head straight for old DU this afternoon."

"Two chairs," said Oan's roommate.

"The IP what?" said Oan, befogged.

"T," I said, which made me thirsty.

"But what in Abe's name is an IPT?"

"Instantaneous personal transport. Teleportation thingummy. Move from Spot A to Spot B in a flash. Invented by Isaac Newton himself, if memory serves. Why, it's how I travelled today."

"Surely you're joking, Mr. Feynman," she said, gargling, or possibly laughing lightly. "You say the strangest things. There's no such thing as instantaneous transport. There never has been, and there never will be. That's what this article is about," she added, tapping the I-Ware datalink she'd conjured earlier. "Professor Newton made an announcement just this morning. He has proved beyond any doubt that teleportation is impossible."

Chapter 5

You're probably thinking that Oan's recent *obiter dictum* must have shivered the Feynman timbers, but it didn't. On the contrary, her statement about the IPT failed altogether to shatter my customary aplomb. If there's one thing life in Detroit Mercy has taught me, and taught me well, it's that you can't put too much stock in the ravings of hospice dwellers, not even those who are bunged into the place through unfortunate misunderstandings. Nor was I bothered by the fact that Oan's fatheaded pronouncements were supported by some digitized slab of yellow tabloid journalism. "Fake news," I might have said to myself had I been in the mood for soliloquies. I wasn't fussed in the least. The recollection of arriving by IPT that very morning was still fresh in the Feynman bean, and I remained confident that I'd take my departure by IPT as well. And thus it was that not a trace of despondency or agitation etched my finely chiselled features when I absorbed Oan's suggestion that teleportation was a mere thingummy of the Feynman imagination.

Indeed, it's fair to say I was in a breezy mood when I bid farewell to Oan and her scorched pal, and breezier still when I checked in with Dr. Peericks. Shoving the Feynman nose a few inches into his office, I cordially toodle-ood in the chump's direction, punctuating my farewell with an assurance that I'd return post-haste equipped with props and documentation designed to cajole Oan's little grey cells back into working order. This seemed to satisfy the old brain scrutinizer, who thanked me several times before I withdrew.

And I'll tell you why my m. was breezy. When I'd arrived at Detroit Mercy, shaking from stem to stern at the prospect of being recognized as a recent escapee, I'd been beset by doubts and qualms. Would I find myself consigned to a padded cell? Would my quest grind to a halt before I made it through chapter 4? Or would the Author, in His wisdom, drop bread crumbs in the vicinity of the hospice, leading me toward the trails of my twin quarry, viz, Isaac Newton and Zeus? But now, after my tête-à-tête with Oan, the mists had cleared and my path was set. The Isaac situation, hitherto veiled in mystery, would be solved by a few well-chosen words warning him off whatever ill-advised experiment he'd started. Isaac would, no doubt, be so sincerely grateful for my helpful words of caution that he would rally 'round and help Oan fly the hospice coop, which would in turn allow Peericks to pitch his woo, leading him to unseal his lips with respect to Zeus's current locale, thus strewing happy endings all around. All as simple as *do re mi*, as the expression is. So it was with a song in my heart that I hitched up at the local IPT hub in search of instant transportation to Isaac's lair, viz, the faculty offices at Detroit University.

Except it wasn't an IPT hub. It was a bus depot, of all ghastly things. And if there's anything more depressing than a proletarian bus station awash with gloomy transit users, it is a bus station that takes the place of the teleportation thingummy on which your strategy depends.

The thing about life that's always baffled me, and probably always will, is the way that, as soon as the hand of fate eases matters a little by taking something off your mind, it then sidles up behind you and shoves on something else, as if seeing how much the traffic will bear.

I saw in an instant that there was but one explanation for

this most recent fly in the ointment. The Author had, for whatever reason, seen fit to make yet another blasted retroactive revision to His manuscript — all without regard for my own preferences. After spending an idle hour erasing references to Feynman's prior sojourns at the hospice, He now thought it shrewd to remove Detroit's IPT network and replace it with fleets of rusty, ill-upholstered motor coaches. Dashed inconvenient of the chap, I'll admit, but He must have had His reasons. Perhaps He wanted to have a crack at penning a travelogue and felt that instantaneous whooshing from spot to spot unduly hastened the hero's journey. Or perhaps some fatheaded critic of His previous work had opined that the Author had spent too little time describing the various slabs of geography found between Plot Point A and Plot Point B. Whatever His reason, though, there was nothing for me to do but buy a ticket and settle in.

And on thinking about tickets, it occurred to me that I had one in my pocket — the ticket for the IPT journey which had whisked me hospiceward a few hours earlier.

I fished it out for inspection. My deductions proved true. I saw at a glance that this item was no longer a ticket for a trip through the IPT, as it had been that morning, but a receipt for a bus trip all the way from the Riviera to the station nearest the hospice — the very depot where I now stood. The Author had, I perceived, been dashed thorough in His revisions, replacing a stub which had hitherto been marked *IPT 6F* with another which read *Detroit Transit Commission — Bus 34A — Detroit Mercy.*

For me, the task of tracking down this station's ticket seller, doling out an appropriate sum, and securing a spot on the next bus bound for Detroit University was but the work of a moment. Within minutes, I was perched on a fairly gum-free bench, where I equipped myself with a handy, printed copy of the *Times*.

I took this opportunity to drink in the full contents of the article about Sir Isaac Newton, hoping it would provide much-needed intel about the next stop on my voyage.

And provide intel it did, in heaping measure! Poring over the article, I learned that Isaac was not only the Grand Poobah of scientists at Detroit University, but also the patron saint of high-tech entrepreneurs. He'd made sackfuls of the right stuff by churning out new types of I-Ware at regular intervals, and he'd dabbled in what is known as "social media," creating various platforms with catchy names along the lines of I-Chat, I-Spy, I-Chirp, and whathaveyou, sites which seemed geared toward keeping folks updating their I-Ware and acquiring the latest gizmos he'd invented. It was clear that one could never accuse this Newton chump of being shortsighted. Having taken the step of commercializing his scientific scribblings, the chap was now sitting on piles of gold and as rich as Creosote, if Creosote is the oofy chap I'm thinking of.

Not long after I'd finished my spot of intel gathering, flipping through every page of the *Times* lest I miss some relevant slip of rapportage, I boarded the bus and set sail — or rather wheels, I suppose — toward the next waypoint on the Feynman grand tour.

I've said it before and I'll say it again: I am the most devoted and forgiving of the Author's disciples and never one to serve in the role of literary critic. But one does have one's preferences. If it had been up to me, for starters, I'd have cheesed the IPT revision and left the teleporters in place until Our Hero had made his way to and from the university. I mean to say, this would have saved me a longish ride in an omnibus which had, based on all available evidence, a long and storied history of transporting the great unwashed hither and thither as they carried bagged lunches featuring cabbage rolls, cheese, and improperly sealed sardines. And to suggest the journey passed quickly, featuring only pleasant scenery and a musical montage or two, would be to stretch the bounds of credulity. It was long, it was dull, and it came within an inch of abrading the Feynman spirit.

Teleportation had, hitherto, caused many an anxious moment for the uninitiated traveller — the sort who grows queasy at the prospect of fading out of existence in Spot A and reassembling in Spot B without all of their bits intact or with their limbs and other anatomical whatnots rearranged in some surprising and inconvenient manner. But weighed against trifling fear was the irritation of a road trip which involved sharing a bathroom with the sort of people who share bathrooms.

And so the long day wore on, featuring self nestled into seat 9C, about midway between the bus's stem and stern, cheek-by-jowl with an assortment of transit-goers who were similarly desirous of making their way to the university. My fellow passengers included a brace of eager-looking students, a handful of slump-shouldered workers, a pair of Napoleons gabbling away in their heathen lingo, and a dozen or so others who, whatever their individual merits, struck me as the sort of people who manage to make their ways through life's journey merely blending into the background. It was while I sat in a reverie, reflecting on the effective camouflage provided by humdrumishness, that a siren pierced the usual din of bus travel and gripped the Feynman senses.

The bus pulled over. Its front doors opened. And when they did, they admitted two of the surliest-looking policemen it has ever been my displeasure to smack into — the sort who chew tin cans for dinner and refer to their respective biceps as "the guns."

They goose-stepped down the aisle, right past yours truly without even glancing in my direction, and then stomped to a halt several seats behind me.

"What have we here?" demanded one of them, sticking to the constable's handbook of easy-to-memorize repartee.

I swivelled the bean. And in doing so, I saw that these two gendarmes had positioned themselves adjacent to the Napoleonic chaps in row 12, seats A and B.

The Napoleons seemed to take no notice of them, but persisted in jabbering away at high speed. It's their way. Show me a pair of Napoleons back and forthing in their gibberish and I'll show you a pair whose attention cannot be gripped by any measure short of beaning them with a baguette.

"I SAID, WHAT HAVE WE HERE!" bellowed the shorter and larger-headed specimen of Detroit's finest.

"Looks like a pair o' Napoleons," said his taller, thicker, and duller-eyed companion.

"*Qu'est-ce qui se passe?*" said Napoleon 12A, at last perceiving that he was abutting the Full Majesty of the Law. And I remember thinking he was getting off on the wrong foot. I mean to say, you can't go around qu'est-qui-se-passing at policemen in Detroit, or rather you can, but only if you're keen on being hauled off to the nearest hoosegow for a bevy of unscheduled cavity searches.

"Sounds like Napoleons, too!" said tall and dull.

"Yer comin' with us!" said the shorter specimen, whose face looked like it had been carved by a sculptor who'd studied her craft by correspondence and gave up before lesson three. He gripped a Napoleon by the shoulder and hoisted him up.

"Now see here, officers!" said a loudish, officious-sounding voice, registering no small measure of pique. And you can imagine my surprise when, after a moment of reflection, I realized this officious voice had issued from me. This sense of surprise was heightened by the discovery that, on uttering my remarks, I had risen imperiously from seat 9C and stepped within a confrontational pace or two of these specimens of Detroit's Thin Blue Line.

"Ho!" said short and sculpted, raising his one face-spanning eyebrow in my direction.

"Ho!" said tall and dull, flexing an arm or two.

It was at this point, when I found myself in close proximity to these rozzers, that something struck me as rather odd. As I was standing there, looking up at one and down at the other, it registered that these were no run-of-the-mill policemen. A man of my irregular habits meets his fair share of coppers on life's journey, and he cannot help but come to recognize certain traits, or commonalities, which are shared by every member of The Force. On close inspection, these two specimens didn't square up with the specs, both featuring too little forehead and too much neck, each of them having been fashioned more along the lines of back-alley bruisers or Hospice Goons than graduates of the constables' academy. And there was a certain . . . how should I put this? . . . a certain ogreishness about them. A sense of knuckle-dragging, glassware-chewing menace coated with a thickish layer of dull, species-hating whatdo-youcallit — a trait which I had not hitherto associated with the folks in blue. In sum, the two exhibits now confronting me seemed less apt to "serve and protect" than to hector, vex, and abuse.

"Mind yer business," said the short one.

"But officer," I began, "you can't simply barge in here and—"

"But officer nuthin'," he retorted, which rather derailed my train of thought. "We have a warrant. A warrant fer the arrest of any an' all Napoleons found travellin' to or from Detroit Mercy. Since these two 'ere are Napoleons, and this 'ere bus is headin' from Detroit Mercy, we has what you call 'judicious authorization'—"

"Joo-dish-ull," suggested his colleague, with some effort.

"Judicial authorization to take these 'ere two in fer further questionin'."

He flourished a piece of official-looking paper and then tucked it away instanter, precluding thorough inspection.

He could have displayed the thing all day. We Rhinnicks have a wide array of skills at our disposal, but distinguishing a bona fide warrant from something pulled from a fortune cookie is not among them. So I made a vaguely impressed noise, doing my best to sound tentatively satisfied while still preserving a hint of the wary skeptic.

"Admitting, for the nonce," I offered, adding a magisterial spin to the voice, "these two persons are Napoleons, you are mistaken in thinking they've come from the hospice. I've spent a good deal of time in Detroit Mercy and am well informed of the current personnel. Indeed, I'm presently engaged as a professional consultant by the chief Quack-in-Residence, Dr. Everard M. Peericks," I added, mustering as much hauteur as I could manage in the circs.

"Them bein' Napoleons, and them bein' on this bus, is enough for us to take 'em in."

"On what charge?" I demanded, for I'd read a few procedurals in my day and knew this was the sort of question one could use to stymie a cop.

"That," said short and sculpted, "is none o' yer business." And on saying this, he met my gaze with a look which was pregnant with the suggestion that I was approaching a line it wouldn't be wise to cross. "Now you just turn yourself around, set your arse back in yer seat, and mind yer p's and q's so as we don't find a reason to bring you in, too."

I saw the force of his argument, largely because there was so much of him. I mean to say, a pair of undernourished pip-squeaks would have found me less cooperative. The same calculus must have escaped the chump seated across the aisle in 12D, for he now stood, brushed a speck of imaginary lint from the sleeve of his corduroy jacket, and gave speech. And what he said was this:

"Pardon me, officers, but I'm afraid that's not right. I'm a second-year law student and—"

On the cue "law student," the taller officer drew back his arm, preparatory to hauling off and striking the student across the mazard — a project which I imagine he would have carried to fruition had it not been for the sudden appearance of several dozen small screens being held aloft in roughly half of the hands found on the bus.

I don't know if you've ever ridden a bus, but if you have, you might be less surprised than I to learn that every rider seems to carry a handheld computing thingummy, possibly with a view to avoiding eye contact with fellow travellers. I could see at a glance that many of the doodads wielded by my busmates were part of Isaac's I-Ware line, they having been featured in the article I'd just read. And I recalled from my perusal of the *Times* that these handheld gizmos came equipped with what are known as "high-def cameras," instant uplink access, and a host of other features which, in the present context, added up to a dirty cop's least favourite two-word phrase.

"Public scrutiny!" I announced, rather pleased with myself and my fellow travellers. And my oration was punctuated by the clicks and bloops and other sound effects which meant pictures were being snapped, statuses were being updated, and what I had hitherto written off as anti-social media did its bit for the rule of law.

This seemed to cast a spell on the officers, if they were officers — something which seemed increasingly unlikely the more I observed them.

"Everybody back off!" shouted the taller of the pair, cracking a knuckle or two and flexing his arms, doing his best to silverback us into submission.

I don't know if you've ever lain awake at night somewhere outside the city and observed the twinkling of stars, but the sudden flash of datalink cameras had much the same effect. Dozens of pictures were taken in a snap, as the expression is, and I imagine just as many were posted to I-Sight, I-Book, I-Chirp, and I-Chat, four of the more popular fora created by Isaac Newton for the sharing of pictures, ill-thought-out political opinions, outright lies, and anonymous critiques of one's fellow persons.

"Erm," said the shorter of the two . . . well I can't keep calling them "officers," can I? "Galoots" seemed more appropriate.

"Erm," echoed exhibit B.

"We're bein' recalled!" announced the shorter slab of damnation.

"Recalled by whom?" I asked, much interested. "I've only met you just now, and haven't much to recall about either of you, apart, perhaps, from the scent and general air of misanthropy — if misanthropy's the word I want."

"Recalled to the station!" he announced. "The call just came in over my earpiece."

"But we 'aven't got earpieces, Phil," said the larger and thicker thug.

"Yes we do! And don't call me Phil. And we're goin' to leave now, without these two Napoleons, on account o' we're bein' recalled to the station where," he added, a bead of persp. erupting above his nose, "we can double-check with the sergeant about our orders, neither of us wantin' to do anythin' inappropriate or newsworthy."

"Oh. Right!" said tall and thick.

And so saying, he joined his fellow thug in what is known as hightailing it from the bus, leaving the rest of us in peace and all of a twitter.

We remained all of a t., speculating on what we had seen, until the bus finally hitched up at its final destination, viz, Detroit University, where I and my fellow travellers disembarked with mutual expressions of esteem and gratitude for having come to journey's end in relative safety.

The two Napoleons, for their part, slipped off the bus and buzzed off I know not where, passing out of the Feynman orbit forever. At least I thought they did. I lived under this naive misapprehension for several weeks, blissfully unaware of the dire circumstances which would cause us to foregather in later chapters.

Chapter 6

Detroit University's Central Campus is one of the more pic-turesque blobs of real estate you'll find on any list of points of interest in Detroit. Apart from the grand old buildings fea-turing clock towers, spires, domes, and other architectural features suggesting higher education, the campus was home to well-manicured lawns; flowering trees in full bloom; artifi-cial ponds; and a whole host of birds, bees, squirrels, and other fauna doing their thing. It was, in short, a green and pleasant land which any honest alumnus or alumna would be proud to name as his or her *alma mater*.

While you might not know it to look at me, I myself am an honoured alum of ol' du. Thrice over, in fact. After spending a few years tootling around in a general arts program and receiv-ing my first degree, I took two shorter diploma programs — one in literary composition, doing the Author's work, as it were — and the second in first aid, being one of the less popular programs at DU, given the basic facts of biology in Detroit. But the point I mean to drive home is that my association with the university had been a long and happy one before it became for-ever etched in the Feynman memory as the place where my pal Zeus had lost his marbles. For it was here — in a buffet line at Conron Hall, to be precise — that Zeus and self had found our-selves in the crosshairs of the assassin Socrates, whose memory-wiping bullets had penetrated Zeus's hide, causing the latter's memories to disappear more quickly than a nest egg in a casino

— an incident which, I think you'll agree, could cause even the most jocund soul to drain the bitter cup. And while this spot of unpleasantness had cast something of a gloom on the nostalgia I've always held for old DU, I must admit that seeing it now, with the cherry blossoms blossoming and the birds fooling about in their winsome way, the old fondness resurfaced. I still like the old joint, despite recent associations. And besides, it's not as though you can blame the entire academy for the hideous fallout of the Socratic Method.

My specific destination on this day was the physics department, housed in the old science building at the end of "Scholars' Walk," a yew alley liberally besprinkled with park benches, bird baths, and bits of statuary depicting men and women who, despite the graceful lines and noble faces carved by the sculptor, probably had something or other to do with university administration. It wasn't long before I reached the end of the yew alley and fetched up at my destination. After this it was a simple matter of obtaining directions from a student here and a caretaker there until I zeroed in on an impressive door marked *Professor Isaac Newton, OA, Lucasian Chair of Mathematics*.

So far, so good, I remember thinking.

"You're here for the Lucasian professor?" said a voice from astern. I one-eightied on the spot and saw the voice belonged to a bespectacled young stripling of the thin and pimply variety.

"You're here for the Chair?" he said.

"I am."

"Well, he's not there. He's in one of the lecture theatres. That's where you'll generally find him. He likes to work things out on the boards," he explained, middle-fingering his glasses up to a higher spot on his nose. "I can take you there, if you like."

"Lead on, officious youngling!" I riposted. And within the space of a few ticks this kid had chivvied me through various hallways, staircases, and quadrangles until we hitched up at what I might rate as the most impressive set of oaken doors I'd ever glimpsed. And as these doors currently stood in what you'd call the "ajar" posish, I could see beyond to the object of my quest.

Isaac stood there, not ten yards from yours truly, scribbling numbers, letters, and squiggly things on a blackboard already bedecked with arcane symbols. After only a moment's reflection, I was nimbly able to recognize this as maths.

My pimply guide said something I didn't bother to listen to and shoved off.

I cleared the throat.

Isaac swivelled his bean.

It was, I could see, the time to lock horns with my prey.

He stared at me for a moment. We both blinked. I was on the point of speech when he beat me to it.

"Oh, there you are!" he said, beaming. "I hope I haven't kept you waiting. I was absorbed by a bit of work on waveform collapse and quantum decoherence and rather lost track of the time. Come in, come in, come in!"

I need scarcely say that this exuberant welcome, to one who barely qualified as more than a passing acquaintance — not to mention one whom Isaac must have regarded as being aligned on the opposing side of life's Parcheesi board — warmed my heart a good deal. It was with a feeling that this Isaac's attitude did credit to academic hospitality that I followed him across the lecture theatre and through a nearby door into a large adjoining room liberally cluttered with worktables, beakers, microscopes, and assorted doodads not readily described by one whose talents, however diverse, do not include the taking of accurate inventories in labs. The room also featured a couple of well-stuffed wingback chairs flanking a big bay window overlooking a nearby garden. It was toward these chairs that Isaac steered me now.

We took our respective seats and Isaac rang a bell for tea. Some species of domestic person manifested himself, took Isaac's order, and shimmered off. When Isaac returned his attention to yours truly he found me perusing a small, leather-bound notebook which I'd spotted beside my chair.

"One of yours?" I said.

"Why, erm, yes," said Isaac.

I detected a note of caution in his voice, like a police detainee wary of being hornswoggled into what is known as self-incrimination.

"Not your usual output, what?"

"No, no!" he said, chuckling. "Pseudo-scientific stuff. Just some thoughts I was exploring some months ago to fill an idle hour — musing on non-verifiable phenomena. It's a hobby of mine. Why, I once wrote an entire book on alchemy, not that I expect anyone to read it. Merely an interesting diversion. That notebook runs along the same lines — a simple exercise for the mind, letting it focus on flights of fancy."

"I see, I see."

"An amusing distraction from my work."

"Nifty title," I said, examining the cover. "*Principia Pre-Morta*. A book about the beforelife, then?" I hazarded.

"Well spotted!" said Isaac. "But again, nothing of consequence. I merely posit a hypothetical world in which the beforelife is real for the purpose of exploring an impractical thought experiment."

I thumbed my way through the journal's pages while he spoke — a procedure which seemed to make him sweat for reasons unknown to me. The fruit of my thumbing was the discovery of a series of printed pictures tucked away within the volume.

"Norm Stradamus!" I said, great-scotting and withdrawing the first pic which caught my eye.

"You know him?" said my host.

This surprised me. I mean to say, the last time I'd hob-nobbed with this maths fancier, we'd both been in the presence of Norm Stradamus and his gang of loony disciples. This Norm, if you'll recall, serves as the High Priest and chief prognosticator of the Church of O, a cultish group devoted to belief in the beforelife and the worship of someone or other said to live there. But the point for present purposes is that Isaac ought to have known I'd recognize this chap at first sight, the three of us having been spinning in each other's orbits in the fairly recent past.

It didn't take more than a couple of ticks for the famously keen Feynman powers of deduction, honed by recent experience, to discern just what in Abe's name was going on. Perhaps you've figured it out too. No? Well, let me connect the dots. It's about all of these bouts of Rhinnick-centred amnesia: Peericks & Co. forgetting who I was, Oan failing to recall that I'd been a patient in the hospice, Isaac forgetting that he and I had once stood cheek-by-jowl with Norm Stradamus — these weren't episodes of amnesia at all! These apparent episodes of forgetfulness were, I could now perceive, simple editorial changes, not unlike the Author's choice to erase all references to the IPT network. For whatever reason, the Author was making retroactive revisions in His work and had deleted various tidbits from my history. Things I remembered having experienced were no longer strictly canon, as the expression is. As for why the Author would leave my memory of these non-canonical episodes intact, who can say? Perhaps as a safeguard, or backup, in the event He wished to restore a previous version. But what mattered now was that I was hep to a timeline Isaac Newton hadn't experienced, and I shrank from the prospect of revealing this to him. I mean to say, having tried to explain the Author and his Works to various parties in the past, I've come to learn that these conversations generally lead to strange looks being exchanged, a series of whispered conversations, a couple of surreptitious phone calls, all finally culminating — if culminating means what I think it does — with self being sent on a forced vacation at some quiet retreat featuring straitjackets and ten to twelve sessions of psychotherapy. I decided I should put a lid on any discussion of my prior association with Norm Stradamus, keeping all related data under the hat.

"I know of him," I said, which seemed to land as a safe response.

"Interesting fellow," said Isaac. "Leads a congregation of devotees who believe in the beforelife and worship someone called 'the Great Omega.' He claims to have done some revelatory research on the boundaries between our own world and the beforelife. I've looked into it — purely out of curiosity and professional courtesy, of course, one researcher looking in on the work of another, I mean. All hogwash in the end, but I've never shied away from a line of inquiry."

"So you really don't believe in the beforelife, then?" I asked, knowing Isaac had — at least in the version of history currently stored in the Feynman bean — been rather thoroughly wrapped up with events which had, for anyone paying attention, conclusively drained the bath on any notion that the beforelife *wasn't* the genuine goods.

He cleared his throat and stammered a bit, doing a passable impression of an academic bullfrog. "Ahem. Well, I mean, there's just no evidence on which to found any such belief," he said, and I perceived that he blushed a little. "No evidence at all. Why, even if it did exist, we've no way to observe it. No, no, any question of the existence or non-existence of the beforelife is best left out of any description of the observable world. But now, I'm curious," he said, once again leaning forward in what you might call a marked manner. "Do *you* believe in the beforelife?"

"Oh, ah," I said, unprepared for this sudden dose of table-turning. But we Rhinnicks are quick thinkers. "I have a pal who does," I said. "Chap named Zeus. Thinks he's been there and back a number of times, sometimes as a man, once as a dog — a Yorkshire Terrier, if that's of any interest. A complicated case. But turning back to this journal of yours," I added, thumbing through it rather freely, "it seems to suggest that you had at least *some* faith in the possibility that the beforelife—"

"It's purely hypothetical," he snapped, if you can snap a word as long as "hypothetical." For some reason not revealed, this number-pusher seemed to be growing rather hottish under the collar, and he carried on in what you might call a harried tone.

"As I said, I merely employed the assumption that the beforelife was real in pursuit of a thought experiment aimed at assessing human thought processes, decision-making, and memory in a climate of non—"

"Quite, quite," I said, waving a placating notebook, for it was clear that I was steering this man of science toward a spot of uncomfortable terrain. I hadn't wished to unsettle the old egg. My goal, after all, was to gain this bimbo's trust, inquire about his experiments, and see how his scientific musings stood to damage the here and now, all while convincing him to lend a hand in bringing an end to Oan's incarceration. His thoughts about the beforelife were a side issue at best.

I was saved the effort of assuaging the old gumboil's rankled feelings by the return of the domestic chap with tea. He did his noble work, adding here a lump of sugar and there a splash of milk, before he shimmered off and left us.

I set the notebook aside as though it didn't matter a single damn, which of course it didn't.

"Talking of scientific whatnots," I said, adroitly steering the conv. toward less controversial topics, "I'm interested in what you were working on back there." I punctuated this by aiming a thumb over my shoulder toward the lecture theatre with the crowded blackboards.

"Of course you are!" said Isaac, his enthusiasm springing back so forcibly that he almost upset his tea. "Some of my most interesting work. A pair of problems, in fact, which keep bumping into each other in unexpected ways. On the western blackboard, as you might have noticed, I'm grappling with the problem of quantum superposition: the hypothesis that the state of nature we perceive is comprised of multiple, different substates that collapse into what might loosely be called reality — the state that we perceive through scientific measurement or sensory observation. And on the eastern board I'm working on what a layperson might describe as the ostensibly unidirectional nature of time."

He then uttered a bit of gobbledygook which might have been an equation, for it featured a larger number of exes, deltas, taus, and references to entropy than you usually hear.

"Time, eh?" I said, keeping up as best I could.

"That's right. One of my most recent diversions is the problem of time travel — moving from one set of temporal coordinates to another. I toyed with the idea that a device might be constructed that would allow us to perceive the flow of time in what might be called the reverse direction — seeing effects precede causes, endings before beginnings, even peering into the past. It's through this work that I managed to develop the basic precepts of time travel."

"Hmmm," I said, stroking the chin and undertaking to show a hint of interest. Of course I was thinking, as you probably are, that here was a scientific babbler who'd fallen off his nut. Effects preceding causes, forsooth. But I didn't see any harm in feigning interest and encouraging the man with word and gesture. By doing so I might even get on this science booster's good side and convince him to let me in on whatever dangerous experiments he might have in the hopper. I continued hemming and hawing, giving the ass the run of his tongue.

"I know what you're thinking," said the professor.

"You do?" I said, surprised.

"Of course I do! You think travelling through time might be dangerous."

That hadn't occurred to me at all. Why, on reflection it seemed to me that I often travel in time without perceiving the slightest risk. Yesterday, for example, I was situated in yesterday, and today I am firmly grounded in today. I fully expected that tomorrow I'd be in tomorrow, travelling from one bit of time to the next without ever breaking a sweat. I must have mused on this for quite a number of ticks, effortlessly travelling through time once again, for Isaac decided to interrupt my bit of musing.

"Going back in time and interfering with history, I mean. Changing the order of things. Becoming the first man in Detroit and preventing Abe from ruling. Or stopping important scientific discoveries. Interfering with causality — all sorts of perils that have been posited by those who've explored the notion of travelling back and forth through time."

I uttered a mild "oh, ah."

"But those perils don't arise," Isaac continued, and I found myself unable to tell whether he thought this was good or bad. "You can't change history by moving backward in time," he added. "It's just not possible. The only feasible form of time travel I've struck upon is useful for observation and little else. The time-stream, at least insofar as physical interference is concerned, seems to have an inherent self-correcting mechanism built into it, preventing anything from moving into the past and changing history. Theoretically, one might step back through time and observe historical goings-on, but there's no risk of treading on butterflies and unravelling history."

He'd rather lost me with the butterfly remark, but he didn't seem to notice, for at this point he threw in another equation or two, as if I'd been stringing right along and needed some maths to complete the picture I'd been developing.

"I've gotten as far as producing a prototype device," he continued, dipping a hand into a pocket and producing something which I might have called a Swiss Army watch, being a timepiece bedecked with all manner of bits and bobs which had been tacked on for some undisclosed purpose, probably scientific.

"It ought to work," he said, brow furrowing deeply, "but it doesn't."

"Too bad," I said.

"All of my calculations are in order. All of the principles are sound."

"No doubt," I said.

"But it consistently fails to work."

"How like life," I said, philosophically.

"I keep testing it by trying to go back in time to observe my installation as the Lucasian Chair — a day that's seared into my memory more than most. A banner day for science. The university set the date to coincide with the 300th manifestival of the department's founding Chair."

"The founding Chair, eh?"

"That's right! Galileo. Clever man. I've set this chrono-device to that date for testing purposes and tried to move myself through time so I can watch the goings-on, but nothing happens."

I mourned in spirit for the poor fish. I could imagine his frustration.

"Perhaps it'd work in the beforelife," I said, feeling that it never hurt to shove an oar in.

This seemed to catch the Lucasian Chair off guard.

"The beforelife? What in Abe's name makes you say that?"

"Time's different there."

"How do you mean?"

"It runs out. If I understand the basic set-up, your average chap puffs along for a space of eighty years or so, and then poof: no more beforelife. His time aboard the mortal coil comes to an end, and he winds up here. Surely that affects your equations."

The serial leaner leaned toward me once again and raised a baffled brow or two, and my heart swelled at the thought that I was holding my own with a named Professorial Chair at old DU. It'd have done my old schoolmasters and schoolmistresses proud to have seen me debating what I believe are called "temporal mechanics" with a chap who, whatever his faults, was good with figures.

"Explain," said Isaac, eyeing me warily. And something in his manner made me shrink an inch or two and left me feeling a good deal less certain that I had any notion of what I'd been driving at.

"Oh, just making conversation. You see where I'm going though, surely. From a human chap's perspective, time's infinite in Detroit. Shorter for the recently manifested than for Abe, I suppose, but infinite nonetheless, if you follow. Keeps ticking along forever. It doesn't end. But that's not true in the beforelife. Each chap gets a shortish chunk. And if I remember anything at all about mathematics, it's that infinite math and finite math are two wholly different things, they being offered in two completely different semesters. I didn't go in for either of them, but I do remember seeing both appear on the class schedule."

This seemed to strike the man amidships. He just sat there looking stunned for a couple of ticks, before fishing a scrap of paper out of his pocket and scribbling down a note or two. And as he scribbled he aimed a fishy eye at me as if he wasn't sure what to make of the handsome blighter staring back at him. I wasn't sure whether he was about to clap his hands and shout eureka or, by sharp contradistinction, cuff me on the earhole and banish me from his sight. He seemed to choose a middle course, steering the conv. in a new direction.

"You've given me much to think about. Perhaps I'll explore that notion later. For the time being—"

Here I laughed heartily, for I had assumed he'd intended this as comedy. "Time being," I mean to say. But Isaac didn't seem to get it, for he shushed me with a glare and carried on.

"I'm approaching the issue by reference to quantum super-position," he said.

I mmm-hmmmed politely, though I hadn't the foggiest notion of what he was saying. But he carried on in this vein, wantonly unleashing an assortment of monstrous phrases like "orthogonal function," "density matrix," and "multiple eigenstates" until I thought my head might spin off its axis, fall off my shoulders, and roll out the door. The whole thing reminded me forcibly of poetry — it sounds well enough, but doesn't mean anything.

"But enough about that," he said at length. "I appreciate your willingness to indulge me, but none of this is why you're here."

"It isn't?" I said.

"No, no! You want to know all about my Stygian expedition."

"Oh, you went to the Styx, did you?"

I seemed to have said the wrong thing. He goggled at me.

"Didn't you know I'd launched a Stygian expedition?"

"Nobody tells me anything."

"I should have thought they'd have briefed you at the office. Seems silly to send a reporter all the way out here to investigate a story without telling him what they're sending him for."

I'm pretty astute and I saw there'd been a mix-up somewhere.

"Were you expecting a reporter?"

"Of course I was. Aren't you here from *The Detroit Review of Neurological Science*?"

"Sorry, no."

"I thought you must be the fellow who was coming to hear all about my work on the neural flows. I had a fleet of drones plumb the deepest regions of the Styx, gathering data for over a month. But if you're not a reporter, who are you?"

"Rhinnick Feynman!"

"Feynman? Never heard of you. Why in Abe's name are you here?"

I saw the time had come to get down to the *res*.

"Now that you ask, I'm here for not one, but two reasons. First to ask about any dangerous experiments you might be designing, and second to ask a favour for a friend."

"Friend? What friend?"

"Dr. Everard M. Peericks."

"From Detroit Mercy Hospice?"

"Oh! You know him?"

"Of course I do. I met with him weeks ago to negotiate the release of patient records in support of my work on memory. Records relating to mindwipe victims, princks, Napoleons, any patient who has atypical memory patterns."

"And did he give them to you?" I said, a bit more eagerly than I'd planned. The reason for this sudden rush of enthusiasm will, I expect, be clear to all. If this earnest professor had gotten hold of these patient records, he might have copies of records pertaining to Zeus. Opportunity was knocking, and Rhinnick was keen to open the door.

"No, he didn't. It was odd, really. We'd spent hours discussing appropriate measures to protect his patients' confidentiality while still allowing me to carry out my work. We had put plans in place to redact names and to exclude any personal data that wasn't relevant to my study. But when Peericks went to examine the records I needed he found that several had disappeared."

"Disappeared?"

"That's right. Stolen. And once the police got involved the doctor said he was no longer allowed to release any patient records at all."

"That's a shame," I said, for it never hurts to strike a note of sympathy.

"It is — and quite a blow to my work. But I can understand the reasons. All of the stolen records pertained to Napoleons, and all the Napoleons had escaped from Detroit Mercy some months earlier. Peericks felt the mass escape and the theft of the records might be linked."

I was pleased to see that at least some parts of this information squared up with my own data. As you'll recall, provided that your memory contains the same information as mine, I — along with Ian Brown and Zeus — had been among the escapees who travelled with the Napoleons when we decided that we'd spent quite enough time cooped up in the hospice. The Napoleons had been instrumental in the escape. And as I said, I was pleased to learn that this particular sequence still appeared in my biography. I'd started to worry that the Author had rewritten me as an insurance salesperson or actuary, or some other goshawful flavourless specimen, and was relieved to discover that at least one spot of colourful derring-do had survived the Author's cull. But while I did recall, rather vividly, the Napoleons' flight from the hospice, I'd heard nothing about the theft of any records.

"Very odd," I said. "Peericks didn't mention that to me when last we spoke."

"He didn't?"

"No, not a word."

"So why did he send you?"

"He didn't. Not directly, at any rate. Peericks has a patient who has a brace of bizarre memories which Dr. Peericks thinks are delusions. But the patient, who goes by the name of Oan, says you can verify her bizarre claims, thereby sliding her from the 'insane' side of the ledger into the 'sane.' Whether this is true or not, who can say? But Peericks's diagnosis of this patient would be assisted if you'd chime in with your own version of the events which she describes."

"What does she remember?" said Isaac, keen as ever to keep abreast. And as he once again leaned forward in his chair, hanging on the Feynman lips, I could see this was another of those times when a spot of caginess was the order of the day. I mean to say, I knew my own memories jived with Oan's and that both of us remembered Isaac's presence in the cavern. But based on our earlier exchange about Norm Stradamus, Isaac didn't seem to recall that I'd been present on that occasion. It was for this reason that I responded with a touch of wariness in my voice, hoping to suss out the boundaries of this scientist's recollections.

"Oh, something or other about a turn of events in a cavern some months back. Pretty apocalyptic stuff involving the City Solicitor, some chap named Ian, a bird named Tonto, and the previously mentioned Norm Stradamus cheered on by a ber-obed flock."

"Egad!" he said, which surprised me. I mean to say, I myself am a fairly frequent egadder, but apart from me you don't bump into many. It was nice to meet another chap from the club, as it were. And now that we'd established that Isaac, too, was one of the boys, I felt a sense of camaraderie and kinship which I hitherto hadn't felt when rubbing elbows with this gifted twerp of science. I leaned forward, too, my interest in this chump having been intensified.

"She must be referring to the struggle between the City Solicitor and Ian Brown's wife," he said. "An ultra-powerful entity named Penelope. No wonder Dr. Peericks thinks this friend of yours is mad. If I hadn't seen those events myself I'd have a difficult time believing they happened."

"So your memory jives with Oan's?" I said.

"Of course it does. I was there. And those events would be impossible to forget. It was the events this Oan describes that inspired me to pursue my current research."

"So you'll help Oan?" I said, hope swelling within my bosom. "You'll go to the hospice and add your voice to Oan's, convincing Peericks to whip out his 'certified sane' stamp and apply it directly to Oan's head?"

He frowned deeply and shook the pumpkin.

"I'm afraid I can't," he said. "It's impossible. I'm at a highly sensitive stage of my most important work — work that could shake Detroit to its very foundations."

Chapter 7

"But dash it, Isaac," I said.

"I'm sorry, but there's nothing I can do," said the arithmetical poop. "The loss of the Napoleons' records was a blow. If I had access to them, any of them at all, I might be able to fill the gaps in my research and make the time to help this Oan person you mentioned. But as it stands I have to remain here and focus on my work."

"But why do you need the Napoleons' records?"

"To further my work on human memory."

This floated past me, and I must have looked befogged, for Isaac chipped in with additional data.

"It's because of their unique memory patterns," he said. "All Napoleons have a highly specific pattern of memories — or rather a highly specific pattern of *false* memories, I should say. They claim to remember not only living in the beforelife but also making multiple visits to it. Reincarnation, they call it. They claim to remember dying multiple times and remanifesting in the Styx. Die, manifest, reincarnate, and repeat. Highly unusual, yet replicated across virtually all Napoleonic subjects. If I had access to a Napoleonic brainscan or two — or better yet, access to a live Napoleon — I might be able to save myself hundreds of hours of work."

"It's too bad I didn't know about this earlier," I said. "There was a pair of Napoleons on the bus with me today. I could have brought them to you."

"You saw a pair of Napoleons? I was told they'd disappeared!"

"These ones hadn't. Although, now that you mention it, a pair of coppers seemed to be trying their level best to disappear them."

"Can you get in touch with these Napoleons?"

"Sorry, no. We were ships passing in the night, as the expression is. Just fellow travellers doomed to share innumerable trouser-wrinkling hours on public transit. I wouldn't have met them at all if the IPT hadn't disappeared."

This was another of those moments when I'd let the Feynman tongue get too far ahead of my mental filter, briefly forgetting that the existence of the IPT was one of those things best left unmentioned now that the Author had expunged it from His text. But I hadn't imagined how this particular statement would land on the science nib blinking at me across the tea-tray.

He took it big. Indeed, he dropped his teacup the moment the IPT was mentioned, punctuating my remarks with the tinkle of breaking china.

"What do you mean, IPT?" he said.

"Oh, nothing. I must have been thinking of something else."

He stared at me intently and unleashed a bit of logic in my direction.

"No. You said you were only on the bus because the IPT had disappeared. And you'd only have said that if you knew what the IPT was."

"Independent Premium Taxis," I said.

"Mr. Feynman—"

"Interesting Passenger Trains?"

"Please, Mr. Feynman," said Isaac, "it's very important that you tell me the truth. What do you know of the IPT?"

"What do *you* know of the IPT?" I asked, goggling.

"I asked you first," said Isaac, which of course he had. And I could see that we'd be at this all day if one of us didn't give up the goods. I took a chance and rolled the dice.

"Fine then," I said. "The acronym refers to a teleportation thingummy, a device one used to whoosh from spot to spot throughout Detroit. The letters stand for Instantaneous Personal—"

"Transport!" said Isaac, chiming in and harmonizing quite well for an amateur.

"You know of it, too!" I said, rejoicing, for I'd been finding it rather lonely to be the sole repository of prior drafts of the Author's work.

"Of course I do. But the question, Mr. Feynman, is this: how are you able to remember the IPT?"

"Ah, now there you have me," I said. "Perhaps some hidden whatsit in my character sketch. But for whatever reason, I seem to be the only one who notices when history is rewritten."

Once again my words had caught this Bunsen-burner enthusiast off guard. But this time the surprise appeared to have been an agreeable one. He sat back in his chair, gazing up at the ceiling, before running a hand through his hair and repeating my words back at me.

"History is rewritten," he mused, savouring the words. "An excellent way to put it, Feynman. History *is* being rewritten. And you can perceive the changes. That's fantastic. But why, Feynman? That's the question. That, and more importantly, what do you plan to do about it?"

"The only thing one can!" I said. "Just keep calm and carry on. However history is rewritten, I shall have to bear the burden of my perceptions and do whatever I can to serve the Author's will."

This seemed to come as yet another spot of exciting and welcome news. I don't remember ever meeting anyone so moved by every word that crossed my tonsils.

"Most excellent, Feynman! That's the spirit," he shouted, punching the air. And so merry was his mood that I think he might have uttered a "yippee" if the expression had been known to him.

"Wonderful news!" he continued. "So you'll help me with my work!"

Now I was the one surprised. The chap's most recent remarks seemed to qualify as one of those non sequitur things you hear about in logic lectures. I mean to say, I'm always happy to chip in with a spot of aid for those in need, but I didn't see why Isaac felt my resolve to carry out the Author's will would translate into an offer to lend a hand with Isaac's own scientific fiddling. Perhaps he assumed, rightly or wrongly, that the Author wanted me to give a leg up to science.

It was while I pondered this that another thought occurred. Follow this closely, for it's dashed clever. It seemed to me that, if I could make myself useful to this blighter, then he might pitch in back at the hospice and shill for Oan's release, thus convincing Dr. Peericks to lift the veil on Zeus's current coordinates. Weighing against this, of course, was the fact that Abe had warned me Isaac's work would imperil the fabric of Detroit, or words to that effect, and here I was being offered a role in pushing this work along. This was a time, I could see, to watch one's step.

"Help you?" I said, that touch of wariness resurfacing in my timbre. *"Perhaps."*

"Perhaps?" said Isaac.

"Yes, perhaps. I suppose the answer depends on what you're doing. Nothing dangerous, I presume?"

"No, no! Not dangerous, Mr. Feynman. Necessary, and *fundamental!*" he said, applying a goodly amount of weight to the final word. "It's what drives all of my work — my work on quantum superposition and waveform collapse. My work on time travel. Even my work on neurochemistry and memory. It's all aimed at the same, worldwide problem: the failure of empirical observation to conform to calculation."

I eh-whatted.

"Nothing works like it's supposed to."

This had been my experience, too. I'd purchased blenders, lawnmowers, roller skates, and any number of other goods which had gone phut moments after their warranty periods had expired. The habit of goods giving up their ghosts just when you needed them unbroken is the whole reason my friend Vera — the medium and small-appliance repairperson whom I think I mentioned earlier — had any career at all. But it seemed a goofy focus for serious scientific thought.

"So you want to fix broken thingummies?" I said, stringing along.

"I want to fix the world," said Isaac. "The whole universe."

I raised a couple of eyebrows and encouraged annotations. I mean to say, you can't go about the joint saying you want to fix the whole universe without offering up a slab of explanation.

"Consider the planets," he said, rising slowly from his chair, lifting his arms and slipping into what I might have called a soliloquy but for the fact that he was saying it to me. Perhaps "lecture" is mot juster. But whatever you want to call his little slice of exposition, its contents ran as follows:

"I've spent hours calculating projected planetary orbits. I've taken account of every conceivable variable. My results are indisputable, my equations elegant, my solutions perfect. And yet the orbits we observe — those actually followed by the planets — deviate from those predicted. Unacceptable. And take the rate of the expansion of the universe," he continued, now pacing around the room. "Based on the models I've developed and the calculations I've run, the universe should expand more quickly than it does. My calculations also predict observable supersymmetry, dark matter, cosmic strings, and detectable multiverses. Yet none of this is observed. Black holes behave incorrectly. And I've found similar discrepancies in the context of cellular regeneration, DNA mutation, chemical decomposition, weather patterns, light refraction, stand-up comedy, folk music — phenomena from every field of inquiry. In every context I examine, phenomena fail to correspond to my calculations."

"Perhaps your calculations are off," I said.

He gave me an austere look. It was the look of a chap whose calculations are *never* off.

"No," he said, gravely. And then, even gravelier, he added, "It's reality that's wrong."

Now, I don't know how this last slab of dialogue landed on you, but it struck me as a bit thick. I mean, setting aside the narcissism of it all, it seemed churlish to shake one's fist at the universe simply because it was bad with figures. "Give it a break," I might have said, had Isaac and I been on matier terms, "I'm sure half of the things I do in a given day fail to square up with your ruddy calculations." But I kept these thoughts to myself. I suppose the failure of the universe to string along with your mathematical thingummies might vex any chap who draws his weekly envelope by fiddling with numbers and occupying Lucasian Chairs. I therefore refrained from interrupting and let this overconfident number cruncher press on, hoping he might soon sum up, as it were. Besides, I could see that he was enthralled by his own speech. His eyes were alight with a fire I had hitherto observed only behind pulpits or under tinfoil hats.

"Virtually nothing behaves as it should!" he continued, now displaying something you might call ecstasy — a word I wouldn't have thought could come within several nautical miles of maths. "Even some of my own inventions follow this pattern. My own I-Ware! Wherever I relied on observation in creating my devices, rather than designing them through pure mathematical models, I saw the same pattern. These devices shouldn't work, but they do. My subsequent calculations, based on after-acquired data, consistently prove these devices shouldn't have ever functioned at all. They were doing things that ought to have been impossible! Just as it was with the IPT! It worked in practice, but calculation proved it impossible. The inescapable conclusion is that there's an unexplained *wrongness* in the universe. A wrongness that touches everything — physics, chemistry, biology, the very building blocks of reality. I couldn't fathom its source until I observed the City Solicitor's battle within the cavern."

"So what's the source?" I asked, intently.

"That's not important," he said, waving off the inquiry like a picnicker shooing away a wasp he hadn't invited. "I've determined that we can exclude any reference to the source from our solution. What matters, Mr. Feynman, is that I've found a way to correct these errors: I can adjust the world itself — the very fabric of reality — so that it corresponds to my calculations. I can make it work as it should! Thus far, I'm able to make only slight adjustments — correct minor discrepancies and marginal deviations. But my methods are improving. I continue to refine them. With your help, I'll soon have the power to change everything all at once."

My heart stood still. It was as if a chilled, spectral hand had gripped my shoulder. For as soon as the confirmed egghead had uttered the words, "I'll soon have the power to change everything all at once," I knew that here must be the threat that had put Abe's knickers into a twist. I had, unless I was much mistaken, zeroed in on whatever it was that led Abe to declare this Lucasian chump, this Mathed Maurauder, to be Detroit's most dangerous man. I gathered my wits about me and probed for further details.

"Change everything?" I said. "You wouldn't care to amplify that, would you? Explain precisely what it is you propose to do?"

He levelled an icy gaze at me — and if you'd care to describe this icy gaze as piercing, or as one that featured several black holes' worth of gravity, you wouldn't hear an objection from me. Only after subjecting me to this piercing, icy, gravity-laden stare for several heartbeats, apparently peering through my physical person and assessing the Feynman soul, did Isaac finally surface and come across with the goods.

"It's the most ambitious experiment anyone has ever conceived," he said, as though reading from a grant application. "What I propose, Mr. Feynman, is nothing short of universal readjustment. The wholesale reweaving of the fabric of Detroit."

"Golly!" I said.

"I've seen beyond the veil," he continued, in a rapturous sort of way. When he spoke again, his voice was husky with emotion. "With your help, I'll achieve my goal of changing Detroit at the quantum level."

My ears perked up. I sat up straighter. What he had said had set my glial cells aflame.

"The quantum level, you say? Your goal — all of this work you're pursuing — is aimed at changing Detroit *at the quantum level*?"

"It is!" he said.

"This great experiment — this reweaving of which you speak — you mean to tell me your efforts are focused exclusively on quantum whatnots? Those thingummies that whiz around, unseen, inside everything, but which can't be detected without several thousand quid worth of government-funded lab equipment?"

"Well, yes," said Isaac, looking at me as though I'd lost a marble or two.

What this chump didn't realize was that he'd underestimated the suave and debonair guest before him and that I was hep to his science jargon. I'd read all about this quantum business in the fairly recent past, having discovered the May edition of *Popular Science* in my powder room at the Hôtel de la Lune. I perused an article on quantum thingummies for the space of at least fifteen minutes before concluding that the title "Popular Science" had been intentionally ironic.

"So," I said, preparing to demonstrate the fruits of my encounter with this *Popular Science* rag, "your attention is directed solely at quarks, bosons, gluons, and whathaveyou?"

"Precisely," said Isaac. "The key to my plan lies in adjusting reality at the subatomic level, manipulating the eigenvalues of elementary particles and their constituents."

"And by subatomic," I said, just to ensure I'd collared the gist, "you mean, in fact, smaller than atoms. This reweaving you describe, your experiments, all of your fiddling with the fabric of Detroit — it is focused entirely on messing about with subatomic thingamajigs?"

"Absolutely," said he.

"So . . . just *teeny tiny things*, then?"

"I suppose so, but—"

"Your efforts are confined to the realm of the infinitesimally small? The teensy weensy? The 'I can't even see the bally things without a couple of highly powered microscopes' level?"

"Yes," said Isaac, a touch defensively. "But when I implement these quantum-level changes—"

"I've heard enough!" I said, waving a dismissive teacup, for I had, in fact, heard enough. And as you might imagine, my relief at what I'd heard was stupendous. It's not going to far to say that only the circumstance that I was sitting in a chair kept me from dancing a carefree step. This officious number cruncher was, as Abe had foreshadowed, tugging at the very threads that formed the fabric of Detroit. But he was doing so on such a minute scale that it didn't matter a single damn. The quantum level, I mean to say! If he wanted to poke around with subatomic doodads, snipping a lepton here and a gluon there, then who was I to stand in this chump's way? "Carry on, Newton," I might have said, "and may Abe speed your efforts!" for now I saw that Abe had gotten the thing all wrong. He could be forgiven for this, of course, not being privy to the hot news I'd uncovered. Abe must have heard that Isaac was, to use the fellow's own impassioned, hyperbolic lingo, mucking about with the very fabric of the universe, or shaking Detroit to its very foundations. But what Abe failed to realize was the laughably small scale of Isaac's fiddling. This science fancier was no cloven-hoofed terrorizer of the innocent but merely a peevish nerd intent on fiddling with infinitesimally teensy weensy things which even the meanest intellect could perceive would be of no consequence to anyone. I knew in a heartbeat this was one of those misunderstandings you often get — those laughable cases where one half of the world doesn't know what the other three quarters is up to.

The quantum level. That's all it was. An amoeba might take note of Isaac's experiments, but nothing but an amoeba, and even then, only an amoeba with a magnifying glass.

Now that the scales had fallen from mine eyes, as the expression is, I realized Isaac wasn't a danger to anyone at all, with the possible exception of undergraduate students who messed up their long division. He certainly wasn't a candidate for the office of "most dangerous chump in the world." Let him tinker with his quantum thingummies, and I hope he has a fine day for it. I breathed a heartfelt sigh of relief.

I suppose nothing is more uplifting than having a major task struck off of one's to-do list. My quest to put a stop to Isaac's mischief was at an end, and I could now turn my attention to the less esoteric problem of tracking down my missing pal. I was so braced at this turn of events that I sat there grinning for a space, forgetting to hold up my end of the conversation. Coming out of my reverie, I recalled that Isaac had suggested I might help him with his tinkering. If he was right — if I might help him push along his quantum business — this could have the effect of putting the old egghead in my debt and convincing him to lend a hand in my efforts to locate Zeus; something he could readily do by convincing Dr. Peericks that Oan was sane. I steered the conversation back in that direction.

"You were saying I might help you," I said, cheerily.

"Yes! Your ability to perceive what you refer to as the 'rewriting' of the universe makes you a uniquely useful aide."

"It's my pleasure to be of service," I said, inclining the bean.

"Excellent!" said Isaac. "But before we get to that, I need more information about the Napoleons. Their memory patterns hold the key to the aberrations I've observed in neurochemisty. I need to understand why this particular pattern remains consistent across subjects — why so many Napoleons seem to remember multiple visits to the beforelife, and how those specific memory engrams can be replicated or changed."

"And with Napoleons disappearing left and right, you need access to their records?" I ventured.

"Exactly! The records are of the essence. I can't see how we'll proceed without them. Now that all of these records have been stolen—"

Here he broke off. Not so much because he had finished what he was saying, but because at this point I leapt up from my chair and danced a few of those carefree steps I'd forgone earlier. And the reason I danced was this: I had just been struck by one of those bolts of inspiration which always seem to come along just when you need them.

86

He eyed me strangely.

"Perhaps not all of the records have been stolen!" I said, cheesing the choreography and returning to position one.

"What do you mean?"

"Well, when you've known as many Napoleons as I have, you get to know a thing or two about their condition. And one thing only the cognoscenti know is that a small whatdoyoucallit of Napoleons are misdiagnosed."

"Misdiagnosed?"

"With Arc Disorder. Happens to female Napoleons all the time. Show me an honest-to-goodness female Napoleon, and I'll show you a beazel who, nine times in ten, will not be counted as a Napoleon at all but will instead be lumped in with those who suffer from Arc Disorder — a closely related but medically distinct malady. Why, one of my good friends experienced that very thing, and it cheesed her off no end. A pipsqueak called Nappy. Friendly sort. Chummy with my pal Zeus. She was proud to be a Napoleon and chafed visibly at the notion that she might be something else."

"So what's your point?" said Isaac, trying to rush to my crescendo.

"My point, impatient egghead, is this: the blighters who stole the records from Detroit Mercy may have stolen only those of patients officially diagnosed with Napoleon Syndrome. They may not have known to look among those who were diagnosed with something else."

"So you're saying—"

"Nappy's records may still be in Dr. Peericks's medical files! And if I can lay my mitts on Nappy's records—"

"They may assist me in my work! They might even lead to this Nappy person herself. And if you could bring her here, I could perform my own neurological scans and get on with my experiments!"

"Precisely!" I said, now smiling a secret smile. And I'll let you in on the secret behind that s. If I was an astute judge — which I think we can all agree I am — then it was highly likely that any trail that led to Nappy would also take us several furlongs closer to Zeus. I mean to say, the two of them were almost as inseparable as Zeus and self had been during our time in Detroit Mercy. And at the very moment that I had left Zeus behind, suffering the effects of Socratic bullets, I had left him in the care of this same Nappy.

Once again the Author had set my course Zeusward, tossing bread crumbs on my path.

And thus it was that, having divined the Author's will, I tied my lot to Isaac Newton's, and signed up to assist this personal-secretary-cum-Lucasian-Chair with his current work.

Chapter 8

For me it was the work of a moment to book return passage on the overnight bus bound for the hospice. And as my return trip was one of those dullish, yawn-inducing sequences in which nothing of consequence happens, I shan't waste our collective time bunging in any superfluous descriptions, if superfluous is the word I want. The one thing the trip did provide in heaping measure was time for planning my next steps.

I don't know about you, but one thing that has frequently struck me is just how dashed elusive a plan can be. I mean to say, you see your aims and objectives dangling tantalizingly on the horizon, but however you strain your eyes you can't see a path to reach them. Take the problem of Nappy's files. They were, as Isaac had said, "of the essence." They were needed. Without those files, Isaac's work would run aground and no competent bookie would rate my odds of finding Zeus at better than 100 to 8. But how could I lay my mitts upon them? I mean to say, I couldn't just saunter up to Peericks and say, "Ahoy there, psychiatric pinhead, let's have a look at your files." The doctor would issue a *nolle prosequi* quicker than I could say "what, ho!" And even if I were to explain that these files were needed by Isaac Newton in service of scientific inquiry, the old mule-headed dimwit wouldn't budge. As Isaac himself had already specified, the recent theft of patient records had cheesed any chance of Peericks willingly forking over the goods.

Nor was there any percentage in a plan to purloin the things. I mean to say, had I still been a resident of the hospice, clad in the standard-issue white robe and able to blend in with the native loonies, I could move hither and thither about the joint without fear of attracting attention. But as it was — now that Feynman had been designated a stranger in a strange land — I was scarcely able to move from spot to spot without an escort. True, I had developed a talent for sneaking stealthily about the hospice via the air ducts and other secret paths, but in those happier days the prospect of being collared while marauding merely raised the trivial risk of being sent back to my room, or hearing another lecture on civil conduct from Oan, Dr. Peericks, or Matron Bikerack. If I was discovered stealing files in my current state, I ran the risk of landing myself in the jug for forty days without the option of a fine.

Casting my mind back to my midnight hospice raids summoned another line of thought, this one supporting a strategy I call "power politics," but which others, in a less charitable vein, might call blackmail.

I had, if you'll recall, spent several years hitched up in the hospice, and if there's one thing you can say about a lengthy sojourn in a mental facility, it's that it affords the opportunity to gather scads of useful data about the other denizens of the joint, particularly if you're inclined to skulk around at night picking locks and opening cabinets. And while I hadn't uncovered anything you might call *damning intel* concerning the man up top — by which I mean Dr. E.M. Peericks — I had, while rummaging through his personal desk, discovered the fact that this mental hygienist dyed his hair and wore a rubbery somethingorother about his tum — one of those girdle-like devices designed to improve the silhouette of anyone who, like Dr. Peericks, is somewhat fonder of pies than he is of jaunts on the treadmill. And while you might be thinking these trivial nods to vanity don't amount to state secrets or solid blackmail material, you're forgetting about the aims and aspirations of the vain object in question. Dr. Peericks was, unless I was much mistaken, hoping to woo Oan, and Oan had frequently established that the trait she values most is staying true to one's "authentic self," of all the dashed silly things. Show me a man who cinches a girdle about his waist and dyes his hair with Madame Jourard's black-umber number 7, and I'll show you a chump who has thoroughly disqualified himself from plighting his troth to Oan. I mean to say, in this life you can chart one of two courses: you can hitch up with a bird who says "to thine own self be true," or you can waddle about the joint wearing girdles, not both. Thus it occurred to me, in a moment of whimsy, that I might sidle up to Peericks, elbow him in the ribs while winking one of those conspiratorial winks, and inform the vain quack I was aware of his cosmetic conceits, and that only by coming across with Nappy's files could he avoid the dire consequence of me revealing all to Oan.

I toyed with this idea throughout the night, as the bus meandered along its route. But by the time I'd reached the hospice I'd rejected the plan *in toto*. Not because it was unseemly — why, the bounds of seemliness are murky when it comes to any strategy that holds the promise of helping a pal in trouble. No, I rejected the blackmail angle because I was sure it wouldn't work. The only thing presently stopping Peericks from pitching his woo in Oan's direction was a hospice rule preventing the staff from fraternizing with crazies. Peericks had shown by his deportment that he wouldn't break the rules for love alone. And if he wouldn't break the no-fraternizing rule in service of his affections, he surely wouldn't break the rules regarding secret patient files. It's how the man's brain was wired. As specious as this medical blighter's reasoning was, at least it was both predictable and consistent.

I needed another plan. But another plan being precisely what I didn't have, I simply showed up at the hospice and hoped for the best.

On my arrival I wasn't met by another one of those bolts of inspiration for which I had hoped, but by a receptionist who informed me that I'd been added to Oan's guest list, preparatory to chivvying me directly to Oan's room in a brusque manner.

On entering Oan's quarters I found myself alone with the weird old bird, her roommate having apparently moved on to greener pastures. And while any man of regular habits couldn't help but enter Oan's presence with a feeling of trepidation, I was heartened to find that nothing could have exceeded the warmth with which I was now greeted.

"Oh, Mr. Feynman!" she said, beaming over a plate of eggs and b. "I'm so glad you returned. Did you have a comfortable journey?"

"Oh, rather," I said, falsifying the data in order to skip the dreary details of my to-ing and fro-ing via Detroit's transit system. "Everything was boompsa-daisy. Most efficient, the transit service. Back and forth without a hitch. And how about you? Everything still pretty bobbish?"

"Why yes, Mr. Feynman. I don't know that I've ever been happier."

"Good, good!" I said, displaying the suavity of the perfect in-room guest. "No doubt your mood is assisted by having the barracks all to yourself. The bunkmate has checked out, has she?"

"Why no, Mr. Feynman. She's in a meeting with Dr. Peericks. He's helping her with her memory."

"Still harping about two chairs?"

"She is, but now she's saying so much more! She improved almost immediately after you left! Why, you hadn't been gone more than an hour when she started saying the strangest things

— things about two chairs defining men, both freeing and binding, uniting twin souls and—"

"Most interesting," I said, interrupting the addle-minded babbler, for I found myself in no mood to delve into the ravings of crispy character who, whatever her qualifications, still warranted a long-term lease in a padded cell.

"She still remembers very little," said Oan, apparently keen on fleshing out the roommate issue. "Dr. Peericks thinks he can help her. That poor woman. She doesn't remember who she is, but does seem to remember some things about other people. She even said she remembered you, Mr. Feynman."

"No doubt. We met yesterday."

"No! She had other stories about you; several of them. She said she remembered riding an elevator with you in City Hall, returning your hamster to you when he'd been lost, and helping you search for hidden clues concerning someone called 'the regent.'"

On the cue "returning your hamster to you," I fished about in my pocket to ensure Fenny was still among those present. I was relieved to find that the little chap was still minding the store with his usual air of quiet dignity. This brief taking-of-inventory had caused me to rather lose the thread of Oan's babbling.

"Do her stories seem familiar?" asked Oan.

"Familiar?"

"The stories about you in an elevator in City Hall, or about the regent, or someone returning your hamster to you? If these stories seem familiar, they might be clues to who she is."

"I'm sorry, no," I said. "The sequences you describe fail altogether to ring any bells."

I was conscious, as I said this, of a certain amount of doubt. I mean to say, the last two days had shown that the Feynman memory, though sound as a bell as far as early drafts of the Author's text might be concerned, now failed to correspond with the memories stored in the beans of secondary characters, all of whom seem to have been updated with the Author's latest edits. Once again, I resolved to keep my responses on the cagey side of par.

"I mean to say, one has ridden elevators a time or two, accompanied by assorted hangers-on, but none who seem to meet the description of your roommate, either in a pre- or post-charbroiled state. And Fenny and I have parted ways when he's had errands to run elsewhere, but like a boomerang, or one of those well-trained pigeons you sometimes meet, he's always made it back under his own steam."

"And this regent person?"

"Doesn't prod the Feynman memory banks at all!"

"But why would she report these memories if they're not true?"

"Ah. That we shall never know. But I'm not here to talk about elevators, hamsters, regents, or roasted roomies. I'm here, as you might have guessed, to talk about our plan to get Isaac Newton to chip in and tell Peericks you're of reasonably sound mind and fit to circulate with the masses."

Here she blushed and took a seat on her bed, where she spent a moment or two picking at her coverlet and tracing some sort of pattern on the floor tile with her toe.

"That won't be necessary," she said, a slight blush mounting her map.

I corrugated the brow, for the bird had baffled me.

"What do you mean that won't be necessary? I've just travelled to and from the university and secured the chump's agreement to sort things out. Conditionally, at least. He did bung an obstacle or two in the way of our path to victory, but will, I am sure, finally come to the aid of the party. Isaac will back up your story and Peericks will have to let you out."

"I mean it won't be necessary to have Professor Newton confirm my story. It doesn't matter any more. I've made a decision."

"What decision?"

And when she spoke, her voice trembled with a soppy sort of rumminess which at the time of writing, with the benefit of hindsight, I now realize ought to have struck me as sinister.

"A decision . . . of the heart," she said. Her eyes were alight with burning pash and her cheeks flushed with emotion.

"How do you mean?"

"I've been thinking about everything you told me, Mr. Feynman. About the aching heart that cannot speak its love. The heart that yearns to be with me, but cannot make its intentions known so long as I remain a patient."

"I'm with you so far," I said.

"And now I've made a decision."

"Yes. You mentioned."

"I've decided to change my story. I'll deny my true memories. I'll do it for love. I shall tell Dr. Peericks that I imagined everything that happened in the grotto; that my dealings with Norm Stradamus didn't end in any apocalyptic struggle. I'll deny everything I've told him about the cavern; perhaps suggesting that some unnamed member of Norm's flock brainwashed me and made me think all of those things I said before. I'll explain all of this to the doctor and clear the path for love."

"You surprise me," I said, for the old bird had. "What about all that rot about being faithful to your authentic self, speaking your own truths, remaining grounded on the path of whatdoyoucallit?"

"I'm prepared to make that sacrifice, Mr. Feynman. I'm prepared to surrender my will to the Laws of Attraction, yielding my own personal truths — for I do these things in service to the greater truth of love."

She blushed again, and I can well understand why. You can't go around saying things like that without a certain amount of shame making its presence known. "Oh, ah," was about all I could manage as response. I mean, what can you say when confronted with a bird who's on the verge of reciting sonnets?

"So you see, Mr. Feynman, there's no need to involve Isaac any further. I'll tell Dr. Peericks what he wants to hear. I'll convince him there's no longer any need to keep me confined. And then our path will be made clear."

Here she rose, and clasped her hands in front of her bosom preparatory to unleashing her crescendo.

"No obstacles will remain," she said. "Everything will be in place. The Laws of Attraction will respond to the true calling of our hearts. I will marry you, Mr. Feynman."

"WHAT!" I said, leaping convulsively from my chair. "You . . . you'll marry ME?"

"I will, Mr. Feynman," she said, still clasping her hands together over her heart as though she was gripped by the soul's awakening. "I've always known I would, ever since we first met in the sacred grotto. I saw you there with the Intercessor and I knew — I knew the Universe had brought you to me through the Laws of Attraction. I would stand at your side, true partners in carrying out the Omega's will. And when you presented yourself to me, here at the hospice, and you stammered out those pathetic, halting words, talking of aching hearts that yearned for love — why, your meaning was plain as day."

"It was?"

"To me, Mr. Feynman. For you and I are twinned souls, star-crossed lovers, preordained to share one path."

I gaped at the bird and struggled for words. It's doubtful that anything so goshawful has happened to you, whatever your circs, but if it had, you'd have struggled to find words, too.

"Oh . . . quite" is all my vocal cords could manage. I mean, what is a chap supposed to say when a woman bungs her heart at his feet, convinced that she's his twinned, preordained whateveritis, and proceeds to accept what she, in her fatheadedness, mistook to be a proposal of marriage? You can't back out. If a member of the gentler sex thinks you've proposed and then proceeds to book you up, you can't explain that she has gotten her wires crossed and that the thought of linking your lot to hers gives you indigestion. You can't set these things straight without embarrassment on both sides. The mere thought of this hideous shame had already rendered my pores moistish and overheated my collar. I could see there was nothing to do but let the thing ride, hoping against hope that the Author would scrap this whole betrothal sequence, hauling me out of both the frying pan and the fire and saving me from the fate that is worse than taxes.

And talking of sequences that the Author ought to scrap, I wonder if you, like me, have allowed your mind to drift back to the exchange in which Oan first got the notion that I might be keen on a trip for two down the centre aisle. Looking back on it, now, with the aid of hindsight and all that, I could see where this old freak had gone off the rails. Intending only to keep Peericks's name out of the thing, purely out of courtesy and propriety, I'd pleaded his case without specifying an ID for the aching heart in Detroit Mercy. And in doing so I'd gone and given this soppy specimen, this pinheaded misunderstander, the idea that I'd been plighting my own troth, uttering those appalling and regrettable words on my own behalf. And now here I was, sweating at every pore, running over my earlier dialogue and fully understanding how an incorrect and dreadful construction could be put on my previous *obiter dicta*.

It goes without saying that the thought of being engaged to a bird like Oan — one who talks of authentic selves, life paths, Vision Boards, and Laws of Attraction — was enough to put any man of regular habits off his feed. Yet here I was, with nothing to do but register for the china patterns and order the boutonniere.

I mused along these lines for the space of several ticks until I realized that Oan had continued babbling. By now she'd reached the point of planning the guest list and wondering aloud whether Norm Stradamus would officiate the thing and be the one to pass the sentence. I was spared the horror of mooting these points when the door burst open, and who should blow in but Oan's barbecued cellmate, looking somewhat less crispy and draped in a hospice robe. Her burns were still extensive, fully obscuring her ID, but one could see she was on the mend. Where she would have qualified as well-done at our last encounter, I now perceived her to fall somewhere between medium and medium-rare.

"Heya!" she said, on catching sight of yours truly. "Look who I found in the hall." And, like one of those conjurors you see yanking kerchiefs from surprising parts of their person, she withdrew Fenny from the recesses of her robe.

I patted my pocket in vain, finding it short one hamster. It dawned on me that the little chap must have slipped his moorings a minute or two earlier when I'd done my bit of convulsing.

"Grrmph," said Fenny.

"Fenny!" said I.

"Mr. Feynman and I are going to be married!" said Oan.

"Nice!" said the medium-well specimen. "But before that happens he'll need these files."

And on that cue, once again displaying considerable skill at the art of prestidigitation, she reached behind her back and produced a thin cardstock folder bearing the legend *Patient 2-02-1836: Arc Disorder.*

Chapter 9

"How in Abe's name did you get those?" I asked, agog.

"I pinched them!" she said, now thumbing through the folder. "Easiest thing in the world. I was in Peericks's office for treatment, and when he stepped out for a couple of minutes I popped the lock on his filing cabinet and fished it out."

"But how did you know I'd need them?" I asked, even agogger than I'd been a moment earlier.

"You told me," she said.

"No I didn't."

"Sure you did."

"No, I didn't, and I can prove it. It didn't occur to me that I'd need those files until I was hobnobbing with Isaac at Detroit University. And I haven't seen you since. QED, as the fellow wrote. There's no way I could have told you that I had need of those files."

"Weird," said the file-conjuring roommate. "I was sure I remembered you telling me. But then my memory isn't what it used to be. Or maybe it is. I can't really tell, but I do have a clear picture in my mind of you telling me you needed these files to help Professor Newton and find Zeus."

"How will the files help?" asked Oan who, up until this point in the conversation, had been oscillating the bean back and forth between me and my interlocutor, doing her best to keep abreast.

"Ah," I said, turning Oanward. "Ingenious plan. These files will give Professor Newton a leg up with his experiments, and may, as our singed friend suggests, help me zero in on Zeus — though I'll be dashed if I know how our singed f. knew any of that. But even if the files hold no clues to Zeus's whereabouts, Isaac will be so glad to lay his mitts on the files that he'll report to Dr. Peericks and corroborate your grotto story."

"But we don't need him to corroborate my story," said Oan. "You can forget my grotto story. As I told you, I'm going to tell Dr. Peericks I was mistaken about the grotto; that it was some kind of dream or hallucination. I'll convince him that I'm cured. He'll release me, and then you and I will be free to marry!"

"No," said our singed companion, rather forcefully. "You can't lie to Dr. Peericks. You have to speak the truth to save the world."

"Save the world?" said Oan and I in unison.

"Save the world," said the roommate. "If you lie to Dr. Peericks, we're all doomed."

It seemed to me that it wasn't so much the world in need of saving as it was Feynman, R. I mean to say, the prospect of taking the wedding glide with Oan is one which could freeze even the warmest gizzard, and if anything did imperil the world at large at least it might have had the effect of putting off the exchange of vows. I was musing along these optimistic lines when the bride-to-be piped in again, seeking notes and clarifications re: this world-saving gag.

"But . . . but how can that be?" said Oan, and I remember thinking this was an excellent question.

"I don't know," said the crispy, cryptic roommate. "It's just something I saw. Not in my memory. Not exactly. But something . . . something like a memory. Except it hasn't happened yet. It's like I saw the whole thing from a distance, like I was . . .

I dunno . . . separated from what I was seeing, like it was a memory sent to me from an outside source. It was like—"

"Good gracious!" said Oan, initiating another round of hand-to-bosom-clasping. "You aren't remembering things! You're peering into the future! Remotely viewing things that have not yet come to pass!"

"I am?"

"You are! You are truly blessed. It's the rarest of gifts! It's called—"

"Television!" I ejaculated, if ejaculate means what I think it does.

"I think I remember people calling it that," said the roommate. "Or rather I will remember people calling it that, some time in the future. It's hard to keep track."

I drew an astonished lungful of air.

"Abe's drawers!" I said.

And I'll tell you why I cursed. These recent revelations about the inner workings of this charred bird's mind had given me all the clues I needed to piece together her hitherto obscured ID.

"You're Vera!" I exclaimed.

"I am?" said Vera.

"Who's Vera?" said Oan.

"The lightly fried exhibit before you, Oan. Do try to keep up," I said. "Vera's a popsy I met some months ago, a day or two before the grotto sequence. She rather graciously helped Ian, Zeus, Nappy, Tonto, and self out of a perilous spot of bother."

"I did?" said Vera. And I perceived that the task before me, viz, bringing both Vera and Oan up to speed with respect to those bits of Vera's biography that were known to yours truly, was going to take a goodish helping of exposition. I could only hope, as I dished up the details, that my memories of those past encounters with Vera weren't among the things that had been blotted out by the Author in one of His recent rounds of revisions.

The difficult choice facing me now is how much of the ensuing exposition I should bother recording here. One of the hitches one bumps into when telling a story like this one, viz, a story featuring characters who've popped up in previous episodes of one's life, is gauging the right amount of flashbacks, reminiscences, and background thingummies to bung into the works. I mean to say, recount the entire history of every past acquaintance you encounter, and those who've strung along with your memoirs from the get-go are apt to get itchy. "Old stuff!" they'll cry, chucking the volume binward or heading toward another aisle in the library or shop. But if, on the other hand, you leave out any explanation of how a recurring character fits into a web as intricate as Rhinnick Feynman's history, new readers — and old readers whose powers of recollection have gone phut through the passage of time — will raise a baffled brow and plead for a glossary of terms, a concordance, and a full index of characters. A difficult problem, and one I've yet to solve. But as I'm only responsible for the first draft, leaving future revisions to the Author Himself, I suppose I should get on with the show, erring on the side of brevity, and letting the Author bung in any footnotes or explanations He desires.

So let us return to Vera, the hitherto anonymous charred beazel standing before us. When last I met her she had, as previously indicated, been going by the name Vera Lantz. Having been blessed with television — the power to see faraway things and tell the future, this beazel spent her time peering into the future for friends and patrons, all while serving as the proprietress of an establishment called "Vera Lantz, Medium and Small Appliance Repair," this name being something of an ambiguous pun designed, I gathered, to confound the forces of darkness.

Now that I'd managed to put a name to Vera's charred-but-healing face, I was able to see how she'd gotten herself into her current state. Stop me if I've told you this before, but my last encounter with Vera involved an imminent attack by the assassin Socrates — a gloomy chap who had a habit of leaping out of the darkness and robbing people of their minds. This Socrates, intent on inflicting a bit of no good on myself and my companions, was on the verge of cornering us in Vera's emporium, and seemed to be on the point of carrying out his nefarious plans — if nefarious plans are the things I'm thinking of. And just when we thought it might be time to throw in the towel, Vera helped us make our getaway by whooshing us to safety via her homemade IPT — though I'd have to check back and read the Author's recent revisions now that IPTs aren't real. But in any event, however she managed to secure our flight to freedom, Vera — in one of history's finest displays of all-around good-eggishness — risked her own skin by staying behind to handle Socrates all by herself. And by "handle Socrates" I mean she waited around for the blighter with a bomb, setting it off once she was sure we were safely on our way. This had the effect you might naturally have expected: it blew both Socrates and Vera sky high, as the expression is, scattering their blasted bits over several square miles of valuable downtown real estate.

The Vera standing before me now had, I suppose, regenerated from one of the larger chunks of flesh to haul itself out of the debris, and she was still showing the signs of her ordeal. As for her memory, I can only assume Socrates had done his dirty work, using his mindwiping venom to muddle the poor pipsqueak's brain. So far as I could tell, though, Socrates' mindwiping trick had left this heroine's psychic circuitry intact, allowing her to go on peering into the future and the past, picking up scraps of something similar to memory here and there. One could only hope that, given time, this psychic peering-about would allow this well-done, rare medium to piece her memory back together through the watching of what I believe are called "reruns." I supposed that only time would tell.

"My word," said Oan, after I'd finished with the expository whatnots. "How very brave you must be!" she added, eyeing Vera with the reverence she was due.

"Now it's your turn to be brave," Vera riposted. "You have to stay put. Stick to your story about the grotto. Rhinnick and I have to leave. It's vital that I go with him. He'll need my television to help him through the next leg of his quest to save the world. I'm sure you'll play your own part in all of this — but for now, you can't lie to Peericks about the grotto, and you can't be released."

Here I expected a good deal of cross-examination from Oan, probing Vera's claims and instructions. But what proceeded next from the old disaster's mouth caught me off guard. What she said was this:

"I understand. I will do as you ask, Vera, for I see you for what you are. You are gifted; you are a conduit for the Great Omega's will. The Laws of Attraction have brought you to us — to Rhinnick and me. You are exactly what we need, and you've arrived just when we need you. I will do as you ask, and bide my time here in the hospice."

"A point of order," I said, having remained fairly silent for a paragraph or two, "but there's one thing you've said that I think requires a stitch of amplification."

"Oh?" said Vera.

"It's this 'saving the world' business. It doesn't compute. While you'll find no one keener than Rhinnick Feynman when it comes to any quest designed to shove Detroit out of harm's way, or to shield it with my own body when the bludgeonings of fate are getting down to business, on this occasion you find him baffled. What does the world need saving from?"

I suppose on reflection it ought to have been "from what does the world need saving," but that didn't occur to me at the time.

"Isaac Newton, ass," she said, punctuating the remark with a silvery laugh. "Don't you remember? You were sitting here with Oan, back when I couldn't think of anything but 'two chairs,' and you decided that one of Isaac's experiments would put Detroit in jeopardy, and it was your job to save the day. I can help you with that."

I could see that this was another moment to bring this psychic gumboil up to speed. As adroit as she was at peeping into the future, she seemed to have a dashed difficult time with current events.

"Ah," I said, rather tolerantly. "Events have overtaken you. I've already been to Isaac's lab, where I inquired about his experiments."

"And what did you find out?"

"There's nothing to fear. Everything's boomps-a-daisy. Isaac can carry right on fiddling with his test tubes, telescopes, and electron-scanning thingummies 'til the cows come home, and I hope he has a fine day for it. Nothing he's doing poses any danger at all."

"Oh!" said Vera. "That's a surprise."

"But what about Abe?" said Oan, her eyebrow furrowed with concern. "I thought he told you Isaac was dangerous. The most dangerous man in the world. Abe can't be wrong, can he? It's more likely that we've misunderstood his warning. We merely assumed that any danger caused by Isaac must relate to his experiments. If his experiments are safe, maybe Isaac is up to something else that will put us all in danger. Maybe we should investigate Isaac's—"

"Dismiss the notion!" I said, for I could see that this Oan was making the same error as Abe. "You're making the same error as Abe," I said. "You see, Isaac's experiments *sound* dangerous, to the untrained observer. But if there's one kind of observer Rhinnick Feynman isn't, it's an untrained one. While it is true that Isaac remains intent on changing the world, he means to do it in an entirely sciencey way."

"A sciencey way?" said Vera, looking askance, and I recalled that she herself was something of a dab hand with science and engineering.

"You know," I said, attempting to make matters clear for the meanest intellect, "in the way all these science nibs want to change the world. Invent a more efficient mousetrap. Create a hangover cure. Find a way to keep dress shoes from coming untied. In Isaac's case, his aims and objects are focused entirely on teensy weensy quantum doodads and maths. He seems to think the aforementioned quantum thingummies don't jive with his mathematical models, causing him much agitation and alarm. Thinking that some sort of agreement between the aforementioned doodads and models would just make his day, Isaac has set out to bridge the gap, bringing harmony between, as I think he called it, observation and calculation."

"And that's not dangerous?" Vera asked.

"How could it be dangerous?" I said, chuckling tolerantly, for the young boll weevil amused me. "Isaac is, by his own admission, fiddling with only the most subatomic of subatomic things. And only where they don't square up with his figures. Mucking about with things on that scale couldn't harm the smallest flea. Like all academics, Newton's merely shedding a bit of pseudo-light upon non-problems."

"Well, I suppose you know," said Vera, "but it does seem strange that this Abe person would send you on a quest without realizing there wasn't a point to it."

"We all err from time to time," I said. "Even Abe. So you

see, the world doesn't need saving. The old thing is ticking along nicely."

This seemed to deflate the young prune, who must have been looking forward to a bit of world-saving at the side of yours truly. Never wishing to disappoint the delicately nurtured, I offered whatever I could by way of consolation.

"There's still my quest to track down Zeus," I said. "You could help with that if you like. And in so doing you'll be aiding the cause of science by helping Isaac with his experiments."

"How do we do that?" said Vera.

"With those files you've brought with you. Buried within their contents may be data which will help me hone in on my friend Nappy — and if I know Nappy, she won't be more than a stone's throw away from Zeus, provided she has any choice in the matter."

"And helping Isaac with his experiments?" said Vera, still thirsty for information.

"He needs brain scans, psychological profiles, and other data relating to Nappy's memory. Something to do with aberrant memory patterns and their relationship to quantum whatnots, I gathered."

"Oh," said Vera, still seeming a trifle puzzled by it all. "I was sure I remembered seeing something in the future about you and me teaming up to save the world. And I remember seeing that Oan can't come with us. I'm sure it's true. I still think it's best that I stick with you."

"I agree," said Oan. "The Laws of Attraction have brought us someone blessed with the gift of foresight, and —"

"We all know the one about gift horses and mouths," I said, completing the thought.

Then, perceiving it was about time to get this show on the road, I asked Vera to hand over the files, and the three of us spent a goodish bit of time poring over the contents. And what we found can be all be placed under a single, bold-font heading, viz, "Nothing Bloody Useful." This file was bursting to the seams with test results and medical data but had nothing in the way of personal info, all of which must have been coded and shoved aside for safekeeping. There was no forwarding address, no contact info, no way at all of tracking down the Napoleonic bird whose brain scans, test results, and psycho-assessment thingummies filled these pages.

"You're sure this is Nappy's?" I asked.

"I am," said Vera. "Television. But there's nothing in here that will help us find her."

"What do we do now?" said Oan.

"There's only one thing to do," I said. "We take the files to Isaac and hope they'll be of use to him. If they are, they'll speed his experiments, and he'll make time to hasten to the hospice and convince Dr. Peericks to set you free. Grateful for the gesture, Peericks will, I hope, unseal his lips with respect to Zeus's current abode."

And it was at this point that I was struck by an idea.

"Vera," I said. "You showed excellent initiative — if initiative means what I think it does — in pinching Nappy's file from Peericks's office. No chance of you pinching a nice round number of files, then, and laying your hand on Zeus's, too?"

"No," said Vera. "I looked for them. I remembered you would ask. Nothing filed under Z, nothing filed under *Princk*, nothing filed under *Beforelife Delusion complicated by canine past*. Sorry."

"Dash it," I said, and if I registered a spot of despair, who could blame me? While we Feynmen are renowned for keeping the upper lip stiff, the head bloodied but unbowed, there still comes a time when the slings and arrows of outrageous fortune start to wound the spirit. At this point in my affairs I had become fed to the eye teeth with fate's habit of sidling up behind me and kicking me in the pants. I mean to say, I am the hero of this story, but I do have my off days.

It was at this moment that Vera came through with a honeyed word aimed at curing my spot of dudgeon.

"Don't worry, Rhinnick. It's still possible that he has a file on Zeus stored somewhere else. Maybe he set it aside for safekeeping once he knew you were interested in it. But unless he cooperates with us, we're sunk. There's no hope of finding them without Peericks handing them over."

"That settles it, then," I said, bracing myself for the coming journey back to Detroit University. "I'll have to take these files to Isaac and hope for the best."

"I'm coming with you," said Vera. "Like I said, you'll need my help."

"But how can you?" said Oan, raising a point worth threshing out. "You're confined here in the hospice. You may be able to use your television to retrieve some of your memories, but will Dr. Peericks believe you? He wouldn't believe what happened to me in the sacred grotto — who knows what he'll think if you tell him you're able to see the future?"

"She's right," I said, surprising myself by agreeing with one whom I had hitherto pencilled in as the loopiest specimen ever to cross my path. "It's not as though you can saunter up to Peericks, tell him everything's okay because your television's back in working order, and whatever you lack in memory you make up for in 'messages from beyond.' He'd probably pat your head, say something along the lines of 'There there, it'll be all right,' and install you in one of the hospice's special rooms with softer walls before you can say what ho."

"Just let me worry about that," said Vera, "I have a plan to deal with Peericks."

"Wonderful," said Oan, suddenly beaming rather freely. "And while the two of you visit Professor Newton, I'll stay here and plan the wedding!"

I winced as though she'd touched an exposed nerve. What with the rush of events that began when Vera blew into the room with Nappy's files, I'd largely managed to sublimate any thought of my betrothal to this disaster, if sublimate means to bury a dashed hideous thought into the darker unexplored bits of one's mental storage locker. Whatever you call it, I had almost forgotten that this loopy bird had signed me up for a trip to the altar rail, filling the air with v-shaped depressions bearing down on Feynman, R. Once again, all I could manage to say in response was "oh, ah," and it occurred to me that, if these nuptials came to fruition, a good deal of my future life would be spent staring dumbly at the adored object and groping for something civil to say in response to her latest flood of goofy pronouncements.

"I do hope you'll be able to join us at the wedding, Vera," said Oan, brazenly pouring salt on the w.

"Wouldn't miss it," said Vera. "Now let's get out of here. The world ain't saving itself."

And in the space of a couple of ticks Vera and self were headed down the hall toward Peericks's office, where Vera would let loose this plan to free herself from captivity. And when you hear what her plan was, and how she intended to execute it, you'll have no choice but to agree that, while Vera's strategy might have earned an A+ for its ability to fling wide the hospice gates, the plan promised nothing short of desolation for yours truly.

Chapter 10

I don't know if you've ever broken out of a loony bin, but I have, and I can assure you that these things take some doing. The last time I'd ditched this particular brain infirmary, kicking its dust from the Feynman shoes and legging it for the open spaces, the plan had involved the use of three explosive devices, four or five Napoleons, a getaway van, and the assistance of a particularly resourceful supermodel ninja who'd committed herself to the cause. Zeus had been there, too, lending his tree-trunk arms in yeoman service of our escape. On the present occasion I had no such resources at my disposal, and I hadn't a notion of what Vera had in mind when it came to extricating — do I mean extricating? — herself from the watchful eye of Peericks and his cronies. Nor did she seem especially fussed about vouchsafing the plan to me before we nosed our way through the door of Peericks's office.

On our arrival in that sanctum, we found the doctor deep in thought, furrowing a brow or two over his datapad (another of Isaac's I-Ware models) as if doing long division or working out a complex sauce.

"Oh!" he said, looking as startled as a nymph surprised while bathing. "Mr. Feynman — I wasn't expecting you."

And on seeing that it wasn't Feynman alone who'd darkened his door, the poor blighter's bafflement only deepened.

I did my best to put him abreast. I mean to say, I didn't get into the business of purloining Nappy's file and using it to convince Isaac to make his way to Detroit Mercy, as dishing up this bit of the plan to Peericks seemed to be well outside of the realm of practical politics. Instead I began by telling him that I now found myself in a posish to solve a mystery for him, viz, the identity of the lightly charred beazel at my side whose identity had hitherto been cloaked in mystery. I wasted no time in making the formal introduction.

"That's right!" said Vera, once I'd supplied the informash. "By the time I went back to my room, my burns had healed enough that Rhinnick recognized me straight away! It's so lucky that he was there. The one man who was sure to know me on sight — at least, once I started to look more a bit like myself."

"You . . . you know each other?" said Peericks.

Before I could get a word in edgeways, Vera charged ahead with something unexpected.

"Know each other?" she said, laughing merrily. "Why, of course we know each other! Mr. Feynman's my fiancé!"

I reeled. It's not going too far to say you could have knocked me down with a pencil, for this pipsqueak's statement had unmanned me.

What do you call that feeling you get when, after hours and hours of staying half a step ahead of the gaping jaws of fate you turn 'round and realize that, rather than giving up the chase, said jaws are gaining on you and they've been joined by a pack of even more ravenous friends? It starts with an X. Zeus would know. *Exasperated*! That's the bunny. I was feeling a good deal exasperated by the vicissitudes of life here at the hospice. If one wasn't finding oneself signed up to wed a goofy Sharing Room Director, one was finding oneself engaged to a psychic beazel, if not both. And I don't mind telling you that the target of this recent exasperation — the principal source of all of my troubles — was neither of the two popsies who seemed intent on taking me off the spousal market, but rather the Author, Himself, in person. I'm sure you'll agree that He'd been making my life a dashed sight more difficult than any man would like, and the fault lay squarely on this apparent habit of His of making changes to the Feynman bio without consulting with yours truly, or even bothering to advise me of His revisions, something you'd think both professional courtesy and politeness would require.

Take the case of this young Vera. She now claimed openly to be affianced to me, and I'd be dashed if I remembered us being anything more than mere acquaintances. I mean, I did loan her my hamster on one occasion, and I suppose it's possible that this could be a marker of betrothal in some far-flung cultures, but if it was, that was news to me. At a loss to explain how any of this could be, the only answer I could find was that the Author had revised the Feynman archives such that Vera was now slated in as a long-term romantic interest and I was now en route to becoming Mr. Rhinnick Feynman-Lantz. Had He asked for my input — a thing the Author seldom does — I'd have assured him with word and gesture that a marriage between myself and Vera was not something that would draw applause from the reading public. "Out of character!" they might shout, complaining over a glass of wine or two at a book club. For these readers, no doubt eager to keep up with my adventures, would be keenly aware that Feynman — at least as far as he'd been presented in prior volumes — would never link his lot to a girl like Vera. To be sure, I admired the young prune, and thought most highly of her prowess at getting self and others out of a jam in an hour of need, but there are women who — though highly respected and revered — one would readily run a mile in tight shoes to avoid marrying. This Vera I counted among them, what with her strange habit of peering off into the distance, losing the thread of conversations, and coming up with some pronouncement that, likely as not, would land Feynman rather deeply in the soup.

But then again, I mused, for one always likes to weigh both sides of a thing, I could do a lot worse than hitching up with this Vera. Take Oan, by way of example. A marriage with Oan would be far worse. And thinking of Oan, I suddenly realized that Vera had done me yet another good deed by not immediately objecting to Oan's recent announcement that she and I were soon to be bride and groom. I mean, here was Vera, fully convinced that she herself was on the verge of donning the veil and fusing her soul with mine, suddenly hearing Oan proclaiming the bans and exclaiming that I would be her groom. "What do you mean!" Vera might have cried, rising to her full height and confronting us, "You can't have him; he's mine!" — a situation which, I think you'll agree, would have caused a good deal of embarrassment and confusion on all sides. But she hadn't done any of that. Instead, she had taken Oan's announcement on the chin and simply stood there, rather stoically, letting Oan carry on with planning the wedding. Vera kept her words to herself, perhaps hoping Oan's views on wedding Feynman were some sort of temporary attack of the crazies which would pass before yonder sun had set. But for whatever reason, she had avoided what one might call a "scene," and in doing so she deserved well of Feynman. Yes, if the Author had pencilled me in to become the groom to this bride, I supposed that, as far as marital choices went, I could have done a good deal worse.

I mused on this for a space before realizing that events were overtaking me, as they so often do. When I popped out of my reverie I perceived that Vera was still embroiled in her tête-à-tête with Peericks and had apparently apprised him that her memories were restored. She gave a good deal of credit to Peericks's memory treatments, giving the chap the old oil, as it were, but also claimed that some of her mental rebooting was due to me, I having recognized her now that her burns were healing and wasted no time in supplying the missing details in her biography.

To say that Peericks responded by chanting hosannas would be to deceive my public, because he didn't. Not by a jugful. No, this psychiatric louse sat there regarding us rather skeptically, like a man who's just been told that the used car before him has only ever been driven on a private driveway on Sundays during the summer.

"So," said Dr. Peericks, steepling his hands in that inspectorish way of his, "the two of you are going to be married."

It didn't sound like a question, but seemed to call for a response. I stammered a halting "well, yes," while Vera, in a much more exuberant vein, said, "Absolutely, as soon as we can!"

"And your memories have returned," said Peericks, still registering the rummy skepticism I suppose one has to foster when serving in the position of chief loony-wrangler.

"They have!" said Vera. "I'm certifiably good-to-go! No more problems. Why, I suppose there's nothing stopping you from signing my release papers on the spot!"

"I'd like to run some tests," said Peericks.

"You needn't bother," said Vera. "Everything's back to factory specs. Besides, as my fiancé, Rhinnick here can sign me out."

I'm fairly familiar with hospice rules — I having been a long-term resident in at least some versions of the Author's prior work — and I could see what the popsy was driving at. Having been discovered alone, without any memories, Vera had, no doubt, been bunged into the hospice on the director's own warrant, rather than having been ordered here by a magistrate or other official busybody. In those circs, a family member could sign her out so long as she didn't pose a danger to self and others. She seemed to have Peericks by the short hairs.

Peericks didn't admit defeat. Keen as always to keep his loonies under guard, he threw a spanner into the works.

"I'd need proof," he said. "There are forms to be filled out, records to be filed. In a case like this we'd need a copy of your marriage license, for example. As well as official copies of your ID. You arrived without any form of identification. We have to make sure these memories of yours are accurate, that you are who you think you are, and that you really are engaged to Mr. Feynman."

"I say," I said, shoving an oar in. "I can understand you not trusting Vera, because she's here as an inmate. But surely you can take it from me that—"

"I'm sorry, Mr. Feynman. There are rules that must be observed. I'm afraid that, without that marriage license, I can't release Vera to you. She'll have to stay with us in the hospice until I say she's ready to leave."

"But dash it," I said.

"We'll get you the marriage license," said Vera. "And the ID. No problem at all."

"We will?" I said.

"Of course! We'll just pop over to City Hall. They'll have the license waiting for us. We registered for it right before my accident."

"We did?"

"We did! So if you'll just slip me a day pass," said Vera, addressing Peericks, "we'll pop right up and pick up all of the papers."

Peericks seemed poised to object to this day-pass idea, but Vera wiped the words from his lips by carrying on with her oration.

"You can see I'm making improvements," she said, a melting tone entering into her voice. "And you can take Rhinnick's word that he'll keep an eye on me while I'm out. He's a responsible citizen! And we'll be able to check in at City Hall, pick up copies of my ID and the marriage license, and be back before you know it. I expect I'll be here in time for supper."

And blow me tight if the doctor didn't agree. Such was the magic of Vera's personality that, no sooner had the shrimp finished her case for the defence than Peericks had drawn the day pass up, shoved it across his desk, and bid the two of us a safe and happy journey. We were out of his office and making our way for the open spaces before Peericks could say "what, ho!"

"I can't believe that worked," I said, as Vera and self left Detroit Mercy's grounds and instituted a round of cab-hailing. "I'd have thought Dr. Peericks, as rule-bound a medical blighter as has ever pushed a pill, would have had a bevy of objections ready to shove into the path of your release. How in Abe's name did you know he'd let you out?"

"Easy," said Vera. "I remembered you telling the story of my escape to Ian Brown."

"To Ian Brown?" I said, agog.

"Yes, to Ian Brown," she said, "sometime next year." She topped her answer off with a laugh that, while silvery, sounded to me like nails on a chalkboard.

It occurred to me that, once we'd finish with the "will you, Vera, take this man" business, we'd have to have a talk about all of this scrying into the future and prophesying. It seemed unfair that one member of any marital union should have privileged access to intel from the future. The soothsaying half of the sketch would have the other over a barrel. I mean to say, the prophetic partner could pick and choose what visions to share with her helpmeet, more or less bending him to her will by claiming that she knows, from reliable sources beyond the veil, that ruin and desolation will ensue should the hapless husband have a second martini, spend a night out with his pals, or fail to support some goofy purchase by his bride. The thought that this would be a permanent feature of our happy union made me wince. If I've said it before, I don't mind saying it again: unless managed carefully and shared equally by both parties, television can ruin a marriage.

Chapter 11

I wonder if I've ever told you about Detroit's City Hall. It's an imposing old edifice, surpassing even the most striking buildings to infest the grounds of Detroit University. I believe the thing is listed as one of the four ancient wonders of the world, and the only one featuring toilets and municipal offices. The outer walls of the place, crawling with ivy and heavily gargoyled, rise to a height of thirty metres, give or take a turret or two, and must have kept an army of stonemasons busy for at least couple of centuries.

We arrived at these outer walls, passed through a series of gates and things, and made our way into the vast, marble-tiled foyer of the building's north wing, where Vera assured me we'd find personnel able to point us in the direction of marriage licenses and IDs. We presented ourselves to one of those automated screen thingummies that tell you where to go, and it directed us to the fourth floor.

We made our way to the elevator bay and summoned the machine. On entering the carriage I aimed an eager finger at the button marked 4, but was stopped short of my objective when Vera grabbed my outstretched arm and stayed my hand. She then smiled what I believe is called a wry smile, and, after winking at me, leaned into the speaker mounted on the elevator panel and spoke as follows:

"Sub-basement nine. R'lyeh."

The machine spoke back, repeating the soothsayer's words without delay. I then perceived that the elevator was travelling downward, into the bowels of Detroit.

"Sub-basement nine?" I said, bafflement no doubt spreading across my map.

"Sub-basement nine," said Vera.

"And . . . did you say 'R'lyeh'?"

"I did say R'lyeh," said Vera.

I instituted further inquiries. Hitherto I'd never encountered the word "R'lyeh," and it seemed to me to be dashed useful, both for conversations with elevators and for getting out of a pinch in a game of Scrabble.

"But what in Abe's name does it mean?" I asked.

"Search me," said Vera. "It's the password. You can't get into sub-basement nine without it."

"But why are we heading to sub-basement nine? If my maths check out, that's about nine sub-basements and four above-ground floors away from marriage licenses and IDs."

She laughed another one of those light, silvery laughs, a practice to which she'd become far too addicted.

"Silly ass," she said, still laughing, "we're not here for a marriage license. We're here to find out what's going on in sub-basement nine. It's critical to your quest to find Zeus and save the world. It's one of the first things I saw when my memories started back: you and me riding an elevator to sub-basement nine in City Hall—"

"Abe's drawers!" I said, remembering. "Oan told me about that while you were out of the room."

"While the two of you were busy planning your wedding," she said, unleashing another of those wry smiles.

Of course this caught me amidships, but I forced myself to rally. I'd spent a good deal of the time since we had left Detroit Mercy waiting for this particular conversational shoe to drop, as it were, and trying to come up with some scheme for extricating myself from the bouillon. But I'd be dashed if any idea worth the name had presented itself. I mean to say, I couldn't say anything suggestive of the fact that my engagement to Oan had been a mistake and that the real plan had been to hitch Peericks's wagon to that of the weird old bird, as such a claim could well fall under the heading of "speaking lightly of a woman's name," and wouldn't be couth. Nor could I tell Vera that my engagement to Vera herself was news to me, and that the Author must have bunged this into my history via edits which were unknown to yours truly, for I didn't wish to take this young prune's marital hopes and dash them to the ground. Now that the time had come, and I was caught in Vera's crosshairs, I gulped like a landed trout and said, "Oh, ah."

This didn't appear to satisfy. Vera just stood there, staring at me, grinning in what seemed to me to be a mischievous fashion.

"Well, about that marriage to Oan," I said, still gulping, "No doubt you've perceived that there's been something of a mix-up, what with self appearing to have become affianced to more than one potential bride. That wasn't the plan, I mean to say. I intend no disrespect to the polyamorous, if that's the word I want, but Rhinnick Feynman — if he intends to marry at all — intends to be a one-woman man."

"Go on," she said, crossing her arms and leaning back in a manner that seemed about fifty thousand times more relaxed than I could have managed at the time.

"Well, you see, there are times when one finds oneself overtaken by events. I mean to say, set adrift on the seas of vicissitudes one didn't precisely see coming."

"I see," said Vera.

"And these vicissitudes," I said, orating like nobody's business, "well, they've put me into a spot I should very much like to explain."

"It's all right," said Vera. "You needn't bother. You should know I'm—"

Here she broke off. Not so much because she'd finished what she had to say, but because on the cue "you needn't bother" the elevator had said, "Sub-basement nine" and opened its doors.

"Saved by the bell," said Vera.

"What bell?" I said.

"Just an expression." And so saying, Vera stepped out of the door and into the darkness cloaking what, I'd been given to understand, was sub-basement nine.

The elevator closed behind us, and the darkness was complete. The air was filled with a low, chest-squeezing "thrumming" sound, like the breathing of a vast engine with a touch of pneumonia. The air chilled me to the bone, as though some penny-pinching miscreant had failed to pay the heating bill. I could have seen my breath had I been able to see anything at all.

"You go left, I'll go right," said Vera. "Grope along the wall and look for a light switch."

This I did, and found success a moment later. I flipped the switch and bathed our environs in an eerie, greenish light.

"Abe's drawers!" Vera exclaimed through teeth which chattered with the cold, and I couldn't blame her. For the sight that now confronted us wasn't anything I ever expected to see, let alone something you'd plan on finding beneath an army of municipal paper pushers and file clerks. What I saw, as the greenish lights flickered on, was a warehouse-sized space filled with row upon row of innumerable metallic, table-like thingummies topped by what appeared to be high-tech torpedo casings, each about seven or eight feet long. Each was thoroughly festooned with lights, wires, panels, and alphanumeric keypads suggesting that, whatever the purpose of these torpedo contraptions, it quite possibly involved science.

We moved in for closer inspection.

What I saw sent shivers down the Feynman spine. Well, I mean to say, the spine was already shivering, what with the chill that filled the air. But the shivers now redoubled their efforts. For when we moved toward the nearest torpedo casing, what we learned, unless our eyes deceived us, was that these did not, in fact, encase torpedoes. Each of the eyesores in question contained no weapon, but rather a sleeping human person. One could perceive the face of each slumbering occupant through a transparent, frosted glass-ish panel near the end of each casing.

Vera wiped the frost from one of these transparent panels and peered within.

"Gosh!" she said, and I couldn't blame her. The young shrimp's frost-wiping actions had revealed that the occupant of the doodad, like the casing itself, was liberally adorned with tubes and wires which seemed to penetrate the skull.

"Gosh indeed," I said.

"They're dormant," said Vera. "Some form of cryogenic stasis. Suspended animation. And all of these wires penetrating their skulls — they're forming relays between each of these . . . these tube things. The people inside them are connected to each other."

"Connected?" I asked.

"At the cerebral level," she said, her fingers dancing along the keypad of the cryo-whatsit. She paused to examine a readout on the screen. "I think — I think they're all sharing the same thoughts. Their brains are somehow being . . . I dunno . . . synchronized. All of these people. They're physically dormant, but their brains are connected, thinking together as one. All part of a single, centrally governed network that extends between all of them."

"Like some sort of warehouse-wide-web," I said, marvelling at the lengths to which scientists will go in pursuit of a grant.

"Exactly," said Vera. "They share memories, thoughts, ideas. And look here," she said, pointing toward a thickish tube that penetrated the side of the cryo-thingummy and continued straight into its occupant's bean. "These tubes are pumping some kind of solution into their brains. I think it's — it's altering their brain chemistry."

"Their brain chemistry?"

"Yes. It's changing their memories," she said, still drinking in whatever gobbledygook was being displayed on the infernal machine's display. "Whoever controls the cerebral network," she added, tapping her way through a few more screens, "can control what everyone in it thinks. They can . . . well . . . rewire their memories, it seems. Completely change their perceptions of the world. They might even change their personalities."

"How in Abe's name could you know all of that?" I asked. "You can't have read it all on that screen."

"I just know it. It comes naturally. It's what I told Ian when your gang first came to my shop — I can almost always see what things are for. I think it's related to my television. As soon as I see any kind of device, I know its purpose. Helps a lot with my repair work."

"No doubt," I said, remembering that the moppet under advisement spent as much time fiddling with machinery as she did perceiving the future. And while I'd never really be fond of the idea of marrying anybody, it occurs to me that, if one absolutely must don the sponge-bag trousers and shuffle up the aisle, one certainly saves something from the wreck by hitching up with a woman who knows her way around an engine.

"Sarcophagi," said Vera.

"Gezundheit," I said.

"No, no. These tube things. These cryogenic storage devices. The word 'sarcophagi' comes to mind. I've no idea where the word comes from, but I think it's the right word for these devices."

"Sarcophagi, eh? I suppose it's as good as the next word. Certainly mot juster than 'cryo-thingummies' or 'person-freezers.'"

"Sarcophagi, then," said Vera, pressing a few more buttons on the one over which we were still hovering. She examined the effects of her button pushing. She tapped a few letters and numbers onto the keypad, read the response, and came across with a diagnosis. "Whoever put these people into these sarcophagi is giving them new memories. These chemical compounds mirror the changes that take place in the human brain when long-term memories form."

"Why in Abe's name would someone want to do that?" I asked.

"Who knows?" she said. "Maybe if I can figure out who's stored in these things . . . let's see if I can pull up a name."

She instituted a brief stage wait while tapping away on the sarcophagus's keypad, waited for a response, and then gave something of an excited cry.

"They're decamillennials!" she yipped. "I recognize some of the names. Kushim. Harad. Iselle. Tubal-Cain. Fanny!"

"Fanny?"

"Short for Tiffany. An ancient name. These are some of the first people to cross the Styx — the first people to find Abe in the barren wastes that formed Detroit. The ones who helped him tame the wild. I've read about them in history texts. And there are a lot of other names here that I don't recognize."

"But why in Abe's name would someone keep a warehouse full of freeze-dried decamillennials?" I said.

"They have to go somewhere," said Vera. "I mean, loads of decamillennials go dormant. We learned all about it in school. Their sense of time changes as they get older. Once you're past about eight or nine thousand years old, any timespan shorter than a few months passes like the blink of an eye. What seems like a year to you might seem like a minute to them. Most of them can't carry on conversations with younger people — there are only a few anomalies, like Abe, Hammurabi, or Woolbright Punt, who manage to keep the same rate of time-perception as newer arrivals. The rest of them just sort of . . . go to sleep, I suppose. Until today I hadn't thought about where they went. I certainly didn't know that any of them were being kept together in a warehouse under City Hall."

"And what's with the tubes and wires then?" I asked, still baffled. "Why fiddle with their memories?"

"Search me," said Vera, once again plugging away at the keypad. She spent a minute or two poring over the information displayed on the unit's screen before she finally resurfaced.

"It's very strange," she said. "It's almost as though the programmer wants these people to have . . . well . . . to have different views of the way things work. To change their understanding of things. Their brains are changing to make them remember scientific principles that weren't discovered until after they'd gone dormant. Upgrading their knowledge, I suppose."

I raised a disapproving brow. I didn't condone this unnatural tampering with the beans of frozen ancients.

"Seems like a waste of time to me," I said, not masking my disapproval. "These decamillennial chumps have done their time. They've hung around Detroit, doing their part, for epoch upon epoch. Probably pitched in with Abe, from what you tell me. It seems to me that they deserve a good long nap and not to have that nap interrupted by liquified extension courses, however informative, about science. Leave schooling and self-improvement to the young. Let sleeping chumpsicles lie, I say. They've earned it."

"But I just don't get it," said Vera. "Why would anyone want to reprogram some of the most ancient and powerful minds in history — why make them see things differently? Why create

126

a network wired to change the minds of ancients? It doesn't make any sense."

I could readily agree with the psychic twerp on that score, but didn't see this lack of sense-making as any cause for alarm. I mean to say, it had been a good long while since I'd counted on things to make sense.

"A point of order," I said.

"What's up?" said Vera.

"You mentioned that we had to come down this elevator in order to find Zeus and save the world. Unless your directory of names suggests that Zeus is chilled inside one of these tube thingummies—"

"Sarcophagi."

"—these sarcophagi, as you say, then I don't see how this brief pit stop advances the quest. No Zeus, no hint of Zeus, no maps toward Zeus's location. A total bust. And as for saving the world—"

"I'm sure this is important," she said. "I just don't see why. I mean," she continued, tapping rapidly on the keypad and making a series of quick gestures on the touchscreen mounted beside it, "why in Abe's name would someone be teaching decamillennials all about . . . let's see . . . this one's twelve thousand years old, and within the last twenty-four hours she's learned . . . what . . . that teleportation is impossible."

This caught me in the vicinity of the third waistcoat button.

"What do you mean she's learned that teleportation is impossible?" I said.

"What do you mean, what do I mean?" said Vera. "Teleportation *is* impossible. She wouldn't have known that. Theories supporting the possibility of teleportation have been around for years and years. Nothing ever came of it, though. It was recently shown to be an absolute impossibility — a total violation of physical laws. But if she went dormant years ago, she likely expected that teleportation might eventually be possible."

I stroked the chin. This struck me as probative — though probative of what, I couldn't be sure. I mean to say, just one day ago I'd travelled by teleportation, only to see the whole teleportation industry retroactively burned from the threads of Detroit's history because (a) the Author had apparently decided He was better off without it, and (b) in His wisdom the Author had given Isaac Newton the means to prove that teleportation failed to square up with the physical laws that governed Detroit. It was dashed inconvenient of the Author to make these changes while I was midway through a quest that required a good deal of mobility, but one learns to take the rough with the s.

"What is she being taught now?" I said.

"That's odd," said Vera.

"What's odd?" I asked, though in the circumstances it probably would have been easier to point out anything nearby that didn't qualify as odd.

"Their most recent memories. They're all focused on one topic. But it's very strange."

"In what way?"

"It's just — why on earth would decamillennials need to know about new approaches to quantum mechanics?"

Chapter 12

On the cue "quantum mechanics," I had, of course, started visibly. I was about to relay a few well-chosen phrases concerning how, in recent days, this quantum note had been entering my life more often than one generally expects, when the words were dashed from my lips by a booming mechanical voice which seemed to explode all around us.

"NEW DATA RECEIVED," it cried, if you can call it a cry when a voice erupts from an automated doodad which, whatever its capacities, presumably lacks emotion.

"COMPOUND GENESIS IN PROGRESS."

This utterance coincided with an increase in the volume of the pervasive thrumming sound, which was now harmonized by a chorus of buzzings, whirrings, and pings from various bits of machinery stationed all around the periphery of sub-basement nine.

Whether it was the announcement which called Vera to action, or the buzzings, whirrings, and pings, I cannot say. But whatever the cause, Vera bustled away from the sarcophagus in a sou'sou'westerly direction, heading toward a large computer thingummy standing some yards off. She passed her fingers nimbly across its touchscreen, calling up a variety of numbers, symbols, and pictographic whatnots which meant nothing to me but seemed to make an impression on her.

"Someone's changing the compounds. The liquid pumping into the decamillennials," she announced. "They're revising the memory upgrades — changing what they're being taught."

"Who do you mean by 'someone'?"

"Who knows?" she said, fingers still tap-dancing along the touchscreen, "but I've traced the flow of data back to Detroit University."

For the second time in the space of about three minutes this young boll weevil had unmanned me. From what she'd tried to explain to me thus far, I had gathered that some person or persons hitherto unidentified had been tossing spanners into these decamillennials' memories for some inscrutable purpose. The thrust of this meddling, it seemed, involved jacking up these dormant persons' knowledge of quantum mechanics. And now it seemed the person or persons responsible resided in — or at least sent transmissions from — Detroit University. Well, I've never been one to believe in coincidences, and it seemed to me that all indications pointed in one direction, viz, Newton comma I.

"Isaac Newton!" I said, sharing my deductions with the class. And if a note of triumph entered my voice, who can blame me? I dislike being baffled, and the piecing together of these clues brought me no small measure of intellectual satisfac.

"What about him?" said Vera.

"He must be the blighter who's keeping these decamillennial fogies in cold storage, hooking them up to this cranial web, and pumping their heads full of new ideas!"

"Why would he do that?"

"Now there you have me. But I'm sure that it's him doing it. We got together in his office at Detroit University just yesterday, and he vouchsafed to me he's more or less obsessed with quantum thingummies. Brain patterns, too. He didn't go deeply into the whys and wherefores, but he did say it had something to do with making sure his calculations matched up with what he referred to as 'empirical observation.'"

"So you think he's using these people to do what — double-check his figures?"

"He didn't strike me as a chap who needs his figures double-checked."

"But why would he be feeding them data? Why would he want to change their memories?"

"Making great minds think alike, as it were?" I said, and even as it crossed my lips I realized that, so far as gags go, this wasn't one of my best. It thus came as no surprise that Vera didn't respond to this slice of repartee by slapping the Feynman back and issuing peals of rib-rattling laughter.

Her actual reaction wasn't one I would have expected.

She just stood there, looking about as stunned as a landed cod. I mean to say, she stared off vacantly into the distance, her lips moving slightly as though she were attempting to recite some forgotten snatch of poetry which she'd memorized in her youth.

I knew at a g. that this was not some passing bout of psychosis or other mental whatdoyoucallit, for I recognized the symptoms: this was television at work. Though Vera was physically with us, her mental self was elsewhere, remotely viewing some tidbit from the future, or from her past, or from some far-flung, hitherto hidden spot in the present.

This carried on for the space of eight or nine seconds, and I was on the point of prodding the young shrimp to see if I might achieve anything in the way of rebooting her software, as the expression is, when her eyes suddenly widened and gave the impression that they were about to leap from their parent sockets.

Vera unleashed an exuberant cry. "The Rules!" she cried, "I'll bet it's all about The Rules!"

"What Rules?" I said, taken aback.

"I just had a vision."

"So I gathered. You mentioned Rules."

"The Rules that make Detroit tick. You must remember. The images just came back to me. You were in my shop when I told Ian he'd never find his wife until he managed to learn The Rules. He found his wife, didn't he?"

"Yes."

"So he must have learned The Rules!"

"It stands to reason: QED."

"And you were there when he found Penelope, right?"

"I was."

"So what were The Rules?"

"I haven't a notion. I was preoccupied at the time. Thinking of this and that. You can't expect a busy man like me to keep track of everything."

She seemed to take this in stride.

"That's okay. It's just — well — it seems to me that Ian's quest to learn The Rules must be related to what's going on here. I mean, if Isaac's teaching all of these decamillennials about his experiments, about any new discoveries he's made, maybe he wants them to know The Rules that Ian was searching for. The 'Rules' must be things like quantum mechanics, classical physics — he wants the ancients to know The Rules that govern Detroit."

This seemed like a massive stretch to me, but I didn't wish to wound the enthusiastic pipsqueak, so I strung along.

"I suppose that's possible," I said. "But why bother teaching any bally 'Rules' to decamillennials? What's the motive? That's what I want to know."

"Who knows?" said Vera. "But we know Abe told you that Isaac is the world's most dangerous man. You know he's interested in gathering data about brain patterns — especially those involving people with Beforelife Delusion. And we've just figured out that he — or someone else at Detroit University — is pumping ancients' brains full of serums that rewrite their memories and make them seem to 'remember' modern science."

"Which takes us where?" I said, a touch more eagerly than I'd intended, for she seemed on the precipice of a climactic revelation, if precipices and climactic revelations are the things I'm thinking of.

Her answer came as a disappointment, for she simply shrugged a shoulder or two and said, "Search me."

"So what do we do next?" I said.

"I suppose we head to the fourth floor."

"The . . . the fourth floor?" I said, suppressing a shudder. With the recent rush of events, I'd briefly lost sight of our reason for being in City Hall in the first place, and this reminder of our fearful purpose washed over me like a sudden wave of nausea.

"You mean . . . the floor where they issue . . . marriage licenses?" I said, doing my best to sound brave, but failing to come within several miles of it.

"Among other things," she said, laughing heartily. "We'd better get up there before the office closes."

It was a deadline I'd have been happy to watch whoosh by. Say what you will about the futility of putting off the inev., the procedure can, if timed just right, buy you a couple of extra gulps of free air. Vera did not appear to subscribe to this philosophy, for she wore the fixed, determined expression of one who would count the day lost if yonder sun were to set without her having an official marriage license gripped in her mitts.

"Do you — I mean — does it strictly require both of us in attendance?" I said. "I mean, couldn't you, perchance, look after this bit of administrivia yourself?"

I'm the last man to heap burdensome errands upon the delicately nurtured, but I am a man of spirit: if I'm to be condemned to the electric chair I've no intention of checking the plugs and throwing the switch myself.

"I can handle it," she said. And then this young stripling, revealing herself as a pearl of the fairer sex and a champion among all women, said words for which I shall forever be grateful. They ran as follows: "I noticed a bar in the lobby. 'Off the Record,' I think it's called. Why not pop down there and have a drink or two while I take care of the paperwork?"

This came like manna in the w. Indeed, it's not going too far to say that I have rarely heard a suggestion which I liked more. It occurred to me once again that, when it came to a choice of marital fauna, one could have done far worse than this prophetic gem in human shape. I mean to say, if one is forced to climb the scaffold, one is lucky to be spared an itchy rope, and it's hard to imagine a cozier instrument of strangulation than this Vera Lantz. I took her suggestion on board and adopted it as the official Feynman Party platform.

For me, it was the work of a moment to pop back into the elevator and ride the thing to the lobby, bidding Vera a quick farewell as she rode on to the fourth floor, where she would, I presumed, set about the task of making this engagement of ours an official government-sanctioned sentence.

I made my way to the bar, quietly thanking Abe for having the foresight to provide his civil lackeys with handy access to the blushful Hippocrene throughout the course of their working day. I could understand the need. A dismal career spent poring over applications, stamping licenses, and filing triplicate forms in service of bureaucratic masters is enough to blot the sunshine from any life, and could be rendered bearable only through frequent, large-economy-sized doses of high-octane lubrication. The lubrication Abe provided flowed through this ground-level saloon which, as Vera had portended, went by the name "Off the Record," which I presumed was some journalistic gag about the passing of state secrets. The bar was fully furnished with plastic upholstered booths and shiny barstools which had been polished, no doubt, by the equally shiny trousers of municipal workers in need of mind-numbing refreshment.

I approached the bar as harts do when heated in the chase, eager to get my hands on a much-needed tissue-restorer.

"What'll it be?" said the apple-cheeked pubman manning the taps.

"A spot of brandy," I replied. "Or perhaps a double." And then, reflecting on the fate which lay before me, I amended the order by pleading for him to fetch the cask.

Having supplied me with the needful, the bartender stood nearby, engaging his stool-occupying patrons in entertaining chit-chat. For the next few minutes I contributed nothing to the proceedings, most of my attention being focused on getting a shot or two of brandy across the tonsils before joining the rep-artee. When I did finally bend an ear to the buzz of ongoing conversation, what I overheard was this:

"Three more of 'em, eh?" said the barman.

"That's right! Three more Napoleons," said a chap who seemed to be midway through a bucket of something fizzy and green and decorated with cherries — the drink, I mean, not the chap, who was decorated with appropriate workday fashion.

"You don't say," said the barman. "That's how many this week. Eleven? Twelve?"

"Fourteen," said green and fizzy. "And at least . . . hic . . . twenty-five last month. But wha' would anyone want wif Napoleons?"

"I've met some nice ones," said a lanky, bright-eyed bird perched on an adjacent stool. She was wearing a feathered cap and nursing a stein of something frothy. "Some very nice ones. Napoleons can be friendly."

"I'm not sayin' they ain't friendly," said green and fizzy. "But why would anyone take 'em away? They can't be . . . hic . . . disappearin' all on their own. Mark my words. Someone's takin' 'em."

"I haven't seen one for days. It's like they've all disappeared," said Frothy Stein.

"I'll bet it's Abe," said the barman, who didn't literally tap the side of his nose in a conspiratorial manner, but by his facial expression and tone of voice implied a certain amount of side-of-nose tapping. "Probably gathering all of them up for treatment. They're all princks, you know. Napoleons. They think the beforelife's real. Can't have them runnin' around, stirrin' up trouble."

"I've heard that, too!" said green and fizzy, belching a volley of greenish fumes which could have powered a small engine. "The beforelife stuff. Part of the wossname. Thingy. Agnostic somethingorother. Criteria."

"Diagnostic criteria," said Ms. Stein. "It's a feature of the disorder. All Napoleons think they've lived somewhere else before Detroit, and they think they'll go back to that life some time in the future."

"Makes no sense. How would you get from here to there?" said the barman.

"More to the point, there's no 'there' to get to," said the stein. "The beforelife isn't real."

"But where are they disappearin' to?" said green and fizzy, in wanton contravention of any number of grammatical conventions.

"Like I said," said the barman, "they've gone for treatment. Mad as hatters, every one of them."

"But they haven't," said the stein. "Gone for treatment, I mean. I work on the eighth floor. Health insurance. We keep track of the treatment centres — and Napoleons have been disappearing from them, too. Every hospice, every psychiatric facility — they all report the same thing. Their Napoleons have gone missing."

"Eerie," said green and fizzy, and I remember thinking that, however addled the blister's mental faculties were as a result of his drink of choice, the chap was right.

It was at this point, when I had drawn enough strength from the cask to engage in a bit of conversational give and take, that the project was rendered null and void by the sudden advent of the woman to whom, if I judged correctly from the self-satisfied aura she projected, I was now officially betrothed. She strode into the bar, making a beeline for yours truly.

"I've got it!" she said, advancing rapidly with a triumphant note in her voice.

"You . . . you do?"

"I do!"

I could think of no two words I liked the sound of less.

She gripped my wrist and drew me from my barstool, directing me to a corner booth tucked away from prying eyes and other sensory organs. She leaned toward me.

"You'll never guess what I got," she said, beaming.

"A . . . a marriage license?" I asked. And if I quailed in the asking, who can blame me?

"Never mind about that," said Vera, shooing away my remark. When next she spoke, she spoke in a whisper. "When I was at the registrar's desk I told them I was trying to plan a wedding. But I also told them I was short one maid of honour. I told them I had a friend who I'd met in Detroit Mercy Hospice, and that the two of us had promised to stand as maid of honour at each other's weddings."

All of this was news to me. I tried my best to collar the nub.

"You — you had a friend in the hospice?" I said.

"Try to keep up," she said, and patted my head in a manner I felt offensive. "I said she and I — my friend in the hospice,

I mean — became best pals during our treatment, but that I'd been discharged before her and lost track of her when I left. I told them I'd called at the hospice but they wouldn't release her address. I knew the registrar would have access to some kind of paper trail — property tax filings, municipal fines, license applications, that sort of thing. Loads of things that could help them track people down, even people who don't want to publicize their address. I put all of this to the registrar. Anyway, one thing led to another and this registrar person must have been a lapsed Girl Guide who hadn't kept up with her good deeds. I hadn't been with her five minutes when she did a bit of searching and then gave me the info that I needed. So now we have the address!"

"Which address?" I said, befogged.

"1024 Bethnel Green, Hadley Apartments."

This failed altogether to ease my bafflement. I pressed for further details.

"Don't be a dunce!" she said, and if I hadn't dodged adroitly she'd have tousled my hair once more. "It's the address for Maria Ramolino."

The name came close to ringing a bell, but missed by a whisker. Dashed familiar, I mean to say, but not so much that it called up pictures and character sketches. My befogged state must have been evident to Vera, for she supplied additional clues.

"Maria, Rhinnick. Your friend. Lived at the hospice. I mean — you didn't think they were all actually *named* Napoleon, did you?"

The mists parted. All was clear.

"Abe's drawers!" I said, the shingles having fallen from my eyes. "You've managed to track down Nappy's address!"

Chapter 13

For Rhinnick Feynman, to think is to act, and so it was without a moment's hesitation that Vera and I settled up with the barman, bid adieu to my fellow patrons, and ditched the bar in favour of a taxi stand outside. We hailed the first cab on the spot and, quietly thanking Abe for the efficient address-supplying skills of his municipal desk attendants, slipped the relevant geographic details to our driver and proceeded in the direction of 1024 Bethnel Green.

It has often struck me that the chaps in charge of naming streets must be fans of irony or sarcasm. Take this Bethnel Green, for example. If any neighbourhood failed to live up to the name "Green" it was this one. It was one of those moody, heavily graffitied, ill-maintained urban stretches you some-times see on life's journey, generally after making a lengthy series of wrong turns or bad investments. The names "thug alley" or "desperation row" would have fit the place like paper on the wall, but not "Bethnel Green," unless of course the place was named after some distinguished local personage, say, Josephine Bethnel Green, who had some historical connec-tion to this stretch of urban blight. But for whatever reason, this place was called Bethnel Green, and we'd been assured Bethnel Green was the street where we'd find Nappy's abode.

The driver deposited us in the vicinity of our destination, accepted payment and tip, and tootled off with a friendly yodel. Vera and self mounted a set of concrete stairs which led to the door marked 1024. And the first thing that struck us, apart I suppose from the dismal, grey, soul-dampening drabness of the place, was the fact that the door was slightly ajar and showing signs of having been jimmied, if jimmying refers to what I think it does.

I held Vera back with a bracing arm and assured her that, so long as the pair of us were sliding into parts unknown where thugs wielding truncheons might lie in wait, the first person across the threshold was going to be Feynman, R. Say what you will about we Feynmen, but we do not shield ourselves behind companions when tiptoeing into peril. Unless of course the companion is Tonto or Zeus, who provide their own shielding and are a dashed sight better equipped than self to deal with life's marauders.

I prodded the door gingerly with the tip of my umbrella. It squeaked just loudly enough to add a sense of menace and alert any lurking ne'er-do-wells that a pair of juicy targets were approaching. I quietly cursed the landlord for not keeping the hinges oiled.

We stepped through. The sight that met us didn't so much resemble a cozy apartment suitable for a single Napoleonic pipsqueak, but rather a frat house after a cataclysmic blowout or a garage sale that had been staged during an earthquake. Chairs and couches were overturned, drawers were pulled from their parent shelves with contents strewn wherever gravity might take them, and framed photographs lay smashed on the floor alongside piles of assorted detritus of domestic life. The word "ransacked" sums it up nicely. But on the credit side of the ledger there was one notable entry, viz, whoever had done the ransacking showed no sign of having stuck around. Vera and self appeared to be alone, if you can call it being alone when there are two of you.

"Halloo?" I called, just in case.

"I don't think anyone's here," whispered Vera.

"Apart from us, you mean," I said.

"What do you suppose has happened?"

It seemed to me that there were two possibilities. Either Nappy's condition was more complicated than she had hitherto let on, and she'd developed a habit of pillaging her own home, or the place had been disarranged by someone else — possibly someone looking for Nappy. I put these possibilities to Vera.

"It looks to me like whoever did this was searching for something," said Vera. "They've pulled the cushions from all the furniture, they've rifled through all the drawers. They've been through everything."

"Well one thing's certain," I said, rummaging through a nearby pile of Nappy's worldly possessions, "the motive wasn't robbery."

"How do you know?" said Vera.

"Intact piggybank," I said, withdrawing the named object from the pile. It was large, pink, unbroken, and — as I determined through the administration of a few well-executed shakes — still full of a largish quantity of coins.

"I haven't seen one of those in ages," said Vera. "Not since I was newly manifested."

"Another retrieved memory?" I asked.

"Not exactly," said Vera. "More of a vision of myself re—"

"Yes, yes, I understand," I said, dismissing her pedantic straw-splitting with a gesture. "You can't retrieve your old memories because your memory has been wiped. But you can have new visions of past events, which essentially amount to the same thing. Six of one, half dozen of the other, what?"

"I suppose," said Vera. "But these visions aren't exactly like memories. They're more accurate. They're not distorted by time. I see them as clearly as I can see you right now."

"And are you seeing anything that might prove more useful than the piggybanks of your youth?" I asked, placing the object on a shelf. "Say, a vision of who may have done all this? A bit of soothsaying to point us in the direction of Nappy's current locale?"

"Sorry, no. But I'll bet it wasn't Nappy who made this mess. Her pictures are smashed. All of her stuff has been treated like garbage."

"A fair point. But if not Nappy, then who?"

"Someone looking for Napoleons. I mean, it stands to reason. All these Napoleons disappearing, and Nappy out on her own . . . whoever was gathering up Napoleons must have wanted Nappy, too. They must have come here to find her. And if she wasn't here, they may have trashed the place trying to figure out where she'd gone."

"Determined blighters," I said. "Not to mention dashed untidy. It wouldn't have hurt them to have spruced the place up a bit once they'd found Nappy had gone."

"They must have left in a hurry. Either that or they didn't care if they were found out."

"Shall we dust for prints?" I asked.

"Dust for prints?"

"I read about it in one of those mystery novels."

"Do you know how to dust for prints?"

"The police do it. How hard can it be?"

"Who knows?" said Vera. "It might be easy as pie. But as I've no idea how to do it, or how to do anything with any prints we find—"

"I imagine the procedure calls for dust," I suggested. "Plenty of that on hand."

"Maybe you'd like to sweep for DNA, while you're at it. Look, the best we can do is search every room for any sign of what's happened to Nappy. You take the bedroom, and I'll start in the bathroom."

"Surely not!" I said. "I mean to say, you can't expect me to poke about in a woman's private bedroom. It wouldn't be seemly."

She appeared to be on the precipice of arguing this point when something seemed to catch her eye. She bent over, pushed aside a midsized pile of clothing, and picked up a mechanical clock.

"Is that the time?" she said.

I reached into my jacket pocket, scratched Fenny behind his ear, and withdrew my pocket watch.

"It is," I said. "5:25 pm."

"I have to call Dr. Peericks!" she announced. "There's a payphone out on the street. I'll go out and let him know we'll be late. He'll be expecting me back by now."

And without further preamble, she tottered off, leaving me alone to decide whether the more prudent, gentlemanly, and seemly course was for me to search through a single woman's bedroom or to conduct an investigation of what Nappy probably called her *salle de bain*. Not much in it either way, so far as I could tell. I flipped a coin and it came up heads. Seeing this as a cosmic indication that the loo was the room picked by fate, I dropped the coin in Nappy's piggybank, rolled up a metaphorical sleeve or two, and got down to business.

The first thing that struck me as I entered was how dashed undisturbed it was. The living room, or parlour, or whatever you choose to call the room that I'd just left, looked like it had been rearranged by a long succession of Class 5 tornadoes, while the bathroom looked as though it had just been cleaned. The medicine cabinet remained steadfastly fastened to the wall, the cupboard drawers were tucked away and good as new, and the shower curtain — an opaque plastic number featuring blue and yellow fish displaying unrealistic smiles — remained securely attached to the rod, doing its noble work of hiding the tub and shower-bath from view. I started my search in the medicine cabinet, as one always does whenever one finds oneself alone in another's home.

My initial investigation unveiled nothing probative. I mean to say, there was the usual assortment of ointments, creams, unguents, and bathroom whatnots you'd expect to spot, but nothing out of the ordinary. Lacking any immediate leads, I was leaning in to examine the use-by dates and SPF levels on a couple of bottles of sunscreen, when the project was cut short by the sudden rending of the shower curtain behind me. I spun round just in time to see a crazed-looking Napoleonic chap emerging from behind the curtain and waving a knife. He clambered clumsily out of the tub, cursed a bit in his Napoleonic lingo while extricating his arm from the curtain with which it had been entwined, secured his footing, and positioned himself between the undersigned and the bathroom door.

I stood there gaping all the while. It's what Churchill would have done.

I knew at a g. that this knife-waving chap was no ordinary Napoleon. Nor was it Nappy, the friendly, female Napoleon in whose bathroom I now stood. No, I was able to ID this fiend in human shape as Napoleon Number Three, a former hospice resident of my acquaintance, and one who'd taken to calling himself by a number of loony pseudonyms including "Bonaparte" and "Jack."

Recognizing that it may have been some time since you last perused the archives, I expect you'll need a refresher on the biography of this particular lump of wasted flesh. He was, as I mentioned a moment ago, one of a handful of Napoleons with whom I'd hobnobbed at the hospice, he being designated Napoleon Number Three. When last we'd met this blot on the landscape he'd been trying his best to thwart my aims and objects by preventing self and assorted hangers-on from going awol from the hospice. He'd gone so far as taking me hostage, holding yours truly at knifepoint while threatening to carry out a bit of amateur surgery with a view to determining the colour of my insides. I remember thinking at the time that his motives seemed unclear — he'd babbled somethingorother in my ear about destiny, following orders, and acting at the behest of some person named "Alice" but had never fully explained why his destiny called for me to be held at the business end of a knife while he screamed threats at my friends and colleagues, just ruining our day. It all worked out in the end, of course. My best pal Zeus took a good deal of umbrage at seeing his chum in a spot of peril, and leapt into the fray without delay, thus reducing this Napoleon, if that's what you'd like to call him, or Bonaparte if you prefer to the level of a fifth-rate power. After seeing that this Napoleon was, in the wake of Zeus's beating, little more than a spot of grease on the hospice lawn, we'd flicked the dust from our metaphorical sleeves and gotten on with our lives. And as we'd moved off from the wreckage, I imagined this was the last we'd see of this particular pustule on the backside of Detroit.

Leaping back to the present, I didn't celebrate my reunion with this blighter by leaping into a series of fond reminiscences. Instead, I merely stood my ground and shouted, "Bonaparte!"

This seemed to nettle the blighter. He pointed his knife at me in a marked manner.

"Call me *Jack*!" he shouted, his jaw muscles moving freely.

"Or 'Jack,' if you prefer," I said, cordially. "We needn't quibble about details. But the issue arising now, and one which raises numerous points of interest and could use some threshing out, is this: what the dickens are you doing here?"

"Vat are *you* doing 'ere?" he said. And I remember thinking that he rather had me there. I mean to say, it's not that I had any particular right to be in Nappy's apartment, and I was — if one was to take a strictly legalistic view of the thing — a mere trespasser in her home. I decided it was best to give an account of my presence on the scene, and was emboldened in this conviction because, as I might have mentioned before, the chap inquiring about my presence was holding a knife.

"I'm looking for Nappy," I said.

"*I* am looking for Nappy," he riposted, rather warmly.

"She isn't here," I said, shrugging a shoulder and gesturing broadly. "Biffed off, it seems."

"I came 'ere to see eef she was safe," said Jack, if that's what you'd like to call him, and it struck me right away that this failed to square up with my sense of the blighter's *modus operandi*. I mean to say, here was an unscrupulous dreg of humanity who threatened people with knives, hid behind shower curtains, held fellow hospice patients hostage, and generally came across as one of the landmines hiding in life's lawn. He wasn't exactly a man to whom the motto "safety first" would apply.

"Let's thresh this out like gentlemen," I suggested, giving diplomacy a go. "Why not put down the knife, and you and I can—"

That sentence, had it been permitted to come to fruition, would have ended with the words "put our heads together and sort out what might have happened to Nappy." But those words never crossed my lips. For on the cue "put down the knife," Jack's eyes had widened to a degree I wouldn't have thought possible, seeming to burn with what I believe is called a "baleful light," and he interrupted me with a low, threatening voice, which reminded me of the growl a tiger might unleash before chowing down on its daily villager.

"Zees is Alice!" he growled, brandishing the knife in a most uncordial fashion. And I could see, when he brandished it, that its hilt was carved in the shape of a ballerina, only adding to

146

the overall air of brow-furrowing mystery that surrounded this little excrescence.

"Hallo, Alice," I said, my voice quavering more than I might have hoped. "Now, Jack, there's no need for Alice to get involved in our discussion. Perhaps if we just — I don't know — chatted further about what brought us here, maybe some productive course of action might emerge."

"Zey are coming for us," he said, inching toward me in a disconcerting manner. "For all of *les Napoleons*. I do not know where zey are taking us."

"Who is taking you?"

"I do not know. But zey 'ave Nappy."

"Let's work together to find her," I suggested, for if I'd ever learned anything from Oan's Sharing Lessons, it's that nothing promotes mental health better than team-building exercises, and here was a chap who could use all the mental health he had coming to him.

He eyed me narrowly, as if sizing me up for some unknown purpose.

"I remember you," he said.

"Well of course you do. Rhinnick Feynman, esquire, at your service. We were inmates together in the hospice. We spent many an hour revelling in each other's society, playing Brakkit, hearing Sharing Room lessons, trying—"

"No!" he shouted, or quite possibly "non," for the difference is subtle and I was distracted by the knife. "I remember ze last time I saw you."

"Oh, quite," I said, hoping for a quick change of subject. I mean to say, I for one might have preferred to leave our last interaction unventilated, lest the blighter be reminded that he'd failed to finish the job of using Alice to conduct an exploration of my insides.

"Your friend . . . zis, zis ZEUS person. 'E attacked me!"

"To be fair," I said, diplomatting like nobody's business, "he may have perceived some provocation. You had threatened to—"

Here I broke off, not so much because I'd finished what I'd been about to say, but because the uncouth wretch had suddenly lunged at me, Alice aimed directly at what I believe is called my central body mass.

I won't say that I actually charged headlong into the fray, because that would be deceiving my public. What I did do was shriek a good deal, wave my arms wildly, and wish that in my younger days I'd gone in for martial arts instead of stamp collecting. I can't precisely recount the ensuing string of events in perfect detail, as the fracas didn't vouchsafe me time for detached reflection. At various points in the skirmish I did find myself lying prone on the floor, and at other times clinging to Jack's back with my arms twined around his neck. In one particular sequence I recall grabbing at Alice's blunt ballerina hilt. But at some point that immediately preceded what we might call the climax of the proceedings, we found ourselves essentially where we'd begun, with Jack blocking the door, brandishing Alice in what I perceived to be a threatening fashion, and self backing away toward the toilet.

What happened next caught both of us off guard. For while we had both been focused intently on what might be achieved through defensive use of shower curtains, toilet brushes, and other handy items, neither of us had noted the presence — in the vicinity of Jack's immediate rear — of a certain fortune-telling woman with strong wrists bearing a ceramic piggybank, which she brought crashing down on Jack's head with what some call a dull, and others a sickening, thud.

Jack collapsed on the floor. Well, I mean, of course he did. It's not as though he would have collapsed on the ceiling.

Having completed its task the piggybank broke up into several shards, the largest of these raining down on Jack, followed by coins.

All the while, Jack just lay there looking peaceful.

"Vera!" I cried.

"Heya," she said.

"Thank Abe you were here!"

"Where else would I be?" she asked, which was a fair question. "I heard you shrieking and came running back in as fast as I could."

I paused for a moment to ensure that Fenny had been unharmed, fearing that the little chap may have been caught in the crossfire, as it were, having been nestled in my inner pocket throughout my recent altercation. Seeing that he was sleeping happily as though nothing out of the ordinary had happened, I turned back to Vera.

I would have said something about having the matter well in hand before her advent, but I do like to give credit where credit is due, and was dashed grateful for her assistance in what had threatened to become a rather painful slice of the Feynman biography. I thanked her again.

"Let's get out of here," I said, once I was through with my bit of thanking. "Though presently crushed to earth, Jack is sure to rise again. And from what little I know of him I think he might be the sort of fellow who wakes up cross."

"Do you think he'll come after us?"

"I wouldn't put anything past him."

"The least we can do is slow him down," said Vera. "Why don't we cut off his head or something? It'll probably take weeks for him to regenerate, and by then we could have everything sorted out. Maybe send the police to collect him."

"Abe's drawers!" I cried, staring at Vera with a touch of wariness. "You can't go about decapitating chaps simply because they go about acting as fiends in human shape. Isn't there something or other in the book of rules about 'doing unto others'?"

"He did attack you with a knife."

"Twice in recent memory," I said. "But still — we Feynmen do not crush the vanquished beneath the iron heel, nor do we go about the place chopping heads or rending people limb from limb."

"Don't be such a chicken," she said.

I drew myself up. "A man isn't a chicken merely because he balks at dicing a fallen foe!"

Here she made a sound that reminded me of maracas.

"What are you gargling at?" I asked.

"Not gargling. Laughing," she said. "At you. You said 'chicken.' And then 'balk.' That's very funny."

"Is this the time for merrymaking?"

"It's just that chickens say 'bawk.' You know, 'bawk bawk bawk,'" she added, punctuating the remarks, if you can call them remarks, with another of her silvery laughs.

This whole exchange was starting to make me pretty dubious about the young shrimp's eligibility to be at large from the hospice and circulating among the masses.

"Do try to remain on task," I said. "We have to decide what to do with Jack. And we're *not* going to butcher him."

"Well, you at least have to let me tie him up."

"Tie away, and may Abe speed your knotting."

"All right then," said Vera. "Just give me a minute and I'll get to it."

She then crouched down beside the recumbent Jack and initiated a rather personal search of the *corpus delicti*, as the expression is. She searched through every pocket, unfastened every button, and unzipped every zipper until she'd produced a pair of items she deemed useful. These were, in the order found, (a) a set of car keys, and (b) a crumpled note.

The keys she pocketed. The note she uncrumpled and flattened out on the countertop beside me.

The note was written in lipstick — a lipstick that, if I was any judge, precisely matched an exhibit found in Nappy's medicine chest. And it was written in a script that, if the undersigned was any judge, could not have proceeded from Jack's hand. Having received several IOUs from Jack following hospice Brakkit tournaments, I was aware that this chap's handwriting, if popularized as a typographical font, would be more likely to be called "Psychopathic Sans Serif" than "Cursive Script." The hand that had written the crumpled note was light and fluid, more accustomed to writing out formal invitations than ransom notes and threats.

"That's Nappy's handwriting," I said.

And what the handwriting wrote was this:

TO NORM STRAD.

THEY'RE TAKING ME.

"What's it mean?" said Vera, and I was pleased I was able to put her at least partially abreast.

"Someone took Nappy!" I said. "As for who, I cannot say, for the pronoun 'they,' taking the place of a proper name which might provide more information, has laid me a-stymie. But I can help with the first bit. You see the note is addressed to 'Norm Strad.' This must mean none other than Norm Stradamus, another member of your soothsaying circle and one who serves as Grand Poobah of a cultish gang of princks who call themselves the Church of O. His flock not only believes in the beforelife but also worships someone called 'the Great Omega,' some sort of self-help guru who resides in the beforelife. I met Norm at the outset of that apocalyptic cavern sequence which has become such a topic of interest at the hospice. That cavern, or grotto if you prefer, was the seat of Norm's church, complete with scripture-quoting, robe-wearing loonies, a chorus who shouted things in capital letters in praise of the Great Omega, and plans to chuck my pal Ian into the Styx with a view to wiping his memory."

"You do have interesting friends."

"No friends of mine!" I protested. "This Norm is a relative stranger, and struck me as one of those bug-eyed, bearded weirdos who wear sweaters woven of hemp and perceive messages from beyond whenever they eat alphabet soup — no offence meant to the more level-headed and sensible members of the future-scrying fraternity. But he did, I'm forced to admit, have a relatively important speaking part in my last quest."

It was at this point in the conversation that the recumbent Jack groaned. At least he seemed to stir a bit, and make a noise that was in the ballpark of the groan. Vera oh-goshed in his direction, gave him a solid, nonchalant boot to the upper slopes, and once again knelt down beside him. This time she removed his belt and shoelaces and began the important work of trussing him up like an Abe-Day hen.

"And Nappy knew him?" she said, somehow unruffled by recent events.

"Nappy knew who?" I said, goggling.

"Do try to keep up," said Vera. "Norm. You were telling me about Norm. Was Nappy involved with him in some way?"

"She knew of him. She was present at Detroit University when, after a certain amount of gunfire and generalized panic, she stayed behind to tend to my pal Zeus while self and others were chivvied away toward this Norm's lair. She might have heard us mention our destination."

"Or maybe she already knew him. You did say she was a princk. All Napoleons are. Could she be a member of his church?"

"It's possible," I said, tapping a skeptical finger or two on the countertop, "but I doubt it. You'd think she'd have mentioned

prior association with another fortune teller when we first introduced her to you. It stands to reason, I mean to say. It's not as
though Detroit has honest-to-goodness prophets camping on
every street."

"Maybe," said Vera. "But we know she knows of him now.
You don't write a letter like this to just anybody."

"An excellent point well made," I said, eager as ever to give
credit where it was due. "She knew she was being taken by
unnamed persons, and she addressed this warning or cry of
help to Norm."

"She must have wanted him to see it."

"True. And the letter implies Nappy expected Norm to
know who it was who took her. I mean to say, you don't write
a letter saying to Norm saying 'they're taking me' if you don't
expect that Norm Strad will know at a g. who 'they' are. No
point in being opaque when being kidnapped, I mean to say."

"It stands to reason," said Vera, tearing a strip or two from
Jack's clothing and deploying them in the trussing. "So what's
the plan?" she added, tightening a knot.

"We take this letter to Norm!" I said. "We find out who
'they' are, and why they've taken Nappy, and solicit Norm's
assistance in tracking her down, thus pushing along the quest
to help Isaac and find Zeus."

"But how do we get the letter to Norm?" Vera asked, getting
straight to the nub. "Where do we find him?"

"There you have me. Things grew a little apocalyptic in
his little grotto-getaway when last we put our heads together,
and a certain amount of earth quaking, stone melting, and geographic upheaval seemed to have dropped property values in
the vicinity. I doubt he stayed put. But I'll bet—"

Here I broke off. And in doing so, I must've become somewhat greener about the gills, for Vera turned to me and asked
me what was the matter.

"I think I know who can lead us to Norm Stradamus," I said.

"Who?"

"The one person I know who mentioned hobnobbing with Norm ex-post-grotto."

"Who's that?" said Vera. And it pained me to give the answer.

"Oan," I said, dully. "We have to go back to the hospice to speak to Oan."

Chapter 14

"Oh, good!" said Vera, and if this causes you to flip back to the last sentence of the preceding chapter just to see what she was oh-gooding about, I won't stop you. I'd have done the same thing in your posish. For not only did this "oh, good!" arrive hot on the heels of a break in chapters, after which you may have turned in for a night, done a spot of shopping, turned to a neighbour to recommend picking up this book, or whatever it is you do when chapter X transitions to chapter X plus 1, but it also followed a revelation — if revelation means what I think it does — that had nothing jolly well worthy of an "oh good" about it.

Allow me to amplify, just in case you're listening to the audio version and can't face rewinding. I had just told Vera that, if we were to track down Norm Stradamus with a view to handing him Nappy's note and pushing along our quest to find this lost Napoleon, we would first have to pop by the hospice for a vis-à-vis with Oan, she being likely to have information re: where in Abe's name Norm Stradamus might be found. And for a man in my posish, viz, a man who finds himself engaged not only to this Oan, but also to the Vera travelling with me, the prospect of bringing these two fiancées together for a conference was an undertaking calculated to bleach the Feynman hair.

"Of course it'll be a bit awkward for you," said Vera, arching an eyebrow at me, and this also surprised me. What surprised me was that she had an eyebrow to arch at all. At the beginning of our travels this Vera had resembled little more than a walking scab as a result of her recent dust-up with Socrates. Her recovery, within the last few hours at least, seemed to have stomped the accelerator and started working on all twelve cylinders. She was almost recognizable, and now equipped to convey emotion through facial expression.

One thing I've always found tricky to navigate is the extent to which one should comment upon another person's injuries. There are some folks who respond well to sympathy and encouragement, and others who'd much prefer that you didn't mention their convalescence at all, preferring to put on a brave face, cope privately, and carry on as though they'd never been torn limb from limb, exploded by a bomb, digested by alligators, or otherwise inconvenienced by the vicissitudes of life. Judging Vera to be settled somewhere near the open-bookish end of the distribution, I ventured a vague comment.

"Err, your eyebrow," I said.

"What about it?"

"You have one, I mean to say. Or rather two. They've grown back."

"Oh. Well, that's two fewer things to worry about I suppose," she said, breezily.

"And you arched one of them, just now."

"I did."

"Sardonically, I gather."

"Maybe a touch sardonically. Sorry. I just can't imagine what it'll be like for you to deal with Oan now that she's gotten herself convinced that the two of you are engaged."

"What do you mean, 'gotten herself convinced'?" I asked.

"Don't play coy with me," she said, and her eyebrow got a bit more arching done to it. "It's obvious that you hadn't any intention of getting engaged to Oan. Some misunderstanding, I suppose. And now you've got to go dig yourself out of it."

"But dash it, how can I?" I asked. "When a bird's gone and

convinced herself that you've bunged your heart at her feet and are ready to take her for richer or poorer, you can't just haul her aside and tell her, 'Oh, sorry, you've gone and made a bloomer, and I haven't the slightest intention of hitching up with the likes of you.' Embarrassment on all sides, I mean to say. I can't say for certain that such a discussion would fall within the bounds of scorning a woman, but it's most certainly in the same zip code as a scorn, and you know what they say about scorned women."

"That's a difficulty. Like I said. It's going to be awkward."

"Have you anything to suggest?"

"You'll have to wing it. Or maybe you can convince her to chuck you aside."

"But how can I?"

"I dunno. Say something rude about the Laws of Attraction. Or tell her you've taken up smoking cigars. Get a weird tattoo or start learning the bagpipes. Anything that'll drop your appeal as husband material."

This was, I could see, a thought — but on reflection, not one that had a snowball's chance in mid-July. This Oan, as fatheaded a goop who had ever worn a beehive hairdo, was convinced I was a figure of myth and legend — the Hand of the Intercessor, she called me — and one who, whatever his bad habits or views on Sharing Room philosophy, was pretty hot stuff matrimonially. It would take a lot more than a few cigars to wriggle myself out of this spot of soup. I was about to relay this bit of reasoning to Vera when she, now putting the last few finishing touches on the binding and gagging of Jack, resumed speech.

"I suppose you could just tell her you're marrying me."

I winced.

"No good," I said. "We're back in the realm of women scorned."

"I suppose you're right," said Vera. "Unless she's fond of bigamy, in which case you aren't any further ahead. No, you'll have to think of something else. I'm sure you'll manage. You've wormed your way out of tighter spots than this."

"Nothing to do but trust the Author," I said, mopping the brow.

"All right then," said Vera. "Jack's not going anywhere soon. Let's get out of here before he comes to."

A moment later we were back in the open spaces of Bethnel Green, I still mopping the troubled brow, and Vera pointing Jack's car keys at vehicles in the street, pushing buttons on the key fob and hoping for results.

"I think we ought to divide and conquer at the hospice," she said. "You deal with Oan, get the coordinates of this Norm Stradamus person, and leave Peericks to me."

"Peericks?"

"We've got to check in with him. I'm on a day pass from the hospice. He's waiting for you and me to return with proof that I'm your fiancée and ready to be discharged."

"Oh, ah," I said, remembering. And this particular remembrance, featuring yet another landmine that had been planted squarely in the Feynman path, led me to muse upon the topic of just how dashed confusing life had become in the last few orbits about the sun, or rotations of the Earth, or whatever astronomical thingummy signals the passage of one day. I mean to say, a simple quest to find Zeus, supplemented by Abe's request to thwart whatever dangerous plans Isaac Newton might have hatched, had turned into one of those Byzantine scenarios thrown together by amateur playwrights who, long before learning the wisdom of keeping things simple, see their audiences scrutinizing the playbill for explanatory notes, scratching their heads, and sneaking out of the theatre at the first intermission. Consider my current state of affairs: having determined that Isaac's "dangerous plot" was the sort of dangerous plot you surround with a pair of quotation marks — indicating that it isn't in fact dangerous at all, but rather a goofy science project aimed at messing about with quarks — you'd think the path before me would have become a dashed sight simpler, reducing my list of quests by fifty percent. But no. Now that I was left with but one quest, viz, tracking down Zeus, this quest has now bifurcated — do I mean bifurcated? — into a rabbit warren of side quests, backup plans, and distractions. My list of aims and objects had been fruitful and multiplied to the point that I was in danger of losing track. Thus it was that, when we finally managed to find Jack's car (a loathsome compact number painted green, with an orange rag protruding from where the gas cap ought to have been), I edged my way into the passenger seat and withdrew my journal, keen to take stock of my current posish. As Vera put the steed in motion, if you can call a compact car a steed, I set about the task of preparing an up-to-date to-do list. It took shape as follows:

Rhinnick's To Do List, Wednesday, Abeuary 21:

1. *Find Zeus, the parent quest from which all others spawn;*
2. *Help Peericks woo Oan — a task which has become a dashed sight more complicated by Oan, in her fatheadedness, thinking that I am the one doing the wooing — so Peericks might unseal his lips regarding Zeus's current location;*
3. *Convince Isaac to corroborate Oan's story about the apocalyptic goings-on in the Church of O's grotto, thus allowing her to be released from the hospice, clearing the path for item 2 (Peericks's woo-pitching), above;*
4. *Push along Isaac's quantum-altering efforts by tracking down Napoleons and supplying relevant*

data regarding their brain scans, psychological profiles, and whatnot, all in aid of achieving item 3 above, viz, convincing Isaac to string along with Oan's story;

5. *Fish Nappy out of the soup, wherever she might be found, thus enabling her to assist with item 4, namely, Isaac's quantum doings; and*

6. *Track down Norm Stradamus, who seemed likely to have data regarding Nappy's whereabouts, which would place item 5 within the realm of practical politics.*

Not to mention side quests 7 through 208, which involved whatever steps might be required to sort out the slew of Rhinnick-centred betrothals which seemed to be spawning like the very rabbits whose warren my life now so resembled.

Having compiled this list, I checked it twice. Then I checked it a third and fourth time. I read it forward, I read it backward. As a matter of fact I seem to remember *smelling* the thing. And the upshot of all of this list-obsessing was this: it was a pensive Rhinnick Feynman who, chauffeured by Vera Lantz, finally hitched up at the hospice at about half-past eight p.m., far later than Vera's day pass strictly allowed. She parked the car, we crossed the lot, and after a few steps found ourselves in the lobby, where Vera was eagerly greeted by a phalanx of hospice staffers who seemed intent on stuffing her back into her cell. She offered a few well-chosen words of explanation and was chivvied off in the direction of Peericks's office, while I, now apparently a trusted member of Oan's treatment team, was escorted to her room.

I stood at the door. I swallowed. I reached into my jacket pocket and patted Fenny for good luck, and then braced myself for the inev. Two knocks and a "come in" later and I found myself once again vis-à-vis with my betrothed. Or rather, my accidentally betrothed, not to be confused with the other betrothed who'd apparently been thrust upon me without notice through the Author's recent revisions.

"Mr. Feynman!" she said, although "effused," "exulted," or "gushed," may be mot juster, for she was beaming like any woman would after finding herself on the verge of being married to the Hand of the Intercessor. She continued beaming rather freely for the space of a few ticks, before adding, "I'm so glad you're here. There's so much I wish to tell you!"

"There is?" I said, bracing for impact.

"Oh, yes! I'm sure you'll be ever so pleased," she said, gushing rather freely. "I remembered your deep love of great literature — you spoke of it often, in the grotto. It's one of your most admirable traits. Many adherents of the Church of O remarked on how deeply moved they were by the reverence in which you held authors."

The Author, I might have corrected, had I been able to get a word in edgeways.

"It's because of this great reverence, Mr. Feynman — because of my own heartfelt wish to honour the fusing of our souls, and to share in your commitment to the sanctity of the written word — I've started writing a book!"

"A . . . a book?" I stammered, suffocating beneath the mounting dread. I mean to say, the mind boggled at the thought of the hideous bilge that might drip from any pen gripped by this prized slice of fruitcake.

"I'm going to call it *For Love Alone: My Journey to Join the Hand of the Intercessor.* Oh, Mr. Feynman," she added, still gushing, "I can't wait for you to read it!"

I'd rather see the thing consigned to the flames, I might have said, but for the fact that, at this fraught stage of my affairs, speechlessness had marked me for her own. As it was, I merely stood there, overcome by dumb anguish, and tried to separate my tongue from the front teeth with which it was now fully entangled. Oan took my moment of silence as a chance to rub a bit of salt in the wound.

"And I've been making plans for the wedding!" she said. "I was thinking Dr. Peericks should give me away."

I might have remarked on the outmoded and patriarchal nature of this wedding custom but for the fact that Oan still seemed intent on hogging the conv.

"Who do you think should give you away?" she asked. "Your friend, Zeus? I do hope you've managed to find him."

These last words were like manna in the wilderness. I was so grateful for this sudden change of subject that I latched on to it like a drowning sailor might grasp a kisby ring — those things that are sometimes called "life preservers" in the beforelife; a name which, I think you'll agree, makes no sense in Detroit.

"It's . . . it's about Zeus I've come to see you!" I said, now regaining the power of speech. "I haven't much time to explain all the ins and outs," I said, "but it turns out my errand to reunite with Zeus has taken a turn, and that turn has set me on a course which leads straight through Norm Stradamus."

"Norm Stradamus?" she said, befogged.

"You remember him," I said. "Religious chap. Saw the future. Spoke in quatrains, if that's the word I want. Bearded bloke who—"

"Of course I remember him. It's just that I'm . . . well, I'm shocked that you should desire to see him. You see," she said, eyes widening, "I'd just been thinking you need to confer with him before we marry."

"You had?" I said, for most of this had floated past me.

"I had. And I suppose it should come as no surprise that the Laws of Attraction have made your desires align with mine!"

Here she blinked in a doe-eyed fashion which only height-ened my desire to be elsewhere.

"I think it's only proper that we should seek his blessing, after all," she continued. "I mean, he is the head of the Church of O, and the Great Omega's greatest prophet. I'm sure he'll grant his blessing — the Laws of Attraction assure me of it — but I still believe it's only proper for us to see him in advance. He'll want to perform the ceremony. He may require the whole flock to be in attendance! It's an auspicious event for all. It's not every day that the Hand of the Intercessor takes a partner to share his path!" she added, more doe-eyed than ever.

I did my best to swallow my chagrin and soldier on. I mean to say, there was no sense being defeated by all of this wedding-planning stuff when I was hot on the trail of Zeus. I wanted to meet with Norm, Oan wanted me to meet with Norm. It seemed our interests were aligned, as the expression is.

"There's just one thing," I said.

"What is it?" she asked.

"I haven't the foggiest idea of where to find him. I mean to say, Norm and his flock had fled the grotto like rats leaving a sinking ship last time I checked, and I've no idea where they might've regrouped. I thought I should check with you."

"Oh!" she said, looking surprised. "You must have forgot-ten. I told you last time you were here — I haven't any idea of where Norm and the flock might be. If I did, we could have just asked him to corroborate my story, rather than troubling Isaac Newton."

"Abe's drawers!" I said, smacking the forehead. My fore-head I mean, not Oan's. "You *did* say that, didn't you. It slipped my mind. So you haven't a notion of where to find him?"

"Sorry, no. We held our meetings in the grotto and the sur-rounding catacombs. They were abandoned after the battle between the Intercessor and the forces of darkness. I've no idea where Norm and his flock may have gone."

This was an unexpected turn. I mean to say, just when life offers a bit of a leg up, it sneaks around behind and lays you a juicy one right on the seat of the trousers. This pattern of one step forward, two steps back was beginning to wear on me.

"We might try a Vision Board," said Oan. "Surely you've heard of Vision Boards, Mr. Feynman. They help us harness our positive mindforce, and bring harmony between our authentic selves and the world around us. Through a Vision Board — one featuring representations of Norm Stradamus and the church — we can manifest our own deepest desires. We can use the Laws of Attraction to bring the information we seek."

It amazed me that even a sloppy pest like Oan, in the face of the obvious loopiness of this idea, was able to put the dashed thing forward with every appearance of sincerity. And it pained me to think this sort of goofy drivel could be a daily feature of life in the Rhinnick-Oan household, unless of course our conversations would come to be dominated by explanations of why an additional spouse named Vera kept popping up at the breakfast table.

"Perhaps you can have a whack at setting up a Vision Board," I said tolerantly, for I didn't wish to wound the freak. "I mean to say, perhaps my own efforts might be better directed elsewhere. Knocking on doors. Placing phone calls. Turning over rocks and logs. But in the meantime, can't you think of anything Norm might have said to indicate the location of his post-grotto HQ? A forwarding address? A hint of where you might look him up? A favourite bar he might stop by when moving house?"

"Let me think," said Oan, instituting a bit of a stage wait as she looked off into the distance. "I don't know where he lived before the grotto and never saw him elsewhere . . ."

"Any magazine subscriptions? Favourite pizza delivery

shops? Anyone to whom he might have given a heads up about his future whereabouts?"

"He was most concerned that he might be found by sinister forces. You'll recall that the grotto was invaded by the church's enemies. He would have made every effort to keep his location secret."

"Even from you?" I said. "I mean to say, you were one of his steadfast whatdoyoucallits. He would have wanted you to find him."

"I always expected he'd send word to the hospice. He knew he could always find me here, and I assumed he'd send word once he had established the church elsewhere."

"Have you checked today's mail?" I said, teeing up a long shot.

"Yes. Not a peep from Norm Stradamus."

I sat down and massaged the lemon. I mean to say, how is one supposed to find a bloke who's making every effort to stay hidden from all and sundry? We Rhinnicks are resourceful, but if we're going to be resourceful we insist on a precondition, viz, that there be resources upon which we can draw. I was at a loss.

"I'm at a loss," I said.

"Me too," said Oan. "What shall we do?"

And before I could respond — though what I might have responded with remains beyond my ken — there was a brief knock on the door followed by the advent of Vera.

You can imagine my chagrin. I mean to say, as fond as I am of the young pipsqueak, and as accustomed as I'd become to being in Oan's room, the effect of their combined presence was enough to make anyone drain the bitter cup and take on the general aspect of a bloodhound who had received bad news. But I bore up philosophically. I mean to say, you can't show alarm and despondency simply because you're in the presence of two birds who've both made plans to sign you up for better or worse. Or rather you can, but it wouldn't be chivalrous, and we Rhinnicks are practically famous for being chivalrous. So I bore up, as I just said, philosophically, and welcomed Vera with a debonair "hello."

"I've just come from Peericks's office," she said. "He's given the all-clear!"

"What do you mean?" asked Oan.

"I'm free to go. But I've got to be going straight away. Places to go, people to see, that sort of thing. No time to dawdle. Rhinnick," she said, turning to me, "would you be a lamb and give me a lift back home? You have a car with you now, and it'd save me the bother of hopping on a bus."

I raised a puzzled brow. Vera knew the ins and outs of my growing to-do list, and ought to have been hep to the fact that carpooling hither and thither wasn't written on the agenda. But I reminded myself that we were in the hospice, and that Vera had just been closeted with Dr. Peericks, and these things have been known to take a toll on the cognitive whatnots of even the most level-headed bimbos. So rather than issuing a flat-out refusal or telling the bird to go and boil her head, I softened my response, hoping to gently jiggle her grey cells back into proper working order.

"I . . . err . . . I was just asking Oan where I might find Norm Stradamus. You remember Norm Stradamus? I need to pinpoint this chap's whereabouts so I might push along the quest to—"

. . . find Nappy, take her to Isaac, convince him to help Oan, and unseal Peericks's lips regarding Zeus's current locale, I might have said, had my sentence been allowed to come to fruition, but it didn't. Instead I was interrupted, or cut off, if you prefer, by Vera insisting there was no time for extended chit-chat.

"We've got to get going. I know where we have to go next."

"You do?" I said, bewildered.

"I do. Television," she added, tapping her bean.

"Oh, ah!" I said, cottoning on. "Right then. Tally ho. Next stop, Norm Stradamus!"

This drew a sharp intake of breath from Oan, who had spent the last several seconds watching the exchange between self and Vera like a spectator at Wimbledon. And she followed this sharp i. of b. with an exhortation.

"Be sure to ask for his blessing!" she said.

"Whose blessing?" asked Vera.

"Norm Stradamus's blessing," said Oan. "If Rhinnick and I are going to be married, we'll want to have Norm's approval. He'll give it, of course. Oh, he'll be so pleased that we've asked. And I'm sure he'll want to conduct the service himself. He's such a—"

Goof, would have been how I'd have finished that sentence, but Vera once again showed herself a champion interrupter and insisted that we get on with the show.

"No time to chat," she said. "I'll make sure Rhinnick asks Norm for his blessing. You have my word." And so saying, she sauntered over to Oan, leaned down, and gave her a warmish sort of hug that must have lasted at least three seconds.

"Shall we pack your bags?" I said, wanting to help push things along.

"No time," said Vera. "I have an appointment."

"Well then, cheerio!" I said, facing Oanward, while opening the door and letting Vera glide through.

"Come back as soon as you can, Mr. Feynman," said Oan. And what she said next blanched the skin beneath my tan, for it seemed precisely calculated to shatter the undersigned's aplomb. It was this, spoken with a sickening sort of treacly rumminess which unmanned me:

"Or rather, come back as soon as you can, *darling*."

Doing my best to suppress a wince, though every fibre within me was wincing like billy-o, I bade farewell once more and exited stage right.

Chapter 15

"What ho!" I cried, and I'll tell you why I cried, "What ho!" The moment I'd loosed myself into the hallway I found that my elbow had been grabbed and I'd been chivvied, at a rate of considerable mph, up the hall without what is known as preamble. And the person who had attended to the chivvying was Vera.

"What in Abe's name are you doing?" I said, mid-chivvy.

"Getting out of here," she said. "Just play along."

And while playing along is a thing that I'm always keen to do, I find it a dashed sight easier to do when I know what it is I'm playing along *with*. I prepared to unleash a few well-chosen words in order to put this point to Vera, but she shushed me with a gesture. She then increased our speed, hauled me through a couple of doorways, and then pulled me around a corner where we collided with a solid, fleshy wall of white polyester topped by a whiter pillbox hat.

The fallout of this collision was a tangled mass of arms and legs, a dislodged pillbox hat, an impromptu, no-holds-barred wrestling match involving all three collidees, and a cry of "Matron Bikerack!" from yours truly.

Of course you'll remember Matron Bikerack.

No? Oh, surely. She's the boss-nurse of the hospice, the scourge of Detroit Mercy, and the sturdiest light-heavyweight to ever push a pill or chill a bedpan. Second only to Dr. Peericks on my list of hospice-based medical-louses-to-be-avoided, this Bikerack was not only a pain in the neck to end all pains in the neck, but also the Officious Meddler who had, more often than not, been the chief party responsible for making my time in the hospice a drudgery and a penance. She had an unmatched capacity to lower the boom on anything that might be loosely described as fun, remorselessly scuttling any attempt at merriment or frivolity in favour of the soul-crushing application of niffy ointments, stinging syringes, and other medical treatments that I daren't name in mixed company. While I've frequently been assured that she means well, and that her efforts are aimed at boosting the mental whatsits of her charges, I maintain that she stands alone as a world-class damp rag, dark cloud, and party-pooper. I couldn't begin to count the times that this sturdy enema-giver had gotten herself in the way of my legitimate aims and aspirations, though she'd never gotten in my way quite so literally as she had at the moment of going to press.

Disentangling myself from the wreckage, I rose from the floor, dusted off the Feynman trousers, and extended hands to help all and sundry regain their footing.

"Matron Bikerack," I repeated, just in case the last one had been swallowed in the mêlée.

She contrived to steady herself and seemed to sway a bit before regaining the power of speech.

"What the . . . I . . . well I never . . . I mean . . . who in Abe's name are you?" said the matron, taking a moment to glance around and absorb the scene. "And what are you doing running through the halls with . . . with . . . is that patient 89-427?"

"It is!" said Vera, who seemed to have come away from our recent collision without any ill effects. "But call me Vera. That's my name. And this is Rhinnick, my fiancé."

"Abe's drawers!" said the matron, in an astounded sort of way, replacing her pillbox hat and taking a step closer to Vera. "I barely recognized you. Your burns — why, why they're practically healed," she continued, moving in for an even closer inspection. "Dr. Peericks told me you'd improved, and that your memories were returning, but I — well I had no idea that — wait, did you say 'fiancé'?"

"I did!" said Vera. "Rhinnick Feynman. And as much as I'd like to stick around and make more formal introductions—"

"Rhinnick Feynman?" said the matron, now rotating on her axis and fixing me with a fishy eye. "The man Dr. Peericks called to help with Oan's treatment?"

She stepped closer, subjecting me to the sort of penetrating scrutiny which she had, during my previous sojourns at the hospice, generally employed in the examination of rashes and unexpected growths. At least, she had done so in the version of history known to me. Based on her dialogue thus far it was clear that this Matron Bikerack was yet another victim of the widespread epidemic of Feynman-centred amnesia, or someone whose previous encounters with yours truly had been blotted out by the Author without Him bothering to send me his latest revisions.

"Y-y-yes, that's me," I said, inclining the bean.

"And you just happen to be engaged to Oan's roommate?" she said, still subjecting me to the fishy eye. "An awfully odd coincidence," she added.

"N-n-none odder," I agreed. "But coincidences do happen. That's why we have a word for them. And no one could have been more surprised than the undersigned when I learned — that is to say, when I realized — that the charred husk stationed in Oan's room, staring off into space and chirping about two chairs, was really my old comrade-in-arms—"

"Fiancée," said Vera.

"—was really my old fiancée, Vera Lantz, for whom I'd been searching for years and years."

"Weeks," said Vera.

"Weeks," I agreed.

I didn't seem to have assisted matters. The fishiness of the matron's gaze intensified.

"We do have to be going," insisted Vera.

"Going where?" said Matron Bikerack, crossing her arms and pivoting — if pivoting means what I think it does — into a position between Vera and the only road to freedom. "Dr. Peericks hasn't signed any discharge orders," she added.

"There isn't time," said Vera, who, apparently keen on getting our show on the road, proceeded to kick her pace of speech up a notch or two, landing somewhere between Auctioneer and Regimental Sergeant Major. "Not today, at any rate," she began. "I presented Dr. Peericks with our marriage license so Rhinnick could sign off on my release. You know, responsible family member accepting responsibility, that sort of thing. Anyway, that's all been attended to but Peericks didn't receive my paperwork until after business hours. So he just gave me another day pass and told me to push off until tomorrow. I'll come back for the final discharge papers then. Here's my pass."

Pausing for breath, Vera hastily withdrew a piece of paper from the recesses of her costume, waved it briefly before the matron's eyes, did something resembling a half-curtsy, and turned to leave.

"Not so fast!" said the matron. "Let's have another look at that pass."

I couldn't blame the old disaster. There was an obvious sort of shady, dubious-rumminess in Vera's behaviour, and the speed with which she'd flourished her paper at Matron Bikerack invited suspicion. It occurred to me in a flash that this Vera, keen as ever to keep my quest on course, had falsified the data about Peericks allowing her to vacate the hospice, and that the putative — do I mean putative? — day pass might not withstand careful investigation. I could see this was a moment that called for action.

But what action? That was the q. As the matron stepped toward Vera, hand outstretched, my mind returned to my last escape from the hospice, when I'd facilitated my own departure by beaning the uncooperative Dr. Peericks with a book, much in the same way Vera had beaned Jack with a heavy ceramic pig containing coins. And while the act of bringing heavy objects crashing down on a subject's head is one that shouldn't be cultivated as a habit, it occurred to me this might be another instance where a bit of upper-slope-clubbing might be indicated. But where the beaning of Jack had been attended to in an apartment featuring heavy piggybanks, and the beaning of Peericks had unfolded in an office holding a wide assortment of sturdily bound books, the present encounter was situated in an open, sterile hall containing nothing that might serve in what you might call a bean-biffing capacity.

On further reflection I was glad to have found myself weaponless, for it occurred to me that, while the assaults on Peericks and Jack had occurred in circumstances that practically cried out for a bit of justified beaning, the bonneting of Bikerack could be regarded as unsportsmanlike in the circs. I mean to say, there she had been, shuffling along in a corridor and minding her own business, only to be waylaid by a pair of speeding escapees. Topping off the encounter with a final, parting shot to the matron's melon seemed offside. I therefore ditched the notion of further physical confrontation and gave diplomacy a go.

"Aren't you the same Matron Bikerack who attended to Ian Brown?" I said.

"Ian Brown?" she said, turning. "Ian Brown? Why, yes, he was a patient here a few months ago. He escaped with the help of a DDH Guide and a gang of Napoleons. That's the gang that stole my pass card!"

Here she paused to shimmy a bit, wiggling as though the memory had made her itch, and I regretted that my little attempt to distract the old juggernaut had dredged up an irksome slice of her recent past. I contrived to redirect the conversation.

"Ah yes," I said, "well, I crossed paths with Ian Brown some time ago, and he assured me that his entire recovery and present well-being could be laid squarely at the feet of Matron Bikerack, nurse extraordinaire, and one whom Ian said, and I quote him verbatim, could easily out-Florence any Nightingale. 'Abe's gift to mental health,' I think he called you."

Here she shimmied again, as though a feather had been drawn up her spine or her spirit had been gripped by irresistible island rhythms. I couldn't recall her having been a compulsive wiggler during our past associations, so I imagined this was some new tic or habit she had developed in recent days. Perhaps another of the Author's strange revisions.

"Oh!" she exclaimed, rather excitedly, suddenly wriggling like a hooked halibut.

I'm a keen observer of human behaviour, and I perceived that something was amiss. Vera, too, seemed to sense that this sudden mobility on the part of Matron Bikerack might be a sign of trouble brewing.

"Are you all right?" said Vera.

The matron didn't respond. Or rather she did, but her response didn't come in the form of anything you might describe as language. She grunted something that may have been a word but seemed to be focused on other things. She redoubled her shimmying efforts and started tugging forcefully at her nurse's uniform in a way which seemed to suggest her supporting structures and guy-wires might have become entwined. Her troubles seemed to localize in the vicinity of her bosom, and she pulled repeatedly at the pectoral regions of her uniform in a manner that risked the hospice's PG rating.

My gaze drifted chestward — not for any unseemly purpose, but only, as you'll understand, because of this matron's ongoing struggle. And once my gaze had settled at ground zero, as it were, I perceived the source of the matron's trouble. For when she tugged, a gap appeared in the field of view, revealing slightly more of the matron than I was accustomed to drinking in. And what I saw was an eyeful. For what emerged from that gap was the last thing I might have expected: a small, familiar furry face blinking dazedly and looking as though he'd recently seen things that would now and forever be emblazoned in his memory.

"Fenny!" I cried.

"GAH!" cried the matron, or something that sounded like "gah," as Fenny, now nestled in the valley of doom, started scrabbling toward the summit of Mount Matron in a frenzied bid for freedom.

The matron cried aloud again, but I paid no heed to her hullabaloo, my sympathy and concern being earmarked for the tiny, intrepid hamster who now perched himself mid-bosom and dodged the matron's grasping hands. I daren't imagine the perilous passage he'd just made, making his way bravely through dark and secret paths, only to emerge to the open spaces where ham-sized hands flailed wildly and sought to fling him from the perch where he now nestled. I won't say that my next act strictly qualified as chivalry, but it wasn't intended as non-chivalrous, and it had the virtue of having been motivated by the same primordial force which compels the mother bear to charge ahead to save her young with no regard for self.

I reached out for Fenny.

The matron swore and swatted my hand.

Fenny leapt as far as his little legs would take him, and he alighted on the matron's neck.

This seemed to be more than she could take. For this matron, now cursing and gyrating like a furious ballerina, did a

174

final series of frenzied pirouettes before collapsing in a heap on the very tiles from which she'd arisen minutes before.

I remember thinking that it was an impact like this one that did in the dinosaurs.

Fenny did the shrewd thing, escaping the avalanche narrowly and legging it up the hall in an every-creature-for-himself sort of way, somewhat encumbered by various ropes and strings and things which had entangled themselves about his person during his ordeal. I gave chase, Vera bringing up the rear. We left the matron in our wake, now snorting like a gas explosion and cursing a good deal — as was natural for a person in her posish — but showing no sign of any continuing interest in the bona fides of Vera's documentation.

Providence, in its wisdom, gifted hamsters with short legs, so I was able to overtake the little chap in the space of ten or twelve strides — counting mine, not his, which would have numbered somewhere in the hundreds, if I'm any judge.

I scooped him up. And blow me tight if the little chap hadn't — as he had done so many times before — escaped from a hideous peril while at the same time doing his part to save the day. For in saving his own skin, in escaping the hidden sights that lurked beneath yon wall of white polyester, and in risking his reputation as a preux chevalier and gentlehamster by treading in places where no rodent ought to tread, Fenny had hooked his jaws upon a perfect solution to our troubles.

He wiggled free of the things encumbering him and, registering no small measure of triumph, spat the perfect solution into my hand.

"What's he got?" asked Vera, and I forgave the grammatical slip, for what my tiny companion had purloined, what this prince among diminutive furballs had just released from his jaws, left me gaping in wonder.

I showed his prize to Vera.

"Abe's drawers!" she said. "The matron's lanyard."

"With her new pass card affixed!" I said, goggling. "The little chap must have heard the matron mention her pass card when I asked about Ian Brown. Reasoning, no doubt, that this pass card was just what his old pal Rhinnick needed in order to pry himself from the slavering jaws of doom, he wasted no time in risking all to plunder the matron's trove, as it were, in order to make off with the swag."

Vera eyed me skeptically, but I paid no mind. I had collaborated with this rodent before and knew of his unmatched capacity for fishing buddies out of the soup. But never before had he faced such jeopardy, never before had he showed such enterprise, or made such supreme sacrifices when rallying 'round and steering me clear of the bludgeonings of fate. It makes one wonder why such a fuss is made about those half-a-league, half-a-league onward chaps who rode into some valley or other. They didn't have to face the unspeakable shame of clambering through a gyrating matron's undercarriage. Heroes they might have been, but Fenny stood alone.

I looked down at Fenny reverently, much moved by the lion heart in his hamster frame, and patted him on the head. He blinked at me, twice, and I knew he understood my depth of feeling.

Within two shakes of a hamster's tail we had taken our leave of Detroit Mercy, making appropriate use of the matron's card and a handy employee's-only exit. Thanking Abe for tiny friends, we bunged ourselves into Jack's car, placed Fenny in a place of honour upon the dashboard, and set our course for freedom.

Chapter 16

"Set a course for freedom!" I cried, as we drove on.

"Sounds good to me!" said Vera. "Where to?"

"What do you mean 'where to'?" I said.

"I mean where do want to go?"

"To Norm Stradamus's hideout. At least I presume that's where you're taking me. You told me that, in the wake of your meeting with Dr. Peericks, television had shown the way, and that your soothsaying machinery had directed you toward the next waystation on our quest, which I presumed to mean the new and hitherto hidden HQ of Norm Stradamus."

"I didn't exactly say that," said Vera.

"Whatever you said, that's where we ought to be headed. So as I was saying, set our course for Norm Stradamus and don't spare the horses. First star to the right and straight on 'til morning. Continue giving the machine all of the gas at your disposal."

"I don't know where Norm's hideout is."

"But in the hospice you said—"

"I know what I said in the hospice. I was lying. I had to get you out of Detroit Mercy and into the car."

This unmanned me. I mean to say, however skeptically one regards the babbling of garden-variety fortune tellers, palm readers, astrologers, and other purveyors of cryptic bilge, this particular soothsayer had always been a credible source. It's true that her prophesies and predictions could be opaque at times, or even misleading if carelessly misinterpreted by the unwary, but out-and-out lying wasn't in this Vera's nature. Whether she'd been a Girl Guide I couldn't say, but her behaviour up 'til now indicated a good egg, and one who could be trusted with state secrets. Why, I'd always thought her word could be counted on more reliably than my own fingers and toes.

"But why lie?" I asked. "You could have just asked me to come along and I'd have gladly—"

"There wasn't time for explanations. I had to get you out in a hurry."

"But why? That's the matter that needs threshing out. I can readily understand the desire to put a healthy slab of terrain between self and hospice, but why the sudden urgency? Why all of this up-tempo, shake a leg, prestissimo charging about? It's not as though we were paying for hourly parking."

"I had to get out of there before Peericks woke up and sicced the Hospice Goons on us."

This perplexed me. I'd known Peericks for years and years, and he'd never been known as an on-the-job napper. I pressed for particulars.

"What do you mean 'before Peericks woke up'?"

Here she paused, as though reluctant to explain. She fixed her gaze on the road ahead, swallowed hard, and took on board a couple of extra lungfuls of air.

"Dr. Peericks was asleep?" I said, pressing the matter.

"In a certain sort of way," said Vera, trailing off.

I gaped. There was a fishy sort of rumminess in this young beazel's manner, and her tone raised the gravest suspicions. It was the way she'd said Peericks was sleeping "in a certain sort of way." Unless I was very much mistaken, I had divined the meaning of those vague words right off the bat.

"You beaned him!" I exclaimed.

"I had to!" she cried. "You told me yourself that you did the same thing when—"

I raised an interrupting digit, for I couldn't allow this doctor-clobbering pipsqueak to cite me as a binding precedent. "While I admit that I did, on one occasion, ko the good doctor in a bid to extricate — do I mean extricate?"

"Yes, extricate. Or remove."

"Right. Then I'll admit I did ko this doctor in a bid to remove or extricate self and others from the hospice, but I did so only as a last resort and at the unmistakable prompting of the Author. I mean to say, everyone knows you can't go beaning hospice officials on a whim without the merest provocation. But when the Author places a book called *Cranial Trauma* at your elbow, just as the doctor moves his occiput into prime beaning position, you've no other choice but to bow to the Author's will and get to biffing. But the crucial thing is to choose your wallops wisely. Take my example. I'll admit freely that in our recent tête-à-tête with Matron Bikerack, it occurred to me more than once that a well-placed slosh on the occiput might have been an effective ploy. Yet I suppressed the urge to biff. Not every head which the Author places in your path is ripe for beaning. Other solutions should be exhausted before you give in to the impulse and start raining blows on those around you or the thing becomes habit-forming and you gain a reputation."

"Other solutions my eye," she said, peevishly. "Peericks wasn't about to let me go. He didn't buy my story about the engagement, and he was going to stick me into a higher-security wing of the hospice. He said I was a flight risk. A flight risk!"

Well, I mean, she *was* a flight risk, of course, and that risk had come to fruition. She'd proven the doctor's point by flying the coop this very night. But I didn't raise this point with Vera. If she chafed at being labelled a flight risk, despite ample justification, I was happy to let the matter rest. Besides, she had raised another issue which called for exploration, viz, the doctor's refusal to accept her claims about our engagement. I called for additional information.

"He didn't accept the marriage license?" I said.

"There isn't any marriage license."

"Did you lose it?"

"I never had it!" she said. "All I got from the clerk at City Hall was Nappy's address."

"It seems to me it would have been prudent to get the license while you were there."

She turned her head in my direction, taking her eyes from the road ahead just long enough to aim an exasperated look at yours truly — the sort of look that says "how can a thick-headed brick like you be allowed to mix freely with the public?" And while anyone seeing this look would have no trouble divining the meaning it conveyed, I couldn't see why it was indicated in the circs. I'd merely pointed out the obvious error of her ways. I was on the point of drawing myself up to my full height — at least as much as this was possible while occupying the passenger seat of a compact car — and giving Vera one of my own austere looks while demanding an explanation, when she sighed an exasperated sigh which seemed to come from the soles of her shoes.

"What's done is done," she said, dully. And then seeking a change of subject, or possibly just a distraction from our present plight, she fiddled with the appropriate knob on the car's dashboard and activated the radio, which began emitting offensive noises indicating country music.

Reasoning that there was enough sadness in the world without this twangy din polluting the air, I changed stations, finally settling on one that featured the daily news. This seemed like a sound choice: if police had started setting dragnets far and wide for a pair of fugitives on the lam from Detroit Mercy, it was best that we get word of it here and now. But rather than dishing up a story about an escaped mental patient and her debonair fiancé, the news was featuring a story on the disturbing trend of disappearing Napoleons. Practically all Napoleons, said the radio, had disappeared without the merest trace, and public authorities remained baffled, having no clue as to where the Napoleons had gone or what might have caused their disappearance. Complicating matters was the fact that Abe the First, Mayor of Detroit, was still awol from his office, and the bureaucrats he'd left in his wake hadn't a notion of how to proceed, but merely scratched their collective head for want of any clear solution.

"We've just got to find Norm Stradamus," said Vera. "Remember Nappy's note. It was addressed to Norm and said, 'They're taking me.' She must have believed Norm would know who took her. And whoever that is must be the person who's making all the Napoleons disappear."

I agreed with the young pipsqueak's diagnosis. It seemed unlikely that there was a widespread public fad of scooping up random Napoleons left and right, and far more likely that a single person, organization, or gang with a Napoleonic fixation had been responsible for the scooping.

"But where could Norm Stradamus be?" I asked. "And how do we find him? We can't just wander about Detroit going door to door and asking folks if they've spotted Norm or caught wind of anyone spouting cryptic quatrains, what? Does your television say nothing?"

"Sorry, no. Not a peep out of it today. It's been pretty quiet since all of that stuff about 'two chairs' and the vision that led me to pinch Nappy's files." And on the cue "Nappy's files," the beazel's face spread into a wide-eyed, eureka sort of expression and she slammed on the brakes, skidding Jack's car to a halt and sending Fenny hurtling forward into the windscreen. He stuck there briefly, looking like a displeased furry pancake, and then slid back down to the dash, where he shook his head for a space and gave Vera a piercing glare of indignation.

"Nappy's files!" Vera repeated. "Why don't we take them to Isaac? He's the one who wanted to have them in the first place. And if he's so interested in Napoleons, he may have some clue about why they've all been disappearing."

I hated to pop this young prune's balloon and dash her hopes to the ground, but I knew this idea was a dead end. Isaac, I explained, had been just as baffled as me when it came to the motive-force behind the sudden Napoleonic shortage. He needed Napoleons in his research but hadn't a notion of who else might want them or why they'd all been disappearing into thin air.

"But Isaac still might be able to give us a hand," said Vera. "If we just give him Nappy's files—"

"But to what end?" I said. "The whole point of giving Nappy's files to Isaac was to push along his research, thus obliging him to return the favour by confirming Oan's story, convincing Peericks that Oan's grey cells are firing correctly and she's fit to return to duty."

"Right," said Vera, in a quizzical sort of way indicating that she hadn't seen the problem.

I could see the time had come to put her abreast. "What you're failing to see, young shrimp, is that the ultimate goal of that strategy, the foundation upon which our whole foreign policy has been built, has well and truly gone phut. The only reason we had for helping Oan get out of storage was to assist Dr. Peericks, and the reason for helping Peericks was to put this peerless twerp into my debt, convincing him to fork over whatever information he had about Zeus. But consider our situation now! Assume that Isaac shows up, assists Oan, and Oan is returned to her gig as Sharing Room Director. So far so good. But mark the sequel: I return to reap the rewards, asking

Peericks to give me Zeus's coordinates. Peericks then looks at me and says something along the lines of, 'Ah yes, you're the fugitive who helped Vera waylay the matron, steal her pass, and escape from the hospice rather than waiting a day or two for banns to be read and marriage licenses to issue. Please come right this way and I'll get you a comfy padded cell.' I understand you wanted out, and I understand beaning the doctor and charging through the hospice gates felt like the surest path to freedom, but in your hot-blooded haste and naïveté you've missed a key part of the equation: my name at the hospice is now mud, and all hope of fishing info out of Peericks is now lost. Why, even if Zeus is still a resident of the hospice, I'll never get word of it from Peericks."

"I hadn't thought of that," said Vera.

"There's your error," I said, tolerantly. "Always think of everything."

"You could have stopped me," she said. "You didn't have to use the matron's pass card. When she fell you could have—"

"My dear ass," I said, "we were in the heat of the chase! You can't expect a fellow confronted with tumbling matrons, heroic hamsters, stolen pass cards, and lightly charred fiancées making a break for the open spaces to stand calmly, weigh the situation in a dispassionate manner, and formulate solutions. The adrenaline kicks in and overwhelms what psychological types refer to as the *executive function*. It wasn't until we were in the car that the heated blood had cooled enough to allow for detached reflection."

"Should we go back?" said Vera. "Clear things up with Peericks?"

I lowered the boom on this suggestion with the greatest of promptitude. One didn't need television to see where that incautious strategy would lead us. We'd both be locked in the hospice before you could say "what ho." And while it was possible Zeus himself was in the hospice, and my own incarceration would result in merry reunions, it seemed a dash sight more likely that I'd be stuck cooling my heels in Detroit Mercy while Zeus got on with his life elsewhere. And as if that weren't enough to cloud the brow, I'd be stuck in a loony bin with a pair of fiancées. I issued a clear *nolle prosequi*. Vera's recent rash actions, I explained, had taken the hospice off the list of practical destinations.

"Well, at least I've solved one of your problems," she said, putting the car back into motion.

"How do you mean?"

"Your problem with Oan. Word of my escape will spread around the hospice like wildfire. I don't think Oan will be keen to marry the man who broke me out."

I shook the loaf. If this Vera had one flaw, apart from a growing habit of biffing every bean that was lowered in her presence, it's that she failed to account for the sheer magnitude of loopiness within the hospice walls.

"I'm not so sure," I said, slumping a pair of despondent shoulders. "First, Oan is understandably besotted with yours truly. She sees me as a religious icon — the Hand of the Intercessor — and is unlikely to be swayed in her views by something as minor as our recent flight for freedom. And second," I continued, making the score plain to the meanest intelligence, "Oan knows about your television. She heard you tell me your prophetic powers had plotted a course to Norm Stradamus. She'll think our dust-up with the matron, and our escape from Detroit Mercy, were all part of some preordained scheme designed to clear our path to Norm Stradamus's hideout so that you could keep your promise."

"What promise?"

"Your promise to seek Norm's blessing! You gave your word to the old disaster. And no one puts more stock in the word of prophets than this Oan. When a bird who can see the future gives her solemn promise that she'll spare no effort in seeking a blessing from another sayer of sooth, Oan is sure to consider the matter settled. She'll be convinced that everything we have done, however weird or unseemly, has been set in motion by the ruddy Laws of Attraction, or Destiny, or the Great Omega, or whatever force a goofy stargazer like Oan blames for everything that happens."

"That's a difficulty," she said.

"And we still don't know where to go next," she added, filling the dead air.

I pulled a suggestion from the metaphorical hat.

"The Hôtel de la Lune?" I said.

"Why there?"

And there she had me. I suppose the idea had coalesced because I couldn't think of anywhere else to go, and in the absence of any plot-furthering destination, one might as well plant one's flag in the lap of luxury. I was about to explain all of this to Vera, and to describe for her the wonders of the Detroit Riviera, when I was rudely interrupted by a police cruiser barrelling into the side of our compact car, stopping us in our tracks and crushing everyone within.

When I awoke, some unspecified time later, I was wearing a silk dressing gown and lying in a four-poster bed, found in a room that was so luxurious that it made the suites in the Hôtel de la Lune look like a one-star airport hovel on the wrong side of the tracks.

Chapter 17

I shook the melon with a good deal of vigour, hoping to clear out the cobwebs and determine whether the sight that met my eyes was a mere hallucination or illusion.

The vision held.

I was in a vast room that was, as previously specified, about the most palatial spot to have ever housed the Feynman frame. The four-poster bed in which I'd awoken, for example, was bedecked in fine silk sheets, flowing draperies, a rather sumptuous duvet, and an entire platoon of well-stuffed pillows. The walls were liberally besprinkled with a museum's worth of art — principally landscapes and portraits framed in gold — and the wall that faced my current posish was home to one of the most imposing hearths to ever cook a log. Other prominent features of my surroundings included couches, tables, chairs, bookshelves, busts, knickknacks, and tapestries, all drawn from the swanky slice of the spectrum and practically screaming the word "posh."

I could see at a glance it was the sort of place where Rhinnick Feynman belonged. Fenny, too, seemed right at home, for the little chap was snoring on a cushion nestled snugly on the passenger side of the bed.

The port side of the room featured a floor-to-ceiling window at least thirty paces wide. Through this window I could see I was several storeys up and looking out on a swath of primordial forest abutting a shimmering blue lake. There were mountains on the horizon. It added up to the sort of scene

I'd hitherto spotted only in those high-definition background photos that decorate the computing machines of people who spend most of their days trapped in cubicles. "Picturesque" about sums it up.

The room also featured several large wooden doors. One of these was slightly ajar, and I perceived that it led into the sort of marble-laden loo you'd imagine you might find in a spot like this. But it was the door nearest the window that collared the lion's share of my attention, for it now opened, permitting entry to some form of domestic fauna backing into the room pulling a wheeled, metallic cart.

This domestic denizen pivoted on his axis.

And while I won't say that his advent qualified as one of those thunderbolts that shoot from the heavens and shiver your timbers, I *was* caught by surprise, and I uttered a mildly astonished, "Why, Abe love a duck!" when I realized who he was.

"William!" I said.

"Good morning, sir."

"Grrnmph," said Fenny, burrowing into the sheets, apparently not wishing to hobnob with the help.

"What in Abe's name are you doing here?" I asked, which was a bit odd, now that I think of it, since I hadn't a notion where "here" was. William saw through this snafu and supplied the data.

"We're in the home of my new employer, sir. The regent."

"Your new employer?"

"Yes, sir. The regent."

"And who is that?"

"A wealthy ancient, sir, and a princk. She was recently a guest at the hotel. While there, she kindly expressed appreciation for the manner in which I attended to my duties, and offered to add me to the strength of her staff here. I agreed, and took office as the regent's personal attendant just last week."

"Last week?" I said, scoffing. "You've miscalculated, my dear old luggage handler. It's only a few days ago that you and I were bandying words at the Riviera."

He shook the loaf. "I'm afraid you're mistaken, Mr. Feynman. You've been convalescing here, in one of the regent's guest quarters, for eleven days and nights. You've been asleep since your ordeal."

"My ordeal?" I said, befogged. And then it hit me like a police cruiser, or like a large ceramic pig containing coins. Memory returned to its throne, as the expression is, calling for an immediate change of subject.

"The police car!" I cried, a cry I amended a moment later by appending: "Where is Vera?"

"She, too, is recovering, sir," said William. "In another wing of the house. Her recovery has, if I may say so, been somewhat more rapid than your own. She has responded well to nature's soft nurse and has been conscious for some time."

"Nature's what?"

"Soft nurse, sir. The allusion refers to sleep, sleep that knits up the ravell'd sleeve of care, sore labour's bath, balm of hurt minds, and chief nourisher in life's feast. Vera slept for seven days and then awoke, fully recovered. Her wounds healed quickly."

"I don't doubt it," I said. "She's had practice. The poor blister recently bounced back after an explosion which blew her limb from limb. No doubt her various bits and pieces are getting used to sorting themselves out and knitting themselves together."

"It is conceivable, sir."

"She's all right, then? Suffering no whatdoyoucallits from our imbroglio?"

"She's doing very well, sir. Indeed, when last we spoke she seemed to be in jocund mood."

"Good, good," I said. "And how about this regent chap? What's his story?"

"Not a chap, sir. The regent is female."

"Right. I think you mentioned. What's her name? And what's she the regent of?"

"I am not privy to those details," said William.

"You signed on without knowing who she was?"

"It seemed advisable, sir. There is a tide in the affairs of men which, taken at the flood, leads on to fortune. Omitted, all the voyage of their life is bound in shallows and in miseries."

It took me perhaps a quarter of a minute to work this out. "It seemed like a good idea at the time, you mean?"

"Precisely, sir. I took the current when it served."

I might have pressed this point further, but I had bigger fish to fry. I mean to say, if a chap wants to buttle for a beazel without knowing who she is, or what she might be the regent of, this may be a mystery worthy of a bit of exploratory sleuthing, but only by someone who knows where in Abe's name he's holed up and what's been going on in his life for the last week and a half. And if William could be trusted, that wasn't me.

"And you say I've been out of commission for ten days?"

"Eleven, sir. Tonight will be the twelfth night."

"Golly," I said.

"Have your preferences in the matter of tea changed, sir?" said William, hauling a tray from his cart and setting it on a table beside the bed.

I assured him they hadn't, and might have suggested something a good deal stronger than tea had the present moment not been a time for clear-headed thinking. There appeared to be numerous points of interest concerning which I would soon be needing particulars, and I foresaw that all of my brain cells would need to be firing on all thrusters, as the expression is, if I was to have any hope of making sense of the sitch.

William passed me a strengthening cuppa and I drank deeply, giving myself a moment or two to marshal my wits before carrying on.

"What can you tell me of where we are?" I asked. "This house, I mean. Definitely not a bungalow. And judging by the trees outside the window, and the mountains on the horizon, we aren't back at the Riviera."

"No, sir. We are, to use a popular expression, deep in The Wild. Far away from the city centre. The regent prefers to conduct her affairs in places far removed from mayoral scrutiny."

"The mayor's scrutiny reaches everyone," I riposted, and I meant it. I was one of the many in attendance when Abe the First, Mayor of Detroit, had let loose with a touch of hitherto undisclosed omnipotence, on the occasion when he had butted into the battle between the City Solicitor, subsequently ID'd as some chap named Plato, and Penelope Somethingorother, aka Ian's wife.

"That may be the case, sir," said William. "Nevertheless, the regent prefers to reside in secluded locales, far from prying eyes. She prefers her actions to remain cloaked in anonymity."

"So how did I get here, then. IPT?"

"IPT, sir?" said William, corrugating his brow. "I'm unfamiliar with the expression."

"Oh right," I said. "I'd forgotten. Never mind. But leaving that aside for the moment — how did Vera and I end up in the regent's home?"

"Her summer home, sir," said William, proving a good deal more pedantic than I remembered. "You arrived here, as I said, some eleven days ago. The two of you came by helicopter, and were brought in by a pair of the regent's agents, dressed as policemen."

"Why on earth were we dressed as policemen?"

"Forgive me, sir. It was the regent's agents who were so garbed."

"Two chaps dressed as coppers brought me here?" I said. And then the significance of this fact penetrated. "You mean — you mean to tell me that the two jonnies who rammed self and Vera, the two blighters who wrecked our car and squashed the pair of us with their cruiser, thought it best to add to the mounting list of charges by kidnapping their victims and—"

"I fear you misjudge them, sir," said William. "While it is true that the same two agents who, as you say, rammed your car, are the ones who brought you hither, they did so without any malice or *mala fides*. They acted for the public good. They thought you were Napoleons."

"Why should they think I was a Napoleon?"

"You were in a Napoleon's car, sir. The gentlemen had been tracking it."

"Even allowing for the fact that they might, as you suggest, have thought I was a Napoleon, that doesn't explain why the blighters brought me here. Not by a jugful. I need an answer from you, William, and a categorical one at that. Answer me now with a simple yes or no. *Why* were these pretend coppers hoping to nab a Napoleon or two and bung them into the regent's home?"

I half expected my stern tone to cow the chap where he stood, causing him to lose an inch or two of his height or seek shelter behind the sofa. He didn't so much as shuffle a foot. He just stared back at me flatly, like a penguin who'd been entirely unmoved by something another penguin had said. Then he answered, matter-of-factly.

"They did so at the regent's behest, and at the urging of her colleague, Norm Stradamus."

"Did you say 'Norm Stradamus'?"

"Yes, sir."

"You don't mean Norm Stradamus."

"I do, sir."

"You're sure you've got the name right? Stradamus?"

"Yes, sir."

"Norm?"

"Yes, sir."

"A prophesying chap who wears robes, forgets to shave, and babbles in quatrains at the merest provocation?"

"Precisely, sir."

"The regent works with Norm Stradamus?"

"She does, sir. Indeed, Norm Stradamus is here among us. He has come with much of his order, the Church of O. They've retreated to the temporary seclusion of this locale."

"Well I'm blowed!"

And I'll tell you why I was blowed. Ever since I'd set off hot on Zeus's trail, and then on Nappy's, and then finally on the trail of Norm Stradamus, I'd become so dashed used to failing to find any trace of my prey that I'd become something of a cynic and had come within a hair of throwing in the towel. Had I known that all fate required was for me to tangle with a police car and suffer a bit of a coma before I'd be parachuted into my quarry's lap, I'd have chucked myself under the wheels of the nearest cruiser a few days sooner.

"You surprise me, William," I said. "I had Norm and his flock taped out as hermits, rejecting the comfort of great houses in favour of crevasses, crags, and holes. And here you stand telling me that he's checked into this five-star palace. What in Abe's name brought him here?"

"He is here for scientific research, sir."

This surprised me, too. From what I knew of Norm and his troop they were all atwitter for prayer, penance, and piety, but not so hot when it came to what you might call "facts" — things to be sussed out through the use of Erlenmeyer flasks; telescopes; and small, medium, or large hadron colliders. Those devices might have made Isaac's heart skip a beat or two, but not Norm's.

"What kind of scientific research?" I asked.

"Research into the beforelife."

"Ah," I said, inclining the bean. "The scales fall from my eyes. I mean to say, I catch your drift." And I'll tell you why I caught his d. Norm and his hangers-on had always been mad-keen on the beforelife, believing that the goddess or prophetess they served, a bird called the Great Omega, lived there and doled out gifts to deserving members of her gang. I ought to have known that, if Norm and his weird, robe-wearing cronies had hung up the prayer beads and shawls in favour of lab coats and mass spectrometers, it would have something to do with the beforelife.

"But what have Napoleons got to do with research into the beforelife?"

"That, sir, is the question; the very mystery that Norm Stradamus and the regent seek to solve. They wish to understand the link between Napoleons and the beforelife. Both the regent and Norm Stradamus believe that all Napoleons reincarnate multiple times, leaving Detroit and returning to the mortal coil repeatedly. The regent seeks to replicate this process. That is why her ladyship and Norm Stradamus have gathered all Napoleons here. They've been sequestered in a hospital that the regent had installed on her private grounds."

"Abe's drawers!" I exclaimed. "You can't mean to tell me the regent and Norm Stradamus are the ones behind the mounting Napoleon shortage."

"They are indeed, sir."

"Taking people against their will?"

"I'm afraid so, sir. The regent's project has necessitated some actions that, while highly regrettable, are for the public good. This has included taking Napoleons by force."

"But you can't go about the place kidnapping Napoleons!"

"Conscience doth make cowards of us all, sir. The act is unavoidable, but a cruelty born of kindness. As I said, both the regent and Norm Stradamus share the view that all Napoleons have the capacity to return to the beforelife multiple times. They further believe that, if they can learn why this is so, they may find a route to re-enter the beforelife themselves, allowing passage for all who wish to make the journey. That is their ultimate goal, sir. This is why they capture Napoleons, why they study them, and why they prefer to conceal their plans from public view. Though this be madness, sir, yet there is method in't."

"Gosh," I said. "You've seen a lot in your first week on the job, what?"

"I have indeed, sir. I could a tale unfold whose lightest word would harrow up thy soul, make thy two eyes, like stars, start from their spheres, thy knotted and combined locks—"

I shushed the man with an impassioned gesture.

"Kindly cheese the flowery lingo," I said.

"Yes, sir."

"I mean to say, there's a time for blathering on about stars and souls and eyes and things, and a time for taking tides at the flood and jolly well getting the show on the road. This is decidedly the latter."

"Very good, sir."

"And, talking of minding one's tongue," I added, for this had given rise to a new line of thought, "will you get in trouble for spilling the beans to me?"

"I do not believe so, sir. The regent wished for you to be apprised of her activities."

"She did?"

"She did, sir."

"Well, then may I see the Napoleons? And Vera?"

"You are an honoured guest, sir. The Hand of the Intercessor.

I've been instructed to extend every courtesy to you. I'm sure the regent will permit you to visit with anyone you wish, with the possible exception of the Napoleon whose car you'd taken. He has proven most difficult, sir."

"You don't mean Jack is here!" I yipped.

"I do, sir. The Napoleon who calls himself Bonaparte, or Jack, arrived shortly after you. Once it was realized that you'd taken his car, it was no great effort to retrace your steps and locate the missing man. The regent sent her agents to bring him in."

"Well then," I said, "no sense lolling around here in silk pyjamas and jabbering with the help. Point me toward my clothes and take me to your leader."

"All in good time, sir," he said. "I imagine that, before you meet with the regent, you'll wish to reunite with your fiancée."

I stared at the man. Indeed, it's not going too far to say I gaped. I sat there, blinking at William, groping for a response for the space of several louder-than-average heartbeats. I mean to say, when he'd suggested I might wish to see my fiancée, the only response that had occurred was "which one?," a response that — I think you'll agree — invites judgment, censure, and disagreeable backchat. It's true, I knew that Vera was in the house, and the smart money would have bet it was she who wished to see me, but Oan had been known to travel with Norm, and I wouldn't put it past the Author to land her on me here and now. Indeed, He might have gone even further and added a third or fourth betrothed into the mix while I was sleeping.

"Oh, ah, she wishes to see me straight away, does she?" was the best response I could muster in the circs.

"She does, sir. And she waits without. Shall I admit her?"

"Bung her in," I said, dully.

And so saying, I straightened myself in bed, adjusted the silk pyjamas, and hoped for the best.

Chapter 18

I don't know if you've had the same experience, but I've always found that, even if you muse rather freely on a looming crisis in your affairs, anticipating its advent and steeling yourself against whatever vicissitudes it might bring, you can still be fairly gobsmacked when it finally shows up on the horizon, burns through several layers of atmosphere, and comes crashing down upon you. Broadly speaking, that was the state in which I found myself at the time of going to press. A mere paragraph or two earlier I had mooted the possibility that Oan would be the fiancée to whom William referred and that she'd blow into my room and trouble an already troubled mind. And when the door to my bedchamber did open, and Oan *did* blow in as I had feared, I found that all of my mooting, predicting, and musing hadn't prepared me in the least. Rather than taking her arrival with suavity, aplomb, or insouciance, possibly flicking a fleck of dust from my pyjama sleeve and letting this Oan's advent pass over me like the idle wind which I respected not, I reacted as though fate had once again snuck up behind me and administered what I believe is known as a wedgie. Gobsmacked, as I said before. The blood pressure rose, the heartbeat quickened, the palms moistened, the throat dried, and the eyes, had they not been anchored in their sockets, might have ricocheted off the opposing wall.

Oan didn't seem to notice these physiological whatnots. She had, upon entry, uttered a passing nicety or two in William's direction, rushed across the room, and then flung herself into the ornate chair beside my bed, taking my hand in hers.

Fenny noticed the arrival and emerged from his little nest beneath the sheets, grrnmphing at Oan in a cordial fashion. William, for his part, shimmered off discreetly, leaving what he must have regarded as two long-parted lovebirds to exchange their soft words and get a jump on the tender reunion.

The very thought of this turned me green.

"My darling!" said Oan, and I greened more thoroughly than I'd ever greened before.

"Oh, ah," I said.

"I'm so relieved to see you awake," said Oan, "so very, very relieved. It warms my heart. I did my utmost to hasten your recovery by appealing to the living Universe; focusing all of my energies and attention upon the Laws of Attraction, that they might manifest my desires. Oh, my darling! How I yearned for your revival. I recorded my desires within my book — *For Love Alone* — allowing the manuscript to serve as a totem of my wishes, like a Vision Board, calling you back to health — back to me — as soon as possible. Oh, how deeply and constantly I worried about you, my darling."

I found myself pining for my coma. But remembering that it's important to be civil, whatever the circs, I babbled a word or two of thanks.

Oan steamrolled on.

"What else could I do, knowing that my betrothed, the very Hand of the Intercessor, was lying here, alone, in a coma, unaware of his surroundings, and laid out by his terrible wounds? The regent's best physicians hadn't any notion of when you might awaken. So I came to you every day, and every night. I tended to your wounds. I added to *For Love Alone* while at your side. I kept my silent watch as you slept, knowing all the while that—"

"You . . . you watched me as I slept?"

"Of course I did. Has anyone who ever loved done any less?"

I had to rerun that one through the processor once or twice before it penetrated, and when it did I felt the answer had to be "yes, probably loads of times." But I didn't bother mentioning this to Oan. I had noticed — and perhaps you did as well — that the theme of "love" had been wontonly lobbed into the field of conversation numerous times, and I hoped a change of topic might serve as a bit of in-the-bud-nipping before the thing had a chance to metastasize and become dashed untreatable.

"But how are you here at all?" I asked. "When last I checked you were locked up at the People's Pleasure and doomed to be kept in store until Dr. Peericks certified you as *compos mentis*. Did Newton turn up and back your claim? Did you do something to convince the hospice staff that your loopiness had subsided and you were now fit for general circulation?"

"Doctor Peericks agreed to release me to the Order," said Oan.

"The order?"

"Yes, the Order. Capital O. The Church of O," she said, specifying. "Dr. Peericks agreed to release me to their care at the regent's request. Or rather, at the request of her court physicians — the regent herself prefers to work behind the scenes. But she has an impressive entourage, one that includes highly regarded mental health professionals. The doctor released me to them for treatment."

I corrugated the brow. This didn't seem right to me at all. I mean to say, the doctor was, unless I'd misread the chump entirely, absolutely besotted with this Oan. He wouldn't have let her out of his sight for any price, no matter how many highly regarded mental health professionals lined up to assist in jump-starting the bird's synapses. This called for further examination. I pressed Oan for details.

"Dr. Peericks was content to let you leave?"

"Not at first," she said. "But the regent seems to have influence with people in positions of power. Several of these intervened with the doctor. They supported my application for release. They cited several conflicts of interest, and claimed I oughtn't to be treated in a hospice where I held a staff position. This seemed to affect Dr. Peericks rather deeply."

"I'll bet it did," I said, stroking the chin in a clue-putting-together sort of way. And I'll tell you why. I had deduced what had transpired in Peericks's head. On the cue "conflict of interest," Peericks must have worried that some bureaucratic bimbo would soon sniff out, as I had done, the fact that he had fallen in love with one of his patients. Small wonder, then, that he'd yielded to the request to have Oan's treatment moved elsewhere. It's no use risking your medical license to serve as psychiatrist for a person you'd like to wed: some committee of Boss Psychiatrists is apt to strike you from the roster if they find you're harbouring burning whatdoyoucallits for a person in your care. Let someone else take charge of clearing the bats out of Oan's belfry, and Peericks would be cleared to woo and win. Yes, that had to be it. It was an ingenious plan. But it did seem to have holes, so I pressed further.

"So Peericks knows where you are?" I said

"No," said Oan. "Not exactly. It was agreed that I'd be released for care at a private facility in an undisclosed location. It's all in order, I'm sure. But the regent doesn't wish for anyone to be able to find us here."

"And what do you know of this regent? I take it she's an ancient of some authority. Secretive bird with heaps of cash. But apart from that—"

Oan didn't seem interested in chatting about regents. She interrupted my peroration, telegraphing the fact that no husband of hers would ever get a word in edgeways. She changed the subject entirely.

"I have wondrous news," she said, her eyes suddenly bedewed and her voice taking on a melting note, two signs which I thought portended trouble for Feynman comma R.

"N-news?" I said.

"From Norm Stradamus. I've spoken to him. I've spoken to him at length, and told him about our plans. Oh, Rhinnick —"

Here she broke off, pressing my hand to her heart in a dashed familiar fashion and allowing her eyes to become even further bedewed. She looked as though her soul had become home to new and beautiful thoughts.

"Rhinnick," she said, although "swooned" would be mot juster.

"Hello?"

"Oh, Rhinnick."

"Still here, old bird, and awaiting your next dictum."

"Oh, Rhinnick! Norm Stradamus has given his blessing."

She then paused to blush deeply before closing in on my position and showing every indication of initiating a shame-inducing hug.

I quaked where I sat, bracing for the inev., when I was saved by the last-second intervention of a vigilant ally.

"EEK!" said Oan, or words to that effect, as Fenny hopped off the bed and into her lap. She followed up with "oh, my word," and other expressions of surprise as the little fellow danced the hamster version of a buck-and-wing dance atop her thigh.

"Ah," I said. "My hamster. Fenny."

Oan gathered her wits about her, settled back into her chair, and let Fenny do his thing.

"I think he likes me," she said.

I might have said something about hamsters being noto-riously bad judges of character, but I didn't wish to wound the old disaster, merely to find some civil way to oil out of the engagement, or at least change the tone of the present conversation before any more of this hugging business might erupt.

"So Norm's blessing," I said, easing into the thing, "this is his final word on the subject? No chance . . . that is to say, no *fear*, that he might entertain second thoughts, change his mind, possibly louse the whole thing up?"

"Goodness, no!" said Oan, once again taking my faint hope and dashing it groundward. "He's most enthusiastic. He sees our union as an important development for the church. Our wedding will be celebrated far and wide by adherents of the Order. Norm wishes to speak to you about it and sort out the details."

The last thing I wished to do was start plotting out seating charts, writing out vows, or otherwise chatting about the details of any dashed wedding, but I saw this as my only chance to extricate myself from a lavish bedroom populated by a determined fiancée in a hugging mood. So I uttered something along the lines of "there's no time like the present," removed my sheets with a flourish, and hopped out of bed with the greatest of promptitude. I then stood still for a space, recovering from the dizzying headrush that ensues whenever a medium-term coma patient rises from his bier.

I bade Oan to lead me Normward.

She handed me my hamster, and we were off.

A couple of shakes later we were standing with Norm Stradamus in some large species of parlour or salon — one that was every bit as lavish as the room in which I'd rested, it being generously decked out with about 378 *objets d'art*, as the Napoleons call them. These adornments gave the room an antiquish sort of air, one that was echoed by the prophet standing before us.

Now, stop me if I've described Norm Stradamus to you before. If you recall, the man styled himself the High Priest, Principal Prophet, and First Prelate of the Mysteries of Omega, and looked exactly how you'd expect a character with that string of titles to look, provided only that what you expected was a slightly hunchbacked, somewhat gristly, eagle-nosed headmaster equipped with a scraggly beard, wispy hair, and parchment skin, the whole portrait being completed by a black skullcap and a dark green robe.

He was standing by a little cart bearing drinks and all the fixings which was, as far as I was concerned, an excellent place to be. He summoned Oan and self to his side, made all of the usual civilities, lobbed a few honorifics in my direction — Hand of the Intercessor and all that rot — and then asked if I'd like one for the tonsils.

I assured him that I would. Indeed, had the man offered three or four at once, I would have taken him up on his offer.

Oan and I stood in a sort of respectful silence while Norm fiddled with the controls, adding here an ounce of gin, there a splash of vermouth, when I perceived that we were not, as I had hitherto believed, a party of three, but rather a full foursome. Off in a distant corner of the salon, or a distant corner of the parlour if you prefer, sat a person obscured in shadow. But despite this camouflage or concealment, I knew at a g. that this had to be the regent herself.

No, check that for a moment. Let's call her the Regent, capital R, because I've rarely basked in the presence of someone who so obviously called for all the capital letters you could muster.

I've never been one for magical thinking, or one who is given to fooling about with metaphysical hokum. I don't read people's auras, perceive the tenor of their vibrations, or assess their attunement with various psychic whatnots. But a certain palpable sort of somethingorother did seem to emanate from this Regent. And if I had to give this somethingorother a name, I think it would have to be "nobility," or possibly "stateliness," "loftiness," or "grandeur" if you prefer. Whether the source of this emanation was a result of the Regent's finely chiselled features, her closely cropped hair, the upright posture she maintained in a seated position, or some combination of these or other factors, I couldn't exactly say, but the overall package reminded me forcibly of a Siamese cat — a creature decidedly manufactured for both worship and adoration. She was ornamented every bit as richly as the parlour in which she sat, being tastefully festooned with every bangle, bauble, and bijou for which she could find an appropriate resting place on her person. This arrangement was finished off by a sort of rich, purple drapery which was cinched at the waist with a golden cord. She was, in a word, Magnificent, capital M. And she just sat there, blinking at us, while Norm expertly speared a couple of olives and presented his finished work.

"Bottoms up!" I said, giving every appearance of making merry while keeping a wary eye on the Regent's corner.

"To happy unions," said Norm, clinking my glass with his.

I drank deeply, feeling this was the best course.

"The Regent," I said, resurfacing and nodding in her direction. "She isn't joining us? A teetotaller, perhaps?"

"She prefers to observe," said Norm.

"It's her way," said Oan.

And while I thought to myself that this violated some precept or other in the Host's Formbook — sitting mutely and gawking while your guests hobnob amongst themselves, I mean to say — I didn't raise the issue or do anything else to cramp the Regent's style. If she wanted to sit like a Trappist monk while I and my fellow standees drank martinis, who was I to get in her way? So I merely drank my drink and gawked back.

"We're so pleased to have you here," said Norm, bobbing in my direction in a way that struck me as unduly obsequious, if obsequious is the word I want. "It's our honour to have the Hand of the Intercessor in our midst as we carry out our important work."

I bristled. I mean to say, all of this "Hand of the Intercessor" stuff was starting to grate on me. It's one thing to be on the receiving end of public adoration; it's quite another to receive it because you're the hand of somebody else. The "Intercessor" to whom everyone kept referring was, if you'll recall, merely an old pal of mine named Ian Brown, the milquetoastiest chump to ever inspire a fit of yawning. I didn't begrudge this chump his ill-deserved fame, nor did I bother pointing out that the only thing interesting about that lump of unflavoured oatmeal was Penelope, his wife. But I now started to chafe at being defined as this chap's hand. We Rhinnicks aren't vainglorious, but we like do like to rest on our own laurels, as the expression is. Call me "Rhinnick, escaper of hospices," or "Rhinnick, knocker-out of psychiatrists." "Rhinnick, helper-out of needy pals in trouble." Or even "Rhinnick, chap who was personally selected by the mayor to safeguard Detroit from apparent (but, as it turns out, imaginary) existential threats," if you like. But not "Rhinnick, Hand of the Intercessor," which was no better in my estimation than "Old Whatshisname, Hanger-on of a More Interesting Pal." Judge me harshly if you like, but judge me on my own merits.

I don't mean to prolong the point, but it was bad enough that Oan — to whom I was in danger of being hitched matrimonially if current conditions persisted — thought of me chiefly as Ian's Hand. But now that I was ensconced here, in a large, stately home apparently filled to the brim with members of the Church of Ruddy O, it seemed as though I'd be hard pressed to take more than a couple of steps without bumping into someone who'd look at me and think, "there's that chap who knows Ian, let's see if he'll introduce us." Why, here was their leader, Norm Stradamus, a character with whom I'd scarcely exchanged three words in my prior adventures, treating me as a popular favourite simply because I'd been standing cheek-by-jowl with Ian when last we'd met.

But though proud, we Rhinnicks know when to keep the upper lip stiff. I stifled my chagrin. I reminded myself that there are times for wallowing in self-pity, and times for swallowing your dudgeon, rolling up the sleeves, and seeing what you can do to help a pal who finds himself treading on life's banana skins. If Nappy's note could be believed, Norm Stradamus was in a posish to give some clues as to who might have taken her. And any step toward Nappy was a step toward Zeus, the two of them having been inseparable the last time I'd checked.

"Er . . . I said we're honoured to have you with us," Norm repeated, pulling me out of my reverie.

"Oh, the honour is all mine," I said, falsifying things a bit. "Oan tells me that your important work has something or other to do with Napoleons."

"It does!" said Norm. "We've gathered all the Napoleons we can find and brought them here."

"Quite a crowd, I'd imagine."

"It is. There are several hundred housed in the Regent's hospital."

"They can't take kindly to that," I said. "Napoleons hate captivity. They're known to be haughty spirits — these Napoleons, I mean — and apt to resent being exiled or otherwise bunged into anything reminiscent of a slammer, however luxurious."

"It's for their own good," said Norm, "and for the public's good, as well. Everything we do is for the public good. We'd never do anything to harm anyone without cause."

As he said this, I thought to myself that it had a sinister ring to it, suggesting that this Church of O was perfectly happy to love thy neighbour only so long as thy neighbour didn't get in its way. Stand between them and whatever it was they wanted and they'd ram you with a police cruiser and bung you into a cage.

"So what's led to all this Napoleon rustling?" I inquired.

It was Oan who supplied the answer. Up until now she had been a silent member of our little circle, she having been experiencing some trouble with an olive which had gone rogue, slipped its moorings, and found its rest on the carpet. Now that she'd attended to this development and rejoined the party, she seemed keen on holding up her end of the feast of reason and flow of soul.

"The High Priest and the Regent are looking for a way to reach the beforelife," she said. "They believe the Napoleons are the key."

"Why in Abe's name would you want to reach the before-life?" I said. "You may not know this, but I'm a princk, and I remember the beforelife. You can take it from me that it isn't all donuts and jam. There are downsides to the herebefore. Take death, by way of example. Dashed inconvenient thing, death. Every time you cross the street, lance a boil, leap from a cliff, or swim too soon after dinner, you run the risk of shuffling off the mortal coil and before you know it you're bobbing up to the surface of the Styx without any memory of who you were."

"That's why the Napoleons are the key!" said Norm. "The Napoleons do remember. They have a deep connection to the beforelife. While we believe everyone starts out in the same way, manifesting in the beforelife and living a full life there before appearing in Detroit, Napoleons are different. Special, I mean. They make the trip back and forth a number of times. Consider the Napoleon whose car you'd taken."

"Jack," I said.

"Right, the Napoleon known as Jack. Upon questioning, and after exposure to various treatments designed to improve his memory, he insisted that he'd been back to the beforelife dozens of times. He's lived any number of lives, and gone by several names. He remembered living as Napoleon, Jack, Judas, Richard, Brutus, Sheila, and at least two chaps named Pope."

"He's been a host of unpleasant people!" said Oan, "Every one of them a scoundrel!"

"I don't doubt it," I said, "and the unpleasantness seems to have stuck. Why, the last two times I've met the blighter he seemed keen on investigating my interior. Probably cheats at cards, too. So what's your theory? A life of anti-social behaviour, or ignominy, if you prefer, gets you a hand-stamp for the before-life equivalent of come-and-go privileges?"

"Not at all," said Norm. "No, it seems to have something to do with the Napoleonic brain — or rather their mindset, the way they perceive the world. It's about their expectations."

"Expectations, eh?" I said, stroking the chin.

"What we learned about in the cavern," said Norm.

"That which was revealed by the Intercessor," said Oan, lowering her eyes reverently and curtsying my way, as though any mention of the inter-bloody-cessor called for a show of respect to me.

"As Oan once taught in her Sharing Room," said Norm, "it seems that, in a very real way, it is our expectations that give the universe form."

"I've experienced the same thing," I said, for I had. "It's what happens when you expect a party to be a bit of a drag and it turns out, despite the host's best efforts, to be a bit of a drag. Your expectations bring it about."

"No, no," said Norm, "it's much more than that. You must have seen what happened when the Intercessor fell into the Styx; when he took the plunge in the holy waters and fulfilled the prophecies of the ancient texts."

His allusion was to what I've previously described as "the cavern sequence" — that slice of my fairly recent past which

Oan had described to Dr. Peericks, causing him to bung her into Detroit Mercy. It was during this cavern sequence that I'd first met Norm Stradamus, encountered his Church of O and observed the fallout of a battle between Penelope — Ian's wife — and the City Solicitor, two fairly omnipotent world-bending characters who'd gotten into each other's way. But I didn't see what any of this had to do with expectations.

"Sorry, no," I said.

"No?" said Norm.

"No," I repeated. "I mean, no, I didn't see what happened when Ian nose-dived into the Styx. I mean to say, I'm vaguely aware that there were some fairly apocalyptic goings-on — flashing lights, exploding thingummies, a bit of earthquakishness trembling the world's foundations — but I'm afraid I missed most of it. Occupied with other things."

"Well," Norm said, "what many of us witnessed made it clear the Intercessor was able to call forth a power—"

"Called Penelope," said Oan.

"That's right, a power called Penelope, and through this power he was able to reshape the very fabric of Detroit. Bend it to his will. Change the very nature of nature."

"We call it Climate Change," said Oan.

Chapter 19

"Climate Change?" I said.

"That's right," said Norm Stradamus. "The power to alter the environment. Change the entire world to fit with your expectations. The Intercessor, through this Penelope figure, had that power. The City Solicitor had it, too. And we believe Napoleons have it in some measure, at least in so far as it relates to remanifesting themselves in the beforelife. So deep is their expectation that they're going to be reborn, so thoroughly are they convinced that life here in Detroit is but a step toward remanifestation in the beforelife, that their expectations are made manifest through reincarnation."

"The Regent has this power, too!" said Oan, exhibiting awe. "The power of Climate Change. She's not as strong as—"

"Enough!" said a commanding, feminine voice from some-where nor'nor'east.

I spun 'round. It was the Regent herself, standing a pace or two behind me. At her side was a sleek, hairless hound with a silver collar, looking at me as though I were a particularly mouthwatering piece of kibble.

I uttered an audible squeak, for I'd heard neither the Regent nor her canine friend approaching. I clasped a protective hand on the pocket of my pyjamas, keeping Fenny under wraps. I'm generally a friend of dogs of all shapes and sizes, but their views on hamsters differ, and I wasn't willing to risk my little pal's future on the undisclosed intentions of this particular dumb chum.

"I apologize, Mr. Feynman," said the Regent, "but the scope of my powers is not your concern."

"I'm so sorry," said Oan, looking abashed, "I didn't intend—"

"No matter," said the Regent, another champion interrupter. "What has been said has been said. We did not bring Feynman here for a discussion of Climate Change. We brought him here to show him the respect that he deserves."

I raised a skeptical eyebrow. I mean to say, as far as I knew they'd brought me here by accident, mistaking self and Vera for Napoleons.

"And now that you are here," said the Regent, who seemed to pay no heed to my skeptical brow and carried on regardless, "we find that you may be well positioned to help us."

My brow rose farther.

"Oh?" I said.

"Indeed," said Norm, looking intently toward the Regent as though he hoped to receive some sort of telepathic directions. "There's been a — well, a development involving your friend Vera."

"What about her?"

"While she slept," said Norm, "she kept repeating the same phrase. Something about—"

"Two chairs?" I asked.

"How did you know this?" snapped the Regent.

"Vera and I were housed together in the hospice," said Oan. "She had suffered terrible injuries, and lost most of her memories. When she came to, all she would say was 'two chairs.' At least, that's all she said until the day she met Rhinnick. Shortly after he'd left the hospice she seemed to enter some kind of trance before reciting a whole poem with these 'two chairs' as the theme."

Here the Regent piped in.

"Two chairs define a man and men;
Two chairs that free and bind;
Two chairs that open worlds and free
The body and the mind;
One chair sought and held by both,
The other coveted by none;
The first chair reunites two souls
Intended to have been just one."

"That's the poem!" said Oan.

"She said precisely the same thing while recovering in our care," said Norm. "She was unconscious, still recovering from her wounds, but sat upright in her bed and said those very words."

"Odd," I said.

"Very odd," said Oan.

"I mean to say," I continued, "I'd never have thought of Vera as the sort of bird who'd recite poetry. Oan, yes, but that's because Oan is one of those soupy, emotional birds given to flights of whimsy, the sort who sings old folk-songs, engages in cross-stitching and writes poetry at the merest provocation. She has what you might call a spiritual complex. But not Vera. Vera isn't the poem-spouting sort. Have an engine that needs fixing? Count on Vera. Need to have your rocket repaired? Vera's the person you need to see. But when it comes to reciting poems, rhyming or otherwise, you can include her out."

Oan seemed to take offence. I wasn't entirely sure why, as everything I'd said was backed by sufficient empirical evidence to withstand peer review, and I was on the verge of citing sources when the High Priest piped in.

"The words were prophecy," said Norm.

"Oh, ah!" I said, cottoning on. "And you recognized the symptoms, you being a soothsaying, prophecy-spouting bimbo yourself."

"That's right," said Norm, "but none of us has any idea what her prophecy means. What are these 'two chairs' to which she alludes? Who are the 'man and men' she mentions? occupying chairs that free and bind?"

"Well, I suppose one of them might be Isaac," I said, thinking aloud. "I mean to say, from what I've learned of him of late, the current version of Isaac Newton, call him Isaac 2.0, is practically famous for occupying a chair. The Lucasian one at the university, to be precise."

The Regent seemed to be deeply moved. She wheeled 'round in my direction, gripped the Feynman shoulder, and stared intently into my eyes with a gaze that could have shucked an oyster at fifty paces.

"What do you mean, 'the current version' of Isaac Newton?" she said.

"Well, I mean to say, his prior iteration wasn't a scientist at all. At least," I continued, for one likes to be precise, "not in any professional sense. He was the City Solicitor's personal secretary, and any scientific pursuits were of the amateur variety. But now, following what must be the latest revisions of the Author, I find this Newton has been recast as a famous scientist who has occupied the Lucasian Chair for years and years."

"The Author?" said Norm Stradamus, looking baffled.

"Pah!" said the Regent, who from her manner seemed to suggest she wasn't inclined to discuss the Author. She kept her gaze fixed on me. "So you perceive Isaac Newton to have changed completely," she said, still boring into my soul, "to have been one thing, and then to have always been someone else — not to have changed sequentially or organically, but through — through what you might call retroactive changes to his life?"

"That's right," I said. "From what I gather he's always been the Lucasian Chair — well, for years and years at any rate, but that's only been true for a month or two from my perspective.

His history's been revised. Nothing to do about that, of course. The Author writes what the Author writes. If He wants to revise His manuscript without telling me, then—"

"Climate Change!" said the Regent.

"Climate Change!" said Norm.

"Oh, my!" said Oan.

"Pish tosh," said I. "I don't want to be a Climate Change skeptic, but the change you're prattling on about is a mere whatnot. A revision. The Author's editorial work. Nothing to worry about at all. Happening all the time, that sort of thing."

This didn't seem to make an impression. The Regent turned toward Norm and carried on as though I hadn't said anything at all.

"This Isaac may be the subject of Vera's prophecy," she said. "One of the men occupying these two chairs."

"He might be both!" said Norm. "Rhinnick says there are two versions. Isaac Newton the personal secretary and Isaac Newton the scientist." He turned to me. "Tell me, Feynman, when this Newton was, as far as you can recall, a personal secretary to the City Solicitor, was he known for sitting in any particular chair?"

"Sorry, no," I said. "I mean, not any one chair in particular. Civil servants are widely known for sitting on their backsides, but not in any specific chair, at least not in Isaac Newton's case."

"Hmm," said Norm.

"Hmm," said Oan.

The Regent clicked her tongue. Or it might have been a hiccup. In either case, her dog responded by rearing up and perking its ears, which I found disconcerting. He didn't appear to be the sort of dog who'd curl up in one's lap, but rather the sort to whom the command "go for the jugular" might evoke a quick response.

"Memphis, down," said the Regent, stroking the dumb chum's head.

I'm fairly astute, and gathered from this that his name was Memphis.

"Not to raise a point of order," I said, stepping an inch or two backward out of the Memphis Zone; "but, why do we care about this poem? I mean to say, I know you've suggested that it's a prophecy, and Vera is known far and wide as a prophetess, but what's the issue? So there appear to be some man or men — one or both of whom might be Isaac Newton — who occupy a chair or chairs, and these chairs have something to do with freeing bodies and minds. What's the big deal? Plenty of chairs to go around for everyone else," I added, shrugging a shoulder to indicate that one needn't give a single damn about either chairs or poems.

"It's because of my own predictions," said Norm. "Years ago I predicted the coming of a greater prophet, one who would guide us toward the Great Omega's realm. And in this prophecy I foretold that the coming prophet's name would be Truth and she would travel with the Hand. You, of course, are the Hand."

"And you think that batting 500 is close enough?"

"Batting 500?" said Norm.

"Fifty percent," I explained. "You say I'm the Hand, but that the prophet's name is Truth. The prophetess of whom you speak is named Vera."

"The name 'Vera' does mean Truth," said Oan. "She fulfills all of Norm's conditions."

"Not entirely," said Norm. "My foretelling also suggested that the prophet would have 'no past but what her prophecies could bring.' I've no idea what that means."

"Egad!" I said. "That's Vera in a nutshell. She had her wires crossed and grey cells scrambled in the recent past, wiping her memory entirely. No past, if you see what I mean. And those memories that she does seem to have are what you might call 'syndicated reruns' which arrive via television: she sees images of herself in the past, or foresees future images of herself remembering things. It doesn't make much sense to me, but it does seem to square up with your predictions. It's amazing how you prophet types work these things out."

"She must be the one foretold!" exclaimed the Regent. "Her prophecy points the way."

"The way toward what?" I asked.

"The beforelife," said the Regent. "Norm's prophecy foretold that this greater prophet, speaking in dreams, would guide the Servant of Truth on the path to the mortal realm."

"Who's the Servant of Truth?" I asked.

"It's one of Norm's titles. Members of the order frequently call themselves the seekers of truth."

"I thought the word was servant," I said, in that penetrating way of mine.

"Norm regards himself as the servant of the Order. It all makes sense," said Oan, although I remember thinking she was straining the word "sense" rather uncomfortably.

"Be that as it may," I said, seeing myself as the only hope for injecting a voice of reason into all of this prophecy chat, "I don't see how we're going to make sense of this 'two chairs' business. Isaac may be one of the chaps in chairs, but there again he might not. It's not as though Vera's poem came with an index of terms."

"That's where you come in," said Norm. Indicating me, I mean, not someone else. "You've known Vera longer than we have. You've spent time with her, you know her habits. She trusts you. We want you to visit with her to see if you can help unpack this poem. Unlock its meaning."

"We know you'll succeed," said Oan. "You cannot fail us. You're the Hand of the Intercessor."

Once again I found myself chafing at this title, and would have ground a tooth or two had I not felt that the act might cause offence. "Hand of the Intercessor, my eye," I might have said, renouncing the title, turning on my heel, and making a quick march to the exit. But I didn't, what with one thing and another. I mean to say, all they'd really asked me to do is hobnob with Vera, a good egg who, as I've said before, it's always a pleasure to see, and do my best to interpret a poem. And while the interpretation of poetry is one of those activities calculated to bore any man of spirit into a comatose state, it wasn't as though I had anything else pencilled into the agenda. My quest to find Zeus was at a standstill. And I was musing on this fact, about to agree to the course of action prescribed by Norm, the Regent, and Oan, when I was struck by a whatdoyoucallit of memory.

"Nappy!" I cried.

"Nappy?" said the Regent.

"Aroo?" said Memphis, or words to that effect.

"My friend, Nappy. A female Napoleon. Not one of the ones you've bunged up here. She's been taken by someone else. And as odd as it may seem to have people on all sides clamouring for the chance to kidnap Napoleons, I give you the straight goods: she's been taken by some person or persons unknown, and suggests that you, Norm Stradamus, might be able to tell me who. Or whom, I suppose."

"What do you mean?" said Norm.

"Do try to keep up," I said. "I have a friend who suffers from Napoleon Syndrome and goes by the name of Nappy—"

"Lots of Napoleons are called Nappy," said Norm Stradamus.

"I suppose that's probably true," I said. "But this one is my friend, and her given name is Maria. Ramolino, if that's of any interest. She was once housed with self and others at the hospice. She passes her time with my friend Zeus, and was recently scooped up from her home by some person or persons unknown, leaving not a rack behind, as the expression is. Except that she did leave a rack, I suppose, if a note or clue left in one's wake counts as a rack. I'd have to look into it. William would know."

This didn't appear to have clarified matters. I tried to elaborate. But before I could roll up the sleeves and get down to it, the Regent silenced me with a glance — she was singularly gifted in this respect, and I imagined that she could silence a whole platoon with little more than a wiggle of her nose or a twitch of her hand.

"This female Napoleon is here," said the Regent. "She is housed with your friend, Vera."

"Abe's drawers!" I said. "Nappy is here?"

"She is," said Norm Stradamus.

"But her note to you suggested she'd been taken by someone else. And that you'd know who'd taken her."

"Ah, yes, the note. Vera showed it to us shortly after she woke up. It said, 'To Norm Strad. They've taken me.' That's the note to which you refer?"

"That's right," I said.

"I'm afraid you've been led astray by Napoleonic grammar," said Norm, chuckling lightly.

This floated over the Feynman head. It didn't seem to mean anything. I asked for amplification.

"They're always getting things backward," said Norm. "You must have noticed. It's the result of some sort of cognitive impairment, we suspect. A common symptom of the Napoleon Syndrome. Instead of saying 'I have to do the laundry' they're apt to say 'the laundry I must do.' Instead of saying 'you require no more training,' they say 'no more training do you require.' That sort of thing. No doubt she overheard our agents say they were planning to bring her to me, and, not realizing they were taking this action for her own good, she left a note, addressed to no one in particular, intending to convey 'they're taking me'

217

to Norm Stradamus.' To Norm Strad., they're taking me. I can understand your confusion. An understandable error."

I nodded the pumpkin, for there was sense in what the bearded chap had said. And the fact that Nappy had, in fact, hitched up at the joint lent credence to his claims. None of this did me any good, though, for this discovery had sucked some of the helium from my balloon. Nappy was with the rest of the Napoleons here, in the Regent's HQ. And unless the Regent's agents had also been kidnapping Zeuses, my hope that Nappy would be a bread crumb on the trail of my missing pal went up in smoke, as the fellow wrote.

Oan seemed to notice the dark clouds forming over the Feynman head, perceiving that my general aspect was now somewhere down among the wines and spirits. She tried to give consolation.

"Don't worry, darling," she began. And you'll realize just how depressed I was when you learn that I didn't bother to cringe at being called "darling" in mixed company.

"It'll be all right," she continued. "You'll go to Vera and help her work out the meaning of her prophecy. If Norm is right, Vera's prophecy could hold the key to solving all of our problems."

I wouldn't have thought it possible, but this managed to take even more wind out of the Feynman sails. I mean to say, it's fair to assume no one's day was ever improved by poetry, and it seemed to me that nothing was to be gained by plumbing the depths of Vera's verses. I've never really gone in for aesthetics, and dishing out poetic interpretations was the last thing I wanted to do at the moment of going to press, unless the poem in question started with "There once was a chap named Zeus," and went on to lay out a series of rhyming clues about his whereabouts. Or maybe a few rhyming couplets with instructions on how to get out of a pair of accidental engagements.

But deciphering a ditty about two chairs was not on my list of ways to lift the Feynman spirits. I saw no profit in parsing a prophet's poems.

I couldn't say any of this with the present gang of onlookers, of course. Norm was a fan of prophecy, and Oan was just the sort of weird gosh-help-us who'd spend her spare time curled up with a poem. So I bore up, kept the upper lip stiff, and agreed to do my best to pitch in.

"Right ho," I said. "I'll do my best. Just point me in Vera's direction."

And at the risk of dishing out spoilers and ruining all of the suspense we've built thus far, I have to say that it was through this supreme act of self-sacrifice — signing on to analyze poems muttered by an unconscious, psychic fiancée — that I put myself on the path that led me straight toward happy endings. There's a lesson to be learned from this, I'm sure, though I'll be dashed if I have a notion of what it is.

Chapter 20

The useful thing about psychics is that they're handy when making plans. I mean to say, just think of the extra room you'd have in your luggage if you had a medium or soothsayer standing by your side to help you pack. He or she could peep into the future and not only predict the weather, but also the number of times you'd spill coffee on your trousers or be called upon to dine in formal dress.

My present reason for musing on the utility of psychics has nothing to do with travel plans — at least, not with any travel beyond the rather trivial journey from the Regent's splendid parlour to Vera's quarters. Instead, my current appreciation for prophets and their prescience has to do with drinks. For Norm Stradamus, foreseeing that anyone who proposes to spend an afternoon deciphering poems would need a bracer or two, very kindly prepared another round of deeper-than-average martinis. This useful round of drinks was doled out to only two imbibers — self and Norm — for Oan indicated something about making wedding plans and shipped off toward her quarters, and the Regent moved off to parts unknown, Memphis stalking in her wake. Norm and I made up for their absence by having a third round of drinks on their behalf.

"Are you feeling braced?" asked Norm.

"I do feel braced!"

"Well then, cheers to feeling braced!" he said, taking up the shaker and producing another round. This one we consumed by toasting the Regent's health, and then Oan's health, by which point we required an additional round in order to toast the health of any we might have missed. It was at this juncture that the two of us, feeling fairly well lubricated, sang a couple of sea shanties before having one for the road, as it were — though not actually for the road, as we Rhinnicks don't approve of anti-social conduct, especially when we've just arisen from a lengthy coma occasioned by a car accident.

Now where was I?

Ah, yes. The sea shanties, the final round, the last toast to one and all, the departure.

The result of all of this whistle-wetting and merrymaking was that, far from being the downcast, drooping, dispirited Rhinnick I had been when first cajoled into trying my hand at interpreting Vera's poems, I'd become a fizzy rejoicer and a friend to all mankind by the time we slipped our moorings and curvetted our way, arm in arm, through an assortment of hall-ways, foyers, and staircases en route to Nappy and Vera.

Norm gingerly piloted me through a security checkpoint — this one involving a stout steel door guarded by a pair of gorilla-sized sentries — when I perceived that the hairs on the back of the Feynman neck were standing on end, as though trying to draw my attention to something I'd missed. And as I was likely to miss quite a lot in my current state — being filled with a gallon's worth of cocktails and notably effervescent — I took a moment to steady myself, take in my surroundings, and subject them to a more penetrating scrutiny. Surveying my environs, I noted the door, the hallway, the prophet, myself, and a pair of guards . . . all seemed to be in order. I ran through it again. Door, hallway, prophet, self . . . and then it hit me.

The guards.

Or rather, one of the guards. They were, as I think I mentioned, gorilla-sized. And the larger of the two — him being drawn from the extra-large economy-sized lot of gorilla-sized sentries — towered to such a height I hadn't caught his face on my first pass.

I noticed it now. It was familiar. Indeed, it was as familiar as my own, and in the present circs it was even more welcome.

"Zeus!" I cried.

Both guards pivoted toward me.

"Zeus!" I cried again.

Both of the guards looked at me as though I'd been having a couple. Which I had, of course, but not on such a scale that I'd been rendered pie-eyed, as the expression is, or unable to identify a pal — particularly a pal for whom I'd been searching for several weeks. I stepped toward him.

"Stop right there!" said Zeus, raising a hubcap-sized hand in a gesture I believe is taught during the first semester in copper academies. His fellow guardsman tucked in beside him, forming a wall of about 700 pounds of sentry.

"But Zeus—" I began.

"Do you know this man?" said Norm, teetering slightly and showing every sign of being as filled to the gills as I.

"As well as I know myself!" I said. It may have sounded more like "aswellazinomyself," and been punctuated by a hiccup or two, but self-respect restrains me from recounting all of my dialogue in the somewhat sozzled dialect which I had, for one reason and another, adopted at this point in my affairs. I proceeded more or less as follows:

"The colossus standing before us is none other than Zeus, my loyal sidekick, pal, and gendarme! We've been friends for years and years! We've shared too many adventures to count. Why, until we were recently separated by misadventure I never set foot outside without him. He's—"

"I've never seen this man before," said Zeus, aiming a fishy eye in my direction and taking a pace toward me.

222

"This is the wossname!" said Norm, slapping me firmly on the shoulder and grinning maniacally. Seeing that this failed to impress, he took another run at the thing.

"The Hand, I mean. Of th'other fellow. Intershesher!" he added, with a note of triumph. "He's . . . he's . . . s'an honoured guest of the Regent." And he, too, finished his oration with a something that sounded like a hiccup.

"It's me, Zeus," I said.

"I thought you said I was Zeus," said Zeus.

"That's what I said!"

"Then who are you?" said Zeus.

"The Hand!" said Norm.

"Rhinnick . . . J . . . Feynman," I said, enunciating as clearly as my current state permitted. And fearing that the name might fail to penetrate, I added the words "I'm your closest pal."

The second guard — Zeus's apparent partner who had, up until this point in the conv., acted as a silent partner, now sidled up to Zeus and eyed me searchingly.

"You know this guy, Terrence?"

"This guy *Rhinnick*!" I said, by way of correction.

"No, Terrence!" said guard number two.

"Who in Abe'sh name ish Terrensh?" said Norm Stradamus.

"My name's Terrence," said Zeus.

"You mean Zeus," I said.

"No I don't mean Zeus," said Zeus, or possibly Terrence, for it was getting harder than average to keep names straight, particularly in my current gin martini–addled state. But whatever you wish to call the familiar side of beef before me, he went on to say, "My name is Terrence, and I've never laid eyes on you before."

This smote me like a blow. I mean to say, when you've nursed a fellow in your personal bosom for years and years, when you're vis-à-vis with a chap with whom you've frequently shared your

223

last bar of milk chocolate, a pal with whom you've plucked the gowans fine, as the expression is, you don't expect him to disclaim all knowledge of you, deny your past association, and look upon you as one who, whatever his merits, is no more familiar than one of those ships that are always passing in the night.

I steadied myself on my pins, drew myself up to my full height, and tried my best to project authority.

"You mean to tell me," I began, "that your name is not now, and has never been, Zeus?"

"That's right," said Zeus.

"And you don't know who I am?"

"You're the Hand of the Intercessor," said Zeus.

"But apart from that," I added, grabbing hold of the nearby wall, as the hall in which we stood seemed to be pirouetting more than I should have liked.

"Does the name Rhinnick Feynman mean *nothing* to you?" I added.

"Sorry, no."

"Perhapsh . . . hic . . . he'sh a bit confushed," said Norm Stradamus, indicating me, not Zeus. Then he stared at me intently through one eye, closing the other as though blocking out an extra Feynman or two who had polluted the field of view.

"You've been through one of thosh things," he said. "Whashicalled. An ordeal. The car acshident. That coma. A few martineesh—"

And he went on in this vein for the space of a minute or two, elaborating upon the theme of diminished capacity, when another couple of thoughts found their way into my bean. The first was this: Zeus had, when last we met, been shot full of Socratic bullets, bullets which contained the very same memory-wiping serum that had been used to great effect on Vera Lantz. And since Zeus lacked Vera's television-based capacity for peering into distant times and places, he wouldn't be able to reboot his memory, as it were, by catching reruns of his past life and associations. The second thought was even less agreeable: it was possible that the Author, in what has been passing lately for His wisdom, had decided to wipe out all past chapters in which the Zeus & Feynman alliance had played a part. It was, I thought, not beyond the Author's scope to delete the character Zeus and reintroduce him — reusing an old and previously discarded physical description — as a giant guard named Terrence. And whichever of these possibilities was the case, poor old Zeus would be in the dark, having no memories upon which to draw.

I saw that this would call for careful navigation.

Norm was still going on about the brain-fogging effects of gin martinis — a topic on which he seemed to be well informed — when I resurfaced.

"Tell me, Zeus—" I began.

"You mean Terrensh, Hand of the Intersheshor!" said Norm Stradamus.

I was about to explain that it was "Rhinnick, Hand of the Intercessor," and "Terrence, Guard of the Door," when I thought nothing could be improved by this correction. I chose instead to shush the High Priest with a gesture.

"Tell me, Terrence, then," I said, and I may have poked him on his shoulder, "precisely how long do you remember being Terrence? About six months? Everything before that's a bit of a fog?"

"How did you know?" said Zeus.

"The Hand of the Intershesher is wise," slurred Norm Stradamus.

"Seems like a crackpot to me," said guard number two, who, despite being nameless, didn't seem to know his place. I ignored his intervention and pressed on.

"And how . . . how did you come to work for the Regent, Terrence?" I asked. And as I did, I was fully prepared to slap anyone who responded with anything along the lines of "the Regent isn't called Terrence."

"She found me," said Zeus. "I was in an accident, she said. The Regent took me in and had her staff nurse me back to health. She's very kind, the Regent. Very kind. When I was healthy again she offered me a job in her personal guard."

"But before this accident," I said, "what did you do before that?"

"I don't remember. The Regent thinks I may have been newly manifested shortly before she found me. But I was wearing bloody clothes. I'd been shot. I didn't remember any of it."

"Aha!" I said, out-Perrying even the cleverest Mason, "That's because you'd been . . . whatdoyoucallit . . . mindwiped by Socratic rounds! Bullets, I mean. Amnesia. Bloody clothes. Practically all the proof you need."

And once again I felt the need to lean on a door frame, though there again it might have been Zeus. This accomplished, I continued.

"They all support my thesis. You are my good friend Zeus, one who was gunned down by Socrates and the victim of a mindwipe," I added, connecting the dots.

This didn't seem to land with the level of oomph I'd expected. Rather than issuing the communal "ooh" or "ahh" for which I'd budgeted, the persons assembled merely looked at me askance, as if to ask if they could have a shot or two of whatever I'd been having.

"Look, mister," said Zeus, laying a catcher's-mitt-sized hand upon my shoulder, "you're drunk. And I think you might be confused. All I know is what the Regent tells me. I was newly manifested, someone shot me, the Regent found me, and that's that. I'm happy here. The people are nice. And I love guarding."

This much, at least, lent credence to my version of events. I mean to say, the chap had been a dog in a former life — some form of Yorkshire Terrier if that's of any interest — and the only things he'd loved more than standing attention at a guard post were chasing postal workers and spinning around three times before curling up for a nap. His basic wiring seemed to be intact, much like Vera's had been post-wipe. The software may have been wiped, but the hardware was still there and still firing on all thrusters. Even his basic preferences still held. I took another stab at rebooting the system, this time using what had, in recent chapters, become a reliable secret weapon.

I reached into a pocket and drew out Fenny, presenting him for inspection.

"My hamster," I said. "Fenny."

It was at this point in my affairs that the Author, in His wisdom, decided to inflict me with about the worse fit of hic-cups ever recorded. I hic'd a couple of dozen times in Zeus's direction after announcing the hamster's name, the effect of which, I gathered from Zeus's reaction, was to undermine the overall rhetorical power and persuasiveness of the tableau unfolding before him.

"He seems very nice," said Zeus, patting Fenny and chuck-ling. "But maybe it's time for the two of you—"

"The three of us," I said, not wanting Fenny to feel left out.

"Maybe it's time for the *three* of you to run along and get some rest," he concluded. And he punctuated this by looking over at his fellow guardsman and winking a conspiratorial wink I found offensive.

He returned his massive hand to my shoulder as if to pivot me bedward — but as he did, he paused in a marked manner and stood absolutely still, as if struck by one of those thunder-bolts you hear about. I knew in a jiffy what had been the cause of this sudden break in the action, for unless I was much mis-taken I saw Zeus, as he grabbed me, draw in an extra lungful of breath, via the nostrils.

I could see where this was headed. Opinions differ in the matter of Yorkshire Terriers, but whatever one feels about them, one must acknowledge that they always have an excellent sense of smell. And it seemed to me that these olfactory gifts must persevere through the reincarnation process.

I stood straighter. I opened my eyes wider. I willed every pore on the Feynman person to open to full capacity, hoping to push matters along by bathing Zeus in my bouquet. Pheromones, I think they're called, teensy smellicules which are said to be equally useful in pitching woo or when being tracked by hounds.

Zeus drew another breath, this one deeper than the last. We were, I could see, mere steps from merry reunions. I did the only thing I could. I took steps which I knew, with every fibre of my being, would seal the deal and bring about the happy ending.

Chapter 21

I don't know if you've ever noticed the same thing, but it's often struck me as odd that you can be dashed sure of a thing, knowing with every fibre of your being that you see the path to victory, only to find that you've made an absolute bloomer and bunged a spanner into the works, fouling up your aspirations and landing yourself in the ditch.

It was that way with this recent plan of mine. I mean to say, perceiving that Zeus's memories were in the process of being sparked by my aroma — memory being deeply inter-twined with scent, and scent being the fastest route to the brain of any dog, former or otherwise — I tried to coax mat-ters along by encouraging Zeus's olfactory explorations with both word and gesture. This was where I made my bloomer. For, as Norm would put it several minutes later, when we were out of Zeus's earshot and en route to Vera's room, you can't go about in a high-security place, smelling of gin mar-tinis, accusing people of being mindwiped dogs, and — this part was key — openly inviting the guards to sniff you. This last step in the procedure, one which I'd pursued enthusias-tically, is apt, as I had found, to cause offence. Only a few well-chosen words by Norm Stradamus — a figure of some influence with the Regent's household guard — enabled me to escape a situation which seemed on the verge of causing a good deal of embarrassment on both sides, and possibly a black eye for Feynman.

"But I tell you he is Zeus!" I said, pressing the case with Norm Stradamus as he chivvied me down the hall and out of the Zeus-slash-Terrence zone. "I know his face as well as I know my own." And I think, owing perhaps to the gallon of gin I'd had a short while earlier, I may have added the words "weller, even."

"S'all right," said Norm, who suddenly struck me as even slurrier than he'd been a moment before. "S'okay. You can call him Zeus if you like. Terrence won't mind at . . . he won't mind at . . . why did you tell him he was a dog?"

"Because he *is* a dog," I explained. "Or rather, he was."

"So . . . issa temp'rary whassit," said Norm.

"In the beforelife," I explained. "The titanic chap you saw guarding the doors is but this fellow's latest form. He's a princk. Like me. Like the Napoleons. And like the Napoleons he's been recycled through the beforelife several times, most recently as a Yorkshire Terrier."

"What's Yorkshire?"

"Some kind of pudding."

This failed to clarify matters.

"Look at it from wossname's perspective. Terrensh. Imagine what he thinksh."

"Call him Zeus."

"Imagine what Zeus thinks, then, Hand of the Intershessher —"

"And call me Rhinnick!"

"Forgive me, Hand o' — forgive me, Rhinnick. I use the title to show, eh, reshpect."

"You don't see me running around calling you 'Pal of Regent,' or 'Spiritual Advisor of Oan,' or 'Chap who won't believe Terrence is Zeus' — wait, that last one doesn't quite fit the pattern. But what I mean to say is that I prefer not to be known as the somethingorother of someone else. I'm my own man, dash it."

"We'll see what Oan has to shay about that after the wed-din'," he replied, grinning horribly and gargling at me, or possibly chuckling.

I shushed him with an impassioned gesture. My heated blood, I perceived, had sobered me up. At least that's how I choose to remember things. The Author may correct me in His revisions.

"Be that as it may," I said, "rest assured that I'm as certain of this as I've ever been certain of anything. The faithful guardian of recent interest is my pal Zeus, former resident of Detroit Mercy and longtime sidekick of yours truly. I've been looking for him for months. I'm not mistaken, and my powers of rec-ognition haven't been addled by martinis, however dry and expertly made. I seem to be having a good deal more success in keeping an even keel than you," I added, noting that the High Priest seemed to be something of a lightweight, "and could recite any number of tongue twisters, walk a mile's worth of straight lines, and recognize missing pals without fail."

Whether or not my speech had impressed him I couldn't say, for he temporarily shelved the topic, suggesting that we moot the issue in greater detail at some future moment. I would have pressed the matter — Zeus's current status and locale being the most important items currently on the Feynman agenda, even above wriggling out of a pair of engagements — but for the reason Norm gave for dropping the matter at this time, viz, we'd arrived at Vera's temporary quarters: the quarters she shared, if you'll recall, with our friend Nappy. Thus it was that, with a feeling that it's best to confront the problem in front of you, I let the Zeus issue rest on the back burner while I attended to forces marshalling on the Vera front. Besides, Zeus appeared to be safe and happy for the nonce, and now that I knew where he was, the chances of hitting upon a formula for ensuring a happy ending seemed high.

We knocked. Vera issued a friendly yodel. Norm bunged me in and toddled off, muttering somethingorother about perfecting his bartending technique and finding someone else with whom he might share an ounce or two of the right stuff.

The room in which I now found myself was well populated with Rhinnicks and Veras, but appeared to be short one Nappy. She, according to Vera, had been whisked away for an interview with some of the Regent's staff. Once these preliminary matters had been dealt with, Vera and self settled into our tête-à-tête.

"You've looked better," said Vera, in that diplomatic way of hers, and I foresaw — even without the assistance of television — this sort of helpful observation might feature prominently in our matrimonial life. But to be fair, for one always likes to look on both sides of an issue, it was true that I had, in fact, looked better. Mine is a face that tends to puff and redden when loaded up with a brace of cocktails.

"Not looking my best, what?" I said.

"No. But then you've just woken up from a coma. I suppose we can forgive you for looking like someone who's been dragged backward through a hedge." Here she sniffed for a moment, Zeus-like, and muttered something about gin.

She instituted something of a stage wait and rifled through a drawer in her bedside table.

"Take one of these," she said, handing over a smallish bottle of pills.

"What are they?" I asked, it being my standard policy to institute inquiries prior to swallowing anything of a pharmaceutical nature.

"Detipsers," she said. "Instant sobriety pills. I'm surprised you haven't heard of them. They're another of Professor Newton's inventions."

I ran an unsteady eyeball over the label. As this soothsaying pipsqueak had predicted, it did claim to contain sobriety pills.

I deftly dealt with the childproof cap and downed a handful, just to be safe.

"Clever blighter, Isaac Newton," I said in heartfelt tones, wishing as always to give credit where it was due. I could feel the effects instanter. I would have praised the inventor further had I not been itching to unleash my latest helping of hot news.

"Brace yourself, my half-baked prophetess," I said, leading up to the thing, "for here is the latest news and this is Rhinnick Feynman reading it: Zeus is here!"

I had expected this to land like a bomb alighting on a munitions dump, but it didn't. Vera's eyes didn't widen by even the merest micron. Instead she looked at me levelly and said she knew.

"What do you mean you know?"

"I mean I know! He's been here for months. Nappy told me. She hasn't been able to talk to him, but has seen him through the bars."

"What bars?" I asked. We were closeted in a room with a well-carved wooden door, but there were no bars to be seen, unless one counted the bar of soap poised on a nearby wash-stand, but context rather ruled that out.

"When she first arrived," said Vera. "They put her into some kind of jail with the other Napoleons."

"Abe's drawers!" I said.

"After I woke up I asked about you right away. They keep calling you the Hand of the Intercessor, and they said they wanted to do whatever they could to help you. So I told them we were looking for Nappy, and that you'd been hot on her trail when the police cruiser hit us. I described her, and it didn't take them more than a few hours to find her and bring her to stay with me. Anyway, that's when she told me she'd seen Zeus when she was kept behind bars with a bunch of other Napoleons. She saw him loads of times, and kept calling out to him, but he didn't answer."

"The poor blighter has lost his memory," I said. "But look on the bright side: we've found him. And it's not as though this Socratic memory loss is always permanent. Look at what's happened to you!"

Here she raised a skeptical brow. She didn't seem to string along with my optimistic appraisal of the sitch.

"Rhinnick," she said, leaning in and clasping my hands in hers, "you know why I've gotten some of my memories back, right? You know it's because of my television. I get visions. Sometimes they're from my past. I don't actually remember those memories, if you see what I mean, but I see them again, as though it's the first time. Unless Zeus has television, I don't know if there's any hope of him getting his memory back."

"There's always hope," I said. "Take this Regent, for example. She's an ancient. She has powers — not at the same end of the omnipotence curve as Penelope, Abe, or the City Solicitor, I'm told, but impressive nonetheless. Maybe she can snap her fingers and magically sort things out for Zeus."

"I thought you told me that even Abe couldn't fix Zeus's memories," she said.

"It's true," I said. "But there again, Abe thought Isaac was the most dangerous man in the world, all owing to some misunderstanding about a bit of scientific fiddling with quarks, gluons, bosons, and other teensy thingummies which don't matter a single damn."

"What's your point?"

"Abe isn't infallible!" I said. "Powerful, yes. Clever, sure. Awash in civic pride and responsibility. But not infallible. Just because he can't find a way to restore Zeus's marbles doesn't mean it can't be done. Haven't you seen anything from your television hinting at Zeus's future condition?"

"I've seen him with you," she said, a cautious sort of

rumminess in her voice, "but that doesn't mean he gets his memories back. I can't tell if that's going to happen."

"Then we'll just have to hope for the best," I said.

"I'll let you know if I have any helpful visions," she said, patting the Feynman hands in a "bear up, little fella" kind of way. It was at this point in our affairs that the door opened, revealing Nappy being bunged in by guard — this one a female guard, rather than a Zeus or a Terrence. Nappy looked to be exhausted.

"Nappy!" I said, once the guard had closed the door and left us alone.

"Monsieur Feynman!" she said, slumping into a chair. She had the aspect of a person who, though glad to enter the Feynman orbit, had just run a marathon or two and lacked the strength for a hug, handshake, or high-five.

"I am so 'appy to see you," she said.

"Your accent's gotten stronger," I replied.

"Eet 'as. Zis always 'appens when I'm around ozzer Napoleons."

"What's wrong?" said Vera, moving over to where Nappy rested, and then kneeling at her side. "You look exhausted."

"Zey 'elped zemselves to blood and spinal fluid," she said.

This seemed to awaken the mother-bear element in Vera's personality, for she responded by shouting, "They've no bloody right to be—" when Nappy waved her off.

"Non, non, eet's okay," she said, taking in a couple of extra lungfuls of strengthening air. "Zey say it will 'elp with zere research, and zis research will 'elp everyone."

"How so?" I asked, leaning in.

"Zey believe zat we Napoleons 'ave a connection to ze beforelife. Zat zey can, 'ow you say, replicate zis connection. Use eet to pass between worlds. Maybe even 'elp us remember our mortal lives," she added, drifting off and seeming to slip into something of a reverie.

"You think this will help Zeus," said Vera, "don't you? That's why you're letting them take your blood."

"Zere is no 'letting zem' about it," said Nappy. "Zey take what zey take. But oui, I do 'ope zat zere research might 'elp Zeus."

"But surely they can push the research along without your aid," I said. "I mean to say, they have dozens of Napoleons, from what I've heard."

"Hundreds," said Nappy.

"Egad," I said. "Well, then they have hundreds of Napoleons. Let them take *their* blood and spinal juices."

"I 'ave to 'elp," said Nappy, suddenly looking a good deal stronger, but tearing up at the same time. "I 'ave to 'elp in any way zat I can. You deed not see Zeus after 'e was shot. You deed not see 'im as 'e lost 'is memory. 'E cried out for me. And for you. And zen eet all just slipped away. I tried to 'elp 'im. I tried to—"

Here she broke off, as Vera pulled her into a hug, muttering something about how we understood what she was doing and would do our best to push along her efforts. I, for one, couldn't see any percentage in what she was doing to 'elp Zeus, as she would put it, for the innate loopiness of the Regent's plan to exploit — do I mean exploit? — the Napoleonic connection to the beforelife seemed to dwarf even Oan's goofy practice of invoking the Laws of Attraction and merely hoping the universe will fork over whatever you need. I didn't say any of this to Nappy or Vera, of course, for I didn't wish to depress the young prunes. So I held my tongue apart from a spot of "there-thereing" alongside Vera, and promising to do whatever I could to help her out. It was perhaps a quarter of an hour before we returned to anything that resembled a productive discussion. And when we did, our discussion turned to the matter of questions that the Regent's staff had been asking their Napoleonic guests.

"Zey want to know what we remember of ze beforelife, of course," said Nappy. "But eet's more zan zat. Zey want to know 'ow we remember — what do zey call eet — 'ow we remember our return passage, ze moments when we leave Detroit before being reborn."

"I hadn't thought of that," I said, because I hadn't. "It hadn't occurred to me before that, if Napoleons do 'reincarnate,' as I've heard it called, if they do take multiple trips back and forth between the beforelife and Detroit, there must come a time when they disappear from here and reassemble in the beforelife."

"I suppose so," said Nappy.

"What do you mean you suppose so," said Vera. "You mean you don't remember?"

"I don't," said Nappy. "I remember my current life en Detroit. I remember bits and piecez of ozzer lives in ze beforelife. Or possibly just one ozzer life. Eet's so difficult to tell."

"Not for Jack," I said. "He remembers loads of lives."

"Oo eez Jack?" said Nappy.

"You knew him as Napoleon Number Three," I said.

This drew a startled yip from the young bird, and she might have leapt a foot or two had she not been sitting down.

"*Zut alors!*" she said. "Napoleon Number Zree eez getting ze worst of ze Regent's treatment. Eet's practically torture. Zey question 'im every day. Zey take his blood. I 'eard 'im scream-ing ze ozzer night — somesing or ozzer about 'ating women, and somesing about someone named Alice. But why do you call 'im Jack?"

"It's some name he picked up in a prior incarnation, if that's the word I want. He's had others, too. Judas was one, if memory serves. But in any event, this Jack, or this Judas, or this Napoleon Number Three, seems to recall more than the usual number of past lives — I've lost count of just how many — and most of these past incarnations appear to have been dashed unpleasant. Not a very nice man, it seems."

"Number Zree always was a bit of une tête de merde," said Nappy.

"No doubt," I said.

"That must be why they're questioning him so forcefully," said Vera. "If he remembers lots of lives — if he can remember them clearly and is certain that he's passed back and forth between the beforelife and Detroit several times — maybe they see him as being even more connected to the beforelife than the others."

"Perhaps being a fiend in human shape strengthens one's ability to pass from one world to the other," I mused. "Though why they'd want to replicate any journey between worlds that results in coming back as a rotten egg is beyond me."

"Perhaps your nature eez . . . *distilled* each time you cross," suggested Nappy. "You become more . . . I don't know . . . more 'yourself' each time you return. So every time Jack passez from one life to ze next—"

"His essential Jackness is intensified!" I said. "That could be the case. Zeus gets Zeusier, Jack gets Jackier — every reincarnating bimbo is repeatedly reduced down to his or her essential self, and the flavour becomes bolder."

"We're not talking about sauces," said Vera. "We're talking about people. I don't think it works that way."

"But it might!" said Nappy, and I remember thinking that she might have a point.

I don't know if you've had the same experience, but I've often found that, when I'm caught up in a discussion of a topic fraught with interest, the minutes whip along like a greyhound chasing a rabbit, and every time you look at the clock you're surprised to see that another hour or two has passed. That's how it was with this discussion. We carried on mooting the ins and outs of reincarnation, and then interrogating Nappy about her prior interrogation, until the hour drew late and we were surprised by the advent of William — who floated in and announced the time had come for me to dress for a late-night dinner with Mine Host. Nappy and Vera weren't, it seemed, slated to join the Regent's party, they being earmarked for something simple served in their own private quarters. I, by sharp contradistinction, was on the Regent's list of honoured VIPs, and therefore required to dine with the folks up top.

"But dash it," I said, at last remembering why I'd been brought to Vera's quarters, "I'd almost forgotten. I'm here about your poem."

"My poem?" said Vera.

"Your poem," I said. "The one about the chairs and two chaps who sat in them."

"You mean my prophecy!" said Vera.

"That's right. What does it mean?"

"I'm afraid there isn't time, sir," said William.

"Of course there's time," I riposted, warmly. "All kinds of it. That explains all of the clocks and watches."

"I mean there isn't time for you to discuss this prophecy at present, sir. The time has come for dinner. The Regent insists that you attend."

It was with a feeling that a guest shouldn't disappoint his hosts that I shrugged the shoulders and decided to shelve further discussion of Vera's poem, placing it on the back burner and pen-cilling it in to be mooted at some future, as-yet-undetermined date. I therefore said my cordial farewells, featuring hugs and shaken hands, and followed William back to my room, having not the slightest notion of what awaited.

Chapter 22

One thing that life has shown me, as it may have shown you as well, is that tastes often differ. Take me, for instance. Despite my well-known tendency to sparkle and shed light upon those around me, recent evidence has suggested I'm not everyone's cup of tea. Matron Bikerack, for example — when she remembers me at all — is more inclined to unleash an acid crack, issue a thumbs down, or swipe left, if swiping left means what I think it does, than to offer a rave review when the topic of Feynman R is raised. Peericks, too — before the Author washed all evidence of me from that medical fathead's bean — couldn't be listed on the roster of Rhinnick Boosters or Feynman Fans. To be weighed against these naysayers are the countless other, better-informed, and wiser beazels who count the day lost when it's not spent revelling in my society, a viewpoint best demonstrated by the increasingly popular fad of signing up to be my spouse.

But the point I'm trying to make, I think, is this: when it comes to Rhinnick Feynman, opinions vary. But somehow all of this seems to change when Rhinnick finds himself at a formal evening meal. You might regard Feynman with indifference or contempt at other times, but throw on the soft lights, push him into Correct Evening Costume, and shove a dinner in front of him, and you'd be surprised.

The set-up for this particular dining binge seemed precisely calibrated to allow Feynman to shine. When William took me to my room, preparatory to setting sail for dinner, I found the finest suit of clothes into which it has ever been my pleasure to climb — all tailor-made to fit the Feynman frame. The Regent appeared to be a traditionalist in the matter of evening wear, having instructed her quartermaster to come across with a full-blown formal get-up including tails and a white tie. Catching a glimpse of myself in a full-length mirror, I was able to offer the wholly objective and unbiased view that I had never looked better than I looked in this upholstery. And however deeply one's brow is furrowed out of concern for amnesiac Zeuses, captive Napoleons, and a higher-than-usual number of accidental engagements, one can't help but feel a certain lightness of spirit after donning gay apparel of this calibre.

Thus it was that I was in merry mood when I, ushered by William, blew into the Regent's formal dining room, completing a party of four comprising self, Oan, Norm Stradamus, and the Regent herself — or a party of five, if you count Memphis, the Regent's dog, who sat at attention beside his mistress, staring down his nose at me as if to suggest that he was keeping an eye skinned in my direction and that any funny business would result in bites, abrasions, and contusions. My own four-pawed sidekick, the hamster Fenny, had opted out of this particular binge, he having intimated that he'd prefer to stay in my room and fiddle with scraps of shredded paper.

The room in which our party dined was about as opulent a joint as you could imagine. The dining table, for starters, was laid out with a feast the likes of which I'd never had the pleasure of inhaling, and featured all manner of dishes calculated to throw even the most indifferent tastebud into ecstatic fits. The room's walls were covered in silk, and tastefully decked out with about a gallery's worth of painted portraits, landscapes, and abstract whatdoyoucallits. The perimeter was dotted with pedestals, stands, and tables of various heights displaying sculptures, busts, urns, shields, and other *objets d'art* which would have produced a pang of envy in any curator who knew his stuff. Much of the artwork seemed to reflect a singular theme or style — a style which I hadn't hitherto come across. Oasis Chic about sums it up. The lion's share of the pieces featured not-so-subtle hints of some far-flung desert kingdom. There were landscapes showing sand dunes, desert flowers, and oases, and several depictions of some sandal-wearing, authoritative beazel smiting sand-encrusted underlings with a rod. A number of the sculptures on display were hewn from heavily pitted reddish stone, others from a shiny black material, and still others seemed to be made of pure gold. Some of the more bewildering works depicted weird chaps who looked all right from the shoulders down, but whose upper slopes had been replaced by the heads of birds or dogs — a peculiar arrangement, and one which seemed unlikely to withstand scrutiny by any licensed biologist or physician. The whole collection had a certain somethingorother about it . . . what's the word? What do you call it when there's a stately sort of ancient grandeur which is dashed impressive and imposing and makes you feel like a smaller than average ant staring up at a mountain? *Dynastic.* That's the bunny! There was something *dynastic* about the Regent's art collection, and it conveyed a flavour of magnificence, resplendence, and unapologetic majesty of which I heartily approved.

One particular piece of artistic flotsam caught my eye as I passed a plate of potatoes to my left. It was the centrepiece on the table. In any normal house this would be a bowl of flowers, a line of candles, or something of that order, but here, *chez* Regent, the table's centre was home to a squat pyramidical thingummy carved out of some material I couldn't quite place. To say the thing appealed to my own artistic sensibilities would be to deceive my public — indeed, it's fairer to say I would have flung the thing from me if I'd found it in my home. But feeling that nothing could be harmed by a bit of kissing up to the host, I opened the conversation by complimenting the eyesore.

"Attractive little bijou," I said, nodding toward it. "Is it granite?"

"Onyx," said the Regent, a tad more peevishly than I'd have liked.

Memphis growled as if he didn't think much of my conversation.

"Oh, ah," I said, adding a spot of *Pheasant à la Regent* to the plate before me.

"It's the prize of the Regent's collection," said Norm Stradamus, presently coping with the potatoes.

"I'm not surprised," I said. "It looks valuable."

"It's priceless," said the Regent, who seemed to be on a diet, judging by the lonely spear of asparagus taking office as the sole occupant of the Regent's plate.

"The Regent uses the pyramid as focus for her powers," said Oan. "It amplifies her connection to the universe, allowing her to use the Laws of Attraction to great effect. It's truly remarkable. I've seen her perform wonders you'd be hard pressed to believe!"

This seemed to draw a sniff of approval from the Regent, which surprised me. The last time Oan had taken a stab at barking about the Regent's powers, she'd drawn a glower of disapproval and a command to hold her tongue. But this time 'round, the Regent sniffed and nodded Oanward in a way that seemed to say, "Well done, thou good and faithful servant."

This sparked the Feynman imagination. This was, as noted above, the second time the topic of the Regent's powers had been ventilated in my presence. She was an ancient, she had powers, and she could use what Oan called the "Laws of Attraction." I'd seen these laws at work before, they having been in full effect during the previously mentioned cavern sequence. On that occasion, the forces of darkness in the form of the City

Solicitor had rolled up their sleeves and set about the task of doing a bit of no good to Penelope, Ian's wife, and had used those laws to such a degree that words like "ultra-powerful" and "omnipotent" came to mind. Both Penelope and the City Solicitor had *deus ex machina*'d all over the place and thrown their weight around like a couple of gods intent on starting up new religions. If the Regent had a modicum of this power — if modicum is the word I want — then I perceived she'd have no trouble snapping her fingers and sorting out any number of difficulties; say, by way of random example, restoring a pal's missing memories or putting the kibosh on a few unfortunate marital mix-ups. I earmarked the Regent's powers as something worthy of further study.

"Talking of the Laws of Attraction," I said, "a rather funny thing happened to yours truly this afternoon."

"Forgive me, Hand of the Intercessor," said the Regent, "but we must discuss the prophecy."

I sensed that the air of debonair gaiety was about to wane a trifle.

"Oh, that," I said. And if a touch of asperity entered my voice, who can blame me? Not only had I been cut off mid-story, but I'd also been called the "Hand of the Intercessor" again, a title which, as I think I've mentioned, was starting to wear thin.

"What did you learn from Vera?" said Norm, leaning forward.

"To be quite honest," I said, easing up to the thing, "I learned nothing at all. I'm afraid that, what with the rush of current events—"

"You learned nothing at all?" said the Regent, giving every evidence of thunderclouds forming behind her eyeballs — not that they hadn't been fairly thunderous to begin with. "Her poem may hold the key to reaching the beforelife. It may chart out the path before us. It holds the promise of—"

"Well, dash it," I said, "there's no use carping about it now.

244

As I was saying, what with the recent vicissitudes I've been undergoing — say, rising from a longish coma, downing a gaggle of martinis, and spotting Zeus at liberty on the grounds, there was so much pressing material to cover when I met Vera that we didn't have time to explore the ins and outs of a scrap of verse. We'll get 'round to it another time."

This seemed to annoy the Regent, but she *was* a host, and I was her guest, so she stifled her chagrin and pushed the conversation along.

"Who is this *Zeus* you mention?" said the Regent.

"That's what I was about to tell you," I said. "That 'funny thing' that happened to me this afternoon."

"Pray, tell us," said the Regent, thunderclouds receding.

"It involved one of your guards," I began, only to find myself being shushed by an under-the-table-kick from Norm Stradamus. This prophet seemed to have sobered up quite thoroughly in the hours since we had parted, possibly having swallowed one of Professor Newton's wonder pills. I think I preferred the blighter when he was still on the slightly sozzled side of the spectrum. For now, rather than cheering me on with drunken word and gesture, this sober chump sought to quash my conversation and gave the impression — through heavy, waggling eyebrows — that the item atop my agenda, viz, Zeus's true identity, was something best left under wraps. I ignored the old ass and carried on.

"It involved one of your guards," I repeated. "A chap named Terrence."

"I know this guard," said the Regent.

"You *think* you know this guard," I said, seizing upon the critical point, "but you don't. Not really. His name, for example, isn't Terrence. His name is Zeus."

Reactions around the table varied. The Regent repeated the name "Zeus" in an interrogative manner, trying the name out on her tongue. The dog Memphis tilted his head and said "Aroo," or something similar. Norm Stradamus said nothing, but merely pinched the bridge of his nose. Oan seemed to choke on her breath a bit and do another bit of swooning, but then chipped in with an "oh, good gracious," which she followed up with a helpful speech aimed at the Regent.

"Zeus is Rhinnick's best friend!" she said. "He told me about him in the hospice. He's been looking for him for months!"

"It's true!" I said.

"Oh, you must be so happy to have finally found him," said Oan. "I know how you longed to see him again. And here we see the Laws of Attraction at their best, manifesting the desires of those who focus their intentions. I'm so pleased for you, my darling. I'll have to write about this in *For Love Alone*."

I blanched at this goshawful reminder of Oan's stomach-churning turn at literary composition, while the Regent merely cocked a head at me and thrummed a finger or two on the table.

"Terrence came to me with no memory. As one who is newly manifested," she said.

"But with gunshot wounds!" I said, glad to be saved from further discussion of Oan's literary garbage. "You don't manifest with gunshot wounds! And while you might have filed this away as one of those insoluble mysteries, allow me to connect the dots and dish up the hidden solution. This Zeus, recently aka Terrence, has been mindwiped! His neurons have been scrambled, his little grey cells cleaned out, and his memories blotted from the copybook, leaving only a clean slate. This is why he popped into your life free of any notion of who he was, or any stories about the old guys and dolls back at the hospice. But Zeus wasn't a new arrival. Far from it! He was a longtime resident of Detroit with a whole host of prior experiences. He was my closest pal and man-at-arms for years and years, and one of the founding members of the Feynman entourage. Most recently he was at my side when I was involved in a brief entanglement with the City Solicitor, and Zeus found himself in the line of fire when Socrates let loose with some of his memory-wiping rounds!"

"Socrates!" said the Regent. Or perhaps "hissed" would be mot juster. The mention of this assassin's name always provoked a strong reaction, but it was usually one of skepticism or fear — most bimbos didn't believe in him at all, and those who did would happily run several miles in tight shoes to avoid meeting up with him. But there wasn't a hint of skepticism or fear on the Regent's map — not by a jugful. What she displayed was nothing short of unbridled contempt. She'd made the sort of look cats make when the subject of dogs is mentioned in mixed company, or the look a shark might make when confronted by another shark from a rival political party.

"Oh, you know him?" I said.

"We've had dealings," said the Regent. She didn't seem interested in supplying further details.

"Well, so have I, so has Zeus, and so has the prophetess Vera, come to think of it," I said. "And in each case we escaped by the skin of our teeth. Vera and Zeus got the worst of it, both bumping up against the Socratic Method and having their memories go phut."

"But Vera seems perfectly fine," said Norm Stradamus, chipping in. It seemed that, after watching mutely as the Regent and I discussed the Zeus and Socrates imbroglio, Norm had at long last concluded that the story wasn't merely the raving of a martini-soaked reveller.

"Vera is fine," I said, "but only because of television. Her prophetic powers have clothed her with the power to peer into both the future and the past, replacing bona fide memories with these visions. Zeus is another story."

"Oooohh," said Oan, still with the soppy melting note in

her voice, "I do hope you can help him. All of those years of friendship, all of those shared experiences, all of his past hopes and dreams—"

"Fear not, old Sharing Room Wrangler," I said, "for the solution lays before us. Or do I mean lies? In any case, the Regent can fix it. She can snatch up her pyramid thingummy if required, lay into those Laws of Attraction you're always babbling about, snap her fingers or do whatever it is she does to exert her powers, restoring Zeus's memories. No fuss, no bother. Probably won't even break a sweat."

Well, I hadn't expected the Regent to clap her hands and leap about, as these forms of expression wouldn't have jived with her M.O., as the expression is, but I thought she might have at least smiled at me or nodded approval. She didn't. She merely leaned back in her chair and steepled her fingers in front of her chin, like some arch-criminal about to board his hydrofoil en route to his secret base inside a volcano.

"That won't work," said the Regent.

"But dash it," I said.

"There is no argument. It won't work. My powers cannot restore what Socrates has destroyed."

"But why not? I can't say that I had a full view of the City Solicitor's battle with Penelope, but from what little I could hear, I got the impression that you ancient, powerful lightning hurlers can do anything you want."

"You fail to understand the nature of Detroit," said the Regent. And, in what I've always thought was something of an odd coincidence, the nature of Detroit appeared to respond.

The room began to shake like a freight train getting underway. Plates rattled, a terrine of soup upended itself, and our party of four gripped at the table like we were grasping at life preservers — life preservers, as mentioned earlier, being something you don't really need in Detroit, but you catch my drift. And just when I thought the rattling might subside, that's when nature really rolled up its sleeves, spat on its hands, and got down to business with a hearty goodwill.

The air rippled all around us, like the surface of a pond into which someoneorother has bunged a sizeable brick. The ripple passed through the dining room, distorting everything in its path. Even the Regent, Norm, and Oan seemed to warp, stretch, and contort as the wave passed through them, looking more like reflections in a receding funhouse mirror than honest-to-goodness chumps who'd dressed for dinner. My ears popped, my head throbbed, and all sound seemed to be sucked out of the world. I briefly felt as though I weighed about six hundred and fifty pounds.

And suddenly nothing.

The wave passed, the rumbling stopped, and Norm asked me to pass the mustard.

I stared at the man.

"But what in Abe's name was that?" I said.

"What was what?" said Norm.

Oan, too, seemed to wonder what I was driving at, for she cocked her head in a manner reminiscent of the dog Memphis. She then made a face which telegraphed a pathetic sort of sympathy, as though I'd turned up for this dinner in floral pyjamas.

"What's bothering you, my darling?" she said.

"The whole rippling, rumbling, world-warping thingummy that just happened!" I said, gesturing vaguely around the room. "The tremor that drove us all to grab the table? The wave of something-orother that tipped the soup and set plaster falling from the ceiling, the ripple that bent us out of shape, the whole—"

Here I broke off, for I looked around the room and saw that everything was in order. No tipped soup, no fallen plaster, no disarray. But something about the room had . . . well . . . *changed*, is about the only way to put it. Like there was a subtle somethingorother that hadn't been there before. The atmosphere seemed thicker, perhaps. The ambient "feeling" of the room wasn't right. The entire setting felt wrong in a way I couldn't put into words, which is saying something, as putting things into words is one of the things that I do best.

The Regent seemed intrigued, for she'd been staring at me, eyes narrowed, ever since the bizarre rippling sequence had passed.

"You perceived that?" she said, with a look that had "agog" written all over it.

"Perceived what?" said Norm.

"The *change*," said the Regent, rolling her tongue on the italics.

"I perceived it like the dickens!" I said.

"And you remember it, now that it's passed," said the Regent. She didn't ask it. She announced it. With an air of mild astonishment, like a seasoned entomologist who has happened upon a millipede wearing shoes. "Tell me," she continued, "while the memory is fresh in your mind. What changes do you perceive?"

"But dash it!" I said, "What was that rippling thingummy?"

"A reality quake," said the Regent.

"Good gracious!" said Oan, gasping.

"Another quake!" said Norm Stradamus, employing one of those whisper cries you sometimes use when you wish to register astonishment without waking the neighbours.

And while the phrase "reality quake" appeared to be one of great importance and deep meaning for those assembled, it didn't mean a dashed thing to me, so I just sat there looking baffled. The Regent noticed.

"Please, Mr. Feynman," said the Regent, "this is important. Describe any changes you see. Anything that has altered since the quake."

I won't claim to be the most observant fish in the sea, but I always do my best to keep an eye fixed on my surroundings. Having been entrusted by the Author with the task of sketching out the first draft of my adventures, I'm fairly diligent about taking in the local environment with a view to chucking in a bit of description now and then whenever I feel that a bit of stage setting might brighten up the text. Take the dining room in which I presently sat. I had taken fairly careful mental notes of its furnishings and accessories when I'd entered, just in case they might prove useful. I now reviewed these notes and compared them to what Isaac would call my current set of empirical observations.

Table? Check. Folks seated around it? Check. Dog? Check. Trays of assorted, scrumptious foodstuff? Check. Pyramidical thingummy serving as centrepiece? Check.

"Pay close attention to details," said the Regent.

I humoured the bird. After all, I was her guest, and she had laid out the spread to end all spreads and treated me with gracious hospitality. I peeped around the room once more.

"Abe's drawers!" I said, at length.

"Tell me!" said the Regent.

"*Everything* has changed!" I said, agog.

Oan gasped again.

"What do you mean?" asked the Regent.

"It's — well, dash it — it's difficult to describe. Everything's broadly the same as it was before this quake, but slightly different 'round the edges. Take the tapestries. Some of the imagery has changed. The little chap with the eagle's head is facing left instead of right. And the pattern on the serving dishes exhibits a bluer hue. The cutlery has changed, too. We're all still wearing the same clothes that we'd been wearing all along, but Oan's necklace has gotten longer. My tie is stiffer. Norm's beard is — "

"And the weather?" pressed the Regent.

"The air seems thicker," I said, remembering. "Harder to breathe. Heavier. Laden with rummy sultriness."

"Very good," said the Regent. "I see things as you do, Mr. Feynman. Before now, I've been the only one who could see such things or perceive the quakes themselves."

I looked around at my fellow guests. Oan and Norm sat there goggling at me in an awed sort of way, like children of tender years who've just witnessed their first conjuror pulling a rabbit out of a hat.

"But what in Abe's name is causing them?" I asked.

"The world is reshaping itself," said the Regent, leaning in. "Detroit is being transformed. The quakes started a few days before we brought you here. The first ones left very few changes in their wake, but each successive quake seems to be stronger."

"It's Climate Change!" said Norm Stradamus. "The reshaping of the world! Everything's just as I foretold."

"The High Priest speaks the truth," said the Regent. "Reality is bending. The very fabric of Detroit is being rewoven."

"Odd," I said.

"Odd?" said the Regent, cocking an eyebrow at me as though she expected Greater Things from one who had mysteriously perceived the recent thingummy.

"It's just an odd sort of coincidence," I said. "All of this Climate Change stuff. You've been noticing these changes in china patterns, atmospheric pressure, tapestries, and whatnot — little marginal changes which don't matter a single damn — all at the same time that I've been taking note of some of the Author's larger-scale editorial revisions: deleting here an IPT, there a protagonist's biographical sketch, and swapping personal secretaries for famous mathematicians. And you now describe these changes as the 'reweaving' of the fabric of Detroit. Yet another rummy coincidence."

"What do you mean?" asked the Regent.

"Nothing of consequence," I said, waving a carefree fork-ful of soufflé. "It's just that Isaac Newton used the same bit of metaphor when describing his latest research. He didn't spell out the details, mercifully sparing his audience a lecture on experimental methods, but he broadly described the thrust of his current work as reweaving the fabric of Detroit."

My three dinner companions now permed a synchronized slack-jawed goggle — all four of them if you count Memphis, for he too seemed to stare at me with a look of wild surmise.

"What is it?" I asked. "A bit of asparagus in my teeth?"

"What did you just say about Isaac Newton?" said Norm.

The Regent shushed him with a gesture, as if she wasn't interested in rehearing what I'd just said. She seemed to be keen on footnotes rather than repetition.

"What's Newton doing?" she demanded.

"Nothing important," I said, surprised at this crowd's keen interest in an academic's work. "Merely science. Your concern is forgivable, though, and has been shared at the highest levels. Abe himself had doubts and qualms about Newton's experiments, fearing that this science fancier might be up to something that could cause Detroit to spin off its axis or otherwise come to a bad end. I investigated the matter and quickly put those fears to bed. Rest assured that all is quiet on the Isaac front. He's is merely fiddling about with atomic whatnots."

This failed to placate my audience.

"Atomic whatnots?" said Oan.

"That's right," I said. "The quantum level. That's what he said. He wants to change Detroit at the quantum level. His grandiose plan, such as it is, is to alter all of the world's quantum thingummies all at once, and he needs my help to do it. There was something in there about Napoleons which I couldn't quite follow, and something else about time travel,

253

but none of that seemed to be of the essence. The nub of the thing is — the thing I mean to impress upon you — is that Isaac Newton's scientific fiddling is confined to this sub-molecular quantum realm, and that anything he does will be on such a teensy weensy, imperceptible scale that it couldn't matter to anyone larger than a virus who smoked in boyhood and stunted his growth."

I'd intended this spot of exposition to act as a balm for their collectively troubled spirits, but it didn't seem to have worked. Indeed, rather than soothing their troubled s.'s my recent statement seemed to have thrown fuel on a fire, for the Regent and Norm Stradamus appeared to respond with no small measure of alarm and agitation. Norm Stradamus suddenly leaned toward the Regent and cupped a hand over her ear, whispering something at her in a flagrant violation of dinner-party etiquette. And the Regent, eyes now bulging, shoved her chair back from the table and stood up.

"You'll have to excuse us, Mr. Feynman."

"But dash it, wait," I said, hoping to pour oil on the troubled waters, "you've got the thing all wrong. These reality-quake thingummies, this Climate Change you fear, this is probably nothing more than the Author scrapping a few unhappy words. Making changes here and there. Some of His changes are barely worthy of mention — tweaking description of the furnishings of this room, by way of example — and others are more macroscopic, if macroscopic means what I think it does. Like the IPT business I mentioned, or my own past biography. Or the transformation of Isaac from a bureaucratic toady to a ruddy Lucasian Chair. It's happening all the time, that sort of thing. I'll admit these changes can occasionally be irksome, but there's nothing to be done about them. Just keep calm and await the Author's next set of amendments. But rest assured that Isaac's messing about is a wholly separate issue, and one which needn't wrinkle the trousers. It's less worthy of grabbing headlines than a newly released batch of Isaac's I-Ware thingummies. Newton's work is the idle scientific puttering of an egghead and something that, like any peer-reviewed slab of research, is probably best ignored."

Once again I'd missed the mark, for rather than calming down, Norm appeared to writhe like an electric blender and the Regent seemed to arm herself with a sort of chilled resolve, her face setting into the steely glare of a soldier setting out for the front lines.

"You said Isaac is changing Detroit at the quantum level," she said. "You claim that he's hoping to increase his power to make these changes. Seeking to change all things at once."

"That's right," I said, "but seeing that you're failing to take this in the proper spirit, I think I should add a word or two in season. What I think you fail to realize, befogged Regent, is that the defining trait of the quantum level is that it's very small. Exceedingly so. Take your favourite amoeba or bacterium and adjust the scale downward. Isaac Newton is fooling about, as I think I mentioned, with atoms, quarks, bosons, Higgs-thingummies, and similar teeny tiny bits and bobs. Small potatoes, I mean to say. So small that you'll never notice. Nothing to worry about at all. What harm could come from poking quarks or splitting atoms?"

This didn't seem to have helped. The Regent looked from me to Norm, then back from Norm to me, and then finally back at Norm. Norm, who'd ceased his bit of writhing, shrugged his shoulders and wiped a hand across his brow.

"We have much to discuss, Mr. Feynman. I'll meet with you in the morning. In the meantime, please return to Vera's room. I will ask, once again, that you do your best to unlock the secrets of her prophecy. This is imperative. Now, more than ever."

And before I could respond, she had thrown down her napkin, picked up the centrepiece from the dining table, said the words "Memphis, heel," and withdrawn. Norm, Oan, and Memphis followed closely on her tail, leaving the undersigned alone and bewildered.

Chapter 23

It wasn't long before William came to clear away the debris and chivvy me to my next appointment, viz, another meet-up in Vera's quarters. The path we travelled en route to Vera's nest took us, as I'd hoped, straight through the door that had hitherto been guarded by my pal Zeus. I was disappointed to see there'd been a changing of the guard, for now some alternative variety of extra-large-sized chap had taken Zeus's customary post, if you can call it a customary post when you've only seen a chap there once. I was therefore in a slightly dejected mood when I hitched up *chez* Vera, as anyone would have been who'd failed to reunite with a long-lost pal and now faced the prospect of a night discussing poetry.

Safely ensconced in Vera's room I exchanged cordialities with both Vera and Nappy and asked if either of them had noticed the "reality quake" thingummy which had disrupted my formal dinner. They hadn't. This matter filed away as resolved, we got down to the apparently urgent business of discussing Vera's poem, aka her prophecy, which ran, if you'll recall, along the following lines:

> *Two chairs define a man and men;*
> *Two chairs that free and bind;*
> *Two chairs that open worlds and free*
> *The body and the mind;*
> *One chair sought and held by both,*

The other coveted by none;
The first chair reunites two souls
Intended to have been just one.

"All right," I said, having gone through the text with those assembled. "So what's it mean?"

"I've no idea," said Vera.

"Search me," said Nappy.

"Helpful," I said, with a touch of exasperation in my v. I mean to say, if you can't turn to the poetess herself when seeking to ferret out the meaning of a short scrap of verse, where can you turn? I remembered a bit of advice I'd once taken from Matron Bikerack — something or other about breaking horrible tasks up into manageable chunks — and went at the thing line by line.

"Two chairs define a man and men," I said. "Let's start with that."

"It seems to me zat zere are two chairs," said Nappy, "and zat bos of zem define a pair of men."

"That's right," I said, "that much is specified. But the question, I think, is this: how can a chair define a man?"

"The Lucasian chair!" said Vera, echoing a notion I'd shared with Norm earlier and reminding me of the gag about great minds thinking alike.

"The chairs mightn't be physical," Vera added. "If anyone is defined by his work, it's Isaac Newton, and Isaac Newton's job is Lucasian Chair."

"Quelle sort de chair?" said Nappy.

"Lucasian," I said. "L as in laparoscopic, U as in ulcerative colitis, C as in—"

"It's the name of the chair that Isaac Newton holds," said Vera, cutting in.

"'E 'olds une chair?" said Nappy, befogged.

"Do keep up," I said, perhaps a touch more impatiently than was warranted. This Nappy, after all, had just been through the wringer alongside countless fellow Napoleons, and couldn't be expected to be perfectly up-to-date with current events.

"Isaac is the Lucasian Chair of Mathematics at Detroit University. He's what you call a 'chair holder' — one who occupies an office of particular importance. Think of the chair of a board, or the chairperson of a committee. Not an actual chair. I was telling Norm, earlier, that Isaac might be one of the chairs in Vera's poem."

"But there again," said Vera, "the prophecy could mean actual chairs. Or maybe one of the chairs is Isaac Newton, and the other's just a piece of furniture. My visions don't usually come as poems, but when they do they're never easy to understand. You can't expect the words to be used consistently."

"We can't even be sure zat Isaac is one of ze chairs," said Nappy.

"True," I said, "but it does seem right. This Lucasian chump seems exactly the type who'd pop up in an oracle's visions. The last time we rubbed elbows he went on at length about the wrongness of the universe and his own plans to fix it. And even Abe, however wrongly, deemed this chap to be dangerous. If any chair is qualified to waft around in the ether and pop out in prophetic poems, it is this Lucasian Chair."

"It feels right to me, too," said Vera. "But you're right: we can't be sure."

"So what's ze ozzer chair?" said Nappy.

"Who knows?" said Vera. "It might be another chair at the university, it might be a lawn chair. It could just be an everyday, garden-variety seat."

The word "seat" lit an unexpected fire in the Feynman bean, and by what I've often thought was an odd coincidence, it struck Nappy in precisely the same way, for at the same time, and with roughly the same volume, we both shouted the words "a seat of power!" as if directed by a conductor.

"Perhaps the ultimate seat of power," said I.

"Abe!" said Nappy.

"*Rem acu tetigisti!*" I said. "That has to be it. One chair is the Lucasian Chair, the other is the mayoral seat of power. I think we've solved it. Let's move on."

Nappy clapped her hands and bounced delightedly in her seat, indicating to those assembled that she, too, was finding poetic interpretation to be a good deal more diverting than expected. Vera, by sharp contradistinction, failed altogether to string along with our merry mission-accomplished spirit. Instead, she sat there in a grey-cloudish sort of way, corrugating her brow at us and saying "hmmm."

"I don't know," she added, with a rummy sort of skepticism dripping from every word.

"Oh, dash it. Stop raining on parades. Chair One is Isaac Newton, and Chair Two is Abe. Or perhaps the other way 'round. Abe did arrive here first."

"You're making an awful lot of assumptions," said Vera.

"No more than two or three," I said.

"But they're big ones. Does the rest of the poem make sense if we assume the two chairs are Isaac and Abe? Does the Lucasian chair both 'free and bind'? Does the mayoral seat?"

"Zey do!" said Nappy. "Ze mayor is, in many ways, free to do 'ow he chooses. But 'e is bound to serve Detroit."

"That's right!" I said, applauding this bit of reasoning. "And the Lucasian Chair, if I understand correctly, frees Isaac to pursue whatever research he likes, yet binds him to the university!"

"Okaaaaay," said Vera, still with a skeptical tone I found discouraging, "but it sounds like a stretch to me. How do these chairs 'open worlds,' or 'free the body and the mind'? How is either seat 'occupied by both,' while the other is occupied by one?"

"Isaac's never occupied the mayoral seat," I conceded, but I wasn't yet prepared to admit defeat. "Was Abe ever a maths professor?"

"I don't think so," said Nappy. "Being ze mayor keeps 'im busy."

"Hmmm," I said.

"Hmmm," said Nappy.

"The trickiest bit," said Vera, "is the part about two souls that were meant to be just one. What's that all about?"

"It's your poem, you tell me!" I said.

"But that's just it," said Vera. "I haven't a clue. But I think that — I dunno — I think that I'd know it if I heard the right explanation. I . . . well I think I'm sure about Isaac being one of the two chairs. It feels right. But Abe? He doesn't fit. I'm sorry, but I just don't think my poem refers to him."

I slumped the shoulders. Say what you will about the weirdness of television and the even greater loopiness of soothsaying via poem, but this Vera had never once, since our association began, led me astray — unless you count an unexpected betrothal and a couple of whitish lies during her escape from the hospice as being led astray. But the point I'm driving at is that she was, and always has been, a good egg, and one upon whose intuition and future-gazing powers it has been safe to rely. She'd even laid down her life on one occasion — at least so far as a life can be laid down in Detroit — to ensure that self and others got to safety. And now she assured us that, despite our best efforts, our attempts at sorting out her poem's meaning had missed the mark. We'd tried our best, straining every nerve in Olympic-level poetic analysis, and failed. So as I said, I slumped the shoulders. My entire bearing must have resembled that of a basset hound with a secret sorrow, for both Nappy and Vera rallied 'round with multiple doses of consolation, patting here a shoulder and there a head.

"It's all right," said Vera. "I'm sure we'll figure it out."

"Just look 'ow far you've come!" said Nappy. "You've found Zeus, you've learned Isaac's plan, you've sorted out part of zis 'two chairs' poem — you should be 'appy, Monsieur Rhinnick!"

"But how can I be 'appy?" I riposted. "Zeus is here, yes, but his memories have gone phut. And Isaac's plan has been revealed, if you'll pardon the expression, as purely academic: a phrase which, I should point out, means both scholarly in nature and unimportant. The quest on which Abe sent me — a quest initially advertised as being of globe-wobbling import — has turned out to be based on a complete misunderstanding and amounted to little more than a walk in the park. As for Vera's poem — well, dash it, why are we even fretting about this slice of verse? The Regent says it's important. Norm Stradamus says it's important. But the two of them, if you don't mind my making a personal observation, seem likely candidates for residence in Detroit Mercy Hospice under the watchful eye of Everard M. Peericks, wetting their pants about Isaac's trivial plans and throwing fits over the Author's editorial revisions. What I mean to say," I added, preparatory to summing up, "is that nothing seems to matter."

Vera's entire demeanour shifted. She seemed stern. Where there had been a mother hen, there now sat a sergeant major. She cheesed the shoulder-patting routine and crossed her arms at me.

"It's time for you to grow some ovaries," she said.

I eh-whatted.

"Woman up," she added.

"What in Abe's name are you on about?"

"It seems to me you have two choices. You can sit here and sulk, or you can roll up your sleeves and see what you can do to help Zeus. His memories are gone? Fine. Then it's your job to help him. And while you're at it you can find a way to stop what they've been doing to the Napoleons. It's not right. They're cooped up in cells and being experimented on. Somebody has to do something, and that somebody has to be us. Especially you. The Regent and Norm think of you as the Hand of the Intercessor, right? Then use that! They think you're important and influential? Tell them to let the Napoleons go! Just stop sitting around and whining. Buck up and get to work."

"But dash it," I said, "how can I? I'm in the midst of one of those things you sometimes get."

"Huh?" said Vera.

"A kind of crisis. They start with e."

"An emergency?" hazarded Vera.

"Egg-zee-stential?" said Nappy.

"That's the bunny," I said. "I'm having one of those existential crises. Like the one I had before — when Ian Brown stood revealed as the leading man in my last adventure, and I was cast in a mere supporting role — Hand of the Intercessor, forsooth. And now . . . well, I'm *fairly* convinced I really do exist — but to what end? I emerge as the protagonist in a book without a plot, and one in which all of my actions have amounted to less than nil."

"That isn't true!" said Vera. "You got me out of the hospice. You found Zeus and made sure he was safe. You've discovered what's been happening to the Napoleons."

"Zis is true!" said Nappy. "Wizzout you, none of zis might 'ave 'appened."

I might have argued the point, but it's dashed depressing to have to explain, in no uncertain terms, that the sum total of the impact of your efforts is less than advertised, particularly when that impact is being hyped up by your pals. They were right, of course, that I'd discovered a good many things in the course of the last few weeks — but these were things that were happening whether I discovered them or not, and I hadn't had any impact on them at all.

Vera's words of encouragement had, however, reminded me of one thing: it wasn't time to throw in the towel. Say what you will about we Feynmen, we know how to keep the upper lip stiff. Faced with the bludgeonings of fate, our heads are bloodied but unbowed, as the fellow wrote. We do not raise the white flag or turn our faces to the wall. We might wallow for a paragraph or two and take stock of our chagrin as I'd just done, but we don't make a habit out of the thing. Having engaged in a bit of this self-indulgent wallowing, we sink our dudgeon and carry on. In a word, we can take it.

The patented Feynman resilience — or resolve, if you prefer — was just starting to kick in, and would, in any cinematographic depiction, have been heralded by a chorus of *Voix Céleste* rising up toward a crescendo. And after they'd made their way through a couple of bars' worth of glory-glory-hallelujah-ing, they'd fade into the background as I kicked in with an inspirational speech.

I was on the point of coming across with the inspirational s., but was interrupted by the sound of a polite cough coming from my immediate rear. This was revealed to be the domestic servant William, once again turning up to chivvy me elsewhere.

"You must rise early on the morrow, sir," he said, in that respectful way of his. "The Regent has called for a meeting of great importance and bids you thither in your capacity as Hand of the Intercessor. If you've concluded your conference with Ms. Lantz and Ms. Napoleon, I shall convey you to your room."

And on that officious note, the evening ended. William ushered me to my room, where I found Fenny curled up with a book and looking as though he hadn't a care in the world. I apprised him of the day's events and tucked myself into bed for a good night's sleep.

Chapter 24

But I didn't get much of it, and what I did get was interrupted by dreams of killer whales chasing me over difficult terrain. Some of them looked like Oan, some of them looked like Isaac Newton, and for some reason I couldn't fathom, a few of them looked like the butler William. When I finally gave up my pursuit of sleep, the day was dawning bright and fair, the sun was beaming through the windows, and these same windows revealed a treeful of about one hundred and forty birds who tootled and tweeted as though they hadn't a damn thing on their collective mind. Fenny was snoring on the bedside table — his habit when we spend the night in unfamiliar quarters — and William, his trained senses knowing just when a guest of the house would be in need, was manifesting himself in the doorway with a trolley topped with tea and all the fixings.

"Good morning, sir," he said.

"It strikes you as that, does it?"

"I beg your pardon, sir?"

"The morning. You deem it good?"

"I do, sir. The weather is extremely clement."

"That's easy for you to say," I said, a touch austerely. And there must have been something in my demeanour indicating that chagrin had marked me for her own, for William's next words indicated that he'd divined my mood.

"Is something bothering you, sir?"

"You bet it is," I said. "It's this dashed meeting with the Regent. I can't face it. They'll be all over me about interpreting Vera's poem, they'll repeatedly call me the Hand of the ruddy Intercessor, and they'll probably insist that we spend some time planning a wedding or two. Not," I added, "intending to suggest anything derogatory about marriage — it's just that all of this fuss and bother about me being something of a Church Icon gives me the pip, as it would any man of spirit."

"That is regrettable, sir."

"But it's not me who's going to regret it. It's everyone else. I'm oiling out. Convey my RSVP in the negative, William. Tell them I can't make the meeting."

"I'm afraid that's impossible, sir."

"Impossible? Just watch me. It's practically the easiest thing in the world — not attending a meeting, I mean. You simply don't turn up."

"But the meeting is here, sir," said William.

"How do you mean the meeting is here? You can't mean to imply that they're holding their official tête-à-tête here in the Feynman HQ, among my bed and luggage and other personal whatnots?"

"I do, sir. In fact, unless I'm much mistaken I hear the Regent and her party approaching now. Shall I show them in?"

As a general rule we Feynmen keep open house and are happy to entertain whatever huddled masses choose to enter our orbit. But I was still in bed, dash it, and not yet prepared to face whatever it was that the Regent and her party — whomever that might entail — wished to unleash in my direction. I was about to indicate this to William when I realized that his question, "shall I show them in," I mean, was one of those questions that aren't really questions — purely rhetorical, if you take my meaning, for as soon as he'd finished asking it he turned on his well-polished heel, beelined his way to the door, and gave entry to the Regent and her p.

And what a p. it was. It included the Regent herself, carrying that little pyramid thingummy from the table and looking like she was about to start shooting flames from both nostrils, as well as the prophet Norm Stradamus, the dog Memphis, and — as if to suggest that this little shindig also constituted a jamboree for the Society of Those-Affianced-to-Rhinnick-Feynman — both Vera and Oan, standing shoulder to shoulder when I'd prefer to have seen them separated by a couple of oceans and impassable mountain ranges. Seeing the two of them standing here, together in my room, made me chafe more than a little — this despite the fact that I was currently tucked to my chin in luxurious sheets of the nigh-infinite thread count variety.

Of course, if there's one thing Rhinnick Feynman has always been nippy at, it's bearing up in the face of impending ruin and desolation. I therefore maintained such composure as I had, smiled a welcoming smile, and bade the party to rally 'round the Feynman bed and pull up chairs.

They seemed to prefer standing, and gave every indication of having no time for civil chit-chat.

"Mr. Feynman," said the Regent, who looked to be in a mood for chewing bottles and spitting nails. "You must tell us everything you know of R'lyeh."

"R'lyeh?" I said, befogged, "I thought you were here to talk about Vera's poem."

"No need," said Norm Stradamus. "Vera's already filled us in."

"R'lyeh, Mr. Feynman," said the Regent, still looking about as ornery as a regimental commander with a toothache. "Tell us what you know about R'lyeh."

I took a moment to shake the cobwebs from my attic and marshal the brain. And just when I was on the point of saying

I hadn't a notion of what she was babbling about, memory regained her throne.

"Oh, R'lyeh!" I said, remembering, and turned toward Vera. "That was the password you used to access the basement of the City Hall, wasn't it? The room with the frozen ancients?"

"That's right," said Vera. And something about her tone — a sort of rummy, stammering, tremulous quality — told me that Vera was not her usual fizzy self. Now that she'd entered the conversation and I'd subjected her to that penetrating Feynman scrutiny which has been so widely publicized, I perceived that this generally rosy-cheeked medium was now about as ashen-hued as you can be without actually lying facedown in the hearth. And whatever views you have on Rhinnick Feynman, you'll have to admit that he does not stand idly by when he sees a pal exhibit a clouded brow.

"There's something troubling you," I said.

Vera stood there, staring mutely.

"It's nothing," said the Regent. "You must tell us about R'lyeh now."

"You want me to tell you about the password?"

"No, the place," said the Regent.

"It's what they're calling sub-basement nine," said Vera, before finding herself caught in a rather caustic glare from the Regent.

"Tell us what you know," said the Regent.

"Please forgive us, Hand of the Intercessor," said Norm Stradamus, in a placating sort of way, "but we really must know. It's of vital importance."

"Please, Rhinnick, do tell us," said Oan, who seemed be chewing her lower lip.

"There isn't much to tell," I said, shrugging a shoulder or two. "It's just a big, warehouse-sized space in the bowels of City

Hall. Filled to the brim with — what did you call them, Vera? It's on the tip of my tongue. Not sarcasm or sarcomas, but—"

"Sarcophagi," said the Regent, once again pinch-hitting for Vera, who stared intently at her own shoes.

"That's right," I said. "The joint was filled to the brim with sarcophagi containing freeze-dried ancients. Vera said they were dormant. And for some reason or other — we weren't vouch-safed time to conduct a thorough investigation — some officious chap, possibly Isaac, was pumping these sleeping ancients full of lessons."

"Lessons?" said Norm Stradamus.

"That's right, lessons. Things about science. New research. All of these sarcophagus-bound oldsicles were joined together in this neural network thingummy which seemed to pump them full of a serum that filled their heads with information."

"And what do you know of its purpose?" asked the Regent.

"Its purpose?" I said, and my shoulders got a bit more shrug-ging done to them. "Why, nothing at all. Why anyone would bother going to all the trouble and expense of building one of these network thingummies, all with a view to putting ideas into the heads of elderly birds, is beyond yours truly."

"I told you," said Vera, apparently to her shoes, "he doesn't know anything."

The Regent shushed her with an imperious gesture — a practice to which she seemed far too addicted.

"What's all this about?" I asked. "And why does Vera seem as though she's been caught stealing coins from the collection plate?"

The Regent turned to Norm Stradamus and cupped a hand over his ear, proceeding to whisper in a way that would have drawn a firm tut-tutting from the author of any book of man-ners. Vera looked up at me and seemed on the point of tears, and Oan stood mutely by her side, still chewing her lip — her own, I mean, not Vera's.

It seemed to me that the time had come for a spot of decisive action. But what action to take? That was the question. Here I was, sitting in bed surrounded by a bevy of church officials and nervous fiancées, with no idea of why everyone in the zip code was acting so dashed odd. I was hampered by my lack of information.

I adjusted the pyjamas, pushed the covers aside, and scooched my way out of bed with as much dignity as I could muster in the circs. Then, doing my best to adopt a haughty air — though possibly not coming within several miles of it — I reissued my demands.

"I say!" I said, preparatory to chewing out the Regent, "I appreciate the lavish bit of real estate you've let me occupy during my convalescence, and I'm grateful that you gave my pal Zeus — better known hereabouts as Terrence — a comfortable post for which he is well suited. You've been my host, kept me beneath your rooftree, and earned a bit of leeway in the area of departing from basic rules of etiquette and civility. And I've been patient. I've done my best to furnish you with all requested information, and I've entertained requests to interpret poems. But there are limits, and strictly defined ones! I now see that you've reduced Vera practically to tears, you've rendered Oan a fairly speechless lip-chewer, and you whisper amongst yourselves in flagrant violation of the book of social rules. I've never been one to invoke titles, but whether I like it or not I am apparently the Hand of the ruddy Intercessor, and I demand that you fill me in on whatever it is that's caused this unacceptable state of affairs."

My earnest rebuke of the Regent's conduct appeared to have unmanned her — if you can call it unmanning when it happens to a woman. Her features softened, her brow unfurrowed, and the storm clouds brewing around her head seemed to abate. To say she stopped shouting orders and started cooing like a dove would go too far, but her manner did improve.

"Hand of the Intercessor," she said, causing me to cringe a bit and regret having invoked that blasted title. "Mr. Feynman," she continued. "I regret keeping you in the dark. There are forces at play that you do not understand."

"Enlighten me," I riposted.

"Tell me," she said, "what do you recall of the battle you witnessed with Norm Stradamus — the contest of wills between the Intercessor and the City Solicitor?"

"You mean the Intercessor's wife. It wasn't Ian who fought against the City Solicitor — or rather, he *did* fight, but his efforts amounted to less than nil. It was his wife, Penelope Somethingorother, who busted up the City Solicitor's plans."

"Very well," said the Regent, "please tell me what you recall about the City Solicitor's battle with Penelope."

"I'm the one in need of information," I replied with a touch of asperity, for I was beginning to grow impatient with this habit of grilling Rhinnick on both sides when he was the one left in the dark.

"Your answer will help the Regent explain matters," said Norm, diplomatically.

"All right," I said, doing my best to appear tolerant. "Well, the City Solicitor popped into the grotto, interrupted Norm *et al.* as they were trying to coax Ian to bung himself into the river, and ruined everyone's day by firing a gun — apparently loaded with those memory-wiping rounds — directly into Ian's brain. I'm given to understand that this was followed by some sort of cosmic battle, most of which took place beyond my line of sight — I having been confined to an oddish sort of amber cocoon thingummy once things really heated up. I did manage to collar the gist, though, and understand that both the

City Solicitor and Penny flexed a bit of omnipotence, flinging thunderbolts hither and thither and rearranging the geography through a psychic battle of wills. Penny won, Abe turned up, and Ian and Penny biffed off to parts unknown. Abe then offered yours truly a quest — my quest to thwart whatever it was Abe mistakenly thought Isaac Newton was planning — and my pursuit of this quest, through twists and turns too numerous to mention, landed me here."

The Regent, Norm, and Oan nodded throughout, as though approving of my oration. Vera raised her head and stared in something approximating slack-jawed wonder, as though indicating that all of this had been news to her.

"Excellent," said the Regent. "And do you recall what passed between the City Solicitor and Ian prior to this battle?"

"You mean apart from the bullet?"

"Yes. What did the City Solicitor say to Ian?"

"Oh, that," I said. "Just some rot about the nature of the universe. Old stuff, really — things Oan covers in those sharing sessions of hers. Not," I added, for I was cognizant of the fact that this same Oan was standing three feet from my bed and clearly hanging on my lips, "that hospice patients shouldn't appreciate those sessions. Vision Boards, friendship bracelets, musings on the Laws of Attraction — always just what the doctor ordered in the realm of mental health. But suffice it to say the Solicitor said a lot of things about expectations and desires forming the universe. What we expect to happen, happens. He added some guff about Abe and other ancients shoring up the walls of reality and preventing things from getting out of hand. I think that covers it."

My answer seemed to have landed well, for Norm Stradamus and Oan both seemed pleased. The Regent never seemed pleased by anything, but even she seemed to register approval.

Only Vera seemed unmoved by my oration, for she once again dropped her eyes and adopted a distinctly dishraggish manner.

"It was all hogwash, of course," I added, not wishing to leave anyone befogged. "What the City Solicitor said, I mean. The truth of the matter is this: the Author, for whatever reason, has seen fit to equip a few select heavy-hitters with extraordinary powers, and these same heavy-hitters — folks like Abe, the City Solicitor, and Penelope — stomp around the local landscape leaving obstacles in the way of the rest of the herd. They're simply a kind of literary thingummy. A device designed to create dramatic tension. The world isn't, in point of fact, formed by anyone's expectations apart from the Author's and, perhaps, the Author's Editor, His Publisher, and His Critics," I added, wanting to avoid any blasphemous failure to give credit to the whole pantheon. "Now, would any-one mind connecting dots for me? What does any of this have to do with anything?"

The Regent stepped closer. Her face darkened. Her voice took on a conspiratorial air, and she seemed to be on the point of letting me in on state secrets. "What you need to under-stand," she said, gravely, "is that the City Solicitor was right. He was right about Detroit. About the nature of the world."

This was nonsense, of course, as I'd indicated a few ticks earlier. But rather than contradicting my host I merely nodded amiably, both out of politeness and the fact that nodding amia-bly is all one can really do when people start flapping their jaws about science and the nature of the world.

"What the Regent means," said Norm, dutifully picking up the Regent's thread, "is that Detroit is not a physical realm. Not entirely. It's a plane comprised of the thoughts, expectations, and desires of everyone who dwells within it. All of the souls within Detroit help to shape its basic reality."

"It's true," said Oan, eager as ever to offer a word or two of Sharing Room philosophy. "The universe listens to our wishes, and shapes itself around them! It's this very phenomenon, rooted in the Laws of Attraction, that has led you to my side."

I suppressed a wince. It's not going too far to say that it took every scrap of my own willpower, whether or not augmented by the Laws of ruddy Attraction or universes that bend to a chap's will, to prevent myself from blanching, writhing, chafing, or otherwise revealing that this Oan's latest pronouncement had given the undersigned the pip. But we Rhinnicks are, as I think I've mentioned before, made of fairly strong stuff. So I wore the mask, sank my revulsion, and bore up.

Indeed, in this bit of the story it was almost as though there were two Rhinnicks, both displayed for the scrutiny and interest of my reading public, but only one of whom was observed by those who'd gathered in my presence. The first Rhinnick — the one who was hidden from the Regent and her gang of onlookers — was all steely-eyed skepticism, unmoved by what he was hearing, and full of confidence in the knowledge that everything presently entering via the Feynman earhole was complete and utter rot. But the other Rhinnick, the one who nodded amiably and uttered encouraging things like "oh yes" and "do tell" at appropriate intervals, was the only one detectable by those present. It was a master class in acting, if I do say so myself, and one which easily justified any number of those little, golden, anatomically incorrect graven images.

I mean to say, it's one thing to know that everything your host is saying is bunk, and it's quite another to let your host know what's on your mind. We Rhinnicks are sticklers for social niceties, and I was — whatever else one wanted to call me — a guest in the Regent's house. It would have been the work of a moment to prove conclusively that everything she was saying was the mere babbling of an unhinged mind:

if the universe was listening to my desires, I wouldn't be standing in my pyjamas listening to a brace of loonier-than-average zealots telling me how the joint worked. But as I said, I held my tongue, not only out of politeness, but also because it occurred to me that, if I was ever going to understand what in Abe's name had been going on in this shack of unrestrained goofiness, my best strategic move was to give the local yokels the free rein of their tongues so that they'd carry on explaining their weird ideas. They'd built their entire foreign policy on their loopy understanding of Detroit's inner workings, and if I let them continue babbling for a paragraph or two, something in the way of useful intelligence might be revealed.

So I carried on with my "oh yes" and "do go on" routine for at least a quarter of an hour.

One thing I think you'll appreciate, having made your way this deeply into the current volume of my memoir, is how dashed difficult it can be for any narrator to keep track of the goings-on while also taking careful notes about his own internal feelings, keeping the readership apprised of what I believe philosophers call the subject's "qualia," or what psychologists refer to as one's subjective experience. It was for this reason that, throughout much of the Regent's babbling, as I'd been paying close attention to my qualia and musing on what I've just told you about "two Rhinnicks" and my desire to hide my true, skeptical nature from my hosts, that I'd rather lost the thread of whatever had passed between those present. I was aware that the Regent had said something or other about conflicting wills and desires, and that Norm had said something reminiscent of Abe's suggestions about the First Ones, or ancients, providing order and regulation, and that Oan, at regular intervals, had added a word or two about the Laws of Attraction. I was also vaguely aware that Vera had carried on in silence while I did my best to stifle yawns. But as I think you'll understand from what I've just said, the substance of the conversation had gotten away from me. And just when I thought we'd carry on in this vein for a couple of years, the Regent finally said something that grabbed my attensh.

"And that," she said, "is why we have to dismantle R'lyeh."

"Dismantle R'lyeh?" I said, intrigued. "Why in Abe's name would you want to do that?"

The whole gang of those assembled looked at me as though I'd sprouted a second head.

"It's what we've just been explaining to you," said Norm.

"Oh, ah," I said. "Right. Perhaps you wouldn't mind crossing a few t's and dotting some i's. You were saying you had to dismantle R'lyeh — that underground warehouse of frozen ancients hidden in City Hall."

"That's right," said Norm. "We have to stop Isaac from meddling with their minds."

This much seemed sensible, at least. I mean to say, these chilled retirees, from everything I'd been told, had earned their rest. They'd been working in Detroit since practically the dawn of time, having popped into the joint when Abe could still be counted as a new arrival. They'd been pitching in and doing their bit to keep the place running for thousands and thousands of years. It seemed the least that one could do is leave them alone now that they'd downed tools and packed it in. Let sleeping ancients lie, I mean to say. It seemed only courteous to prevent any science fancier, however well intentioned, from bothering the somnolent oldsters with involuntary lectures delivered straight to their sleeping brains in liquid form. I registered my approval.

"So you're planning to ask Isaac to cheese the R'lyeh project. Fair enough," I said, smiling broadly. "Abe speed your efforts!"

Once again my remarks seemed to stun my audience. Norm, in particular, looked on me with a disquieting expression which seemed to combine equal parts of pity and bewilderment, a look which I found offensive.

"We can't ask him to stop," said Norm, squinting at me with something resembling incredulity. "He wouldn't agree. It's all part of his plan."

"Right," I said, stretching the word out a bit. "Isaac's plan. I think I see what you're driving at."

I hadn't a notion of what they were talking about, of course. I knew of Isaac's plan to fiddle with quantum thingummies, but anyone could see at a g. that this had nothing whatever to do with his desire to inflict refresher courses in science and natural philosophy on a warehouseful of snoozing seniors.

The Regent seemed to perceive that I was still befogged, for she added what she must have regarded as words of explanation.

"Allow me to spell it out again, O Hand of the Intercessor," she said. "The project at R'lyeh is, as we've been telling you, part of Isaac's plan to change Detroit. He's using his network to change the ancients' minds. He taps into their brains, altering their beliefs and expectations about the nature of the world. He's using their combined willpower to influence reality — to reweave the fabric of Detroit, all with a view to forcing the world to coincide with his calculations. Even Abe and Penelope would be powerless to stop the combined will of so many dormant ancients, acting as one."

"Ah," I said, congenially, though here again I was fairly certain that the Regent was talking out of the side of her head. "I see all. Allow me to restate what I've gathered. Isaac Newton, irritated at Detroit's failure to jive with his figures, is pumping ancients full of science juice in order to alter their perceptions and, through means not fully explained to my satisfaction, bring Detroit in line with his maths. And you're against this plan. Not a fan of his calculations, what?"

"They're the core of the problem," said Norm. "As we've tried to explain, Isaac's calculations are rooted in a purely physical world, not the reality of Detroit. They can't apply here — not fully. Can you imagine what would happen if Isaac succeeded in his plans?"

The answer to this, of course, was "no, I ruddy well can't," for I still hadn't collared the gist of what they were babbling about. I didn't reveal this, and was spared the effort of coming up with something to say because the Regent beat me to it.

"We must stop him before he goes too far. Thus far his work has focused on chemistry and physics, and the results have been far-reaching: the erasure of the IPT; his own transformation from personal secretary to Lucasian Chair. But imagine if he turns his attention to biology. Human biology. It could be the end of everything."

"He could bring death to Detroit!" cried Oan.

"Human Death!" added Norm. "Human aging! Incurable diseases and mortality!"

Caught up in their own lunacy, they'd missed the entire point about Isaac's work being confined to the quantum realm. But you can't explain a fundamental thing like that to yahoos who've gotten themselves riled up and are now frothing at the mouth. The best you can hope to do is point out any minor errors that have shoved them in the direction of their goofy conclusions. I did my best to weigh in and rally their spirits.

"You've made a blunder," I said, rather tolerantly. "A common one, too. I mean to say, you needn't worry about Isaac switching fields, spending a year or two on physics, a sabbatical on chemistry, and a brace of terms on biology. For when you get right down to it," I continued, dredging up one of the things I'd read in *Popular Science*, "it's all just physics at its core. Chemistry, biology, metallurgy, geology — it all comes down to the laws of physics. This is why I imagine Isaac said that once he really gets down to business, he'll be able to change everything all at once. But I'll remind you that his changes are confined to quantum whatnots," I added. "Nothing to worry about at all."

Once again I'd failed to anticipate my audience's response, for their goofiness only intensified as the words fell from my lips.

"We haven't a moment to lose!" said Oan.

"We must stop him now!" cried Norm.

And the Regent, for her part, clenched her jaw tightly and squinted her eyes in a cold-steelish manner, coming across as more stern and resolute than anyone I had ever seen, with the possible exception of Ian's wife, Penelope, in the moments after she'd first emerged from the Styx. The word "imposing" sums it up.

"Inform my personal guard," said the Regent. "We must prepare. We leave for R'lyeh tonight."

Chapter 25

It turned out I wasn't invited.

I mean to say, when the Regent started blustering about assembling her guard, leaving tonight, storming the gates of City Hall, and trespassing upon — or rather beneath — municipal property, I'd assumed she planned to have me at her side, adding to the strength of her troops and hitching along for the ride. "Bring the Hand of the Intercessor," I thought she'd say, "for not only is he a dashed useful chap to have on hand whenever engaged in anything which might be described as derring-do, but he's also been to this R'lyeh joint before, he knows the lay of the land, and he's fairly palsy-walsy with Isaac Newton. Should this Newton chap show up in person, intent on laying our plans a-stymie, who better than Rhinnick F., H. of the I., to grease the wheels?" And in response to this hypothetical invitation or command, if hypothetical means what I think it does, I'd have issued a firm and resolute *nolle prosequi*. "Include me out," I might have said, had the occasion arisen. "N, ruddy O. They won't get a smell of yours truly at City Hall."

I mean to say, I was philosophically aligned with the Regent and her crew when it came to the question of inflicting nonconsensual lessons in liquid form upon freeze-dried senior citizens, but our methods of responding to the situation differed. Where the Regent seemed to be planning something along the lines of storming the ramparts, laying siege to the place, and leaving no sarcophagus standing, the conviction was rapidly steeling over me that something a touch more nuanced — say, a sternly worded letter to the editor — would prove the better response. So, as I said, I planned to RSVP in the negative.

But again, as I said before embarking on something of a tangent: It turned out I wasn't invited.

You might expect this to have bucked me up considerably, given that my current wish was to keep the Feynman nose out of this R'lyeh imbroglio, and this wish had now been granted. But the funny thing I've often observed in others, and which I now observed in me, is that it's one thing to turn down an invitation to a binge you'd give your eye teeth to avoid, and another thing altogether not to have been on the list of those from whom an RSVP is expected. The latter alternative wounds the spirit. It leaves one feeling ostracized and crestfallen. If Rhinnick is to be excluded, let it be me who makes that call.

The Regent didn't even seem to have given the merest thought to inviting me along. For, on the heels of saying, "We leave for R'lyeh tonight," she'd turned upon her heel, exiting stage right, when she looked back over the shoulder — her left, if I recall — and said, "You'll remain here, Mr. Feynman." A command, if you see what I mean. Not a question.

I started to utter an objection — dashed silly of me, I know — when she'd goose-stepped out of the room with Oan and Vera in her wake, she having indicated through imperious nods and gestures that the two were to walk out with her. Norm Stradamus, for his part, stayed behind, wringing his hands and looking at me in a plaintive sort of way, like a chief executive's toady en route to explaining why third-quarter profits aren't quite as high as projected. Or, more accurately, like a High Priest who has to dish up a serving of awkward news to the Hand of the blasted Intercessor.

"I'm sorry, Rhinnick," he said. "The Regent has decreed that you'll stay here."

"Decreed?" I said, trying to sort things out as best I could. "I thought you were the High Priest. Since when do Regents decree to you?"

"It's complicated," he said.

"Just where does a Regent fit in the church hierarchy?" I asked, interested as always in keeping abreast.

"She stands apart," said Norm. "We share the same goal of building a bridge to the beforelife. The Regent has the means to help us achieve this. And any hope of stopping Isaac's current plan will require the Regent's powers."

"But what are the Regent's powers?"

"My apologies, O Hand of the—"

I silenced him with a gesture — a gesture which wasn't quite as imperious as any gesture of the Regent, but it certainly fell within the same postal code. I'd had quite enough of this "Hand of the Intercessor" business, whatever privileges the title might entail, and it was starting to seem that any such privileges were few and far between.

Norm's hands got a bit more wringing done to them, and he carried on apologizing. He looked like a pangolin delivering bad news. Obsequious, I mean to say. Or servile, if you prefer.

"I'm sorry, Mr. Feynman," he said. "I'd be deeply honoured to have you with us, but the Regent felt that for your own safety—"

"My own safety?" I said, bewildered by the bearded chump's babbling. "How's my safety at issue? We're in Detroit. Whatever vicissitudes befall me, life and limb are not at risk. Well, limbs are, I suppose, but they'll grow back. It's one of the many upsides of immortality, if you see what I mean."

"The Regent believes that, should the inclination strike him, Isaac Newton has the power to change whatever he desires. He could blink us out of existence. He could change our histories.

He could burn the Church of O from the threads of history, or stop you and the Intercessor from ever having met."

It took me perhaps a quarter of a minute to sort through this, but I think I collared the gist. I was, I realized, dealing with a mind unhinged. Here was a High Priest who had drunk deeply of the Regent's Kool-Aid, signing up without hesitation to be included on the roster of those who failed to understand Professor Isaac Newton's plans.

Of course you can't explain anything to a True Believer like this Norm. I'd told him several times that all of this "Climate Change" he feared hadn't been caused by Isaac Newton, and that it was simply an emanation — do I mean an emanation? — of the Author's recent revisions. I'd tried on more than one occasion to explain that Newton's plans to "change the world" encompassed only quantum thingummies, and that nothing that you couldn't fit on the head of a pin fell within the purview of this Isaac's schemes, if purviews are the things I'm thinking of. "Do I look like a quark to you?" I might have shouted, rising to my full height and indicating in no uncertain terms that neither I nor anyone else was put at risk by Isaac's plans, but where would that get me? True Climate-Change-Believer that he was, Norm Stradamus would merely shake his head in a mournful sort of way, believing that I was a lost lamb who failed to string along with the flock and that my lack of faith in his words of doom would lead to my undoing. I therefore opted for a slight change in the topic of conversation.

"What about Vera?" I asked.

"What about Vera?" he said, putting a bit of topspin on the word "about" in a way I hadn't.

"Will Vera be joining the assault?"

"It's not an assault," said Norm. "We plan to enter R'lyeh by stealth. Once we're there, we'll disconnect the ancients from the network and put an end to Isaac's plan. I expect that, once that's done, the Regent will want to confront Professor Newton himself. If everything goes as planned, I wouldn't want to be Isaac Newton tonight."

"Leaving aside the question of whether you would or wouldn't like to be Isaac Newton," I said, a touch impatiently, "I return to my previous question. You're going to R'lyeh. The Regent is going to R'lyeh. Some of the Regent's personal guard are going to R'lyeh. Rhinnick Feynman, not so much. But what of Vera? And for the matter of that, what of Oan?"

"We considered bringing Vera," said Norm, still wringing the hands like a champion toady, "but we decided it'd be better to leave her here. Too unpredictable."

"Ironical, what?" I said.

He stared at me, confused.

"Ironical that a person who sees the future would herself be unpredictable," I said, connecting the dots so that even a True Believer possessed of the meanest intellect could perceive them.

He didn't offer so much as a chuckle. Instead he responded in earnest.

"It was her gift of television — her ability to see the future — as well as her knowledge of R'lyeh itself that made us consider bringing Vera along with us. But on the balance the Regent felt she couldn't be trusted."

I raised a censorious brow and took in a lungful of air preparatory to come to this Vera's defence, for if there's any bird who could be counted on to speak the truth as she saw it, it was Vera. Norm Stradamus seemed to perceive my growing wrath and made a placating gesture.

"Sorry, no. I don't mean 'trusted' in that sense. I should have said 'relied upon,' O Hand of the—"

I glared at the man and he corrected himself post-haste.

"I mean, I should have said 'relied upon,' Mr. Feynman. Do

forgive me. The Regent felt that Vera mightn't be relied upon to carry out orders in a pinch. The Regent doesn't know her. Nor do I. And though it'll be a loss to be without her television, the Regent felt that we could rely on my own gift of prophecy."

"But I thought your soothsaying skill was more of the longish-term variety. Peer off into the distance, write a few cryptic stanzas revealing what's to come about several hundred years down the road, and leave them for all and sundry to misinterpret until some vaguely similar event has come to pass, then look back on it and say, 'What ho, Old Stradamus got it right.'"

He looked wounded for a moment but must have seen the justice of my remark.

"Even so," he said, shoulders slumping, "we cannot take Vera with us."

While this old prophet wouldn't have known it, his response had pleased me greatly. This assault on R'lyeh — or this bit of stealthy trespassing, whatever you'd like to call it — struck me as the sort of plan you might get out of a couple of hospice residents who'd been hitting the sauce all night. I mean to say, while Vera and I had managed to slip into R'lyeh once, this had been by pure chance, and we'd lucked into it by dint of one of Vera's handy on-the-spot predictions. Whatever views you hold about City Hall, you'll have to agree it's a high-security joint, and any plan to slip in undiscovered is fraught with peril — peril that I was happy to see that self and chums would avoid.

"Of course, we've already interviewed Vera thoroughly," he continued, "and asked her everything she recalls about your visit to R'lyeh. We've even pressed her to make predictions about the Regent's plan. She was most helpful. She was able to peer into the future and give us insights into guard deployments, security schedules, even a few passcodes that are sure to be highly useful. She seemed reluctant to help us, but the Regent can be most persuasive."

I hadn't liked the sound of that, and would have pressed the man for further and better particulars about the Regent's methods of persuasion, but again he charged ahead, seeming to be fully committed to his plan of hogging the conv.

"Oan, of course, will come along," he added, quickly. "She has proven herself a good and faithful servant of the church, and she understands the stakes. And of course she'll carry your banner. Although you won't be there in your capacity as — if you'll forgive me — as an icon of the church, she'll be there as your betrothed. Rest assured that your — excuse me, Mr. Feynman, are you feeling quite all right?"

I gripped the bedpost, for the room seemed to pirouette around me at the mention of my betrothal and the associated image of Oan waving the Feynman banner — not to mention Feynman waving the Oan banner — for the duration of what could be a lengthy sentence. The prospect of having the Feynman reputation linked with one as goofy as Oan caught me amidships, and something in my bearing and aspect seemed to convey this fact to Norm. It was still early in the day, but I'd have given my left kidney for another one of this soothsayer's patented tissue-restoring martinis.

"Speaking of Oan," I said, composing myself as best I could, "I've been wondering. Do your prophecies, or quatrains, or other future-delving writings have anything explicit to say about the planned nuptials?"

"I'm sorry, no," he said, abashed.

"How about something from the old stockpile?" I said. "Say, an old prophecy you haven't thought about in a while, but that, in the light of recent information, might be interpreted in a way that relates to self or Oan?"

"I . . . well, possibly," he said. "I mean, when Oan announced your betrothal I did peruse my earlier writings to see if any might be stretched to — or rather, reinterpreted in a way that might relate to the blessed news, but as yet I've been unsuccessful. I had intended to keep trying," he added, more abashedly than ever.

It has often been said of Rhinnick Feynman that, whatever his faults, he always bends an ear when opportunity comes knocking. Who was it who, when offered the merest hall pass while on his first sojourn in the hospice, parlayed this simple pass into a chance for self and others to take to themselves the wings of the dove and escape the hospice altogether? Who was it who, down several hands in a game of Brakkit against neophyte player Ian Brown, had made up several plausible rules on the spot to win the tournament? Feynman, R., that's who. And it was this same Feynman, R. who, having listened to Norm Stradamus take the blame for failing to dredge up any dusty prophecies relating to self and Oan, heard the gentle rapping of opportunity at my door.

"Spare no efforts!" I cried. "Strain every nerve! Return to your dusty journals! Dredge up your ancient files! Seek whatever you can find about yours truly. Anything at all. And then," I added, sneaking up to the true stratagem or scheme, "see if you can find anything at all about an unnamed man of mystery in Detroit Mercy Hospice. One who had a substantial career in that institution, but who may have — for reasons cloaked in mystery, or Authorial revision — been forgotten by those who knew him."

The man appeared unnerved by my sudden burst of enthusiasm. I gripped a shoulder and pressed on.

"Hear me out," I continued. "You must see if you can find any prophecies about this stranger — this unknown, forgotten character who lived in Detroit Mercy, hobnobbed with Zeus, bunked with Ian Brown, and embarked on many adventures within and beyond the hospice walls — and see if they match up at all with anything you know about me. See if your prophecies might be interpreted to suggest that I and he are one."

"You and he are one what?"

"One person, I mean. That I am that mysterious stranger."

"But why would a prophecy suggest you were some mysterious stranger? If you're speaking of the time of the Intercessor — when the Intercessor himself was housed in the hospice — then we need only turn to Oan to ask what she knows of this person. You see, at the time in question she was not only a member of the church flock, but also a trusted advisor at the hospice and head of Sharing Room activities."

None of this was news to me, of course, for as you know, I was at the hospice and had been crushed under Oan's iron heel over the course of innumerable hours of her Sharing Room disasters. At least, I had been there in one of the Author's prior versions of my biography. But as I think I'd mentioned before, I seemed to be the only person who remembered that particular chapter of the Feynman bio. Yet if some reminder could be found — some method of convincing Oan I had been her student, and one whom she had counted as a pain in the neck to end all pains in the neck — then this could go a long way toward convincing Oan to extricate herself from our betrothal. Keeping this goal in mind, I pressed on.

"Nevertheless, my dear High Priest," I said, striking while the iron was h., "I urge you to roll up your sleeves, press your nose to the grindstone, spit on the hands, and do whatever else it is that High Priests do when getting down to business and exerting maximum effort. Comb the archives! Leave no quatrain unturned! Assemble the eager, undergraduate acolytes keen to move to higher heights in the church! It is vital to my interests — nay, to those of the established church," I added, putting on some fancy touches, "that these references be found! Prophecies of the mysterious stranger, and the link between him and me, are your top priority!"

I mean to say, I recognize that this was all a bit thick, but if you're going to be stuck with the title of Hand of the Intercessor, you might as well squeeze from it whatever juice you can.

Norm seemed less enthusiastic than I'd hoped.

"Yes, well, of course, O Hand of the, er, that is to say, of course, Mr. Feynman. I'd be happy to conduct a search, and even to involve additional acolytes in the effort. The more of my prophecies we verify, the happier I am. It's just, well, you see, at the present moment—"

"You have other things to do," I said, showing my own gift for prophecy by finishing his sentence.

"Yes, Mr. Feynman. I do promise to review my prophecies, just as you suggest. But first I must attend to the trek to R'lyeh, and the effort to stop Professor Newton. These are now our primary goals. It's not that your wishes are unimportant. Far from it! It's just that the Regent believes Professor Newton's plans for Detroit must take priority, and I agree with her decision. I mean, Newton could destroy everything! He could radically change the way Detroit works! His efforts to change the climate could—"

I raised a silencing hand. I'd heard more than enough of this blighter's misguided babbling on the topic of Climate Change and the fallout of Isaac's plans, and couldn't bear to trouble the Feynman ears with another goofy pronouncement, however well intentioned.

"Have it your way," I said, and if I sighed a bit, what of it? "You busy yourself with the Isaac situation, and I'll hold down the fort—"

"Hold the fort," he said, interrupting.

"Excuse me?"

"You said you'd hold *down* the fort, Mr. Feynman. Forts don't need holding down. They merely need holding. As in, 'The fort is under siege. I'll continue to hold it against enemy intrusion while you pop off on some other mission.' That's what the expression means. One party holds the fort for those who occupy the fort that is under siege, so they'll still have possession of the fort when the other party returns. In the present instance, you'll hold the fort — referring to the Regent's home — while I'll go off to R'lyeh on my mission. 'Hold the fort.' Not 'hold down.'"

"A bit pedantic, what?"

"It's just, well, it's not as though the fort is going to float off into the sky," the chump continued. "It isn't a blimp. Forts are buildings. You'd only have to hold a fort *down* if—"

"Have it your way," I said, waving an exasperated hand. "I'll hold the fort. You buzz off to R'lyeh, unplug the frozen geezers, air your peeve at a maths professor, and I'll hold the fort without holding it down. I shall spend my time conferring with Vera or seeing what I might achieve on the Zeus or Terrence front."

I seem to have said something wrong, as one so often does. And the effect it had on Norm Stradamus was to intensify his hand-wringing, foot-shuffling, apologetic manner. He cast his eyes downward and seemed to blush beneath his beard.

"Ah, well, yes. You see, O Hand of the, er, O Mr. Feynman, that, well, I'm afraid you won't be able to see Vera or Terrence. The Regent has decreed that you're to stay in your room."

I goggled at the man. I mean to say, I hadn't read the occupational description of Hands of Intercessors before I'd landed the gig, but I'd assumed I was at least free to move about the joint on my own recognizance, as the expression is. I put these facts to Norm.

"I'm sorry," he began, and I remember thinking that I hadn't met someone so keen on apologizing since I'd last hobnobbed with Ian, who explained the habit by claiming to be something called a "Canadian." Perhaps Norm was Canadian too.

"I'm sorry, Mr. Feynman," he continued. "It's for your own safety. Strange things are afoot at present. Reality quakes — like the one we experienced in the Regent's dining room — are rearranging the world. Climate Change is afoot! Everything is unpredictable — even, if you don't mind my saying so, for me!"

He smiled as if to indicate this was comedy. Seeing that I was not impressed, he resumed his downcast expression and carried on. "In any case, you'll have to remain here, safe in your room."

"But dash it—"

"I'm sorry, Mr. Feynman. There are forces at work that you can't comprehend, and there isn't time to explain them. But rest assured that you're safe here — that the Regent has made provision for your protection. Isaac doesn't know the location of this home."

"But surely it'd be safe for me to roam the grounds, or at least move freely about the house, hobnobbing with my fellow guests and domestics."

"Sorry, no. The Regent says you're to be locked here in your room."

"Locked?" I ejaculated, appalled.

"I'm sorry, Mr. Feynman."

The thing about Feynmen is that, whatever the provocation, we know when, and when not, to press an issue. I could see that nothing was to be gained by bandying words with Norm Stradamus, so I acquiesced to his decree — or rather the Regent's, I suppose — that I remain stashed away in the Feynman storeroom for the nonce. At least I *appeared to* acquiesce: that was the genius of my plan. For after a few well-chosen words indicating my acquiescence, and a few more well-chosen words in the vein of goodbye-and-see-you-latering, and after hearing the lock click behind the departing Norm Stradamus, I hatched a plan to push along the secret Feynman agenda: a plan I'd put into motion just as soon as the coast was clear.

I knew straight away that it was an ingenious plan, largely because it was one of mine.

Chapter 26

The first step in the ingenious p. was, for a man of my unbridled and untamed nature, the most difficult step, for it involved a good deal of waiting around. Waiting around for most of a day. For I had to bide my time, locked securely in my HQ, until the Regent and her regiment of jackbooted sarcophagus-unpluggers had vacated the premises, giving me the space I required to get down to brass tacks and put the Feynman plan in motion. Only once the coast was clear could I get this show on the road.

One thing I've often noticed, and something I probably ought to have taken up with Isaac Newton when we had our tête-à-tête and he started babbling about time travel and other temporal whathaveyous, is what I like to call the relativistic nature of time. Perhaps you've noticed it too, viz, time's habit of whooshing by like a high-strung rabbit when you're engaged in some pastime that grips the senses, and, by sharp contradistinction, time's alternate practice of dragging its heels and oozing along at the pace of a unionized snail when you're fed up to the gills with whatever it is you're doing and wish it would end instanter. I imagine that the Author, in His wisdom, wished to bathe the world in irony when He arranged matters this way, making the hours whoosh along like a rocket ship when you want them to slow down and then slam on the brakes whenever you want time to stomp on the gas and pick up the pace. This latter aspect of time, viz, its inclination to creep along and smell the roses whenever you're eager for it to zip along, is

— based on my own empirical observations — most frequently experienced during sermons, university lectures, and Detroit Mercy Sharing Room sessions. But the point I'm making now, in case you were wondering, is that I observed the same phenomenon in my present situation. The time between Norm's departure from my room, and the eventual departure of the Regent and her gang, weighed heavily upon yours truly, and seemed to drag along for at least a geological epoch or seven.

I tried to assist matters by whacking up an indoor game, one that involved coaxing Fenny to push bits of paper past a goalpost I'd constructed from bars of soap. This occupied a quarter of an hour before Fenny rejected the task as pointless and scurried off to amuse himself elsewhere. I then read a quaint, printed copy of the *Detroit Daily Monitor* and followed this up with a solid hour spent in a bubble bath — one that was greatly enhanced by the presence of an impressively buoyant duck. A rubber one, as I recall.

William blew in a couple of times, first bringing lunch and then bringing tea. On both of these visits, he filled the air with that flowery prose of his, and then blew out, locking the door behind him. During the second of these encounters I briefly toyed with the notion that, when the time came for me to head for the hills, I could simply press the bell to summon William, biff him about the upper slopes once he'd poked his nose in the room, and then ho for the open spaces, perhaps trousering his keys for future use. But it has often been said of Rhinnick Feynman that, whatever the possible advantages to self, he takes pains to preserve the innocent and keeps them out of the crossfire. The plan of striking William with some blunt instrument did, I'll admit, afford one quick route to freedom, but it would also leave the aforementioned William with a lump on his pumpkin. And it might also, given the Regent's temper and refusal to see sense, cost William his current stream of employment income. Thus I resolved to stick with what we might call "Plan A."

At long last the time came.

It was about 8 p.m., at the time of quiet evenfall, when William oiled in with a nightcap — the potable sort, not the kind you put on your head. I seized the day, as it were, and, through a spot of what must have seemed to William to be nothing more than idle conversation, I coaxed out of this well-spoken butler the crucial information that the Regent and her troops had left the building.

I wasted no further time. Once William had buttled off elsewhere, I shoved myself into a well-tailored suit which I found hanging in the closet — presumably something the Regent had set aside with a view to upholstering yours truly — and prepared to make my escape. And as much as I'd like to portray my bit of escaping as one of those daring spots of adventure you read about in action novels — the sort where the hero dangles from helicopters or dives into volcanoes — the truth is that I escaped the room by using one of my less widely publicized talents, viz, my skill at picking locks. Fenny helped. And between the two of us we tripped the lock in the space of about five minutes, legging it for the open spaces with a song — albeit a fairly quiet song — upon our lips.

I was cognizant of the fact that, by violating the Regent's edict and going awol from my room, I was probably putting a toe across the line of some cultural norm concerning the proper conduct of guests in houses. To be weighed against this was not only the fact that my absence was necessary if I was to have any hope of pushing along the plans I had for Zeus, Vera, and self, but also the fact that if I remained *in statu quo*, as the expression is, I was as likely as not to die of boredom — at least, insofar as death is possible in Detroit. So I dismissed any qualms that might have furrowed an etiquette expert's brow, and buzzed off, Fenny in hand. Or rather in pocket.

I realize, at this juncture, that having described the first step in my ingenious plan, viz, waiting around for the coast to clear before buzzing off to freedom, I've neglected to tell my public what the ingenious plan was. At this stage in my affairs, it became clear that matters on the Isaac Newton front were being covered by the Regent and her cronies, and I could continue to regard that issue as having been handled or rendered moot. Whatever Abe might have felt at the outset of this journey, Isaac was now a spent force, and nothing to be feared by anyone at all, let alone by the all-powerful mayor of Detroit. To be sure, Norm and the Regent had fallen into Abe's error and mistaken Isaac's quantum tootling for something fit for the bold-faced headlines, but they would soon learn, from their foray into R'lyeh, that Isaac's scientific musings amounted to less than a hill of beans. Perhaps the evidence they gathered en route to this discovery would be useful in showing Abe, in his turn, that Isaac could be safely ignored. I was on to other things: reminding Zeus of who he was, checking up on Nappy, checking in on Vera, and — the matter currently at the top of the Feynman agenda — extricating myself from a pair of accidental betrothals.

It was on this last point, viz, my attempt to escape the scaffold, that my current plans focused, for it occurred to me, when Norm was nattering on about prophecies and church doctrines, that there might be something in these doctrines, perhaps relating to the church's rites of marriage, that I could use to throw a spanner into the works with respect to my impending nuptials with Oan. Perhaps we'd find some rule or commandment that prevented the hitching up of mere parishioners with Hands of Intercessors, if you follow, or possibly some scriptural statement that it was an abomination to marry a man you'd met in a hospice — you know how these religious doctrines are: highly specific and arbitrary. Don't mix natural and handmade fibres, don't smoke reefers in the church, don't play tennis against left-handers, don't wear white after Abe Day passes, that sort of thing. So I'd resolved to do some digging through the doctrine, as it were.

Norm had mentioned, if you'll recall, that the Regent was fairly new in her affiliation with the Church of O. This had given me yet another ingenious idea. I intuited that her personal quarters would be a good place to find church literature, the newly converted being, in my experience, particularly zealous when it comes to delving into doctrine. So I'd rather cleverly planned to make my way to the Regent's quarters, dig through her personal effects, find whatever I could about the rules of the Church of O, and hope against hope that something in those rules could be used to cure Oan of her love for Rhinnick or otherwise convince her to cheese the notion of making herself my better half.

Of course, you can't go doing a thing like that without help from your local psychic — or at least you can, but why would you bother? — so I resolved to grab Vera along the way and take her with me. I could ask if she foresaw any roadblocks, implore her to detect any oncoming guards, or possibly, once her brain was jump-started by me explaining my plan to her, she might use her television to see how the whole thing turns out and then be in a posish to give me the lowdown on whatever information we would have learned in the Regent's quarters, saving us the trouble and expense of actually going through with it. Although, come to think of it, I'm not entirely sure that soothsaying works in the manner described. In any event, if I was breaking into the Regent's quarters and seeking information, it was plausible that a certain amount of datapad hacking or password guessing would be required, and Vera was singularly gifted when it came to anything in the nature of fiddling with machines. So as I said, I resolved to hitch up *chez* Vera en route to the Regent's lair.

Having recently delved my current environs and the surrounding halls with the aid of Norm Stradamus, it was for me the work of a moment to wend my way to Vera's room, ducking into doorways or behind trash bins whenever anyone came bumbling in my direction and threatened to cross the Feynman path. And while you might be thinking that all of this dodging and ducking would take its toll on my psyche and wound the spirit, not to mention what it would do to the trouser creases, you'd be mistaken: for inasmuch as all of this furtive skulking wrinkled the garments, it did convey me safely to Vera's door, where I managed to fetch up without provoking so much as a peep out of anyone who might have raised a hue and cry should Feynman's absence from his room have been noted.

I was about to knock gently on the doorway — loud enough to be detected within, yet not so loudly as to summon the local rozzers and land myself in the jug — when the door opened before my knuckles reached it. And I reflected, as it did so, how dashed convenient it was to be pals with a psychic pipsqueak who had advance notice of one's comings and goings.

I slipped into the room, where Vera and self exchanged a few cordialities before getting down to brass tacks.

"Have they gone?" she asked, agog.

"Like the wind," I said. "They blew out an hour or so ago, intent on foiling Isaac's plans."

"Good," she said. "So what do we do?"

For me — as it would have been for any man of sensitivity and fine feelings — this was a moment of the gravest difficulty. For while this Vera had become, partially due to necessity and partially due to pure merit, a close friend and confidante to whom I could generally spill the beans and entrust the files marked "top secret," the act of filling her in on my hope to escape the grip of

Oan's matrimonial plans still was likely to fall within the statutory definition of bandying a woman's name, and we Feynmen shrink from bandying women's names. Moreover, as one who also considered herself affianced to Rhinnick Feynman, Vera was hopelessly afflicted by what is known as a conflict of interest, and therefore not among those to whom I should, according to the book of rules, confide my plans. But to be weighed against this was Vera's general good-eggishness and skill at fishing a pal out of the soup. And the soup, at this juncture, was what I was deeply immersed in, and it was a time for all good men — or in this case, women — to come to the aid of the party and chip in wherever they may. So I decided, on balance, to fill this Vera in on my current plans with respect to the Oan/Feynman betrothal.

I laid out my ultimate goal, explaining my hope to extricate self from this engagement without causing any embarrassment or shame to either the party of the first part, viz, me, or the party of the second, viz, Oan.

She seemed to weigh this.

"Why not tell her you're off the market?" she said.

"Off . . . off the market?" I said, tremulously, for I feared where this bit of conversation may lead. I mean to say, I knew that this Vera also saw herself as one who was affianced to yours truly, and while she hadn't made a fuss on hearing the news that I was also betrothed to Oan, I was reluctant to lean on one betrothal as my reason for ending another. The party to the second betrothal is bound to expect a certain amount of follow-through if you go about using these pending nuptials as an excuse to return other putative fiancées to store.

"Married to someone else, I mean," she said.

"Oh, ah."

"Just tell her you got drunk one day last month and accidentally ended up hitched to someone else, and that you've been too embarrassed to tell her about it 'til now. That'll let you out."

"No good," I said, although I did applaud the St. Bernard spirit displayed by this young prune, who was doing her best to give aid and comfort and map out the path to safety. "Wouldn't work with a bird like Oan. She'd have me before a Justice of the Peace before you could say what ho, and would be yelling for annulments on every side. No. I need another method of oiling out."

"You could always tell her you have a disease."

"A disease?"

"Oh, you know, something hideous and communicable. Nothing puts a person off a prospective marriage partner like the prospect of catching something that leads to open sores and oozing pu—"

"Desist, young boll weevil!" I cried, pointing a chastening pen directly at her upturned nose, "for not only is your suggestion, if it qualifies as a suggestion, unfit for ventilating in mixed company, but it's also dashed impractical. I mean, simply rub two brain cells together and see the flaws in your specious plan. Point 1: I haven't any communicable diseases at present, and I've no wish to contract one for the purposive of evading matrimonial doom. Point B: well, to be frank I've forgotten what point B was, but rest assured that it was stellar and supports my view that your unspeakable idea is fatheaded and ill conceived."

She laughed a silvery laugh at this juncture, for reasons that escaped me altogether. Females are, in my experience, singularly gifted in this respect, viz, emitting silvery laughs in the absence of any cause.

"Fine," she said, apparently gripped by the force of my arguments, "what's this big plan of yours then? Lay it out and I'll poke some holes."

I laid it out.

She mused a bit.

"Hmmm," she said, and then she did a bit more musing. At length she contorted her map into something resembling amused surprise and said, "You're not the chump I took you for!"

"When did you take me for a chump?" I asked.

"I dunno, sometime last Tuesday. I forget what gave me the idea. But I think this plan might work! Let's get a move on."

So we did. And within two shakes we were standing at the threshold of the Regent's personal study, where we picked the lock instanter, and got down to our derring-do.

Chapter 27

"That's odd," I said.

"What's odd?" said Vera.

Well, she rather had me there, as I wasn't sure precisely what it was that struck me as odd. Something was definitely amiss, but for the life of me, I couldn't put my finger on what it was.

I applied the neuroglia, as I believe they're called.

"Hmm," I said, and meant it.

I wonder if you've ever had the experience of having your attention grabbed by something conspicuous by its abs. I'm not referring to something obvious, like when you set your sandwich down on a hospice table for a moment, busy yourself with some distraction, and turn back to find that it's been spirited away or perhaps wolfed down by a roving Napoleon. No, I mean that rummy feeling of wrongness you sometimes get when things don't quite match up with what you expected. It was that way with me now.

"Rummy," I said.

"What are you on about?" said Vera, crossing arms and tapping a foot or two.

I was, at long last, able to fill the pipsqueak in.

"Pathetic fallacy," I said.

"Pathetic whatacy?" said Vera.

"I thought that might be a bit above your head," I said, in that erudite way of mine. "It's a literary thingummy you get when the atmosphere of a place reflects a person's mood or

essence. A storm raging in the background while your protagonist throws a fit. The sun smiling through the clouds whenever
Feynman takes the stage. A heavy fug when a schoolmaster
enters stage left. The person reflected in the place, I mean to
say. At least I think that's what it means. Though why it should
be called pathetic, or what's fallacious about it, is beyond me."

She betrayed a certain impatience. I set to the task of connecting dots.

"It's just this space," I said, waving around the Regent's
study. "An utter lack of pathetic fallacy. Here we have the private lair of a testy bird prone to flying off the handle, one whose
habits include shooting thunderbolts from her eyes, breathing
fire, chewing broken bottles, and howling at passing moons, yet
what do we find when we enter her private sanctum? A house of
horrors? An armoury filled with torture devices, assorted weap-
ons, and the wall-mounted heads of snarling fauna? No. We
find a cozy little book-nook bedecked with lace, crystal whatnots, a couple of decorative vases, a fussily carved mahogany
reading desk, and all the fixings. A gracefully appointed, fairly
luxurious room equipped for contemplation and study, and one
you'd expect to be haunted by a well-to-do librarian. Not a sul-
len and temperamental ancient who organizes nightly assaults
on City Hall or unprovoked attacks on mathematicians."

Vera looked at me as though something was dribbling out
the side of my mouth, but reason must have told her my remarks
were on the nose, as the expression is. For here was a room
that was tidy, artistically designed, impressively furnished, and
adorned with a couple of restful fireplaces and numerous shelves
of books. Not the sanctum of a scowling conqueror or hater-of-
her-species. It was also touch higher-tech than I might have
imagined given the rest of the décor in the Regent's home, this
room featuring a number of shiny black screens and other doodads possibly drawn from the I-Ware line. The aforementioned

reading desk seemed to serve as tech-central, being strewn with datapads and a few additional techish thingummies which I couldn't readily name. There were also draperies, onyx statues, a few soapstone thingummies, and earthen-tone paintings depicting various desert scenes.

One of the lower-tech items on the desk seemed to draw the Feynman eye. It was a large, empty vase constructed of some thickish species of porcelain, positioned on the desk amid the technological doodads. It stood about two feet high — above the desktop, I mean — and was festooned in that peculiar pictographic writing you sometimes get; the kind featuring squiggles and dots associated with the occasional doodle of a dog or cat or a chap who looks all right from the neck down but is topped by the head of a crocodile or other surprising fauna. All gibberish of course, but eye-catching. I mentioned it to Vera.

Vera reminded me that we weren't here on a sightseeing tour, and that porcelain vases, however liberally emblazoned with pictographic gibberish, weren't featured on this evening's agenda paper. We accordingly wasted no further time staring about the joint and breathing in the surroundings, but instead applied ourselves to the task at hand, self haring toward a bookshelf in search of any literature spelling out the doctrines of the Church of O, and Vera — as is her wont — buzzing straight for the machinery scattered atop the desk, grabbing up a datapad or two, and pressing keys. I had just started reading assorted spines — of books, I mean — when Vera yipped from the nor'east.

"I've found a file about the Regent!" she exclaimed.

"She keeps files about herself? A bit narcissistic, what?"

"You carry your own character sketch with you," she said, emitting another silvery laugh. And I remember thinking that, for one who had been mindwiped in the not-too-distant past, she had an impressive knack for using her televisual powers to dredge up inconvenient slices of my past whenever they might refute a point I was making, catch me in a bit of hypocrisy, or prove a charge of pot-calling-kettles-black. This is a trait I've frequently noticed in members of the female sex, whether mindwiped or not, viz, their knack for keeping track of inconvenient bits of history and airing them out precisely at a time when you'd prefer they remain unventilated. I've often wondered whether this talent finds its seat on the second X chromosome.

I did the manly thing and changed the subject.

"Anything interesting?" I asked, pointing toward the data-pad with the apex of my southeast brow.

"Her real name, for starters."

This grabbed me. Hitherto the Regent had been known, to me at least, exclusively as "the Regent," and I'd only met two people in my puff who chose to be called by a job description: the City Solicitor — a chap it's always best to avoid — and this Regent. The former, whose name turned out to be Plato, probably kept his name under wraps because it sounded like something you'd name your pet dog, or perhaps a small celestial body. As for why the latter would keep her name on the q.t., as the expression is, who could say?

"What is it?" I asked.

"Neferneferuaten," said Vera.

"Gesundheit!"

"Neferneferuaten," she repeated, and I perceived that she was speaking.

"Never what?"

"Not never, Nefer. Neferneferuaten."

"Say that again, slowly. I fear it got past me again."

"Neferneferuaten."

"Neferneferuaten, you say?" I said, testing it out on the tongue.

"That's right," said Vera.

"What kind of a name is that?"

"The kind of name that makes you have everyone call you 'Regent,' I suppose. It says here that she manifested around four thousand years ago."

This surprised me. I requested amplification.

"Four thousand years?"

"That's what it says."

"She's *not* a decamillennial, then?"

"No. Not by at least six thousand years."

"That'd make her — what — a quadramillennial?"

"I don't think that's a thing," said Vera.

"Of course it's a thing," I riposted. "But what it isn't is an age associated with any special power or status. This Regent, we've been told, has some share of an ancient's power," I added, a tad perplexed. "A bit young for that, isn't she?"

"She is," said Vera.

"Then again," I said, for one likes to be broad-minded, "I seem to recall the City Solicitor being rather youngish for one who could bend Detroit to his will, and Penelope — Ian's wife — had been here only a few days before rising to near omnipotence, shaking Detroit's foundations and — in what I've always thought was an act of civic improvement — filling the place with Tontos."

"That's true," said Vera. "So you suppose the Regent's something of a prodigy, like them?"

"I think the word 'anomaly' is mot juster."

Vera weighed this.

"But she doesn't seem like Penelope or Plato," she said. "None of this world-shattering business."

"It's true," I said. "She hasn't a tithe of Penelope's power. If she did, she'd snap her fingers and render Newton a spent force, possibly puffing him out of existence, or maybe turning

306

him into a fig. But I suppose these things are graded on a curve. Let's call her fairly anomalous, but not so dashed anomalous as to be counted amongst the omnipotent godlike beings, say, Abe, Penelope, and Plato, who go about leaving their footprints on planets and shifting reality with their whims."

Vera seemed to have stopped listening, her attention having been captured by some other tidbit of information on the pad.

"It looks like she kept a diary," she said, nimbly scrolling through a few screens' worth of data. "More of a manifesto, really. A lot of complaining that Detroit isn't up to snuff."

"A bit of a negative Neferneferuaten, then?"

Vera issued an "mmm-hmmm," which I took to be affirmative.

"She's definitely a princk," said Vera, still running an eye or two over the display. "She seems to remember an awful lot about the beforelife. Before she came to Detroit she was ultra-powerful. Her word was law. She commanded armies, and she had wealth beyond measure."

"Good for her," I said.

"And for some reason she expected to bring her wealth with her when she left the beforelife and rule over everyone in the hereafter."

"The herenow, you mean."

"The whatnow?"

"The herenow. If she regarded this particular slice of terrain as the hereafter while in the beforelife, it would be the here-now now that she's here. QED."

"Whatever," said Vera, waving at me in a dismissive sort of way. "Anyway, it says she felt her wealth, servants, and status would come with her when she — well, when she crossed over into Detroit — and that she'd be worshipped and adored by the people here. With every fibre of her being — that's how she puts it — she felt as though she'd be in charge."

"Bit of a letdown, what?"

"I don't know about that," said Vera. "She's rich. And she's powerful enough to serve as a patron of the church and fund its attempts to reach the beforelife. Just not quite as rich or powerful as she'd hoped."

How like life, I remember thinking, and I reflected on how dashed difficult things must be for someone in the Regent's posish. I mean to say, had she washed up in Detroit expecting to wait tables, drive cabs, tote barges, lift bales, or engage in any other form of honest, character-building labour, she'd have been over the moon to find that she was destined to become a landed proprietress with patronages in her gift. But there again, if she *had* manifested expecting to be a proletarian slice of the huddled masses, she mightn't have acquired the wealth and power that she had amassed in sackfuls since her manifestation — expectations being, if you follow me, pretty foundational to the way things seem to turn out in Detroit. Aim too low, you get what you aim for. Aim too high, you risk disappointment — but even if you miss, you come out a dashed sight further ahead than you would have done had you aimed too low. The way your life turns out in Detroit seems to depend rather heavily on the way it started out. Philosophical, what?

"Abe's drawers!" exclaimed Vera, interrupting my spot of musing.

"What about them?" I asked.

"I was looking for information about the Napoleons. Where they're being kept, for starters."

"What have you found?"

"This explains what the Church of O is doing with them!"

"We already know that," I said, tolerantly. "Nappy explained. They're taking blood samples and things and trying to replicate their connection to the beforelife, of all the dashed silly ideas."

"But there's more!" said Vera, who had the air of one who would have danced a couple of urgent steps had she not taken a seat behind the desk. "They're torturing them! All of them! They started with Jack, but weren't happy with the results. They're still trying with him, but also moving on to the rest!"

"Egad!" I said, and I meant it. "But why? That's the real question confronting us now, alongside 'how do we get them to stop'?"

"It's all part of their plan to reach the beforelife," she said. "They think Napoleons have what the Regent calls 'a specific, limited version' of the power held by ancients — the power to shape Detroit. It says here that, on some deep level, all Napoleons expect to reincarnate. At their core, that's how they expect the world to behave. It's a key part of their disorder. They believe they'll be reborn. The Regent believes this expectation helps to shape the world around them but that it's only one piece of the puzzle. The missing element is *desire* — you can't just expect to leave Detroit, you have to *want* it."

"Want it?" I said, agog.

"Think of Penelope. She didn't *expect* Detroit to behave in any particular way — she didn't know Detroit existed. She just manifested here wanting Ian to be protected. It was Penelope's desire that changed the world to keep him safe — creating Tonto to be his guide, preserving his memories of the before-life, all of the things Penelope did. The Regent thinks it works the same way with Napoleons. It's only when they really *want* to leave Detroit, and somehow believe that it's possible, that they trigger whatever process leads to reincarnation. Let me read it to you," she added, clearing the throat preparatory to a bit of datapad reading. And what she read to me was this:

> *In-depth probing has established that all Napoleons, whether conscious of this fact or not, believe that they are destined to be reborn. They manifest with the expectation that their time in Detroit is temporary,*

and that they will return to the beforelife at some junc-
ture. Nevertheless, while all Napoleons do reincarnate,
each one does so infrequently, generally less than once
per century. Our hypothesis, based on questioning and
examination of the Napoleon Jack, is that the event
of reincarnation requires some trigger stimulus that
presents itself infrequently. This trigger, it seems to me,
is desire: A Napoleon may always believe that he or
she will be reborn into the beforelife but does not do
so until this reincarnation — or at least a departure
from Detroit — becomes that Napoleon's dearest wish.
Only by forcing these Napoleons to wish for their own
rebirth can we hope to observe the reincarnation pro-
cess. This is why we have instituted—

"Oh, Rhinnick!" she cried, setting down the machinery,
"we can't let them torture the Napoleons. Think of Nappy!
They're going to try to force her and the other Napoleons to
wish they could *die*. They want to make their lives so hideous
that they want to leave Detroit and be reborn!"

"And when this happens," I added, testing out the idea in
the Feynman circuits, "they'll be in a posish to witness reincarnation first-hand, jot down their observations, and have a crack
at reproducing the procedure. An ingenious plan, what?"

She didn't subscribe to my assessment.

"It isn't ingenious!" she cried. "It's horrible!"

"Oh, that goes without saying," I said. "Or rather it would
have gone without saying apart from the fact you've now said it."

"We have to stop them!" said Vera. "We have to do whatever
it takes!"

I had not, of course, come to the Regent's study in search
of bread crumbs leading us toward another ruddy quest but
had instead made the trip in search of data that would help

release yours truly from his honourable obligations when it came to marrying Oan — a fate that it was my own dearest wish to escape — though whether or not I'd have accepted reincarnation to do so is something I hadn't yet considered. But the point I'm making, if you were wondering, is that I was knee-deep in research designed to further my own interests and was now being presented with this detour — being "sidetracked," if that's the expression — toward a quest to free the Napoleons from their fate. And these Napoleons, as I think I've mentioned before, included the pipsqueak Nappy, one whom I'd long counted among those listed on the roster of Feynman pals.

If there's one thing for which Rhinnick Feynman has been praised above all others, it's casting a blind eye toward his own trials and tribulations when the time comes to help a pal in trouble. Whatever rocks and hard places present themselves to Feynman, however harshly winds might blow and crack their cheeks, he scoffs and waves his troubles aside whenever he spots a pal in any species of soup. And these Napoleons were undoubtedly up to their noses in the bouillon. It may have taken half a jiffy for me to reach a decision, but no more than half a jiffy, and that only because it took a while to process all the data.

"Well of course we have to help them," I said. "And if this means I end up marrying Oan, well, so be it."

The deep emotion of this moment seemed to get the best of Vera, who rose from her chair like a pheasant rocketing out of the underbrush, and flung her arms about me, a procedure which I'd gladly have avoided. But I understood the welter of emotions and patted her head cordially, reminding myself that any greater showing of camaraderie might be mistaken for something else, casting a further seal upon the Feynman glamour and convincing this young prune — another who saw herself as a future Feynman spouse — that there could be no better plan than hearing the wedding bells ring out while lock-ing elbows with yours truly.

After a heartbeat or two I wriggled out of the embrace. Vera, for her part, suddenly gave me one of those wide-eyed stares you see when someone sits on a tack, and then flung herself deskward, disappearing under the thing like a diving duck. I blinked for a second or two before discovering the motive for this sudden mobility.

Clumping footsteps. Clumping footsteps which were com-ing in our direction, being presently somewhere down the hall but making rapid progress toward the Regent's study door.

Chapter 28

Keys jangled. Locks turned. The study door blew open. It ought to have creaked ominously, but once again pathetic fallacy, if that means what I think it does, appeared to have taken the night off.

The clumper's identity was revealed. At least, it was revealed to me, this famed clumper and opener-of-doors being one who didn't himself have any idea who he really was.

"Zeus!" I cried.

"Terrence," he said, and he followed this up with, "What are you doing in the Regent's private study, Mr. Feynman?"

Whatever it is that Isaac says holds the universe together, keeping its various ingredients from flying apart at the seams, I'm fairly certain that the one primordial constant — the singular force that makes everything tick over and gives the world its form — is the force of irony. I've already noted its habit of rearing its head and messing up my plans several times in this very volume. And here it was, at it again. At the moment of going to press, the core irony was this: I'd spent many a long day on the lookout for my old pal Zeus, and it was now, one of the few times when his presence operated against my policy, that he came bumbling up the hall and through the door in that galumphing way of his.

"What are you doing here, Mr. Feynman?" he repeated.

I caught scent of an opportunity, and ad-libbed.

"I'm looking for proof!" I said.

"Proof?" said Zeus.

"Of your identity. I mentioned before that you're a longtime buddy of mine. You don't remember this because you managed to get in a spot of bother with Socrates who wiped your brain and dished your memories. But my memories are intact, and I perfectly recollect that you are Zeus, you're my best pal, you once lived as a small terrier, and you formerly looked upon Detroit Mercy as your principal address. I surmised that the Regent might have proof of your ID here in her study, so I came for a bit of sleuthing. No luck so far, but the procedure had just begun."

A look of patient understanding suddenly crossed the honest fellow's map — a look I wouldn't have expected.

"It's all right, Mr. Feynman," he said in a cooing voice, while gently patting the Feynman shoulder with one of his ham-sized palms. "I understand. You've been drinking again."

"I haven't!"

"You're pie-eyed," he added.

"I am not!"

"Let me take you to your room."

"I'm as sober as a judge," I protested, "one of the soberer ones, I mean, and I'm intent on proving conclusively that you're Zeus. Perhaps I can joggle your brain cells now that you've had some time to get used to the idea. Have you no memory at all of your life before being press-ganged into the Regent's service?"

"No, Mr. Feynman. Now come with me."

"But . . . but . . . surely you must remember something. A pedantic little potato named Ian Brown? His super-heroic guide, Tonto Choudhury? Our own battle with Socrates and Plato?"

He seemed to weigh this, and gave me a puzzled look, as though coming to terms with something.

"You don't smell like alcohol," he said, indicative of the fact that he still had the wrong idea.

"Of course I don't!" I riposted.

"You really aren't drunk, are you?" he said, possibly recognizing a marked lack of the symptoms. "You really do think I'm someone you used to know."

"You are, dash it! Someone I still know today. Don't you remember life in the hospice? Hours spent playing Brakkit? Sharing Room sessions? Matron Bikerack? Standing guard at the file-room?"

"I've already told you, Mr. Feynman, I don't remember anything before the Regent took me in."

"Your life as a terrier, then. How do you feel about cats? Or postal workers?"

"Come with me, Mr. Feynman," he said. "You're not supposed to be out of your room."

"Of course I am," I protested. "I'm free to move about as I please."

"The Regent gave us strict orders."

"I'm the Hand of the ruddy Intercessor! Not Prisoner Number TK421!" I riposted, recollecting how dashed easy it is to invoke a title that's supposed to carry privilege, even when that title generally gives one the pip.

"I'm sorry, Mr. Feynman, we have orders. You'll have to come with me. And now that I've found you out of your room, I'll have to write a full report for the Regent."

I mourned in spirit for the poor fish, as I knew what it was to have an administrative task chucked upon you through no fault of your own. I regretted that I'd been the cause of extra tedium. But on the cue "now that I've found you out of your room," he had touched upon a point of interest that I wished to explore.

"Now that you mention it," I said, "how did you come to find me at all? I took every conceivable precaution. I stayed out of sight, and hid my tracks. No one caught a whiff of Feynman skulking the halls."

"A light shone from under the door," he said.

"Dash it!"

"And I heard voices, too," he added, making a judgmental face which suggested I wasn't entirely cut out for cloak-and-daggering.

I contrived to look confused.

"V-v-voices?" I said, "how do you mean, voices? I'm here alone. I may have soliloquized a bit. Perhaps you heard me talking to myself."

"You were talking to Miss Vera," he said.

"I wasn't!" I riposted.

"She's hiding under the desk," he added, patiently, extending the long arm of the law in the direction of Vera's hiding place and pointing it out with the showmanship of a chief inspector revealing the ID of the Masked Marauder. "She's been there all this time," he added, patiently.

And I remember thinking, as he said this, that if Zeus had any fault worthy of censure, it's that he was a touch too observant for his own good.

"But dash it!" I began, though I'm forced to admit that what I was going to say next was a bit of a mystery. It seemed like a fair cop to me, with nothing left for me to do but turn myself in and throw myself on the mercy of the Zeus. I was saved the trouble, though, when Vera rose from her little nook beneath the desk, looking a bit like that Venus person stepping out of her clam.

Zeus and I, each in our turn, swivelled our beans in her direction.

"It's no use," she said, in a pale, saint-like voice. "He's on to us."

"On to us?" I asked.

"Yes. He must have been told."

"Been told what?" asked Zeus. And I was glad he did, for I was foggy on this point, too.

"That we're Napoleons," said Vera.

"WHAT?" I cried.

"There's no use hiding it," said Vera. "The Regent must have already told Terrence what she discovered through her research: the two of us are Napoleons who've been hiding our identities. She must have informed him that she plans to have us locked up with the rest of them. That's why we escaped our rooms," she added, turning a plaintive face Zeusward. "We came here to steal any evidence she might have. We're so sorry to have troubled you. It was our only hope of escape."

This seemed to puzzle the colossal former dog, for he now uttered the words "you're . . . Napoleons?" in a halting manner, as though subjecting them to a taste test, while corrugating the brow.

This Zeus, as you probably already know, was no dead-from-the-neck-up dumb brick, despite appearances. People often assume that any extra-large-sized bimbo with pumpkin-shaped biceps, legs thicker than tree trunks, and a chest that crosses multiple postal districts is a spent force when it comes to anything that might be deemed an intellectual feat. People often made this same assumption of Zeus — but it wasn't warranted. He wasn't dull by any stretch. He was what you might call a careful thinker. A slow, plodding, freight-trainish thinker who took a while to build up a good head of steam, but who managed to process data thoroughly and generally came to sound conclusions after spending an hour or two assiduously applying the bean. And I recognized, as a result of our long association, the symptoms of Zeus's data-processing now. You could hear the gears turning, and I was reminded of that snatch of verse that said "though the mills of someoneorother grind slowly, they grind exceeding small," or words to that effect.

He contorted the mouth and squinted the eyes in a way suggesting that he wasn't, at the moment of going to press, quite ready to string along with Vera's claims.

She redoubled her efforts.

"That's right!" she said. "You must have suspected. Why else would the Regent keep us locked away? She suspected it, too. But she wasn't in a position to prove it until tonight. I thought she'd have told you by now. Perhaps she planned on telling you after her raid on City Hall."

"But Mr. Feynman's . . . not a Napoleon," said Zeus. "He's . . . well, he's the Hand of the Intercessor. The Regent told me so."

"You can imagine how shocked the Regent was to find that the Hand of the Intercessor was a Napoleon!" said Vera. "Shocked and angry, I'd imagine. I suppose you'll have no choice, now, but to stick us into the cells with the other Napoleons," she concluded, shrugging a shoulder or two in a fairly good impersonation of the Napoleonic shrug. Gallic, I think they call it.

We Feynmen are pretty quick-witted, and my grey cells finally managed to process all of the convoluted data that was whizzing about the room. The mists cleared. I saw all, including what this soothsaying pipsqueak was driving at. It was a ruse, and by no means the worst of them. She hoped, by convincing Zeus that she and self were Napoleons, to have us deposited with the rest of the Napoleons, where the two of us might be in a posish to make some tactical moves. And because we Rhinnicks are quick thinkers, it was for me the work of an instant to dive in head first and string along with a bit of corroborating evidence.

"*J'ai besoin d'un pamplemousse!*" I declared.

"What in Abe's name does that mean?" said a puzzled-looking Zeus, and I remember thinking that he rather had me there. It was just something I'd once heard Napoleon Number One say in the midst of a game of Brakkit. Or possibly in one of the hospice cooking classes. I couldn't be sure. But I remember thinking it sounded impressive, and it felt rather pleasant rolling off the Feynman tongue.

"Zere is no use," said Vera, unleashing a hitherto hidden talent as a Napoleonic impressionist. "We might as well drop ze pretence. We are caught and will offère no furzer reseestance."

Dashed impressive of her, I thought, to pull that off on short notice. Zeus seemed less taken with the performance, though, for rather than clapping his hands and requesting an encore or two, as a Napoleon might have done, he merely sighed one of those sighs which seem to come up from the soles of the feet, closed his eyes, and pinched the bridge of his nose, a procedure I've seen many times before, generally when people feel they've had more than the recommended adult dose of Feynman.

"Look," he said, "I don't know what's going on here, but you have to get back to your rooms. Enough of this Napoleon business."

"But ze proof eez right 'ere!" said Vera.

"Where?" said Zeus.

"On zis datapad!" said Vera, pointing out one of the instruments laying face-up on the desk.

Zeus bent down to examine it.

"I don't see any proof, biff."

He didn't actually *say* "biff." That was the sound of Vera sloshing him on the back of the bean with the heavy vase which had hitherto been atop the Regent's desk. I suppose the word "biff" doesn't do it justice, as it was more reminiscent of the eardrum-shattering crashes that the famous bull must have made when charging about the china shop — although why the bull was in there is a mystery. I mean to say, he can't have been shopping. But however you'd like to describe it, this loud crash was followed by the sound of pottery shards tinkling to the floor and then a final, dull thud, this one caused by Zeus collapsing floorward where he now lay, looking peaceful.

"Vera!" I cried.

"What?" she riposted.

"You can't go beaning chaps on the head every time it suits your needs!"

"I had to do it!" she protested.

"No, you didn't." I riposted. "The Napoleon ruse was working. We just needed more time to sell it."

"He was onto us!" she yipped.

"Vera," I said, doing my best to calm matters. "This is your third episode of cranial biffing in the space of a couple of days."

"Weeks," she protested, "you spent a long time in that coma."

"Weeks, then," I allowed, for one doesn't wish to give in to hyperbole. "But in any case, you must check this behaviour instanter. No doubt you say to yourself that the thing isn't habit-forming, and that you can abandon the practice of sloshing exposed beans whenever the opportunity presents itself, but after another biff or two the thing will have you in its grip. Just look at the escalation of your burgeoning addiction. First you're biffing Jack, an admittedly deleterious slab of damnation, and already you've progressed to biffing loony doctors and troubled friends. Next thing you'll be biffing everyone who steps within your orbit, beaning heads like a trained percussionist."

"All right!" said Vera, "but what's done is done."

"This is profoundly true," I admitted, "but it raises another issue for discussion, viz, what's to be done now? We can't just leave Zeus lying here on the floor, at the scene of the crime, as it were."

"Of course we can," said Vera. "And we can take his keys!" she added, grabbing the key ring from his belt and secreting it in the recesses of her costume. She seemed heedless of the danger of adding a charge of mugging to what had hitherto been a simple, straightforward assault.

"We can't just leave Zeus here!" I protested. "If we are — as any sensible person would be in the circs — intent on ditching this joint at the earliest possible moment, we have to take Zeus along with us if we're to have any hope of restoring his memory!"

"We have to save Nappy, first. Nappy and the other Napoleons."

"But how do we do that encumbered by an enormous snoozer?" I said, pointing Zeusward to make my meaning clear for the meanest i. "You hadn't thought of that, had you? A fat lot of good it does bringing a medium along when she goes about dishing out sloshes upon the beans of amnesiatic pals without foreseeing what she'll do next! It's one thing to tune into your television, Vera. It's quite another to rub the brain cells together and plan for future events. The former is optional. The latter essential."

"We could tie him up for now and collect him later," she ventured.

"No good," I said. "When he comes to he'll squeal to the FBI."

"What's the FBI?" she said.

"No idea. Just an expression that came to mind."

"We can't carry him. He's too heavy."

"A travois!" I suggested.

"A whatois?" she said.

"Napoleonic expression. It's a thingummy that you use to drag a person around. Take a couple of logs of wood in a roughly V shape, sling some fabric across them, and what ho, you have yourself a conveyance of sorts. We haven't any logs of wood, but we could use one of the Regent's tapestries, laid out on the ground for dragging purposes. We dump Zeus on the thing and tug him along."

"He'll slow us down," she observed, and I admitted that, in this one, limited respect, her prescience was spot-on. But lacking anything in the nature of a superior plan, this was how we chose to proceed. A few minutes later, after we'd strained to roll the recumbent colossus onto a handy tapestry, we heaved-ho and made our way down the hall, I wishing I'd stopped Vera's hand and asked Zeus for directions before the former had brought a vase crashing down on the latter's head.

Now, I don't know if you've ever dragged an unconscious buddy of behemoth proportions around hallways in an otherwise quiet house, but if you have, you'll know it's hard to do these things with any degree of what is called stealth. We did our best to skulk, but still clumped and puffed our way along the hallway with more volume than any proper spy or ninja might endorse. I suppose we managed to stay fairly quiet, but it still seemed to me — what with my overwhelming desire for secrecy and surreptition, if that's a word — that we sounded like the percussion section of an orchestra being dropped through the roof of a conservatory.

"I don't think I can pull him much further," said Vera.

"You've said a mouthful. The chap must weigh four hundred pounds."

"Perhaps we can tuck him into a closet for safekeeping. We'll come get him before we leave. If everything goes to plan we'll have a whole team of Napoleons to help us drag him along."

I weighed this. It was, I could see, an idea. An idea that seemed dashed attractive given the now aching state of what I believe is called my lumbar spinal region. This Zeus was a man of many sterling traits, but one couldn't attribute to him the virtue of portability.

As I sized up Vera's plan, it just so happened that we were passing by a likely spot to hide our recumbent oaf — a smallish sort of door, set in a wall, perhaps four feet above floor level. Some sort of storage bin or other, and one with a door sufficiently dusty that I perceived it wasn't subject to frequent inspection.

I pointed it out to Vera.

She said the word "dumbwaiter." I failed altogether to take offence, for I recognized in a j. what she had meant by the term in question. This was not another opprobrious remark about yours truly, but a diagnosis about the cubbyhole I'd spotted. For it was, you see, one of those elevatorish things sometimes found in great houses, intended to transport goods and materials, rather than personnel, along what is sometimes called the z axis, viz, in an upward or downward motion. They're generally used for moving books or boxes or trays of food and not for storing sleeping Zeuses.

I opened the door and inspected. It was a cozy little nook not more than six feet in depth, and perhaps a few feet across and as many high.

"What do you think?" I asked, admitting, as I did so, that only a folded Zeus would fit.

"I have a knack with machinery," said Vera, who of course did. She then said a good deal about pulleys and magnets and electronic control mechanisms, which she subsequently translated into English: "We can stuff him in, move the dumbwaiter between floors, and then I can jam the mechanism so he'll be stuck in there until we come back and unstick him," or words to that effect.

I subscribed to the plan without delay. There was then a bit of a stage wait as Vera and I engaged in more heaving and hoing than your average Volga boatman, Vera pulling from inside the dumbwaiter and I pushing from behind.

And we were positioned thusly — Vera and Zeus clowncar-ring within the dumbwaiter, with scarcely space to spare, and self pushing on Zeus's lower reaches in order to get the last bits in, when another of those dashed "reality quakes," as the Regent called them, made its presence known down the hall. It took the form of a bulging ripple in the scenery, bending everything in its path and featuring small electrical arcs along its surface.

I had no urge to meet the thing head on. Indeed, I was con-scious of an urge to be elsewhere.

The thing approached. And while a lesser man might have shot down the hallway — away from ground zero, as it were — in the hope of preserving self from the coming thingummy, I felt it best to do what I could to keep the team together. So I did the only thing I could do. I jammed Zeus's remaining bits into the already cramped dumbwaiter, and then jammed myself inside it, right along with the rest of our little gang.

Those who know Rhinnick Feynman have frequently com-mented on his slight, svelte, and pleasingly delicate frame, and I found on this occasion that my figure came in handy, for I was able to fit in the already cramped compartment with a touch of room to spare, but not so much that Fenny, still nestled in my pocket, didn't utter a squeak or two of objection to the condi-tions. I won't say the space was roomy — not by a jugful. To any outside observer we would have looked like a pack of Ramen noodles, a tin of well-dressed sardines, or, more accurately, per-haps, like a pack of unfortunate goofs who'd boarded a standard elevator only to be compressed into our current, compact state through a fall from a great height.

I was just musing on this simile, viz, us looking like we'd suf-fered a fall from a great height, when irony once again spat on its hands and made its presence known. The reality-quake bubble-thingummy passed, bending and stretching the landscape in a way the architects of the Regent's hall had never anticipated, and left in its wake the sounds of cables snapping, gears whirring, and various bits and bobs parting from their moorings.

The air was vibrant with the squeals of unhappy metal.

There were a pair of terrified cries — I imagine they came from self and Vera — as the dumbwaiter plummeted toward the lower floors of the Regent's lair. There was also an annoyed, officious grrnmph from Fenny, possibly indicating that we should have thought things through before jamming several hundred pounds of human flesh into a smallish device designed for carrying tea trays between floors. I found myself thinking, as I've often done in these situations, about how it is that life sometimes hands you lemons, and just as you're hoping to make a bit of lemonade, they turn out to be poisoned lemons with razor blades inside.

There were the beginnings of a crash, and all was darkness.

Chapter 29

I don't know if you've had the same experience, but a longish fall
in a cramped dumbwaiter had a profound impact on me. Not
only did it render me *non compos mentis* for a space — perhaps
three quarters of an hour, according to contemporary accounts
— but it also came within an ace of making Rhinnick Feynman
a cynic. I mean to say, life in the Regent's hall had started out all
right, what with the lavish furnishings, the pristine grounds, the
toothsome provisions, the attentive staff, and other accoutrements
of fine living, but once you really settled in and got to know the
place, or scratched beneath the gilded surface, the whole set-up
seemed precisely calculated to blot the sunshine from my life. I'd
been locked in my room, separated from friends and colleagues,
exposed to a series of reality-bending bubbles, and now I'd been
dropped down an elevator shaft alongside a four-hundred-pound
amnesiatic pal and a fortune-telling beazel beset by problems of
her own. Only an especially sunny houseguest could take all
of this on the chin and keep on smiling. I mean to say, the mere
hustle and bustle of it all was enough to cloud the Feynman brow,
not to mention what it had done to the nervous system, and that's
without even bringing up the fact that somewhere in this house of
horrors dark forces seemed to be tuning up the iron maidens and
thumbscrews for use on Napoleons. And so it was in no jocund
mood that I regained consciousness and inserted myself into a
conversation that was already in progress between Zeus and Vera.

The first voice that presented itself to the Feynman ear was Vera's, saying, "I think he's waking up."

Perceiving that she was correct in her diagnosis, I offered reassurance.

"Egad," I said, massaging the lemon and arranging myself into something that resembled a seated position, before following up with a question aimed at eliciting an important piece of news, viz, where in Abe's name we were. For once I'd opened my eyes and shaken the cobwebs from their moorings, I perceived that we weren't, as you might have envisaged, lying in a tangled heap at the bottom of an elevator shaft, or a dumbwaiter shaft if you want to split hairs, but rather closeted in a smallish, unfurnished, and generally unadorned room which lacked any apparent doors, but featured one wall that appeared to be constructed of a thickish pane of glass — think of it as a cross between a monastic cell and a dryish sort of aquarium. Beyond the glass wall was a corridor, across which I could see another room identical to the one in which we found ourselves, apart from the fact that it was empty.

It looked as though we were on display in some sort of zoo, and the exhibit across the hall had been taken off display to be deloused, or fed, or something of that order.

"We're locked up," said Vera.

This surprised me.

"Zeus too?" I asked, still massaging the loaf.

"Terrence," said Zeus.

"Or Terrence, if you prefer," I said, peevishly, "I'm in no mood to split straws."

"Yes, him too. They think he was working with us."

"Working on what?"

"Escape, I guess. They found Zeus's keys in my pocket."

"Terrence's keys," said Zeus.

"Who are they?" I asked.

"Who are who?" said Vera.

"The 'they' you mentioned. The ones who found the keys and think he's working with us."

"Oh, them," said Vera. "The guards."

"But Zeus is a guard."

"Terrence," said Zeus.

I pinched the bridge of my nose and winced for a space, as the conversation was doing little to ease the growing ache behind the eyes. "Perhaps," I said, "you could supply a brief news update, starting from the conclusion of our descent in the dumbwaiter."

"Dumbwaiter?" said Zeus, or Terrence if you prefer, reminding me that he had suffered his own bout of unconsciousness before the trip in question, occasioned by Vera's deft use of a heavy vase.

Vera ignored his interjection.

"I suppose I woke up in here about half an hour ago," she said. "You were both out cold. I was checking to make sure you were both all right when a couple of guards came up and banged on the barrier."

"You mean the glass?" I interjected.

"It isn't glass," she said. "It's gobbledygook."

She hadn't actually said the word "gobbledygook," but rather something about coherent energy thingummies suspended via somethingorother. Seeing that I seemed satisfied by this response, she moved on.

"Anyway, I asked them what was going on, and they said we were to be held for questioning. Then Zeus woke up—"

"Terrence," said Zeus.

"Or Terrence," said Vera, patiently, "anyway, he woke up and demanded to be let out."

"He can't have been too persuasive," I said.

"I suppose not," said Vera. "The guards called him a traitor and said they'd found his keys in my pocket when they pulled us out of the dumbwaiter wreckage. Since you and I weren't supposed to be out of our rooms, they figured we were making a break for it and Zeus was helping us out."

"Terrence," said Zeus, rather doggedly, which I suppose is to be expected.

Vera ignored the interruption.

"They didn't seem to know what to do with us. I think they're waiting for the Regent to come back and make some decisions about the three of us," she concluded.

"Grrnmph," said Fenny, who I now perceived was sitting behind Vera, nibbling on somethingorother.

"Oh, right," said Vera, picking up the little chap and tickling his chin. "Four of us. Fenny's here too."

I've never subscribed to Oan's Sharing Room philosophy, or believed in Vision Boards, the power of positive thinking, or the capacity of the universe to eavesdrop on your thoughts and manifest your desires, but had I done so, I'd have thanked the universe now for paying attention to yours truly and conveying Fenny safely to the cell. For my heart leapt at seeing the little chap whole and uninjured — it was about the best vision to meet the Feynman eyes all day, and something to which I might have devoted a considerable amount of space on any Vision Board I might have thought of preparing. Hamsters, you see, aren't immortal — or at least I don't suppose they are — so his welfare had been a matter of deep concern.

Fenny's advent didn't seem to bring the same wellspring of joy into Zeus's life, for the latter merely sat on the floor and slumped his massive shoulders in a brooding sort of way, making it clear to all observers that his mood was down among the wines and spirits.

"I was only doing my job," he said, glumly, flexing a bicep or two in a manner indicating that his own vertical journey down the shaft had left him aching.

I did my best to offer aid.

"There, there, old chum," I said, realizing as I did so that no one actually ever says "there, there." I extended a hand and patted a shoulder. "I'm sorry to have gotten you wrapped up in all this. I'm sure the Regent'll sort things out."

"We can't trust her to sort out anything," said Vera, chiming in. "Remember what she's doing to the Napoleons."

"What's she doing to the Napoleons?" asked Zeus.

"She's torturing them!" said Vera. "She's trying to make them reincarnate."

Yorkshire Terriers are, of course, widely known for their expressive little faces, and Zeus had managed to keep this trait in his current form. He now contorted the nose and brows in a censorious sort of way, telegraphing a larger-than-average serving of both skepticism and scorn.

"You people are crazy," he said, and one could see why he'd arrived at that assessment. I mean to say, here was I, a person Zeus regarded as a new, passing acquaintance, repeatedly insisting he and I were bosom pals who used to be bunkmates in a hospice and that he was, as some earlier time, a Yorkshire Terrier. Exhibit B was Vera, who'd tried in vain to convince him we were Napoleons, then beaned him with a vase and gotten him locked up in some species of cell, now accusing his trusted employer of torturing Napoleons for reasons related to reincarnation. If all of that didn't paint a picture of self and Vera as pure padded-cell material, then I didn't know what would.

"Be that as it may," I said, "there's nothing for us to do now but wait and see what happens."

Those who know Rhinnick, and know him well, might look askance at this most recent remark, judging it to be strangely out of character. Rhinnick, you might be saying to yourself, is a dynamic bull-horn-grabbing man of action, not a chump who's content to cool his heels in a cell blithely hoping everything will sort itself out. Rhinnick the gumptious go-getter we know. Rhinnick the seizer-of-the-day we recognize. The chap we haven't met is Rhinnick the submissive, laissez-fairing jailbird who sits pacifically — do I mean pacifically? — whispering *que sera sera* and letting the wheels of injustice do their thing. But if there's one trait I embody more than any other — if there's one thing that ought to be underlined and highlighted in any book reports or character sketches you write about me once you've finished your bit of reading — it is this: I keep the upper lip stiff, I see the glass as half-full, and I readily zero in on the bright spot in any gloomy scene. Whatever trials, travails, and hardships might conspire to blot the sunshine from my life, I can be counted on to keep the eye skinned for silver linings. Take my current predic. Here I was, confined to the Regent's private hoosegow, surrounded by coherent energy thingummies and guards who had been known to resort to torture. Dire straits, you'd have to agree. And while a lesser man might have failed to see any sun on the horizon, the one thing Rhinnick Feynman is not is a lesser man. For within a couple of ticks of becoming aware of the situation, viz, my incarceration on charges of conspiring with traitorous Terrences, breaking dumbwaiters, rifling through the Regent's office, and being awol from my room, I had seen the one, shining entry on the credit side of the ledger: it had a stronger-than-average chance of getting me out of my engagement.

Well, one engagement, at least. The engagement to Vera might still require a bit of sorting out. But it seemed to me that, as far as Oan was concerned, my stretch in the penitentiary couldn't have come at a better time. Oan would never hitch her lot to a chap who runs the risk of getting himself bunged in slammers. You can chart one of two courses in life:

you can be engaged to an idealistic beazel like Oan, or you can serve a stretch in the jug. Not both. I had this Oan taped out from shoe-sole to hairdo, and was supremely confident that, on catching the merest glimpse of me in the cooler, and on learning I'd been put here after a stint of rifling through the Regent's files, she would have doubts and qualms about linking her lot to mine and, perhaps after a day or two of letting these qualms fester, hand me the pink slip and leave the Feynman orbit forever. Nothing turns a girl off more than the thought that future contact with her betrothed will have to take the form of a conjugal v., and this was especially true of Oan. Oan had recently struck me as one of those social-climbing, status-conscious types who are drawn to titles and honorifics like a moth to an open flame. She was hoping to tread the aisle with the Hand of the ruddy Intercessor, a rising star in the Church of O, and not some two-bit crook who lands himself in the stockade every time she turns her back. She was signing up to be Mrs. H of the I., not to be a gangster's moll. I'd have placed a large wager on the prediction that, once apprised of my situation, Oan would shed a tear or two of regret and cast me aside. So as I say, while I'd never really enjoy being stuck in what they sometimes call "the joint," my current confinement had compensations. And so it was with something of a song in my heart that I counselled patience, advising against any kind of rash act that might cut short our incarceration.

"But we can't just sit around," said Vera.

"Why not?" I riposted. "What's to stop us?"

"Grrnmph," said Fenny.

"We have to make a plan," said Vera. "They'll be back to question us soon."

"How do you know?" I asked. "Television working again?"

"Standard procedure," said Zeus. "Besides, they said they'd be back shortly."

"They were very upset with Zeus. They think he must be conspiring against the Regent."

Zeus gnashed a tooth or two and glowered a bit, and I mourned in spirit for the old slab of beef. I mean to say, here was a man I knew from hoof to horns, as the expression is, and whom I'd readily diagnose as the most loyal slice of humanity who had ever bench-pressed a thousand pounds. And now his loyalty was questioned by his comrades in arms, if you can call fellow members of a Regent's private security detail "comrades in arms." Of course you could see their point of view. They hadn't known Zeus for more than a month or two, by all accounts, and he'd been foisted upon them by the Regent as a newly manifested Terrence, only to have houseguests in the form of self and Vera show up and claim that he was an amnesiatic escapee from a mental institution. A certain amount of suspicion was natural in the circs. Finding him in the wreckage of a dumbwaiter in the company of a pair of awol inmates must have pushed them over the edge, as the expression is, selling the view that this Zeus was a traitor.

"I suppose we'll just have to wait and answer their questions," I said. "All will be made clear. It won't be long until they realize Zeus wasn't a willing member of the conspiracy."

"What conspiracy?" said Zeus.

"There's no conspiracy," said Vera.

"There's something of a conspiracy," I corrected. "You and I had been planning to set the Napoleons free and drag Zeus along with us, hoping to prod his memory back into working order. Speaking of which," I added, turning Zeusward, "any change in that department? Did the crash in the dumbwaiter thingummy dislodge any bats from the belfry? Any memories of being Zeus?"

He merely blinked at me in a puzzled sort of way.

"Rhinnick," said Vera, adopting a mother-hennish tone, "I don't think he's going to get his memory back. Mindwipes aren't temporary. I know, I know," she said, staving off my interruption, "you're going to say my memory seems to be working, and I was mindwiped too. But mine's been coming back through television. Zeus is never going to remember being Zeus."

"You were mindwiped?" said Zeus, agog.

"Yes, by Socrates," said Vera.

"Socrates!" said Zeus, agogger than ever. "You mean . . . he's real? And you really did meet him? The other guards talked about him sometimes, but they always made it seem like he was some sort of . . . I dunno . . . some sort of legendary supervillain. A myth. I didn't think he really existed."

"He's real enough, all right," said Vera. "He injected me with his memory-wiping venom when I tried to keep him off your tail. I blew up half a block of downtown real estate with him in it and I barely slowed him down."

"And then he wiped your memory, too, old chum," I added, nodding oafward. "You took several bullets' worth of his memory-wiping Stygian juice straight in the chest while protecting self and others from his attack. Dashed sporting of you, of course, and very much in keeping with your well-known watchdog spirit and your commendable feudal outlook toward yours truly. That's how you ended up as Terrence, if you catch my meaning. I'd hoped to rekindle the mental sparks and remind you you were you."

This last sentence, populated as it was by a few too many yous, took Zeus perhaps a half a minute to sort out. Once he'd done so, you couldn't exactly say he'd been convinced — not by a hatful — but it did appear to give him pause for thought. I suppose nothing causes a chap to re-evaluate his loyalties and beliefs like a pair of sincere well-wishers unreservedly taking up his cause while his fellow guardsmen and guardswomen treat him like a Benedict Arnold, if Mr. Arnold is the traitorous chap whose bit of turncoating has been so widely publicized. Do I mean Benedict Arnold? I should have to check my sources.

It was while I was musing thus, and wondering if Zeus would ever zero in on the truth that he was now, within this cell, among his true friends, when a noise without caught my attention.

"The guards are coming!" Vera whispered.

There was the sound of grinding metal and the turning of heavy locks. Hinges squeaked, and a loud metallic "thud" announced the rather forceful opening of a door.

This door — somewhere down the hall beyond my field of view — must have opened into an area fraught with activity, for when it thudded open our collective ears were assaulted by a hideous cry the likes of which I'd never heard. It was worse than the cry that I myself had unleashed that one time at the hospice when I found that Zeus, apparently feeling mischievous, had slipped a toad between the sheets of the Feynman bed, a toad which I'd discovered when retiring for the evening and deeply feeling the need for quiet, rest, and repose.

The scream of present interest was a hideous, echoing scream from a male tenor with a Napoleonic accent. A male tenor N. who was in considerable distress.

"I think that's Jack!" said Vera, blanching.

"Who is Jack?" said Zeus.

"A Napoleon," said Vera, her voice trembling. "Not a very nice man. But he says that he's been reincarnated loads of times. The Regent thought he might be the key to bridging the gap to the beforelife."

"But why . . . why's he screaming?" asked Zeus, a look of deep concern mounting the brow.

"They're torturing him!" said Vera, still blanching, and her blanching intensified as the voice unleashed another one of those horrid screams.

Zeus pressed his face against the glass — or rather, the coherent energy thingummy that seemed to behave as glass — in a vain attempt to look toward the commotion. The screams intensified, and Zeus, mirroring Vera, started his own bout of blanching, his own hue edging toward the greenish end of the spectrum.

I can't claim that I remained too unblanched myself.

The hideous sounds were silenced by a second, echoing thud, to be replaced by the sound of boots approaching cellward.

A troop of guards appeared outside our cell, pushing a cart bearing an array of contrivances that looked to be vaguely medical in nature. There were four of them — guards, I mean, not medical contrivances, which I hadn't bothered to count. And you can imagine how surprised I was to learn, once this quartet of guards had entered my field of view, that three of them were chaps I'd already met.

Chapter 30

I let out a surprised squeak, followed by a loud, excited cry of "Llewellyn Llewellyn! What in Abe's name are you doing here?"

"How do you know Llewellyn Llewellyn?" asked Zeus, overlapping to some degree with Llewellyn Llewellyn making a similar inquiry.

You might have been wondering the same thing, but only if you've hitherto failed to make a careful study of my adventures — or if you belong to that class of person from whose memory the Author has seen fit to expunge all traces of my previous comings and goings. But if you have dipped into the archives to any extent, and if you do recall earlier chapters of the memoirs, you'll remember this weirdly named Llewellyn Llewellyn chap popped up a couple of times during my brief association with Ian Brown. I first met him about the time of the apocalyptic grotto sequence, when he appeared in the company of the prophet Norm Stradamus and the robe-wearing yahoos calling themselves the Church of O. Ian, I later learned, had met this same chap some time earlier, Llewellyn Llewellyn having been the one who pointed Ian and the gang in the direction of Vera's shop, hoping she could push them along with a touch of prophecy. When last I'd seen him he'd been split apart by a teleportation portal which rather inconveniently opened up in the centre of his person, leaving him bifurcated — if bifurcated is the word I want — in a way that looked as though it might take time to heal. His various bits and pieces had later disappeared, thereby being washed — or so I'd imagined — out of the Feynman life forever. But here he was, apparently whole and undamaged, standing outside the little home-from-home in which I'd been locked with Zeus, Vera, and the hamster Fenny.

I ought not to have been so dashed surprised to see him, I suppose. I mean to say, he was previously known to hobnob in the company of Norm Stradamus, seeming to do the latter's bidding in some mercenary capacity, and his employer had hitched up here at the Regent's abode. Zeus, of course, had forgotten all of this information re: our prior encounters with Llewellyn Llewellyn, Zeus's memory having gone phut through the judicious use of the Socratic Method.

I set about the task of refreshing his memory.

"Llewellyn Llewellyn was the chap who first directed us toward Vera's appliance repair shop. I then met up with him in the grotto where—"

"Shut it!" shouted one of Llewellyn's surly companions, and his manner offended me. Indeed, I rather think I was curling my lip at him and registering no small measure of scorn when I suddenly recalled where I had seen this chap before. This one was the taller and thicker of the two thuggish policemen who'd appeared on the Detroit University bus, seeking Napoleons, somewhere around twenty chapters ago when I was en route for a tête-à-tête with Isaac Newton. He and his colleague, a shorter thug with a head like a pumpkin, who I now perceived was also in the gang outside my cell, had shrunk — or do I mean shrank? — from actually absconding with the Napoleons once confronted with the spectre of public scrutiny. These two thugs were now out of police uniforms and dressed as the Regent's guards, accompanying Llewellyn Llewellyn alongside a fourth guardsperson who was unknown to me: a heavily tattooed guard of feminine aspect who glowered at me as though I were an eel in her commode.

"Shut it" is one of those phrases that doesn't really recommend a specific response. It differs in this respect from "how do you do?" or "good morning" or "lovely weather today, isn't it?" When confronted with anything along the lines of "shut it," some people choose to acquiesce and maintain a dignified silence, others pout and sulk, and still others bristle with defiance, refusing to shut anything and instead mounting a form of verbal protest. In this particular instance, I decided in favour of speech, as the specific dreg of humanity who'd ordered me to "shut it" seemed to have failed to spot the significance of what I was trying to say, viz, that I was not some stranger to be mistreated by surly guards, but a known acquaintance of Llewellyn Llewellyn. So my response was to give tongue in the form of a ready explanation. It started as follows:

"I was merely trying to explain—"

"Well don't!" said Llewellyn Llewellyn.

"Yeah, don't!" said the shorter, male guard, who seemed to expectorate his words, rather than uttering them.

"How did he know your name, Llew?" said the female member of the sketch, arching a shrewd and thinly pencilled eyebrow in my direction.

"We've met," said Llewellyn Llewellyn. "I was working for Norm Stradamus when Brown came to the grotto. This guy was with him. His name's Feynman. Norm calls him the Hand of the Intercessor."

I winced.

"But what's he doin' in a cell with Terrence, then?" said the thickish, tall guardsman, who was built along the same gorilla-like lines as Zeus, but on a somewhat smaller scale and leaning more toward the fleshy end of the spectrum rather than the finely chiselled.

"We'll know soon enough," said Llewellyn Llewellyn. "Let 'em sweat a bit for now. We've got to take care of this, first," he added, patting the cart bearing the medical-looking doodads.

I, for one, didn't like what he was driving at, for it seemed to me that nothing good could come from the application of unrequested medical doodads in my current situation. I won't say I was in especially fine fettle at the moment, what with my recent tumble down the shaft, but I certainly didn't require hooking up to any medical devices, and the idea that I might be hooked up to some against my will, for purposes unknown and quite probably nefarious, led to another bit of wincing. I also won't say that I had a great deal of experience with these mercenaries or guards or whatever they were, but by the look of them, I wouldn't have put it past them, armed with these medical doodads, to inflect their unsuspecting prisoners with the measles or rubella or even that bird flu disease Ian had mentioned when we first met.

It was at this point that Vera decided to make her presence known. Until now she'd just been staring into space in that vacant way of hers, a sure sign that she was on the receiving end of a sudden television broadcast, one apparently sparked by the advent of these guards.

"I've seen all of you!" she said, speaking to the guards, not me, who of course she'd seen frequently. "You're members of the Eighth Street Chapter!" she continued. "You were—"

"SHUT UP!" shouted Llewellyn Llewellyn, in a full-throated and cranky sort of manner. He seemed perturbed, and not keen on merry reunions. Despite the urgency in its tone and the volume with which his words had been unleashed, his shout failed altogether to deter Vera.

"You were hired by Norm Stradamus to get Ian to the grotto. You're Llewellyn Llewellyn," she continued, "and Philly the Rook," she said, addressing the short male guard, "and Kari

340

Slice, and Big Hurt!" she added, completing her little roll call. "I saw your minds being wiped by Socrates. Well, not Llewellyn Llewellyn, but the rest of you were attacked and then—"

"I told you to *Shut. Up*," said Llewellyn Llewellyn through gritted teeth, and also through a coherent energy matrix something or other that separated him from us and prevented him, it seemed, from making any real progress in the direction of preventing Vera's speech.

"What's she talking about, Llew?" said the woman identified as Kari Slice.

"And how'd she know you call me Big Hurt?"

"Ignore her," said Llewellyn Llewellyn.

"But Llew—"

"Look," said Llewellyn Llewellyn, "she doesn't know anything. It's just . . . I dunno . . . some kind of a trick. I've already told you, you all manifested a few months ago in the Styx, along with Thirsty Vern, Alphonse, and the rest of the crew, and I was there to collect you as your guide. Your memories have gotten fuzzy. It happens all the time. But once you were all sorted out I asked you join up with me and Norm Stradamus, and you said yes. And now we're all here at the Regent's place. There's nothing more to it than that. And I don't appreciate," he added, glowering through the energy thingummy at Vera, "anyone stirrin' up trouble or confusing you. It's been hard enough for all of you since the . . . *difficulties* you had at your manifestations."

I arched an eyebrow or two, seeing there was almost certainly more here than met the eye.

"But I've seen it!" said Vera. "They tried to kidnap Ian and were wiped by Soc—"

"ENOUGH!" screeched Llewellyn Llewellyn, this time banging a fist on the energy barrier and following his screech with a series of strange oaths and curses which needn't sully the Author's work. After a moment or two he simmered down.

"Look, lady," he said, his palm resting on the transparent energy thingummy, "I don't know what you think you're doing, but stop trying to put ideas into my friends' heads. They're *my friends*," he repeated, putting a significant amount of topspin on the phrase. "They've been through a lot. They're newly manifested and easily confused. They're good people."

"Good people don't lock other people up for no reason," protested Vera.

"Or accuse other people of being traitors!" said Zeus.

"Or torture Napoleons just because of who they are!" I added.

"That's out of our hands," said Llewellyn Llewellyn. "We're just working with the Regent's guards while Norm is here. I'm not saying I agree with what's going on with the Napoleons. And we're not involved in whatever's going on with you."

"That ain't exactly true, Llew," said Philly the Rook.

"Naw," said Big Hurt. "We're supposed to question Terrence later, like you said."

"I know, I know," said Llewellyn Llewellyn. "But . . . look. We have a job to do. We were sent to prepare the cell, not to argue with the inmates." And once again his attention turned to the assemblage of medical thingummies on his cart.

The spiders that seemed to be crawling up and down my spine when I'd first noticed the medical thingummies now redoubled their efforts.

"N-n-no need," I stammered, doing my best to appear calm but not coming within several miles of it. "We're all fine in here. No call for medical attention or whathaveyou."

"This ain't for you," said Philly the Rook. "Not exactly," he added, and for some reason his pumpkin-shaped head split into a horrible grin.

"This stuff ain't for yous," said Big Hurt. "It's for the cell across the way. Boss says we've got to set up an ivy drip—"

"Not an ivy drip, Hurt. It's an IV," said Kari Slice.

342

"A four?" said Big Hurt, corrugating the brow.

"No, no—"

"But Llew said I-V means four!"

"It means four sometimes," said Philly the Rook. "Other times it means 'in the veins.'"

"That'd be I . . . T . . . V," said Big Hurt, in a halting voice that suggested that this took some concentration.

"Guys," said Kari Slice, "Let's get on with it. It's not as though we're being paid by the hour."

And as interested as I otherwise might have been in the pay structure for the Regent's mercenaries and guards, I was more intrigued by the notion that the cell across the hall was in need of an IV drip. And since there was nothing for me to do but stand and watch as this odd quartet of guardspersons set about their duties, that's exactly what I did. They busied themselves for the better part of ten minutes, doing a fairish job of setting up stands and drips and things within the cell, until I perceived that the door from whence they'd come went through another round of unlocking, slamming open, and slamming shut again, this time without an interlude of screaming, suggesting that the torturers had called it a day, or possibly taken a coffee break.

A further round of clumping footsteps, accompanied by the sound of something being pushed or dragged along the floor, heralded the coming of an addition to our party.

"Bring her in here," called Llewellyn Llewellyn, poking his head out into the hall.

A moment later I caught sight of his audience. It was another pair of guardsmen, these ones dragging along the trussed-up form of another person of my acquaintance.

"They've got Nappy!" Vera cried.

I confirmed the diagnosis. The trussed-up person of my acquaintance was, indeed, the pipsqueak Nappy, now bound, blindfolded, gagged, and zealously wriggling against the restraints.

"What are you doing with her?" Zeus shouted, and one detected the note of disapproval.

"None of your business," said Philly the Rook.

"It's kinda their business," said Big Hurt. "We're putting her here on account o' the fact that she's their friend and says she knows Zeus, and Boss said they'll be more likely to answer our questions and sort things out if—"

Kari shushed him with an elbow, indicating in no uncertain terms that guards were not supposed to enumerate their motivations and schemes when standing within earshot of prisoners.

"Just get her strapped in," said Llewellyn Llewellyn.

On the cue "get her strapped in," Big Hurt hoisted the wriggling Nappy over his shoulder, stepped into the cell, and flung her unceremoniously onto the metal bed. Through her gag, Nappy let out an audible "oof" that made it plain to those assembled that her landing hadn't been cozy.

Zeus didn't take this well. He started hammering on our cell's energy barrier with a hubcap-sized palm, shouting things along the lines of "stop that" and "you be careful with her." These coherent energy barriers seemed to be made of sturdy stuff, for the thing stayed coherent under the onslaught of Zeus's vehement hammering. Nor did his hammering have any apparent impact on the gaggle of guards, for they kept their heads down and turned their attention to the task of strapping Nappy to the bed within the cell, tightening her gag, and securing her to various cords and cables issuing from the trolley.

Zeus's vehemence did have an impact on yours truly, for it gave me pause for thought. This was not, it seemed to me, the reaction of a guardsman merely expressing a regular dose of professional concern for the well-being of prisoners. This was Zeus's watchdog spirit once again making its presence known, rising in defence of one who — though not perhaps remembered on any conscious level — had been one of Zeus's nearest and d. Indeed, unless I'd misread the situation, Nappy and Zeus had been mutually struck by Cupid's arrows, as the expression is, in the time before Zeus's current bout of amnesia. "Young love," about sums it up; a larger-than-average dose of what is called the divine pash.

Observing the big lug now, hammering freely on the energy barrier and shouting exhortations at a gang of persons whom he must have recently counted as colleagues, it occurred to me this was indicative of love swelling in Zeus's bosom as he watched the object of his affections at the mercy of these dark forces.

"Zeus!" I said, placing a placating hand on the chap's enormous shoulder. "Have you remembered? Has Nappy's peril stirred your memory?"

"Terrence," he said, whereupon he cheesed the hammering routine and left his palm merely resting on the barrier. "I already told you. I don't remember anything before the Regent. But you can't do that to prisoners. It isn't right. She's helpless. And she's so small. And there's six of them, and they've got her tied up and are—"

"It's okay, Zeus," said Vera, taking a station at Zeus's other shoulder and mirroring my patting efforts. "She'll be all right. Has Norm told you what I can do?"

"See the future, you mean?" said Zeus.

"That's right," said Vera. "And I know Nappy is going to be all right."

An urgent beeping from the vicinity of the hallway now interrupted the proceedings and caused the action in Nappy's cell to take something of a pause. Nappy was lying on the slab looking peaceful, while Llewellyn *et al.*, now huddled around a beeping datapad or similar high-tech thingummy, possibly I-Ware, looking all of a doodah. And whatever information the thing displayed caused five of their number — Llewellyn Llewellyn, Kari Slice, Big Hurt, and the two anonymous guards who'd brought Nappy to the cell — to buzz off down the hall to greener pastures, shouting back to Philly the Rook that he was in sole charge of the cells and suggesting that he finish hooking Nappy up to the doodads and then see what he might do by way of making Terrence talk.

For the moment, Philly the Rook simply stood there at a loss.

"Where'd they go?" asked Vera.

"None o' yer business," said Philly the Rook, whom I may start calling Phil to lower the word count.

"Why'd they leave you alone?" asked Zeus. "Standard procedure calls for two guards to attend to any prisoner who—"

"Shut yer trap," said Phil, who mustn't have heard the instruction about making Terrence talk. I mean to say, you can't make someone talk by telling them, in any form of vernacular, to be quiet.

"How's the prisoner?" asked Zeus, up-nodding in Nappy's direction.

"That's none o' your business, neither," said Phil, who, now seemingly reminded of Nappy's presence, turned back to the job of hooking up the equipment.

He plugged a couple of plugs into the wall, flipped a brace of switches on the console of a monitoring device, hoisted a bag full of some species of liquid onto a tallish stand, and attached a length of clear tubing between this bag and what seemed to me to be a rather angry-looking economy-sized needle.

"What's in the IV?" asked Vera.

"Just mind your own business!" said Phil, clenching his jaw muscles and grinding a tooth or two in Vera's direction. "Just wait your turn. I've got to finish with the girl."

"Wait our turn for what?" asked Vera, who seemed intent on keeping hold of Phil's attention.

"For questioning," spat Phil.

I'm pretty astute, and clued into Vera's plan. She was, I perceived, attempting to do whatever she could to delay whatever procedure the goon Phil had in mind for our friend Nappy. Eager to help, I shoved my own oar in.

"Questioning," I said, brightly, "why, there's no time like the present. Question away. The Feynman life is an open b. I'll do my best to be thorough."

"Not you," said Phil. "I'm supposed to ask Terrence why he's helpin' you, why this girl keeps callin' him Zeus, and figure out if he's some kinda plant."

"Some kind of plant?" I asked, confused.

"Yeah," said Phil.

"You mean a dog."

"I don't mean a dog. I mean a plant."

"You think Zeus is a plant?"

"My name is Terrence."

"I mean, it doesn't seem very likely," I said. "The terrier story's difficult enough for most people to swallow, but it strikes me as even more improbable that the chap started out as a fern, or rhododendron, or those little bushes you see on the sides of—"

"Not *that* kinda plant!" said Phil. "I mean a spy. The kind who's here to spy on the Regent, or planning to stop her, or working against her plans, creeping around and working against us like some kinda weasel."

I was interested to learn that this was what weasels did, but rather than putting that point to Phil, I simply asked why he and his fellow guards would suspect Zeus would get himself wrapped up with any of that.

"Would you just stop pestering me?" said Phil, whose attentive resources seemed more limited than most. "This part's fussy," he said, eyeing the needle closely and then looking down at Nappy's arm. "And I'm doing it in a hurry."

"What's your hurry?" asked Vera. "And why did Llewellyn and the others take off in such a rush?"

The question seemed to have caught Philly the Rook off guard, for rather than merely telling us to shut up once again, he let the answer slip right out. Or at least it was something approximating an answer, for all he said was "the Napoleons are revolting."

"They're not so bad once you get to know them," I said. "I mean, Jack, or Bonaparte, or Judas, by whatever name he goes, is a horrible little gosh-help-us who can't be trusted with pointy objects, but others are—"

"I mean they're rioting!" said Phil. "The Regent took a whack of guards with her. Looks like the freaks saw this as a chance to get some o' their own back and cause a fuss. A bunch of 'em broke out of the cells and set about the guards. They called for backup."

"Why'd they pick you to stay behind?" asked Vera. "Not much help in a fight? Bit of a glass jaw?"

This rather seemed to rankle, for the chap turned the colour of an irritated beetroot, spat on the floor, and turned his back on self and cellmates, muttering oaths and curses.

His attention finally turning back to the job before him, Phil once again inspected the large, angry needle. Then, in what I thought was a rather unhygienic manner, he licked his thumb and used it to wipe down a spot on Nappy's wrist. This seemed to cause Nappy to stir, for she wriggled a bit and groaned into her gag.

"Leave her alone!" shouted Zeus, more vehemently than ever, once again pounding his palm on the energy barrier.

Zeus's outburst seemed to amuse Philly the Rook, influenced largely by the fact that Zeus was safely ensconced behind the energy thingummy. He turned and grinned hideously, and

I remember thinking that his head now needed only a candle or two to complete the jack-o'-lantern impression.

"Not such a big man, now, are you?" said Phil. "Can't handle what's happening to your girl?"

"She's not my girl," said Zeus. "She's a prisoner. And you can't treat prisoners like that."

"She's a Napoleon," said Phil. "She's only gettin' what she deserves." And apparently "what she deserved" amounted to the insertion of the needle into her arm, for it was at this moment that Phil squirted a bit of the liquid stuff through the tip of the needle, and then took aim at the spot he'd "cleaned," if you could call it cleaning, on Nappy's wrist.

"Leave her alone!" shouted Zeus.

This drew a snicker from Philly the Rook who, sticking a tongue out of the side of his mouth — which I took to be indicative of the fact that he was concentrating on the task before him — placed the needle against Nappy's skin and began to push.

SLAM.

That was an instance of what we literary types call "onomatopoeia." I apologize for slipping into it without warning, but it couldn't be helped, for I can imagine no better way to capture the sudden crash which overwhelmed the senses and sent vibrations shooting through the Feynman person, not to mention all of the other persons assembled. And the source of the slam in question was not far to seek. Zeus, apparently filled to the brim with righteous wrath, had slammed himself shoulder-first into the coherent energy thingummy in an effort to get his mitts on Philly the Rook.

The effort wasn't what you might call a complete success, for while plaster fell from the walls, and whatever ceilings are made of fell from the ceiling, the coherent energy thing remained coherent. At least it seemed to. I mean to say, lights dimmed, the energy field buzzed, and Philly the Rook made a face which made it clear to one and all that he was losing confidence in the ability of the barrier to do its thing and keep him separated from Zeuses.

Zeus wheeled 'round, stepped toward the back of the cell, and with a face that had MAXIMUM EFFORT written across it in large capital letters, he charged full-bore toward the barrier again. He reminded me forcibly of one of those creatures who charge about the savannah crashing into things. What are they called? A sort of armoured-war-hippo, if you catch my drift. Name sounds something like a popular form of surgery . . . rhinoceros! That's the baby — though now that I see it in print I rather prefer "armoured-war-hippo." At any rate, that's what Zeus reminded me of now as he barrelled toward the energy thingummy.

Vera crouched to the ground to shield her head from falling whatnots, I pressed myself to the side of the cell and did a fairish impersonation of wallpaper, Fenny burrowed into the recesses of my costume, and Philly the Rook just stood there looking agog.

SLAM!! This time with two exclamation points and a larger-than-average font.

When the irresistible force finally met the immovable object, a whole host of things happened all at once. Lights flickered wildly, as though we were at some sort of disco-theque or rave or whatever the ghastly things are called, still more plaster rained from the cell's supporting walls, someone uttered a shrill squeak (although whether this was Vera, Philly the Rook, or the undersigned remains a point of contention), and the coherent energy barrier rather failed to live up to its name, for it lost both energy and coherence and no longer amounted to anything in the shape of a barrier. Zeus blew straight through it, leaving sparks and a profusion of fizzling wires in the places where the barrier had met the cell walls. And, as I rather imagine he intended, Zeus ended up being up-close-and-personal with a rather surprised-looking Philly the Rook.

I wonder if you've ever seen one of those large bears who inhabit the western shores of Detroit Columbia, where the Frazier River feeds directly into the Styx — probably not, as most people don't seem to get out that way very much, what with all of the dreary rain and soaring real estate prices. But if you have, you may have observed those economy-sized brown bears — Kodiac, I think they're called — swatting salmon out of the river whenever feeling remotely peckish. It was that way with Zeus now. He was the bear, I mean to say, and Philly the Rook was the salmon, for the former scooped up the latter with a mighty, hairless paw, and seemed to watch him wriggle for a heartbeat or two before slamming him on to the river's shore — the part of which was played, on this occasion, by the wall outside Nappy's cell. There was a dull or sickening thud, a gasp of air from Philly the Rook, and a brief sort of gurgling moan you hear when people receive a tax bill.

Phil lay twitching on the floor, still resembling the landed salmon I alluded to a moment ago, and Zeus, perhaps disappointed to learn that there was no further barrier activated on Nappy's cell, cheesed the hungry bear routine, and also the armoured-war-hippo routine, and simply bounded into the cell.

Vera hopped to her feet and joined him, self bringing up the rear with Fenny carefully pocketed for safekeeping. We rushed to Nappy's side.

Zeus stood there at something of a loss in the flickering lights, which were still doing their discotheque routine in the wake of Zeus's bit of barrier-bursting. Vera faced him from across the recumbent Nappy, who now wriggled against her bonds with renewed vigour, aware of all the surrounding commotion but not apparently cottoning on to the fact that — as I once heard Ian put it — the U.S. Marines had arrived.

"It's all right," shouted Vera, over the buzzing and popping of lights and other electrical thingummies. "It's us. We're getting you out of here," whereupon she busied herself with buckles and knots and things, removing Nappy's blindfold, gag, and the lion's share of her bonds. Zeus completed the procedure by breaking a sort of handcuff arrangement by which Nappy was affixed to the medical trolley, a feat he achieved with no more effort than I might have expended in breaking out of a wet paper bag or snapping a thread.

Zeus helped Nappy to her feet. She seemed more than a little groggy and had the general aspect and appearance of someone who's just crawled through a hedge.

"What . . . what eez 'appening?" she said.

"We're getting you out of here," Vera repeated. "We've got to get out of the Regent's cells and take you somewhere safe."

And before I could offer up any critiques of this notion, pointing out that we weren't sure where in Detroit we might be safe from the likes of the Regent, Nappy seemed to shake the cobwebs from her belfry, if I've got the expression right, and took a more thorough inventory of her surroundings.

"Z . . . Zeus!" she said, looking up at the big chap with what I believe is called a welter of emotion. "You . . . you came for me," she added.

"It's . . . nothing," Zeus faltered, if faltered's the word, as he continued to help Nappy gain her footing. And what I noticed, more than I'd noticed anything else in the recent exchange, was that he hadn't said anything along the lines of "call me Terrence."

The flickering of the lights seemed to play on Nappy's upturned face, revealing a justified tear or two, and then gave up the ghost entirely, leaving Zeus, Nappy, Vera, self, and Fenny — not to mention the snoozing Phil — bathed in darkness. A silence fell. And then, somewhere to the sou'sou'west of our posish, there was a brief mechanical buzzing and a click.

"The door's open," whispered Vera.

"How do you know?" I asked.

"That sound," said Vera. "When Zeus broke through the barrier it must have overloaded the electrical grid. The maglocks on the door have given way."

Well, I won't say that I knew precisely what any of that meant, but Vera did seem to have a way with electrical thingummies, so I deferred to her expertise. I did raise a point of order, though, thinking it to be in everyone's best interest that it be drawn to their attention.

"Doesn't that door lead to the Napoleons?"

"That's what Llewellyn Llewellyn said," said Zeus.

"That's right," said Vera. "We have to help them."

"It seems to me that we already have our favourite one," I suggested, gesturing at Nappy — not that my gesture did any good in the dark. "Besides, Phil seems to have indicated that they'd already broken free and were doing what Napoleons do best, viz, throwing off their shackles, expanding the Western Front, and making a land grab in the vicinity of the Regent's lair."

"We have to help them!" Vera repeated, this time more vehemently than the last.

Well, I don't know about you, but if there's one thing I've always known, it is when, and when not, to raise a fuss. If this Vera — a person who is, I hasten to add, the good egg to end all good eggs — had made it her primary aim and objective to support the Napoleonic rebellion and see it through to fruition, then who was I to bung a sabot into the works? Now was not a time for argument or plea, but a time for all good Rhinnicks to rally 'round and come to the aid of the party.

I uttered a simple and straightforward "well, bung ho, then," preparing to follow this Vera into what I supposed would be something like a battle. True, I was emboldened by the fact that our little entourage seemed to have added a Zeus or

Terrence to our strength, a thing it's always good to have whenever heading toward conditions that might prove difficult, or
when heading any place where thews, sinews, and an intimi-
dating, colossus-like stature might come in handy.

A light shone in the darkness. It was Vera.

That sounded a good deal more romantic and metaphorical than I'd intended, but what I was driving at was that a light
literally did shine in the darkness, and the light did come from
Vera, who had apparently scooped up a datapad from the vicinity of Phil's person and now shone its little screen like a sort of
handheld, digital torch, adding a touch of illumination to the
surroundings. I won't say the thing lit up our path — it's fairer
to say it cast something of a glow within about eight inches of
space around the screen — but its dim halo was enough to
pierce the gloom and help us make our way to the door.

This accomplished, we did the brave thing and hid en
masse behind Zeus, exhorting him to open the door with as
much stealth as he could muster.

Vera shone the datalink on the door. Zeus placed a mighty
hand or two on the handle.

He pushed gently — or at least as gently as one can push
when one has the muscular strength of a whole herd of
weight-lifting elephants.

It turned out that he should have pulled.

He tried again, this time pulling.

There was a click, and the merest suggestion of squeaking
hinges, when our ears were suddenly drowned in the sound of
several dozen Napoleons in full riot.

Zeus flung wide the gates, as the expression is, and our little
party streamed into a madhouse.

Chapter 31

There are some scenes that are too rich for the senses — too thoroughly clogged up with sensory phenomena to lend themselves to ready digestion or description. Scenes that remind you of those spicy soups you get in southern Detroit — I forget what you call them — with too many varied ingredients, tastes, and textures to be sorted out by the human tongue.

A gumbo, that's what it is. We waltzed into a sensory gumbo.

The sound was the first thing to impress itself upon the brain. It was cacophonous, if cacophonous means what I think it does. For not only were there shouts and shrieks of the tactical variety, viz, exhortations to "get down!" or "retreat!" or "get behind them!" coming from guardspersons scattered about the place, but the air was also alive with the animal cries of Napoleons, shouting things like "*zut alors!*" and "*mange ça!*" and "*votre guide porte des bottes de l'armée*" or words to that effect. This was supplemented by the percussion section, being comprised of gunshots, crashing furniture, and the disconcerting thud of feet and fists meeting the fleshy bits of other persons' anatomies. It was enough to make one wish for a sturdy pair of soundproof earmuffs.

But the sound wasn't the only thing one noticed. My initial focus on the aural inputs, as the expression is, is not intended to suggest that the visual spectrum was any less assaulted by the tableau of bedlam spread out before us. No, no . . . once the eyes had adjusted themselves to their surroundings, they were treated

— if one can call it being treated — to what one who mixes metaphors might call an orgy of anarchy in full bloom. The room into which we stepped was one of those two-tiered numbers, with the lower echelon, if that's the word I want, being occupied by guards running every which way, diving behind desks, firing pistols, and hurling cannisters filled with some gaseous substance up toward the upper level. This upper level, which seemed to be lined with cells not unlike our recently vacated home-from-home, seemed to be Napoleon central, for dozens of the frenzied little chaps kept popping up behind the surrounding railing, raining destruction down upon their adversaries and cursing a good deal. The destruction which they did rain down seemed to be chiefly comprised of whatever in Abe's name they could lay their hands upon, this including a large number of bedpans, medical beds, fire extinguishers, and — I apologize for the graphic nature of what's to follow — assorted bits of guards who'd been unwise enough to organize a sortie behind enemy lines.

There was no perfect separation of the Napoleons and the guards, for several members of the Napoleonic contingent had come down from the relative safety of their perch and closed into what I believe is called the "mêlée range." It took a moment or two for me to realize that this forward-line contingent was led by none other than Jack — or Bonaparte, or Judas, or Brutus if you prefer — who seemed to have handpicked a particularly ravenous bunch of mad-eyed Napoleons to follow him into battle. Two of these, I noted with interest, were the Napoleons with whom I had recently hobnobbed on the Detroit University bus. This group descended upon a turtling crew of guards, setting about them with a frenzy which reminded me of a pack of wild piranha meeting up with an unsuspecting knot of bathers. The guards did put up something of a fight. One might even say they displayed the will to win. But Jack and his crew of revolting Napoleons had the bloodlust, and I reflected, in that detached way of mine, that this was one of those noteworthy circumstances in which an unhealthy dose of psychopathy could make all the difference.

As my attention zoomed out from the central battlefield, as it were, I became aware of an upturned table not far from our current posish, behind which crouched Llewellyn Llewellyn and the remaining members of the Eighth Street Chapter. Llewellyn Llewellyn seemed to have formed a makeshift flag-pole out of a chair leg, upon which he waved a white T-shirt, apparently signalling the fact that he'd taken something of a *laissez-faire* attitude toward this spot of mayhem, washing his hands of the current imbroglio and letting the Napoleons go about their business.

I turned my attensh from the fray and looked to Zeus, wondering why this behemoth in human shape, always ripe for a bit of a dust-up, hadn't charged headlong into the brawl.

My q. was answered.

While I had been taking in the full scope of the unfolding anarchy, Zeus's attention was earmarked, if that's the expression, for a solitary spot at the edge of the room. It was a smallish alcove containing a brace of medical beds. Three of them, to be precise, all positioned around a grate in the floor. And it was clear that the principal object of Zeus's interest at this moment was the reddish-brown, notably lumpy fluid slowly flowing through that grate.

It wasn't mulligatawny. Decorum demands that I describe the stuff no further, for I shan't sully the Author's work with what was clearly the fallout of Napoleonic torture. It had a marked effect on me. And Zeus, who wasn't shielded from the sight by my editorial tact, took in the full, unspeakable horror of the scene.

It smote him like a blow. He stood there goggling, rooted on the spot, his mouth opening and closing like a landed whitefish.

One could see what he was driving at. He hadn't known what his brothers and sisters in arms had been up to in this dungeon, and he hadn't expected that his recent benefactor, the Regent Neferneferuaten, might be capable of such horrors. And for a man like Zeus, for whom loyalty is the cardinal virtue, it's rather soul-destroying to learn that the team for which you've been drafted, the side to which you've currently pledged your fealty, is not only unworthy of your allegiance, but also — not to put too fine a point upon the thing — downright evil. It'd be like finding out that your diner's club had secretly been serving you prime cuts of toddler, or learning that your favourite maître d' has been watering down the single malts or replacing them with blends.

Zeus took it big. After staring at the morbid scene for a space and drinking in the extent of its inhumanity, he did what any right-thinking mastadon might have done. He howled something resembling a full-throated battle yodel, charged forward like those half-a-league, half-a-league onward chumps I mentioned earlier, and snatched up one of the pistol-firing guardsmen near the centre of the room.

You read that right. He snatched him up. By the legs, if you want to know. The snatchee seemed to take this philosophically, for he simply made an impassive face as though — like your better-known philosophers — he hadn't a clue what the hell was going on. Zeus now held the man dangling by his ankles, like a fisherperson displaying a gaffed trout. Thus armed, Zeus strode into the nearest knot of guardspersons, now swinging the hapless snatchee like a mace, or morning-star, or whatever you call those blunt instruments designed for bashing in the heads of your opposition.

Some of the swings were golf-like, and some more akin to the baseball variety. But whatever he struck, the impact was the same. Guards flew, seeming to arc toward the putting green or fly into home-run range, landing I knew not where.

With Zeus having left our immediate environs — thus depriving us of cover — Vera, self, Fenny, and Nappy did the brave thing and dove behind the Eighth Street Chapter. It's not that we regarded these chumps as bosom friends, or had forgotten their recent efforts to bring a spot of misery into our collective lives, but to be weighed against these sins was their undeniable utility as human shields.

"Tuck in here," said Llewellyn Llewellyn, scooching over to the side and making room behind the upturned table.

"Tuck in here?" I asked, mildly affronted by the apparent chumminess this Llewellyn chap was showing. "Tuck in here? You expect us to treat you as a warm, congenial host, after all that—"

Here I broke off. Not so much because I'd finished whatever I had been planning to say, but because a couple of bullets whizzed past my left ear, heightening the appeal of Llewellyn Llewellyn's recent offer.

We tucked in.

Nappy was understandably displeased. Once we'd nestled into relative safety behind the upturned table, she glared at the membership of the Eighth Street Chapter with what I've often heard described as a baleful look.

"You bastards," she said through gritted teeth. "I 'ope you get what you deserve!"

"Look," said Llewellyn Llewellyn. "I'm sorry. But we were just following Norm. He said we were serving the greater good and—"

"Serving ze greater good!" she yowled. "Vat kind of good can come of zees? Kidnapping and torturing a . . . an entire people, all in ze name of some crazy beliefs!"

"Look, I get it," said Llewellyn Llewellyn, "but Norm's beliefs aren't crazy. The beforelife is real. He's going to help his people reach it. I've seen some pretty unbelievable stuff since—"

"Seence what?" shouted Nappy, over a fresh burst of gunfire.

Llewellyn Llewellyn looked 'round to see his gangmates were occupied by other things. Apparently satisfied that they weren't hanging on his every word, he aimed a couple of sideways nods at them and mouthed the words "since Socrates."

Nappy didn't seem interested in the Eighth Street Chapter's past entanglements with assassins, for she continued denouncing Llewellyn Llewellyn and his fellows with a string of words and gestures revealing a most impressive command of the obscene vernacular and carried on calling him names beyond the point at which you might have expected both breath and inventiveness to have given out. I was impressed with the vehemence with which she ticked him off, for she displayed not only the lung power of a regimental sergeant major, but also the bravery of one of those first-responder chaps who seem to ignore the danger around them. Her anti–Eight Street Chapter diatribe was punctuated by the regular ping of bullets ricocheting all around us, not to mention other guards, struck by Zeus, flying past at about eye level at regular intervals.

I turned my attensh from Nappy, who seemed to have matters well in hand, to Vera, who nestled at my immediate rear.

She seemed to have taken a brief hiatus from her gig as an appliance repairperson in favour of taking on the role of field marshal, for she poked her head above the table and shouted exhortations to Zeus, telling him when to duck, when to pivot, and where best to aim his blows. This sideline coaching seemed to serve him well, for the chap managed to keep out of the gunfire while swinging his guard-shaped cudgel with what, in any world which didn't feature human immortality, would have been called deadly precision.

And while I won't say that this precisely turned the tide of battle, since the tide was already flowing distinctly in the Napoleons' favour, it did seem to throw matters into sharp relief for the guards. The impact on their morale was clear, and one could see the urge to retreat mounting within them, largely assisted by the image of Zeus battering their brethren and sending them flying who knows where.

Those guards who could still stand did so with great alacrity, dropping weaponry at their sides, kicking the dust of the Regent's hall from their boots and heading for the hills at a significant rate of MPH. Where exactly it is they went I cannot say, for they rabbitted out of sight, into hallways and through doors which I hadn't hitherto noticed, what with all of my attention having been gripped by other things.

Some Napoleons, perhaps taking a page from Zeus's book, gave chase like terriers who've caught the scent of a fox or rabbit or whatever it is terriers chase; but most appeared to understand that their oppressors had been routed, and they stuck around on the spot to savour the victory.

The Napoleon who called himself Jack was among those who stayed behind. And now that he'd cheesed the piranhic-feeding-frenzy routine and finally stood still for more than a couple of ticks, I was at long last able to make a detailed appraisal of his appearance.

It was too awful for words — at least for words that went into any level of specificity or precision. I mean to say, I rarely set myself up as a judge of male beauty, and I don't intend to convey that this Jack was, in his normal state, the sort of chap who'd offend the pupils. But now he was far from being in anything approaching his normal state. Indeed, when I say that his current appearance was too awful for words, I intend to convey that he showed every imaginable sign of his ill treatment at the hands of the Regent's guards and now looked like something that had recently escaped from a butcher's meathook or gone awol from an abattoir. My heart bled for the chap — which is saying something, as the last couple of times we'd crossed paths he'd done his best to make the Feynman heart bleed through sharp-force trauma.

He surveyed the field of victory before him, managed something approximating a subtle smile, and then, no doubt owing to the weariness that comes from a combination of bloodlust and blood loss, he crumpled into an unconscious lump among the carnage.

"No High Priest is worth this," said Llewellyn Llewellyn, still peeping over the table. "We're getting out of here."

"Not before you pay for what you 'ave done!" said Nappy — though here again, "spat" or "seethed" might have been mot juster.

"Look," said Llewellyn Llewellyn — a word of which I think you'll agree he was inordinately fond — "I'm not gonna defend anything we did. Norm was convincing. He was . . . I dunno . . . all religious about this stuff. He made it sound like it was a way for us to make some cash while also doing some good — letting people see the world for whatever it really is, or something like that. I didn't see the harm."

"Didn't see the harm?" shouted Vera, weighing in. "Didn't see the harm? He was having people tortured."

"Not at first!" riposted Llewellyn, but you could see his heart wasn't in it, for he seemed to dish the argument for the defence at this point and just stood there looking down at his shoes. "Crestfallen" sums it up nicely. And then, as if to fill the uncomfortable silence, he muttered something about just wanting to "keep the gang together."

"I'm . . . I'm all they have," said Llewellyn Llewellyn, look-ing over his fellows in what you might describe as a fretful sort of way. And I won't say my heart melted for the blighter, for it's difficult for any heart, however soluble, to melt for a chap whose recent habits included kidnapping, false imprisonment, and the strapping down of your friends for a spot of unwanted medical intervention. But I could, to some degree, under-stand the chump's dilemma. For if Vera's television had been accurate — which I'm fairly sure it always was — then this chap's whole circle of pals had been mindwiped by Socrates in the fairly recent past, and he was straining every nerve and doing whatever was needed to ensure their well-being in their post-Socratic, mind-addled state. I was doing the same job for Zeus and had gotten myself into loads and loads of unexpected scrapes by making the effort. "Put yourself in this blighter's shoes," I said to myself as I watched him mother-henning over his chums and imagined the lengths to which I'd go in order to keep my nearest and d. out of both frying pans and fires. And while I'll admit that none of these lengths would, in my case, have involved kidnapping Napoleons and treating them like pincushions, you have to budget for the fact that this Llewellyn Llewellyn might have been one of those weak-minded bimbos you meet on life's journey, and one who had gotten himself wrapped up with a charismatic, prophecy-spouting religious zealot in the form of Norm Stradamus. These religious z.'s can wrap weak-minded bimbos around their little fingers, as the expression is, and have them doing all manner of goshawful stuff while chanting hosannas about Making Detroit Great Again before you can say "what ho." Why, I once knew a chap who'd been convinced to skip the brace of cocktails before dinner, another who worked himself into a zealous frenzy about others' bathroom habits, and yet another who felt it was a religious duty to steer clear of librarians. Convincing gullible people to act in bizarre and anti-social ways seems to be what zealots are for.

"There but for a functioning cerebrum go I," I remember thinking.

That particular train of thought pulled into its station and ground to a halt when Zeus appeared at our side, kicking his way through the rubble and righting the table behind which we'd been nestled.

"The coast is clear!" he announced.

"Terrence!" said Kari Slice.

"Zeus!" said Nappy.

My colossal gendarme twisted his mouth sideways in a puzzled sort of expression. He had the look of one who, at the halfway point of a long journey, has stumbled upon a crossroads whose presence wasn't announced by the GPS.

He looked at me, he looked at Nappy, he looked at Llewellyn Llewellyn, and he looked at me again. He might also have looked at Vera, Big Hurt, and Kari Slice, but I couldn't tell, for it's hard to keep track of everything someone as tall as Zeus drinks in with a couple of darting glances, he being able to observe things from the high ground, as it were.

He then contorted his face again, replacing the air of bafflement with a mask of firm resolve.

"Call me Zeus," he said at length.

I felt the thing wash through me like a dose of salts, or the news that the horse on which you've bet your little all has taken the crown by a short head.

"Gadzooks!" I shouted, rising, my heart fuller of raw emotion than it had been in quite some time, "You remember!"

He shook the loaf. This surprised me.

"I don't remember anything. Not from before I met the Regent," he said in a downcast sort of way. "But . . . well, I don't think I like the people who call me Terrence, or who I'd turn out to be if I stayed with them. If it's all the same to you," he added, fixing his gaze on yours truly, "I think I'd rather be Zeus, and stick with you."

I can't remember another single paragraph of dialogue that has so quickly gone from stripping every scrap of wind from the Feynman sails to suddenly filling them up with gales. The heart practically burst out of my chest, through my ribs, and ricocheted off a wall or two.

"Of course you can stick with me!" I said, my voice thick with manly emotion.

He turned from me, and glared down at Llewellyn Llewellyn.

"You'd better get out of here," he said. "Take your pals and run."

Llewellyn Llewellyn seemed all for this plan, but Big Hurt voiced an objection.

"But . . . but . . . where do we go? Norm was looking out for us. He paid us to help him reach the beforelife and—"

"Just get out," said Zeus. "Forget Norm. Forget the before-life. I don't think the Napoleons are out for revenge, but if they are, you'd deserve whatever they wanted to dish out."

This roused Llewellyn Llewellyn, who rose to his feet and made the case for the defence: "But we weren't the ones who tortured them!" he cried. "We didn't fight against them in the revolt! We—"

"You let it happen on your watch!" Zeus thundered. "You could have said something, and you didn't!"

Astute observers of this colossus will have noted that, on the cue "and you didn't," a little vein in the nor'nor'easterly portion of his face, right above an eyebrow that he was currently furrowing at Llewellyn Llewellyn and his fellow guards, twitched almost imperceptibly and began to enlarge, though whether it filled itself with blood, or with righteous indignation, is a matter best resolved elsewhere. But Llewellyn Llewellyn seemed to note the transformation, and to understand that it heralded a Zeus who was approaching the boiling point. And although Zeus had dropped his human-shaped cudgel somewhere on the field of battle, he seemed poised to arm himself at any moment, perhaps with another member of the Eighth Street Chapter.

Llewellyn Llewellyn may have weighed his options for a millisecond or two, but if he did there was no outward sign of this hesitation. Instead, he simply gathered up his pals, avoided making any form of eye contact with the members of my troop, and fled out the door through which we'd entered, perhaps to collect Philly the Rook preparatory to entering some type of witness protection program.

And thus is was that the Eighth Street Chapter disappeared from the remainder of my memoirs.

Nappy, rather than hurling objects or curses at the retreating chumps, seemed to have cast these blisters from her thoughts, now having eyes only for Zeus. For she flung herself at him, and the chap had no choice but to catch her in something resembling an embrace.

"It's all right, ma'am," said Zeus. "You'll be all right."

"Call me Nappy," is all she said.

"What do we do now?" asked Vera.

"Search me," I said. "You're the one who has television. Have a peep, and let us know what the future holds for our little gang."

"We're getting out of here," said Zeus, setting Nappy down gently and patting her shoulder in a comforting sort of way. "We've got to get as far away from this place as we can. I know the way out."

"I thought you'd never been down here," said Vera, doubtfully.

"I've studied the blueprints," said Zeus, and once again I felt myself applauding this chap's thoroughly helpful nature.

"Great," said Vera. "But we're taking Jack. The other

Napoleons seem to be all right for now, but I think he's down for the count. Besides, we'll need him later."

"What do you mean we'll need him later?" I asked, agog.

"I'm not sure," said Vera. "Something to do with my vision."

"Not the bally poetry again," I said, bewildered. "I thought we'd left that all behind us."

"No," said Vera. "It's still important. It's about stopping Isaac, and it's the key to bringing this whole story its conclusion. And we'll have to have Jack with us to make it happen."

I was expecting someone present to ask what it was that we were supposed to make happen, and how in Abe's name Jack was involved, but such was the force of Vera's personality that we simply did her bidding, Zeus wading back into the battlefield and scooping up the recumbent Jack preparatory to taking our leave. He slung Jack over a shoulder, Jack uttered a sort of "oof" indicating that life still animated his corpus and that he wasn't doing whatever it is Napoleons do before they reincarnate, and Zeus bounded up a nearby hall, barely encumbered by his passenger.

If you've been playing close attention to the story so far, you'll know I'd have followed Zeus practically anywhere, this chap's well-being being fairly high on my personal list of Things That Matter. So when he turned on his heel to lead us out, I didn't waste a moment before stringing along behind. Vera, Nappy, and Fenny strung along, too, the last of whom had little choice in the matter because he was still tucked in my pocket, apparently waiting for further assurances that we were out of the line of fire.

A couple of ticks later we arrived at an elevator, entered en masse, and Zeus carefully pressed a button marked G.

I, for one, would have assumed that G meant *Ground*, or *Ground floor*, or perhaps *Get ye off the elevator here*. And quite possibly that's what the button-installer had intended. But what he or she couldn't have planned when installing this machinery was that the elevator, on having its G button pushed, would open its doors not on the ground floor — or any floor — of the building in which the bally thing resided, but straight into a lion's den.

I suppose the button should have been marked *LD*.

Chapter 32

If there's one thing I can't abide in any author it's the habit of whipping the same dead horse, by which I mean the habit of recycling an old trope, if trope is the word I want, numerous times in the space of a handful of chapters. I mean to say, you find yourself wading through a slab of literature and enjoying a juicy passage in which it's revealed your antagonist has been hidden by a disguise all the while and actually turns out to be the protagonist's long-lost chum, when three chapters later another bad guy is unmasked and revealed to be another long-lost pal, who later removes another mask and turns out to be someone else, if you see what I'm driving at. A single instance of this plot twist grips the senses and raises the pulse. Three or more of the same twist in rapid succession merely draws a censorious look, a sense the author couldn't be bothered coming up with something new, and a critique of lazy writing in *Publisher's Weekly*. And although I'm the last one to criticize the Author, Capital A, in His literary choices, I felt He was making himself vulnerable to the charges of recycling and lazy writing. I mean to say, just skim through the evidence for the prosecution. Exhibit A: elevators. A fairish number of chapters ago Vera and self had stepped into an elevator at the base of City Hall and ended up in a place that neither of us had intended. A brace of chapters later, on the lam from the Regent's guards and trying our best to hide from a rapidly advancing reality quake, Vera and self had bunged the unconscious Zeus into another elevator — or dumbwaiter, if you're going to nitpick the thing — all with a view to staying put and waiting until the coast was clear. On this occasion, too, the elevator had acted with a mind of its own, moving us from position one and depositing our group in whatever spot the plot demanded.

And here we were on this third occasion, barely a day's worth of reading from the dumbwaiter sequence, entering an elevator in the hope of subtly changing our posish along the Z axis, only to find that when the blasted thing opened we were somewhere else entirely, in apparent violation of previous plot points concerning teleportation. *"Elevator ex machina!"* I might have shouted, had my attention not been gripped by other things. But this slice of teleportation via elevator is the choice the Author made, and it's what happened to yours truly, so there's nothing to do but exercise a bit of journalistic integrity and report these frustrating facts as they occurred. Similar things happened with the topics of memory loss and noggin beaning in what you might call the first few movements of this opus. It's one thing to play a couple of variations on a theme — it's quite another to keep serving the same dish for every course.

So as I was saying before my bit of heresy about the Author's work, the elevator opened into what you might call a lion's den. Not a literal lion's den, but a lion's den in the sense of being a place that held all manner of perils for yours truly and was — at least I thought at the time — exactly the place I didn't want to be.

The door rather inexplicably opened into the lecture theatre where I'd recently hobnobbed with Isaac Newton — the one that was occupied by all of those heavily scribbled blackboards festooned with numbers and things, and that had a little doorway leading into the cozy apartment where Isaac and self had enjoyed our respective cups of tea, if you can call it enjoying tea when you spend an hour or so trying to figure out if your host is bent on global destruction.

We stepped out. And the face that greeted us in the lecture theatre wasn't Isaac's. It was Norm's. He was standing there, apparently alone, wearing the look of a prophet who's been pleasantly surprised.

"Terrence!" he cried, looking to be on the point of clapping his hands and dancing a few steps. "Thank the Omega you've come! I wasn't sure anyone heard my summons. And you've brought everyone with you. Well done well done *well done!*"

"Summons?" said Zeus, looking as baffled as I felt.

"Yes. The summons to bring Jack and the Hand of the Intercessor through the teleportation portal so we could help Isaac finish up his—"

"I didn't get any summons," said Zeus.

"You didn't? Oh. That's odd. Then it's lucky you've turned up. Well, the important thing is that you're here and you've brought Jack and the Hand of the Intercessor with you. Isaac and Oan will be so pleased. You've saved us buckets of trouble. Let's get to it."

He turned on his heel, obviously keen to roll up his sleeves and get to whatever in Abe's name needed getting to, and apparently expecting the rest of us to make like a troop of ducklings and follow along. He'd travelled about twenty steps before he realized my entire baffled troop remained rooted to the spot, blinking at him.

"What are you waiting for?" he asked.

"Enlightenment," I riposted.

"What about?" he asked, ungrammatically.

"What in Abe's name you need with Jack, why you're here at the university instead of invading R'lyeh, and what's all of this rot about helping Isaac ruddy Newton. When last I checked

you were all hotsy totsy about thwarting this chump's experiments, and now we find you eager to push his work along!"

"Yeah!" said Vera, always willing to lend a vocal cord or two
to a righteous cause.

The rest of those present, rather than lending voice to the
r.c., stood by in quiet solidarity and subjected Norm Stradamus
to a collective brow-furrowing that unmanned him. He stood
back on his heels and twiddled his thumbs for a space before
making anything you might call a response. And when he
did give a response, it wasn't what you'd call a master class in
Rhetorical Art, for all he managed was this:

"Well . . . I mean . . . we *did* plan to stop him. That is, we
. . . or rather, the Regent . . ."

His speech trailed off into something reminiscent of a dying
soda siphon.

"Spit it out, man," I said. "You came here with one plan,
changed course for some reason or other, no doubt specious,
and then decided to hitch your lot to the opposition. That
much we can see. That much is apparent. What we want to
know, prophetic fathead, is why you changed your plans. Why
all this side-swapping and redirecting? Why," I added, making
the matter plain for the meanest intelligence, "go from stopping Isaac Newton to suddenly helping him with his plans?"

"It's like he was following your example," said Vera, rather
stalling my momentum.

"My example?" I asked.

"Yeah," said Vera. "I mean, didn't you do exactly the same
thing with Professor Newton? You told me and Oan that he was
the most dangerous man in the world, and that Abe sent you on
a quest to stop him, and you went to the university to — how
did you put it? — to lay his plans a-stymie, or something. But
when you came back you said his plans weren't dangerous at

all and that you'd agreed to help him with his research. Maybe the same thing happened with Norm."

"That's it precisely!" said Norm.

"And it's also the very point I hoped to make!" I said. "I mean to say, the Regent and Norm, all lathered up in religious fervour, got themselves convinced that Isaac Newton would wreck the world, inflicting mortality on Detroit, making retroactive changes, and causing reality quakes that leave the place in disarray, not to mention what they do to people hiding in dumbwaiters. But what they failed to do was listen to my counsel. 'Leave it alone,' I explained to them, as patiently as any chap could, for Newton's scientific tootling was confined to this quantum realm and could have no more impact on Detroit than tying together a couple of quarks, squashing a neutron or two, or possibly splitting a handful of atoms."

At my allusion to splitting atoms, Vera made a face suggesting the only thing preventing her from spitting out her tea was the fact she wasn't drinking any at the time.

The optimist in me had expected my oration to put an end to the argument, but it didn't. Rather than curling up in the face of my iron logic, Norm seemed to feel the need to add a few footnotes and qualifications.

"That's . . . well . . . that's not *exactly* true," said Norm. "I mean — Isaac's plans are significant. They really will change the world. They'll change everything. They'll transform the way people see Detroit, and help break down the boundaries between this world and the beforelife."

It seemed to me that the chap must have missed the entire point of my recent speech, and that the arguments I'd presented had somehow failed to make their way through his ear canals and penetrate the bean. I was about to say as much, and to present my thoughts once again at something approximating a kindergarten level, when Vera weighed in, hogging the spotlight and causing a change of focus.

"And he needs Jack to do it?" she said. And if you cared to describe her tone as dubious, you wouldn't be far wrong.

"That's right!" said Norm. "Jack's the key. I mean, any Napoleon might work, but Jack is best."

"You were torturing him!" thundered Zeus. And while one might accuse the chap of pushing the conv. off the rails and onto a tangent by bringing the torture note to the forefront, no one voiced an objection at the time. This may have had something to do with the tone he'd adopted, and the fact that, in his wrath, he seemed to have grown to the height of about nine-foot-seven.

Norm took two steps backward — always a prudent manoeuvre when staring down the barrel of a fully loaded Zeus. He muttered a word or two of something that seemed halfway between an apology and an explanation, but Zeus wanted no piece of it.

"I don't care why you did it," said Zeus. "But it stops right now. We brought Jack out of the Regent's hall to keep him safe. Not because of any summons, and not so you could use him in any experiment."

"But that's just it," said Norm. "We don't need to . . . well, erm . . . expose him to . . . ah . . . any sort of discomfort. The Regent and I had it all wrong. The key isn't making the Napoleons reincarnate. That's not how we'll reach the beforelife. The key is to adopt a Napoleonic world view."

Once again this prophet had surprised me. I mean to say, I knew he was intent on finding a way to the beforelife, where he would meet this Great Omega beazel in person and do whatever it is religious zealots do when face-to-face with the one they worship, but how this would be assisted by adopting a Napoleon's outlook, gabbling in their goofy lingo, and planning tactical assaults, was beyond me. It was beyond Nappy, too, for this particular Napoleonic pipsqueak, who had hitherto been obscured by Zeus's left thigh, stepped around the behemoth and put the question to Norm Stradamus.

"What do you mean, a Napoleonic world view?"

"It's all a bit complicated," said Norm. "Why not let Isaac explain—"

"She asked *you* to explain," said Zeus, "and we're not moving another inch until you answer."

"Oh. Ah. Right then," said Norm. "Well, you see, it's all about expectations. Isaac explained the whole thing to us. He's been changing the world by altering ancients' expectations — changing their thought patterns and beliefs. You see, the ancients help Abe shore up the walls of reality. They . . . well, they constitute Detroit. It's like Oan taught in the Sharing Room," he added, turning to me, "the world is made up of the expectations of those who live within it. And the most powerful minds have the greatest impact on it. These ancients — the ones who arrived in Detroit shortly after Abe, and who helped him to build the walls of reality — they continue to shore it up when they go dormant."

"They dream the world," said Vera, thoughtfully.

"In a way," said Norm. "Their thoughts and expectations carry on shaping the world and holding it together, preventing anyone else's stray thoughts from changing things and ruining it for everyone else — stopping everyone's conflicting expectations and desires from fouling everything up, as it were. When Isaac realized this — when he observed the battle between the City Solicitor and Penelope — everything fell into place, and he understood the inner workings of Detroit."

At least that made one of us, I thought. But what I said was "Good for him."

"He didn't like it," said Norm. "Not one bit. But at least it made things clear. It explained why the world that he observed failed to correspond to his calculations. He had based his calculations on the assumption that we lived in a physical world, where laws of nature could be known and uncovered through empirical observation, where calculations could predict the movement of everything from quarks to planets. But try as he might—"

"He couldn't get his calculations to work!" I added, dredging up something from my earlier confab with Professor Newton.

"That's right. And it frustrated him more than you could imagine. He'd devoted his life to science and mathematics, only to learn, too late, that he didn't live in a reality where the rules of science and math govern the world. Here in Detroit, the planets follow orbits that the people collectively expect them to follow. Gravity works in the way that we expect. Chemistry, biology, astrophysics — every branch of science operates according to the expectations of those who live in Detroit, guided by minds like Abe, Penelope, and the sleeping ancients."

Vera piped in once again, doing her best to translate this into basic English.

"So if people didn't expect the world to work in a particular way, it wouldn't. Even if Isaac's calculations proved it should."

"Something like that," said Norm. "It's much more complicated, though. I mean, if some new invention or discovery fit with people's expectations, then it might work, even if it's something people hadn't already imagined. If people thought science might someday find, say, a way to reach the stars, then it might be possible to do that in Detroit. Isaac's problems were at the margins, deep within what Isaac calls the hidden universe — things that only a scientist might detect. Microscopic, fabric-of-reality sorts of things that don't correspond to intuition — these are the areas where Isaac ran into problems."

"And those are the things he's changing," I added, a touch of exasperation in my timbre. "Teeny, weeny, undetectable things. Which is why I can't understand what all the fuss is about. Let the chap tinker with these marginal whatnots at his leisure. Leave him alone."

"But why do you need Jack?" said Zeus, who'd managed to maintain his glower right through Norm's bit of exposition.

"It's related to what Vera and the Hand of the Intercessor saw at R'lyeh," said Norm. "Isaac created a way to change the memory engrams and the — well, the science is a bit beyond me," he paused, chuckling, "but whatever you call it that goes on deep within a person's brain, right at the very core of their psyche, Isaac can change that. He can chemically transmit new patterns of thought, so the recipient's world view changes. He takes his own scientific discoveries, his own calculations, and encodes these into a fluid that he injects into the ancients. This changes the ancients' expectations, which in turn changes the nature of the world. Quite ingenious."

"But Jack?" said Zeus.

"Ah, right," said Norm. "If Isaac could encode Jack's neural patterns into this fluid, he'd be able to imprint them on to someone else. And if that person had a sufficiently powerful mind — say, like the Regent—"

"Then that person would now share Jack's conviction that the beforelife was real, and that passage between Detroit and the beforelife was possible," said Vera, cottoning on. "They'd take on the Napoleons' ability to reincarnate."

"Wait," said Nappy. "You mean, eef you can make les anciennes believe what Jack believes, zen everyone will be able to go back to ze beforelife?"

"Perhaps," said Norm, "but we don't want to go that far. We don't need to make everyone believe in the beforelife. We just want to send the Regent there as an emissary. We'll encode Jack's neural patterns, inject them into the Regent, and send her back to the beforelife where she'll meet the Great Omega."

"Won't she reincarnate as a child?" said Vera, which seemed fairly astute, as I hadn't thought of that objection.

"Very good!" said Norm. "She will! But she'll carry some of her memories with her — just like Napoleons do when they reincarnate. What we've learned from Jack, and some of the other Napoleons, is that they reincarnate in the beforelife still remembering some bits of their lives as Napoleons. Isaac is doing something with the Regent's brain — I don't pretend to understand it — that'll help preserve her memories. By the time she reaches adulthood in the beforelife, she'll remember much of her life here in Detroit and make her way to the Great Omega."

"Seems like a dashed silly plan to me," I said.

"Me too," said Nappy.

"I mean to say, why bother with Jack at all? It seems that you, the Regent, and Isaac are all thoroughly convinced that the Napoleons are right, that the beforelife is real, and that reincarnation happens. What's the point of injecting Regents with beliefs they already hold?"

"It's more complicated than that," said Norm. "It's not just about belief, it's about absolute, unshakeable convictions. A level of faith in the beforelife that most will never achieve. A belief so strong it breaks through the boundaries of reality created by Abe and the sleeping ancients, and allows reincarnation despite the accepted 'truth' that the beforelife isn't real."

"But what's Isaac's angle in this?" said Vera. "I mean, why would he help you send the Regent to the beforelife? What's this got to do with him?"

It was at this point that I reached what the Napoleons call an impasse. I mean to say, on the heels of our swash-buckling, nerve-wracking escape from the Regent's lair, we'd suddenly ground to a halt and found ourselves embroiled, if that's the expression, smack-dab in the middle of a dull, dry, yawn-inducing chat about science. This put me squarely onto the horns of a dilemma. Should I, I asked myself, continue my work as the Author's scribe, dutifully jotting down everything that passed from Norm's lips as he explained the ins and outs of Isaac's scientific plans, or should I write in broader strokes, merely giving my public the gist? Give them too deep an account of the whithertos and wherefores of Isaac's ruddy plan, and their eyes may gloss over, the book might tumble from their hands, and my readers, if any, may find themselves drooling where they sit as they slip into a sleep plagued by nightmares in which they're chased by angry lab coats and scanning electron thingummies. On the other hand, if I simply give them what you might call a bird's-eye view of what Norm said, writing something along the lines of "never mind the details, but there's science afoot, and you'll have to take my word that it all makes sense," they'll roll their collective eyes, adopting the justifiable view that one of the minor plotlines in this volume, viz, Isaac's scientific busy-bodying and the original mission on which Abe had sent me, never really amounted to anything or made one jot of sense. You can see the difficulties I'm facing.

I've noted the same issue arising in comic books I've read. You hope to spend an idle hour poring over Wonderchap's acts of derring-do, enjoying his leaps and bounds over buildings and his races with locomotives, when you find yourself mired in a series of dull, boring panels in which an overzealous writer has tried to explain the physics behind the hero's powers, answering questions like "how can Wonderchap propel himself in a vacuum," or "when the archvillain Wickedchump bench-presses a building, why doesn't the whole thing buckle and crumble all around him, leaving him bathed in rubble and ruin?" Yield to the impulse to explain the principles behind these hitherto unexplained fantastical things, and you're apt to find you can't, so you cheat the thing a bit and find yourself hip-deep in mid-ichlorians, or homeopathy, or genetic memory, or some other unempirical weirdness that fails the test of peer review. Pseudo-scientific babbling, I mean to say. The science fails to please the discerning eye, the fantasy is ruined, and the plot is stalled by unnecessary gobbledygook. On the one hand, you ask your public to suspend all disbelief; on the other, you try to explain why all the fantastical bits are firmly rooted in science. I think you'll agree that authors of comic books, science fiction, or fantasy thingummies have to tread a fine line.

In the present instance, perhaps it's best to err on the side of crossing all of the t's and dotting the i's, doing my best to convey the flavour of what was said, while giving impatient readers the option of skipping down about three pages, perhaps until a paragraph or two before the conclusion of the chapter.

Turning back to the present slab of dialogue, Vera had just asked why Isaac gave a tinker's damn about the Regent's perilous passage to the beforelife, and Norm was on the point of offering up an explanation. Here's what he said:

"That's the ingenious bit! And it's why we're going to help him. Isaac's only goal in any of this is to see what happens. He wants to see what happens when someone passes from this world to the beforelife, making careful observations and seeing what he can learn about passing information across the boundary between worlds."

Vera chewed on a lower lip. Her own, in fact. And she followed this up with speech.

"I think I see what you're driving at," she said, which made one of us. "I mean, we already know information can pass between the beforelife and Detroit—"

"We do?" I said, interrupting.

"Of course we do," said Vera. "People come here when they die."

"But people aren't information."

"Of course they are. Information that's encoded in DNA. And memory engrams. And — well — what *you'd* call character sketches. Each of us is information. It's the same principle that underlies the idea of teleportation: transmit all of the information about an object from one place to another."

"Teleportation isn't real. At least it isn't anymore," I said, helpfully.

"Well, it's sometimes real," said Norm, interjecting. "I mean, Isaac can make exceptions. He explained it to us earlier. Not long ago he forced the ancients to believe that teleportation was impossible, which meant that it suddenly was. But half an hour ago he found he needed to make it possible again so that the Regent could, using her pyramidical totem, create the portal that brought you here. So he reintroduced the concept by changing the ancients' minds again, and—"

"We get the idea," said Vera, waving off the bearded babbler before turning her attention back to me in the hope of easing my considerable bafflement.

"The point I'm trying to make is that information can pass between the beforelife and Detroit. When Ian came through the Styx with his memories intact, all of the information stored in his brain came here from the beforelife. That information crossed the boundary between one world and the next. And when the Napoleons reincarnate, moving back to the beforelife from Detroit, that proves that information can move back in the other direction, if you see what I mean."

"That's it exactly!" said Norm. "Isaac wants to observe the passage of information between two worlds. That's all he wants."

"Why in Abe's name would he do that?" I asked. I mean, I didn't precisely care why anyone would want to pierce a veil or two between a couple of worlds, but it did strike me as an odd use of one's time.

Vera surprised me by stepping in and fielding this question, one I'd expected to have been grabbed by Norm.

"Don't you see?" she said, which was a silly thing to ask, because of course I didn't. "He wants to replicate the process. He wants to gather information from the beforelife. Scientific observations. Measurements. That sort of thing."

The look on my face must have indicated that this was going to require some amplification, for she forged on, sprinkling the landscape with necessary details.

"The beforelife isn't like Detroit. It's governed by physical laws. Its rules will correspond to Isaac's math. Here in Detroit, Isaac has to make his calculations in . . . well, in a sort of vacuum. He can calculate all he wants, but if his calculations reveal anything that's outside the collective expectations of the ancients, he can't confirm his math by observation. He might — through his math — prove that dark matter ought to exist, or that black holes keep popping up all over the place, but if these things don't check up with the expectations of the ancients, he'll never observe them here, and never know if the solutions he proposed through his calculations are correct in a physical world. He can't confirm them by observing things, because the world he observes here doesn't conform to physical laws. But the beforelife is different. His observations of how everything works in the beforelife will advance his work and help confirm his calculations. He'll be able to confirm his findings by measuring them against the things he sees there."

"And once he's managed to take stock of the quantum structure of the beforelife, his grand calculations will be complete," said Norm. "He'll fundamentally understand the nature of physical laws. That's all he's ever really wanted."

Why anyone would want this was beyond me. I mean to say, I was merely hearing about the process, and this was enough to cause the eyelids to grow heavy and the mind to wander.

Vera seemed keen to pursue the point, for she seemed to raise some objection or call for a point of clarification. She started by weighing in with the words "but that isn't really true, is it?" at which point speechlessness supervened, due to the advent of none other than Isaac Newton himself.

He tottled into the lecture hall, not seeming the least bit surprised by the presence of an elevator which hadn't been there before. And it warmed my heart to see that, unlike most people I'd met in the last few days, he seemed more than a little pleased to bump into me. Rather than curling his lip, scoffing, or pinching the bridge of his nose on catching sight of yours truly, this Mensa freak clapped his hands, unleashed a smile that any dental hygienist would have been proud of, and said, "Excellent, let's get started."

And if you're anything like me — the sort of chap who pays attention to narrative structure and whathaveyou — then you'll know that Isaac saying anything like "let's get things started" is likely to herald the coming of the end of the present book. Strap in, gentle reader, and prepare for the climax, denouement, and closing words.

Chapter 33

Within about two shakes of Fenny's tail, as the expression is, I found myself back in the antechamber, or sitting room if you prefer, where I'd first had tea with Isaac. I could see at a g. that he'd redecorated a bit, some of the furniture having been shoved out of the way to make room for one of the cold storage units we'd seen in R'lyeh — those mechanical thingummies in which the dormant ancients slept, and into which Isaac pumped his lesson-bearing juice in order to rewire their brains and change their memories.

This one was occupied by the Regent, who seemed to be snoring peacefully within, despite the wires and tubes and things entwined about her bean. Oan stood outside the thing, fiddling with buttons and knobs and things, until she noticed my arrival and gave speech.

"Rhinnick!" she cried, a bit more ecstatically than I'd like, for this ecstasy suggested Oan wasn't hep to recent events, hadn't learned of my recent incarceration or involvement in a Napoleonic rebellion, and therefore still counted Rhinnick Feynman as a king among men and one who ranked in the top echelons — if echelon means what I think it does — of prime marital fauna. She lost interest in fiddling with the Regent's storage compartment and floated straight at me, enfolding me in an embrace that I wasn't able to dodge.

"Grrnmph," said Fenny, from the recesses of my costume,

indicating no small measure of pique at having become invol-untarily entangled in an unwelcome hug.

I rather think Vera giggled at this juncture, but for the life of me I couldn't imagine why.

"Oh, Rhinnick," said Oan. "I'm so glad you're finally here. Once again the universe heard my call and manifested my desires, bringing you to me just when I—"

"Oh, rather," I said, extricating myself from her clutches and doing my best to put an end to this unseemly public display of a. "Wouldn't have missed it for the world. It isn't every day you get to observe Regents winging their way to the beforelife."

"A most auspicious occasion!" said Norm, pulling up along-side. He, too, seemed filled to the brim with ecstasy, and might have broken into a buck-and-wing dance had Vera not stepped in with a question.

"Are you sure this is safe?" she asked, stepping up to the Regent's storage thingummy.

"Don't be silly," said Norm, still effervescing all over the place. "The Regent is perfectly safe. The sarcophagus is merely a precaution — Isaac theorizes that it might help the Regent keep a greater share of her memories once she achieves adult-hood in the mortal world. I don't fully grasp the science, of course. But if Isaac's calculations are correct, which they always are, she'll simply dematerialize and—"

"I wasn't worried about the Regent," said Vera. "I'm worried about the rest of us."

"But why?" said Oan.

"Who knows what'll happen?" said Vera.

"Isaac knows. Isaac seems to know everything!" said Oan.

"He's the one I'm worried about," said Vera. "I don't think he's thought this through."

You might be expecting Isaac to have taken offence at this remark, but you'd be wrong. He wasn't offended by the remark at all, largely owing to the fact that he hadn't heard it. For on entering this room he'd tottered off to the far end, some fifteen metres distant, where now stood a large bank of computers which were connected by wires and cables to the Regent's cozy compartment. He busied himself there with various knobs and switches, blissfully unaware that our little gathering was huddled around a Vera who was speaking in unflattering terms about his foresight and planning.

"Ms. Lantz," said Norm, showing every indication of condescension, "I'm sure Professor Newton has thought this through. He's been thinking of little else for months."

"But what do you think will happen when Isaac peers into the beforelife and sees how everything works? He'll pump his ancients full of his serum and have them change Detroit to be just like the physical world — the *mortal* world."

I don't know about you, but I was fed to the eye teeth with this trend of everyone making more of this professorial chump's science projects than was warranted. So I took this opportunity to oil out of the conversation. I tapped Zeus on the shoulder — the one without an unconscious Jack draped over it — and gave him one of those sideways nods you give when you want someone to sneak off with you.

I'd hoped to slip away unnoticed, which of course was silly of me, because you can't sneak off anywhere if your fellow sneaker, viz, Zeus, is so huge that he tends to blot out the sun whenever he moves from spot to spot. We hadn't moved so much as a muscle when Norm Stradamus and Oan both broke off from whatever they had been saying and indicated, in no uncertain terms, that the Feynman presence was needed.

"You can't leave now, Hand of the Intercessor."

"No!" said Oan. "We have so much to prepare!"

"Include me out," I said. "You seem bent on pushing ahead with this neural, quantum, science business, and I hope you have a fine day for it. But that has nothing to do with me. I'm pushing off."

"But you can't push off!" said Oan.

"Oh right," said Norm, "I'd forgotten. Terrence never received my summons."

"Call him Zeus."

"Why should I call him Zeus?"

"Because it's my name," said Zeus.

"But I distinctly remember you being called Terrence," said Norm. "You introduced yourself to me. I'm good with names. I—"

I pinched the bridge of the Feynman nose with one hand while using the other to silence the fathead with a gesture.

"Please get to the point, prophetic ass," I said, wearily. "What does the ruddy summons have to do with anything?"

"It explained why I need you here."

"You aren't hooking me up to any gizmos and sharing the Feynman brain pattern with the Regent."

"No, of course not. You're needed for the wedding."

His words hit home like a tall bucket of icy water. At least that's how they felt to me. Oan seemed to receive these words like rare and refreshing fruit, while Zeus seemed rather bored with the whole idea, he apparently having eyes for nothing apart from keeping Jack and Nappy safe.

The last thing I wanted to do was ask the obvious question, I personally preferring to leave the whole subject of weddings unventilated — but conversational etiquette dictated that I pick up the thread, rather than changing the topic to politics, or needlework, or the relative merits of tetherball and knitting.

"W-w-wedding?" I faltered.

"Yes, your wedding to Oan," said the prophetic fathead, stating the obv. It's not as though a whole regiment of would-be brides and grooms was in the room.

"But that's months away," I said. "If not years. No need to go on about it now."

"Our plans have changed!" said Oan, who looked happier than a cat who'd caught a legion of canaries.

"We thought we'd have the ceremony here," said Norm, "this evening I mean. To mark the occasion. It was Oan's idea."

Well of course it was Oan's idea, it being one of the goofiest and most half-baked notions to have ever been aired in a public place.

"I thought the symbolism was perfect," said Oan. "The Regent passing from our world into the beforelife, taking her place as the emissary to the Great Omega, as you formally take your position in the church, embracing your role as the Hand of the Intercessor and taking me as your spouse. We start our lives together as the Regent renews hers in the beforelife. It will make a wonderful final chapter for my book, *For Love Alone!*"

I winced like I'd never winced before, and might have collapsed under the weight of events had the Author not built me of sterner stuff. Oan stared at me with a look that a starving lion might unleash on an especially toothsome zebra, and it occurred to me that a more fitting title for her book might be *Eat Prey, Love*.

"It's all so perfect!" cried Oan, still gripped in ecstasy.

I could not subscribe to this. Indeed, it's fair to say that I hadn't heard anything less perfect since the last time I'd been seated in the Sharing Room listening to this very Oan harping about the Laws of Attraction.

"But . . . but . . . surely you can't plan a thing like this at the last minute—" I protested.

"Norm is taking care of everything," gushed Oan.

I grasped the nearest straw.

"We haven't sent any invitations!" I cried.

"All of our friends are here!" said Oan.

"But the wedding dress! The sponge-bag trousers! The vows, and lawyers, and flowers and things—"

"What matters is that you and I are here, together," said Oan. "And that the universe has listened to our desires, bringing us to this day when we'll finally send our emissary to the Omega. Oh, Rhinnick," she said, beaming freely, "this will be the happiest day of my life, and I have you to thank for it. The Hand of the Intercessor! You're making all of my dearest wishes come true!"

Well, I don't know about you, but I could wrack the brain for a dozen years without finding a way to oil out of something like that. I mean to say, here was this loony goofball bunging her heart at the Feynman feet, stating in no uncertain terms that it was her dearest and fondest wish to link her lot with mine, and I, by holding my tongue all this time in order to keep things civil and avoid anything approaching an unpleasant conversation, had done what amounted to stoking the fires of passion. I couldn't turn to the old disaster now and tell her that her dream wedding was going to be short one groom.

I don't know what I would have said — I suppose "oh, ah" would have been about the best I could have mustered if given the chance, but I was spared all effort by the advent of Isaac Newton, who popped up in our midst asking if he might borrow Jack.

Zeus was the first to utter a response, still sticking firmly to the familiar watchdog script which suited him so well.

"You leave Jack out of this," he said. "I don't know what he did, but there's no excuse for torturing prisoners—"

"My good chum," I said, turning Zeusward. "This professorial chump has no interest in torturing anyone. At least, I don't think he does. Isaac," I said, addressing the chump in question, "what exactly is involved in making a copy of a Napoleonic bimbo's brain thingummies? Nothing too intrusive I trust."

"No! He won't be harmed at all. I'll just strap him into that chair," he added, pointing, "and then I'll pop the neural scanner onto his head—"

"The chair!" said Vera, making her presence known and gripping the science nib's arm. He seemed put off by this development — whether because he disliked interruptions or preferred remaining ungrabbed by mediums, who could say — but he quickly regained his footing and addressed her.

"I assure you it's perfectly harmless," he said. "I've been using it on myself. It encodes brain patterns. It's how I've been preparing the fluid—"

"Two chairs!" said Vera.

"Not two chairs," Isaac corrected, "one chair only."

"But you're the Lucasian Chair of Maths!" I said.

"What's all this fuss about chairs?" said Norm.

"It's my vision," said Vera.

"Vera's a medium," I said, bringing Isaac up to speed. "Sees the future. Also the past. Very convenient."

Isaac didn't seem impressed, which didn't surprise me. These sciencey types are often skeptical and dismissive when it comes to fortune tellers and whatnot, but he should have thought of that before partnering up with Norm Stradamus, a known prophet and sayer of sooth.

"I had a vision of two chairs," said Vera. "It came in the form of a poem."

And this poem she proceeded to recite for the benefit of those assembled. I reproduce it here, *in toto*, for your convenience:

> *Two chairs define a man and men;*
> *Two chairs that free and bind;*
> *Two chairs that open worlds and free*

The body and the mind;
One chair sought and held by both,
The other coveted by none;
The first chair reunites two souls
Intended to have been just one.

On finishing this recital, Vera just stood there, all bright-eyed, with an expectant look on her map, as if anticipating that this little slab of verse might win the day and cause Isaac to abandon his plans. Of course it didn't. I mean to say, poetry never convinced anyone of anything, let alone poetry babbled at physicists in the middle of an experiment.

Isaac gave a little shrug, mumbled something unflattering about poets and fortune tellers, and moved off in Zeus's direction.

"You can't really blame him," I said, speaking to Vera. "I mean, the poem doesn't really appear to fit this situation. Which chair unites two souls? Where are the two men intended to be just one? How does Isaac's little neural chair thingummy free the body?"

Good questions all, I think you'll agree, and they left Vera baffled.

"I suppose you're right," she said. "The poem doesn't really fit. But I'm sure Isaac's one of the chairs, and I'm sure we're on the verge of figuring out the poem's meaning. I can feel it in my bones."

Rather than standing there arguing with the bones of a fortune teller, I turned my attensh to Zeus, whom Isaac — through some hidden skill at rhetorical arts — had somehow convinced to hand over the goods and assist in the process of strapping the sleeping Jack in the chair.

"What in Abe's name are you doing?" I said.

"Helping Isaac," said Zeus. "He says this'll be good for Jack."

"It's true," said Isaac, holding a bit of heavily wired headgear which I took to be what he'd called his "neural scanner." "We'll take a full scan of Jack's brain. I'll make my serum from those engrams relating to his memories of the beforelife and his convictions relating to reincarnation and moving back and forth between two worlds. But we'll have access to a record of his whole psyche. I've agreed to give that to Zeus, who can hand the whole thing over to the psychiatrists at the hospice."

"It'll help them treat Jack!" said Nappy. "Stop him from being so . . ."

"Stab-happy?" I suggested. "Anti-social? Downright awful?"

As the last of these words left my lips, it occurred to me that, if anyone in the world could benefit from having a record of his brainwaves recorded with a view to obtaining what I believe is called cognitive readjustment, it was the horrid little Napoleon who sat strapped before me now. I mean to say, one need only revisit my last few meetings with the chap in order to see the evidence: at least two attempts to perforate yours truly with sharp objects, a noted disregard for the well-being of others, and a marked tendency to bite the hand that fed him and make life miserable for any who crossed his path.

"Right ho," I said. "Copy away!"

Nappy and Zeus seemed to agree, for they stepped back from the chair and let Isaac do his thing.

What "his thing" entailed was fastening the last few buckles and zips, placing the neural headgear into place, and flicking a couple of switches.

Nothing appeared to happen except that a few lights on Isaac's computers switched from red to green, and then back to red again.

"There!" said Isaac.

"There?" I said.

"Zere?" said Nappy.

"We've copied his brainwaves. The computer's sorting them now and isolating the ones we've targeted for the transfer. It won't be long until the serum's produced."

"I really don't think we ought to be doing this," said Vera.

"Isaac says that this will help Jack get the attention that he needs," I said. "Not that I'd confidently guarantee that any competent board of medical ethicists would approve the involuntary copying of brainwaves, I suppose — but I think it'll do him good. It couldn't make him any worse, I mean. Horrible little menace."

"That's not what I mean," said Vera. "Isaac is tinkering with the fabric of reality. If he can observe the beforelife—"

"Please, Vera," I said, "desist. I see now that you're convinced by this whole Climate Change theory that Norm and Oan keep mentioning, and you feel that Isaac will upend reality if given a chance to do so. Norm seems convinced of it, too, and he's practically signed on to become Newton's lab assistant. He knows what Isaac is planning. And you don't see him running around in a panic. Chap's busy planning a wedding. He wouldn't be planning weddings if he thought the world would be torn asunder by Isaac's meddling."

And as if on cue, the soothsayer in question, accompanied by Oan, stepped forward and buttonholed me once more, renewing his insistence that I turn my mind to marital matters.

"The time has almost come, Hand of the Intercessor."

"We should start the ceremony as soon as Isaac injects his serum into the Regent's chamber," added Oan.

A muffled *"qu'est-ce qui se passe"* coming from the vicinity of the heavily wired chair behind me, saved the day by turning the conv. away from nuptials. I, for one, had never been more pleased to hear a slice of Napoleonic lingo.

"Jack's awake!" I announced.

"We can see that," said Norm.

"Where am I?" said Jack, and one couldn't blame him.

"You're in Isaac Newton's office," said Zeus. "He's helping you."

"'Elping me 'ow?" said Jack, now struggling against his bonds. "And why am I trapped in zees chair!"

"Best to keep him strapped in, old chum," I said, cautioning Zeus against unbuckling any buckles. "He's apt to be a bit grumpy. Besides, there are any number of sharp objects in the vicinity, and this particular Napoleonic gargoyle can't be trusted to leave them be."

"Let me go!" shouted Jack.

"Eet's all right," said Nappy, offering words of comfort. "You'll be free to return to ze 'ospice after zees."

"What 'ave you done to me?"

"Nothing you'll notice," said Zeus. "They've just copied your brain patterns and—"

"My brain patterns are mine! Zey are what make me! Give zem back!"

"They only *copied* them," said Zeus. "You'll be fine. Just—"

"You 'ave no right! Set me free!"

"Isaac shouldn't be doing any of this," said Vera, taking a spot beside me.

Isaac, still ignoring Vera's protests, stood fiddling with the controls of one of his large computers, and then said, "Serum production in nine seconds."

"If you'll just come this way," said Norm, placing his hand on the Feynman arm, "we can get the wedding started."

"What wedding?" cried Jack.

"Six seconds," said Isaac.

"I don't think you've all considered the consequences," said Vera.

"We really do need you now," said Norm.

"Three seconds."

394

I don't know if you're anything like me, but if you are you might be in need of a headache pill or two, or perhaps something in the nature of strong spirits. I mean to say, there seemed to be six or seven different conversations going on, and none of them was particularly agreeable.

Zeus started explaining to Jack whose wedding was taking place and why he'd be viewing the spectacle while strapped into a metal chair; Vera carried on promoting her theory, if you can call it a theory, that Isaac's plan presented a public menace; Isaac said "serum acquired," and Norm and Oan oiled toward the Regent's storage unit, waving at me to join them. Perceiving that the Wedding Front was the one most in need of my attention, I hopped over to Norm and Oan and made my plea.

"Are you absolutely sure this can't wait?" I said, and if you'd care to add the word "beseechingly" you wouldn't be far wrong. I carried on, making my speech for the defence.

"I'm sure there are others who'd be interested in attending this wedding, it being a fairly Big Deal for the Church of O. Oan's friends from work, for example. Former hospice patients. Dr. Peericks. Why, I'm sure that a whole host of people would like to witness the uhh—"

"Blessed event," said Norm, not noticing that I'd only just saved myself from calling the thing a cataclysm.

"Right you are," I said, "this blessed event. Surely a whole host of people would — wait, do you hear that noise?"

Knowing me as well as you do, having waded through thirty-some-odd chapters of this volume, and quite possibly having made your way through all forty-four chapters of its prequel, you might be thinking I'd uttered the phrase "do you hear that noise" as a kind of ruse or distraction, hoping to throw Oan and Norm off my scent, as the expression is, and turn their attention to something else. But while it's true that I did wish to call their attention to something else, it wasn't anything that might qualify as a ruse. It was a bona fide noise.

"I don't hear anything," said Oan — she apparently having ears only for Feynman and wedding planning.

"Sort of a — what would you say — a crowd approaching in the distance," I specified.

"Now that you mention it . . ." said Norm.

"What you might hear if the Mongol horde were cresting a nearby ridge, preparatory to descending onto the village below for a round of pillaging and plundering and whathaveyou. Occasional blood-curdling scream, that sort of thing."

He heard it now. Nor was he the only one. For Oan, Vera, Nappy, Jack, Zeus, and Isaac — the whole assembled crew — tilted their heads in a curious-puppy sort of way, giving an ear to the distant rumbling.

"It does have a 'descending hordish' ring to it," said Norm.

It was at this point that the true significance of the thing dawned on me, and I gave tongue.

"Did anyone think to close the elevator portal?"

Chapter 34

"What elevator portal?" said Oan.

"Teleportation thingummy," I said. "The one through which we arrived. Something Isaac seems to have arranged to whoosh us here, notwithstanding prior claims about teleportation."

"Now that you mention it," said Norm, for the second time, "I don't think anyone did."

"Ah," I said. "That explains it. It sounds to me like the Napoleons are coming. No doubt they're on the Regent's trail. Intent on exacting a bit of revenge, I'd imagine."

Now that I see those words in print, it occurs to me that there might have been something to Oan's claims that the universe eavesdrops on us when we give voice to our desires and then, when the inclination strikes, sees what it might do by way of answering our requests. Examining all the evidence, I'd have to say it isn't especially competent or consistent when it comes to this desire-fulfilling service, but it does give it a go from time to time. Take the moment of present interest. I had just expressed a wish, however insincerely, that we stall this wedding disaster until such time as we could gather a few more bodies and form something of a congregation. And the universe, failing to perceive that what I really wanted was no wedding at all, presented a crowd instanter, letting a raging horde of Napoleons find their way to the elevator and make their way to ground zero, just in time to watch the vows.

One could hear that they were on the point of making their presence known, the din of their distant approach now reaching levels that shook the walls.

"Everyone stay here," said Zeus, who always seemed to swell a bit in moments like this. "I'll handle them."

"But eet sounds like zere are dozens of zem," said Nappy, making generous use of the letter "z."

"You can't fit an entire platoon of Napoleons in the elevator all in one go," I said, helpfully. "They must be gathered at the other end and sending up a few at a time."

"How many Napoleons can you cram into an elevator?" said Norm.

"Enough to tear apart ze likes of you!" shouted Jack.

"Can you close the portal now?" someone suggested. It could well have been me, but so much was going on at the present moment that it was hard for me to be sure.

"No, the Regent opened it, using her pyramidical totem," said Norm.

"That's a difficulty," I said.

"I helped the Napoleons in the revolt," said Zeus. "I fought on their side. Maybe they'll be friendly if I'm the first person they see."

"They don't sound friendly, chum," I said. "They sound riled up for war. And if they find the Regent and Norm, people whom they, rather justly, regard as the source of their recent troubles—"

"I can handle them," said Zeus, flexing a bicep or two. And so saying, he withdrew, leaving through the door to the lecture theatre and closing it behind him.

Nappy, being a Napoleon, instinctively took up a defensible tactical position, climbing atop the Regent-storage-thingummy with an armload of books, presumably for projectile purposes.

Isaac stood nearby, fiddling with a syringe which, presumably, would fill the sleeping Regent with Jack's brain patterns.

A moment or two later the sound of the coming horde of ravenous Napoleons intensified, and I perceived that a whole dungeon's worth of the little chaps would soon be among us. I could hear Zeus shouting at them, but whatever it was he shouted was drowned out by the sounds of Napoleonic battle cries.

"We can't let them interfere with the procedure," said Isaac, still flicking the syringe.

"Someone should interfere with it," said Vera. And I perceived that she and Isaac descended into something of an argument, she taking the posish that this whole Climate Change plan would lead to ruin and desolation, and he suggesting that whatever ensued would be governed by reason, stable physical laws, and the purity of mathematics, whatever in Abe's name that means. One could see their passions were running hot, like those of attendees at academic conferences when they hear that the liquor license failed to come through and they'll have to make do with decaffeinated coffee and diet soda.

Vera appeared to tire of the argument and took things to what one might call the physical level, for she now tried to snatch the vial-syringe-thingummy from Professor Newton's hands. He dodged, and held it above his head in what I thought was an unsportsmanlike way, given his height advantage.

Nappy prepared a book to launch at any intruders, very decently ignoring any allegiance she may have felt to fellow Napoleons and rising to the defence of those friends who, I think we can all agree, had righteousness on their side.

Norm and Oan, more cut out for planning weddings than involving themselves in anything resembling a mêlée, did the shrewd thing and headed for the back of the room, doing their best to blend in with the furniture.

The sounds of battle intensified. I remembered a line I'd read about someone or other wading into their quarry like a wolf into the fold, with their cohorts all gleaming in purple and gold. Whether or not these Napoleons came festooned with gleaming cohorts I couldn't say, but part of me did feel the undeniable urge to bleat.

"We can't let zem see Jack," shouted Nappy, and one could see what she was driving at. Try as we might, it would be hard to convince Napoleons that we ought to be counted as friends and well-wishers when we had one of their number trussed up like a turkey bound for the oven and strapped into an uncomfortable-looking chair.

Well, I don't know if you've ever been a juggler, but I've always wondered what would happen if you came across one in the midst of his or her act and chucked an extra couple of balls into the mix. Your consummate professional jugglers might take this in stride, calling for extra balls and bats and a few chainsaws to make it a challenge. But your amateurs and workaday jugglers might be a different story. I imagine they'd find the senses overwhelmed, and discover, too late, that they'd taken their eyes off one of the critical balls, and it would spin off who knows where, possibly arcing toward some unlucky audience member's bean and just ruining their day. It was that way with me now, for in the spreading kerfuffle — with Vera and Isaac arguing about Climate Change, and Norm and Oan hiding in distant corners, no doubt planning how the dickens they'd salvage a wedding out of the current hullaballoo, and Nappy shouting encouraging words while standing ready to rain academic textbooks down upon yon invading Napoleons, and Zeus out in the lecture theatre fighting the good fight, I'd temporarily taken my eyes off Jack.

They now swivelled in his direction. They didn't like the sight that filled them.

This Jack had, at various times and diverse places, been bound up by some of Detroit's most seasoned binders. He'd been straitjacketed by the likes of Matron Bikerack and Dr. Peericks, he'd been well copped by the police on many occasions, and he'd been locked up by the Regent and her lackeys. It's also possible that he'd been bound up on other occasions in his personal life, as he seemed the type who might go in for that sort of thing. But as gifted as Isaac Newton was at crunching numbers, scanning brains, and keeping syringes out of the hands of fortune tellers, he had no evident talent for designing sturdy restraints for securing loonies into brain-scanning chairs. I now perceived that Jack had weakened the ties that bind, and, straining every muscle fibre at his disposal, was now on the brink of breaking through his bonds.

This he managed a heartbeat later, bursting every bond that stood between the Napoleonic gumboil and the free, open spaces. And before another atrium or ventricle could give even the merest squeeze, he was free and running straight at Isaac and Vera.

I did the brave thing, shouting a word or two of warning, having seen what Jack was capable of when he set his mind to work. It was good, I reflected, that we found this chap knifeless on this occasion, he having shown a strong bias toward stabbing anyone who came within arm's length whenever he was equipped with something pointy.

He dove upon Isaac and Vera as the two of them carried on struggling for the syringe. A heavy book biffed off his head, and I saw that Nappy was doing her best to give whatever aid she could. The three strugglers — Vera, Isaac, and Jack — went to the ground in a sort of writhing mass of incompetent wrestlers, all three of them seeming to have given physical education a miss during their formative years.

I won't say PE was my specialist subject, either, but I thought there must be something I could do to assist matters. I charged toward the writhing mass, hoping somewhere along the way I might find something capable of serving as a weapon or shield. I was still surveying the landscape, and hadn't taken more than a step or two toward the centre of the action, when Jack managed to extricate himself from the mêlée, rising victorious and holding the syringe.

"Haha!" he cried.

"Give that back!" shouted Isaac.

And in a move we really ought to have seen coming, he gave it back. Business end first. He plunged the syringe straight into Isaac's shoulder, pressing down on the plunger thingummy for good measure.

To say that we took this move in stride would be to deceive my public. I mean, without having made this particularly coherent or explicit, Jack had been arguing in less-than-certain terms against the unauthorized use of his neural whatnots in Isaac's experimentation, Jack perceiving that it violated his right to keep his thingummies to himself. And I won't claim, as I think I mentioned before, that a competent board of medical ethics auditors would have disagreed. But having staked out this claim, he now freely plunged his neural whatnots into Isaac himself, wantonly pushing his own brain patterns into this proton jiggler's person.

Time seemed to freeze for a space.

Isaac stared in disbelief. Jack stared with something resembling mad defiance, and Vera stared into the distance, showing every indication of being off in another one of her television-induced trances.

When time finally spat on its hands and started to function once more, Isaac gripped his arm and cursed Jack with word and gesture, chief among his complaints being that his experiment was delayed, that he'd have to produce another vial of serum, and that non-scientists have no business messing with things beyond their ken.

Nappy smote Jack with another one of her books, still striving to keep the rest of us unperforated.

As if they sensed that the best thing they could do was add to the chaos, Norm and Oan chose this moment to come bounding out of the corner in which they'd nestled, adding their pair of voices to the rising chorus of commotion.

"What shall we do?" cried Oan.

"The experiment!" cried Norm.

"My wedding!" cried Oan.

Jack didn't seem unduly concerned with experiments or weddings, his entire attention being fixated, if that's the word, on the sharp object in his hand and the plethora of potential victims who, as yet, remained unpricked. With a cry that seemed to fall somewhere between "ayeee" and "aaaargh!" he leapt straight at me, waving the syringe in a way that telegraphed his intentions to all and sundry.

I was aware of a "boom" or "crash" somewhere at my immediate rear and a rush of wind as about four hundred pounds of chiselled muscle sped past me. I ID'd this sizeable speedster at a glance. It was Zeus! I won't go into the psychology of the thing, but I imagine that his keen terrier senses, now firing on all thrusters, must have informed him that his former master, if you'd care to call me his master, was in trouble, and that now was the time for all good dogs to come to the aid of the pack.

"Sic him, Zeus!" I cried, infusing every word with feeling.

And sic him he did. Once again those lines about the wolf in the fold came forcibly to the forefront of the mind, with the part of the fold being played on this occasion by Jack. Zeus was on him in an instant. The little chap put up a struggle — he aimed his needle Zeusward, and made some threatening noises — but Zeus paid these no mind. He grabbed Jack by the outstretched arm, spun 'round a time or two as if preparing for the Olympic hammer throw, and then, rather than chucking this Jack skyward — a project rendered impractical by the presence of the ceiling — he simply smashed the ravening loony into the floor.

"Thud!!" about sums it up. With two exclamation points.

Jack lay on the ground moaning some Napoleonic moans, and after expressing my gratitude in no uncertain terms, I put a question to our saviour.

"Why aren't we up to our nostrils in Napoleons?" I asked.

"Oh, them," said Zeus. "They ran off. We had a bit of a dust-up when a whack of them came storming out of the portal. They kept shouting about the Regent, and I said she'd escaped through the other door. One of them bit me on my leg," he added, producing a thigh for inspection. "But after a bit more punching and kicking they ran out the lecture theatre's main doors, hunting the Regent."

"Mon 'ero!" said Nappy, leaping down from the high ground and flinging her arms about the blushing colossus. And I'll admit that I agreed with her assessment of the chap. I also reflected, at this juncture, that our impulsive act of releasing these Napoleons might have had a distinct impact on the average level of goofiness of the world, but an impact that couldn't have been avoided. You can't leave chaps locked up at the Regent's pleasure in a house of ruddy horrors, no matter how weirdly wired those chaps might be. As I'd heard Zeus say before, you can't just lock someone up for being different.

Speaking of this Zeus, his sudden advent, right at the moment when he was needed, raised another important question.

"Zeus," I said, with genuine feeling. "Has the time finally come? Have you remembered Rhinnick Feynman? Did the thought of your friend in danger, caught in the crosshairs of a syringe-wielding yahoo, rekindle the old spark of memory, causing neurons to fire and synapses to buzz in hitherto forgotten ways?"

He swivelled the pumpkin in my direction and furrowed a baffled brow or two.

"Of course I remember you," he said. "I've been with you all day. You just helped me release all those Napoleons from the dungeon. It wasn't right, keeping them locked up like that."

"Ah," I said. "Of course." I topped this off with a pensive "right ho."

I'll tell you why my mood was pensive. It had occurred to me, at long last, that it mightn't be so dashed important that the big chap before me had lost all memory of our prior times together. I mean to say, he'd kept his essential Zeusness — he was still a kindly behemoth chocked to the gills with loyalty, protectiveness, self-sacrifice, and honour . . . a sort of Yorkshire Terrier in superhero shape — all he was missing were a few old stories about his past adventures. We'd have all the time in the world to make new stories.

That is, we'd have all the time in the world to make new stories just so long as Vera was wrong in her diagnosis that Isaac's plan could bring about the end of the world.

Vera remained on her knees, still staring off into space, once again muttering rhyming couplets about two chairs. An uninitiated observer could be forgiven for believing that the vicissitudes of life had finally gotten to this Vera and that the rush and strain of events had left her a spent force fit only for kneeling on floors and babbling. But I knew better. She was still firmly in the grip of television, and would soon, no doubt, emerge and spout off a few details about future events.

Future events, however, not being inclined to wait around for soothsayers to announce their arrival, barged in upon us before Vera could snap out of her trance. They arrived in the form of Isaac, once again fiddling with the knobs and switches on his computer, announcing that he'd reinitiated serum production and would have another batch in about two minutes.

"Friends and colleagues," said Norm, now standing cheek-by-jowl with Oan beside the Regent's storage unit. "We are gathered here to send our emissary to the Great Omega, and also to join the Hand of the Intercessor in wedlock to—"

"W-wait a moment!" I cried, trying to stall the headman's axe.

Oan beckoned me to her side, extending a languid hand and blushing deeply.

"Two chairs!" cried Vera.

"Why hasn't Isaac reincarnated?" said Zeus — something none of us had been expecting to hear. But now that we'd heard it, and now that you've seen it in print, I think one has to admit that it amounted to an excellent question. It certainly grabbed Norm's attention, and it distracted Oan as well. It seemed to pull Vera out of the grip of television, and it made me raise a curious eyebrow in Isaac Newton's direction.

"My colossal gendarme has a point," I said, inclining the bean. "Why in Abe's name are you here? I thought that anyone who was injected with a Napoleon's brain patterns would shuffle off the immortal coil and shoot off toward the beforelife."

Isaac didn't seem to welcome the inquiry.

"Why must I be surrounded by such fools," he cried, raising an exasperated arm toward the ceiling. And then — possibly because these professor chumps can't help themselves when given a chance to lecture — he offered an explanation.

"The neural patterns are only part of the equation," he said, annoyed. "You're forgetting the basic nature of Detroit. The whole place," he added, not bothering to hide his disgust at what he was about to say, "is driven by desires and expectations. Not expectations alone, but *desire* as well. The element of desire is of the essence. If you're going to cross the veil to the beforelife, you can't merely believe it's going to happen. It has to be your heartfelt desire — your most deeply cherished wish. Two minutes to serum production."

"As I was saying," said Norm, "we've gathered here not only to send our emissary to the Great Omega—"

"Come stand by my side, Rhinnick!" said Oan, in that weird tone of voice that sounds like a whisper but is intended to be heard above other chatter. She reached out a hand and made grasping motions at me.

". . . but also to join the Hand of the Intercessor in blessed wedlock to Oan . . ."

"Ninety seconds to serum production."

"Zey are in here!" cried a voice from the door, once again delaying the wedding-bomb that kept threatening to detonate in the Feynman life.

There was no mistaking the source of this distraction. It was a Napoleon — one who'd clearly noticed a marked lack of Regents about the campus and had returned here to try to pick up the scent. Nor was this dogged Napoleon alone, for at this moment he and a handful of bellowing colleagues burst into the room and headed straight for the Regent's chamber.

Norm and Oan, rather than doing the sensible thing, seemed too caught up in their fervour to retreat to the cozy corner in which they'd previously hid. They moved out of the line of fire, ensuring that the Regent's freezing thingummy was between them and the charging Napoleons, but carried on reciting the words that I'd hoped never to hear.

"As I was saying," shouted Norm, "we are gathered here, not only to send our emissary to the Great Omega, but also—"

"Charge!" cried a Napoleon, leading Zeus to throw himself in their path, forming a roughly human-shaped wall of burly flesh between the Regent and this pack of Napoleonic piranha.

"... to join the Hand of the Intercessor in blessed wedlock—"

The sound of a few Napoleons bouncing off Zeus's sternum seemed to penetrate Vera's ear canals and wake her from her trance.

"What's going on?" she cried.

"Quite a lot!" I shouted.

"... to Oan, in the holiest of unions—" cried Norm.

"Why hasn't Isaac reincarnated?" shouted Vera.

"He doesn't want to!" I cried. "That seems to matter a good deal."

"Of course he wants to!" cried Vera. "It's all he's ever really wanted!"

"... and their union will be blessed—" shouted Norm.

"What are you on about?" I cried, shouting at Vera, not Norm, who was pretty dashed clear in what he was on about.

"Isaac wants to live in a world controlled by scientific laws!" shouted Vera. "It's all so clear to me now!"

"Stop biting me!" shouted Zeus.

"... and Oan shall henceforth be known," shouted Norm, above the din, "as She Who is the Spouse of He who is the Hand of He—"

"OH, DASH IT ALL!" I cried at the top of my lungs. And such was the force of my conviction that the chaos that surrounded me suddenly froze in one spot, all eyes turning toward yours truly.

For reasons I cannot fathom, I stepped atop a nearby chair and gave tongue to the gathered masses.

"Stop calling me the Hand of the ruddy Intercessor!" I cried. "That's not who Rhinnick Feynman is! I'm not a man defined as the piece of another man, or a chap who merely served as the Hand of someone else who interceded on some Omega person's behalf. I'm Rhinnick Ruddy Feynman, a human being in my own right. I mean to say, the Author may keep changing my biography, and deleting all recollection of my adventures from those who had played roles in them, but I still know who I am. Which is more than I can say for some of you."

Seeing that they all appeared transfixed by my spot of soap-box preaching, I carried on.

"I mean — why not follow Zeus's example? Here's a chap whose eggs have been scrambled, whose marbles have been lost, and who's had his memories forcibly ripped from his bean, and he still knows precisely who he is: strong, loyal, brave, and an all-around good boy, as the expression is. And Vera, another unlucky popsy who had her memories taken, also carried on being the best Vera that she could be. She was the only one with the clarity of vision — if you'll pardon the expression — to see who Isaac really was."

"I can see who Isaac is," said Zeus, corrugating the brow. "He's the fellow right over there."

"But dash it," I said, "he's not a chap who wants to tinker with quantum googaws, peer into the beforelife, and then reorganize those googaws to align with what he sees."

"I'm not?" said Isaac with genuine interest.

"Of course you're not!" I said. "You're a chap who wants to live in a world governed by physical laws, like Vera said. Physical laws you can discover by calculation. Not some mirror-like, dreamed-up world that can replicate whatever laws you find in the physical world — but an honest-to-goodness physical world for you to figure out. You don't want a . . . what's the word . . . a simulacrum. A world that bends to the will of the ancients, or whomever it is who dreams up what passes for reality in Detroit. You desperately want to be in the beforelife.

"And look at Norm and Oan," I continued, hitting my stride, just in time to be cut off by Isaac shouting "Gah" or something similar. "Gah?" I said, seeking clarification.

"Oh my stars," said Isaac. And, mark this, the chap's skin started to sparkle, and he started to become noticeably translucent.

Reread that last passage if you want to, but it won't change anything. This science fancier started to dematerialize — if dematerialize means what I think it does — and to fade into who knows where. Though, if I follow the trend of his minor plot in the present story, I rather think that he started temporarily fading out of existence, awaiting reincarnation in the beforelife.

And even though I was confident in Vera's diagnosis, viz, that Isaac's dearest wish was to live in the beforelife — a wish now coming to fruition through the medium of the Napoleonic serum — Isaac still refused to string along with this fact, which ought to have been as plain as the dematerializing nose on his dematerializing face.

"N-no!" he cried. "I don't want this!"

"I think you'll find that you do!" I riposted.

Again he protested — this time by haring across the room and picking up one of those gadgets he'd shown to me the last time we'd met.

"What's he doing?" shouted Zeus.

"Dematerializing," I said.

"I mean what's he doing with that machine!" Zeus shouted, specifying.

"Well, there you have me," I said.

Vera was, however, able to field the question. She was, if you'll recall, singularly gifted when it came to identifying the purposes and uses of this sort of technological gizmo.

"A time machine!" she said, agog. "He's trying to move backward in time!"

"That can't be done!" I said, although the word "scoffed" might be mot juster. "It's not possible. You can tell by all of the clocks running clockwise, and failing resolutely to revolve in the other direction."

"I can make it possible!" shouted Isaac, whose voice seemed as though he was calling to us from an especially deep well, or mine shaft, or other sort of hole in which those helpful collie dogs are always finding fresh victims. "I'm going to step back before any of this happened! I'll prevent it from the start!"

He couldn't quite seem to manage to press all of the buttons at his disposal. I mean to say, his fingers seemed to slip in and out of existence, sometimes passing through the chrono-thingummy, and sometimes making contact.

"I don't want this!" he cried, thus ensuring, it turned out, that the last observation of Isaac Newton was entirely incorrect. He manifestly did want this, for he now shimmered more brightly than ever before, winking out of our existence, and dropping his chrono-thingummy to the ground.

With all of the recent goings-on — the eye-popping and gripping drama that had unfolded centre stage, if that's the expression, everyone dropped what they were doing and simply stared in slack-jawed wonder. Even the Napoleons — by which I mean the generic anti-social ones, not Nappy and Jack — stopped their attempts to get 'round Zeus and stood there staring like a handful of sheep who've been stunned by a card trick or an unbelievable spot of news relayed by one of the rams.

It was Norm who broke the silence. This he did by tottering over to the dropped chrono-thingummy and announcing its last reading.

"Time incursion successful," he said.

"What?" said Zeus. "You mean . . . Isaac's travelled back through time? So where did he go?"

"Not where," I corrected, "when!" And I attempted to answer the q. by peeping over Norm's shoulder and running an eye or two over the chrono-thingummy's display.

411

"Ah," I said. "He didn't manage to change the date."

"What do you mean?" said Norm.

"He's got the thingummy set for the date of his installation as Lucasian Chair. He mentioned it to me when he first showed me the chrono-doodad. He said it was an important date, and it happened to coincide with the tri-centennial of some other science fancier's manifestival. Some chap named Galileo, if memory serves."

"So you think he's travelled back to that day?" asked Norm.

"He has," said Vera, still staring off into space. She had an otherworldly aspect about her, showing every symptom of being trapped in one of her televisory broadcasts.

"Or rather, his essence has travelled back to that date. But not here. He was passing between two worlds when he activated his time-shifting device. That date — the date displayed on his device — will be the day of his incarnation in the beforelife."

"How do you know?" asked Oan, agog.

"I can see him," said Vera, still staring off into the middle distance. "Plain as day. He's being reborn. In the beforelife. On January 8, 1942. Exactly three hundred years after Professor Galileo's manifestation in Detroit."

"Oh, ah," I said.

"Congratulations, Mr. and Mrs. Hawking," said Vera. And she topped this off by whispering "two chairs," whereupon she seemed to come back to the surface, popping out of her reverie.

Chapter 35

"What's that you said?" asked Norm.

"Oh, nothing," said Vera. "Just something from one of my visions. I'm fairly certain it solves the riddle of the two chairs — I just can't quite see how."

"Ah," said Norm Stradamus. "It's often that way with prophecy. Some of my own quatrains remain a mystery to me until sometime later, when some clever Johnny figures them out. The Hand of— or rather, I should say, *Mr. Feynman* and I were discussing that very point the other day. And talking of Mr. Feynman, it seems that our emissary won't be going today — at least not the one we intended — and it might be some time before we can send another. I've no idea how Isaac produces this neural serum, and it might take years before we replicate his process."

"Possibly longer," I said, pointing at Isaac's bay of computers. "It seems our band of Napoleons is ensuring that no one else will copy Isaac's work in a hurry."

And I'd said this because this band of Napoleonic loonies was merrily cavorting around Isaac's bank of computers like a band of chimpanzees confronted with a slot machine, and they were tearing wires and knobs and chunks of hardware from their moorings, stomping on the entrails where they fell.

"Oh, my!" said Norm.

"Oh, wow," said Zeus.

"Good riddance," said Vera, which I thought was a little harsh. I mean to say, she'd won the Climate Change war, if it was a war, and there was surely no need to triumph over a vanquished foe.

"But I would like to be getting on with the ceremony," said Norm. "The wedding, I mean."

I goggled at the man.

The fierce rush of life at Detroit University had so gripped my attensh that for about the last five minutes I'd forgotten all about the ceremony. Norm's sudden reminder caught me amidships and unmanned me, leaving me like a landed carp gasping for air. At a loss for words, I mean to say. Tongue-tied, if that's the expression. It's a rare thing for me, but it does happen.

Oan now made her presence known, stepping between self and Norm and asking if she might have a word or two with her betrothed.

I assented — not that I had much choice in the matter — and we moved off.

"Rhinnick," she said.

"Yes, Oan."

"Rhinnick," she said once more.

"Still here, old bird, and hanging on your lips!"

"Your speech," she said, "it reached me."

Well of course it did, I might have said, pointing out that the acoustics in these academic buildings were second to none.

"It touched the core of me, I mean," she said. "It showed me that you truly do see the essential me."

"Oh, ah," I said, and shuffled a toe or two.

She didn't seem inclined to let the subject die and carried on amplifying her remarks.

"It was that part about knowing who you really are. Who you are at the core of your being."

"Yes," I said, eager to push this thing along.

"It's just — it's just that it made me see who I really am."

"Happy to be of service," I said, civilly.

"I mean, who I am, not in relation to someone else, but in the deepest parts of my soul."

This seemed to be getting a bit personal, and I became desperate for a way to oil my way out of the conversation.

"It's just," she said, catching my arm, her voice faltering, "it's just like you said. You're not merely someone else's Hand. You're your own man. And I can't — I mean — following your singular, shining example, I can't define myself entirely in relation to someone else. I cannot be She Who Is Married to He Who Is the Hand of He Who Is . . . oh, Rhinnick! I can't bear to say the words!"

That state of affairs would have been fine by me, as I'd already found the eyelids growing heavy as she'd made her way through this extended preamble to whatever it was she dreaded to say.

Her eyes grew dewy, and then appeared to fill with resolve.

"I mean — oh, please be brave, Rhinnick," she said.

I assured her I'd be brave.

"I mean," she said, stifling a sob, "I mean I cannot be your wife."

"WHAT?!"

"Not now," she said. "Perhaps one day. I must first centre myself, Rhinnick. I must get back to who I am. Be a teacher for those on the brink of spiritual awakenings, not someone who values herself primarily because of a marriage to someone else. I do hope you'll understand."

She placed a tender hand on my elbow as if to offer me support. And I said the only two words I could think of.

"I'll try."

"Oh, Rhinnick!" she effused. "You are so brave."

"Stiff upper lip, what?" I said, and she moved off, sighing another one of those sighs which seem to come from the soles of her size-nine feet. She made a beeline for Norm Stradamus, possibly to break the news.

A snort from the sou'sou'west suggested that my conversation hadn't been as private as intended. I turned, and perceived an entire troop of eavesdroppers. It included Vera, Zeus, and Nappy, all staring at me and smiling.

"All's well that ends well, eh?" said Vera, still with a face-splitting grin.

I wasn't quite sure how to respond. I mean to say, you can't exactly clap your hands and leap about when an old slab of gorgonzola to whom you've accidentally become engaged hands you the mitten and believes she's broken your heart.

"No wedding bells for you, I mean," said Vera.

I raised an eyebrow.

"Well, no," I said. "I won't be marrying Oan. She dumped me like last week's garbage. But I thought you'd take the view that this merely clears the path."

"The path to what?" said this suddenly irksome beazel, making me say the words out loud.

"For . . . well . . . for *our* wedding," I said, no doubt blushing a rather deep shade of vermillion.

She issued yet another one of her silvery laughs.

"*Our* wedding?" she said, snorting a second time. "You didn't really think I was planning to hold you to that, did you?"

I shuffled a foot or two.

"Abe's drawers, Rhinnick," said the gumboil. "I know the last thing you'd ever want to do was marry me or anyone else."

I uttered a word or two of protest. "I never said that!" I said.

"You didn't have to," she riposted.

"And any such feelings, if I had them," I carried on, "would imply nothing derogatory about you. I should feel precisely the same way about marrying *any* of Detroit's noblest men or women, among whom I count you and the others present," I added, waving a hand at Nappy and Zeus.

She laughed again.

"Don't worry about it, Rhinnick. I assumed you realized that the whole idea was just a way to get Peericks to let me out."

It penetrated.

"So, you don't want to hitch your lot to mine?" I said.

"Not as your wife!" said the shrimp.

"You never really thought we should marry?"

"Not for a second!" she said, laughing.

"You mean, you *lied* to Dr. Peericks?"

She assured me that she had. And all was clear. It was a ruse, and far from the least of them. Through a brief spot of dissembling, she'd flung wide the hospice gates, acquiring a day pass from Dr. Peericks, thereby setting our plans in motion. An ingenious idea, I think you'll agree. It might have been nice to have been apprised of the ins and outs of this gag, as the expression is, but one can't ask for everything.

I inspected the terrain. My wedding had been called off. My second betrothal was a ruse. Abe's wish that I stop Isaac Newton — a silly wish, given that Isaac's trivial meddling was, as I've explained numerous times, confined to the quantum realm — had been granted. All appeared to be oojah-cum-spiff. All that remained was the task of figuring out what to do with the Regent and the other freeze-dried ancients stored at R'lyeh — a problem that could be left to someone else. The city councillors, perhaps.

I knew at a g. that this particular entry on the calendar would long be included on my list of banner days. And so it was with a song on my lips that I gathered Zeus, Nappy, and Vera to my bosom, checked to see that Fenny was still secured in my pocket, and bid farewell to the other chumps in Isaac's room

— leaving the cleaning up of the mess (which was entirely of their own making) in their more-than-capable hands.

In no more than a couple of ticks Vera shrewdly found the parking spot for Isaac Newton's car, hot-wired the machine, and we were off.

"Zeus," I said, once the dust had settled, the chickens had hatched, and the chips had fallen where they may. "I don't mind telling you that, while we were still in the thick of it, and before the happy endings were strewn about with a lavish hand, there were moments when I felt things mightn't end so frightfully well. One might even say that Rhinnick Feynman, though no weakling, came within a whisker of despair."

"No kidding," said the honest fellow.

"I mean, one couldn't say that peril didn't loom. It loomed like the dickens. The tortured Napoleons, the corrupted ancients, the bone-chilling brushes with matrimony, not to mention the even graver threat of—"

But then, we've covered that part, haven't we?

Epilogue

I don't know if you've been thinking the same thing, but I'd
been expecting Abe to turn up sooner. Say, just choosing a time
at random, at the moment when I'd finished snootering Isaac
and filled the air with happy endings. I mean to say, while I'm
the first to admit that Isaac's plan wasn't anything you might
call epoch-making, it remained true that stopping his plan,
such as it was, had been the quest Abe had set me, and I had
brought the quest to fruition — if bringing a thing to fruition
means what I think it does. Isaac had whooshed off into the
ether, possibly bringing glad tidings to these Hawking persons
Vera mentioned, and he now posed no further threat to local
pedestrians and traffic. Yet still there had been zero words from
the man up top. Ungracious, what? I mean, I know Abe's a busy
man, but I ask you!

The near-omnipotent blighter didn't show the mayoral face
until I'd conveyed self and party back to the Hôtel de la Lune
for a spot of post-quest celebration. The second day of our orgy
found our little troop frolicking in and around what is known
as a beach cabana, sipping on fruity drinks and making merry
while bedecked in louder-than-average floral shirts and knee-
length shorts. I was in the midst of commenting on the quality
of the local steel-drum band and preparing to make a musical
request when who should blow in but Abe himself, bearing a
tray of what are known as piña coladas.

"Abe's drawers!" cried Vera.

"And ze rest of him!" cried Nappy.

"Who is Abe?" said Zeus, the poor fish.

As for the undersigned, well, I just sat there looking agog. I mean, it was dashed tricky — even for me — to know precisely what to say. On the one hand, I was vis-à-vis with the mayor himself — the most powerful being Detroit had ever seen, give or take a Penelope — and he'd shown up bearing drinks: all suggesting that a word or two of obsequious thanksgiving might be in order. But weighing against this was the fact that I was annoyed at this municipal Grand Poobah, he having failed to lift the merest mayoral finger to assist me in what had, at various times, been a fairly inconvenient series of plunges into the soup. So as I said, I merely sat there looking agog.

Abe relieved me of the need to break the silence, unleashing a genial "Hiya, Rhinnick" in my direction.

"Ahoy, Abe," I said.

"Hello, everyone," he said, inclining the mayoral bean at Zeus, Nappy, and Vera in the order named.

"Hello Abe," they said, more or less in unison, Zeus bringing up the rear, still presumably putting together in fact that the chump under advisement was named Abe.

"Everything's settled, then?" said Abe.

"I suppose it is," I said, dully.

"No questions or anything?" he said.

Vera beat me to the punch. I mean to say, I had about a million issues to pursue with the man myself, and it seemed to me that a brace of burning questions — queries that'd be vexing the Author's readership — remained unasked, let alone unanswered. I mean, how do people get from the beforelife to Detroit in the first place? Does it happen to everyone? When this Hawking chap whom Vera mentioned crosses the Styx, will he be Isaac, or someone else? Does reincarnation really alter one's personality? Important questions, every one. But all these questions bottlenecked in the vicinity of my uvula, crashing into each other and preventing any one of their number from crossing the Feynman lips. All I managed was a kind of gargling sputter, which Vera silenced with a wave of an impatient margarita. So as I said, Vera beat me to the punch, buttonholing the mayor with her own cross-examination.

"Why Rhinnick?" she asked.

"Why Rhinnick?" said Abe.

"Yeah," said Vera, in that informal way of hers. "I mean, you and Penelope can do anything. Why'd you send Rhinnick to stop Isaac?"

An excellent question, I think you'll agree.

"It's hard to explain," said Abe.

"Just try your best," said Zeus, helpfully.

Abe paused to marshal his thoughts, and proceeded as follows.

"It's important to understand that Penelope and I follow the same rules as everybody else. Our expectations give this place its shape. It's just that we, for whatever reason, have a lot more impact than most. And we can control it. Up until now, that's worked out pretty well. But then Isaac found a way to steer the combined expectations of all the sleeping ancients, and when he used them to make changes, it took practically all my power to keep the world on an even keel. At the same time Penelope was — well, let's just say that she and Ian were making things difficult. They decided to have a baby, of all the horrible ideas. And then—"

"A baby?" Vera said, great-scotting, and one could see what she was driving at.

"Un petit bébé?" cried Nappy, "'ow eez zis possible? 'Ow can someone in ze afterlife 'ave un—"

"Sorry, sorry," said Abe, waving them off, "it's a long story, and I can't get into it now. But the upshot is that I've had my hands full. I still do. That's why I wasn't able to be much help to Rhinnick."

"But why push everything on him in the first place?" said Vera. "I mean, why *Rhinnick*, in particular?"

"I thought that would've been obvious," said the mayor. "It's Rhinnick's *ego fabularis*. It came in handy. See, Rhinnick views the world differently than we do. He thinks we're characters in a novel written by some cosmic author."

"He *thinks* that because it's true," I said, piping in a bit austerely.

"Well, it gave you an advantage," said Abe, turning toward me and failing altogether to shrink in the face of my cool asperity. "Isaac kept making retroactive changes to the world — changing things in a way most people wouldn't have noticed. Erasing teleportation. Mucking around with time. When Isaac changed the minds of the sleeping ancients, he retroactively changed the world, and almost everyone fit these changes into their own expectations — what you might call their world view. They believed that the world had always been the way that Isaac had reshaped it. Almost everyone but you," he said, eyeing the undersigned benevolently. "See, everyone else expects the world to be rational and consistent — they expect history to stay as it always was, and they expect things to chug along in a more or less predictable way. But not you. You expect revisions. You believe your author changes things on a whim, and that he rewrites history, character sketches, physical laws, and anything else whenever he likes."

"Well, He does!" I said, briefly eyeing the sky in search of thunderbolts en route to quelling Abe's bit of heresy.

"The upshot is," Abe continued, aiming a smile in my direction, "you were uniquely qualified for this quest. You don't expect The Rules to matter. You don't think things will make sense. When a retroactive change happens, you see the change for what it is. You don't trick yourself into thinking things have always been that way — you just remember how things were, see the change, assume that the author has made revisions, and carry on. Only someone who had that kind of perspective — that way of seeing the world — could navigate his way through Isaac's changes, remain unchanged himself, and—"

"But I didn't remain unchanged!" I protested. "Whole chapters of my biography were consigned to the cutting-room floor! Past sequences that are clear in the Feynman mind have been blotted from my past, and minor characters who ought to remember hobnobbing with me are left in the dark!"

"Sorry. That was me," said Abe.

"You?"

"I hope it wasn't too inconvenient. It's just that you were a hospice patient on the lam, and I didn't think you'd be much help in stopping Isaac if everyone kept trying to lock you up. So I did what I could to alter people's memories — making practically everyone forget whatever it was they knew about you, so they wouldn't get in your way."

I stood there for a space, gaping like a beached herring, for the eternal blister's comments had unmanned me. I mean, I understood Abe was purporting to explain why it was that Rhinnick Feynman, devoted servant of the Author, was The Man The Hour Produced, but I can't say that I kept up with the explanation, it having landed with a thud right between the Feynman eyes. As for the Feynman ears, they registered various grunts of appeasement and enlightenment issuing from the other members of my troop — they seeming to have collared the gist of Abe's revelations a touch more readily than I.

"So let me get this straight," I said, pressing every available grey cell into service, "you're saying that my past *hasn't* changed. That everything remains how I've remembered it all along?"

"That's right," said Abe.

"You mean, I *was* a hospice patient. I *did* square off with Peericks, and I *did* spend years and years alongside Zeus—"

"That's right," said Abe.

"The Author hasn't revised my background? He . . . he's just written a new sequence in which you, Abe the First, took it upon himself to modify the memories of the masses, erasing bits of the Feynman bio from their brains?"

"That's . . . one way to put it," said Abe.

"Well, put them back!" I said, eagerly. "Restore those memories instanter! While I'll admit that the cloak of anonymity comes in handy at certain times, I want those memories back in place! I don't mean to get philosophical, but my stories are all I have! You can't go around erasing what it is the Author wrote. It's what keeps our threads together, if you see what I mean."

Here I pivoted Zeusward, and endeavoured to haul the big chap front and centre.

"Take Zeus!" I said. "He may have lost a marble or two and forgotten who he was, but his story — all of his history — stayed in place. The rest of us, having played parts of varying importance in earlier chapters of his biography, are there to remind Zeus who he was, help him knit together the threads, and prod him along in future volumes. If our histories are erased, then who *are* we?"

This force of my remorseless logic seemed to hold Abe for a space, and he stared off into the distance for a heartbeat or two before resurfacing.

"You're sure that's what you want?" he asked. "I mean . . . you want *all* memories of your history restored?"

"I do," I said. "My history is what makes me me."

"And you're certain?"

"Couldn't be more so."

"You ought to be careful what you wish for."

"I am adamant," I said, for that's what I was.

"All right," said Abe, at length. "I wasn't sure how to thank you for everything you've done for the city — but if this is what you want, then I won't argue. Now hold on. If I'm going to get this right, I'm going to need Penelope's help."

The chap then closed his eyes in apparent concentration, and silently moved his lips in a beseeching sort of way. Then he shimmered like a mirage, and snapped his fingers.

And what a snap it was! Not only did it seem to reverberate through the Feynman bones, but it also had the effect of making Abe disappear in a sudden flash.

I well-I'll-be-dashed. And I don't mind admitting that, in doing my bit of well-I'll-be-dashing, I staggered backward a step or two, overcome by the weight of what Abe had done.

"Rhinnick!" cried Vera, beating Zeus and Nappy by a jiffy or two in hastening to my side and grabbing an arm. Their faces loomed before mine in a concerned, mother-henning sort of way.

"I'm all right," I said. "Or rather, I think I will be."

Their faces darkened. It seemed that something in my demeanour struck them as rummy, and I can't say I was surprised. And the reason for the rumminess of my d. was not far to seek. In restoring all lost memories of yours truly, Abe had, in that thoroughly thorough way of his, flipped the switch on my own grey cells as well, restoring all of *my own* memories in the process. My beforelife ones, I mean. They were suddenly plain as day. I couldn't believe that I'd forgotten them.

"What is it?" said Vera, applying a hand to the forehead.

"Are you all right?" said Zeus.

"I will be," I said, teetering on the spot. "Only . . . well . . . it all comes back to me now, and it'll take some sorting out. I mean, why should I act like a messed-up gumbo of my characters? How did all of this Author-worship stuff come about? And why call myself *Rhinnick Feynman*? The imagination boggles."

425

"Rhinnick . . . what are you saying?" said Vera, still mother-henning like nobody's business.

"I'll be all right," I said, marshalling my composure. "But perhaps, from now on, you might just call me Plum."

RANDAL GRAHAM is a law professor at Western University, where his teaching and research focus on ethics and legal language. His first novel, *Beforelife*, won the IPPY gold medal for fantasy fiction and was a top ten finalist for the Stephen Leacock Medal for Humour. Graham's books on law and legal theory have been assigned as mandatory reading at universities across Canada and have been cited by judges on all levels of court, including the Supreme Court of Canada and the U.S. Supreme Court. He lives in London, Ontario.